Legacy

Legacy

Cayla Kluver

CROWS NEST

Published in the United States by Amazon Content Services LLC in 2009

First published in Australia by Allen & Unwin in 2011

Crows Nest, an imprint of Allen & Unwin
83 Alexander Street
Crows Nest NSW 2065
Australia
Phone: [61 2] 8425 0100
Fax: [61 2] 9906 2218
Email: info@allenandunwin.com
Web: www.allenandunwin.com

Cataloguing-in-Publication details are available from
the National Library of Australia — www.librariesaustralia.nla.gov.au

ISBN 978 1742372402

Cover design by Headcase Design
Cover illustration by Karen Gorst
Interior illustrations by Rosemary Buczek
Set in 15 pt Historical Fell Type
Printed in Australia by Griffin Press

The paper in this book is FSC certified.
FSC promotes environmentally responsible,
socially beneficial and economically viable
management of the world's forests.

10 9 8 7 6 5 4 3 2 1

This book is dedicated to Mom, Nina, and Grandma Frances,

who would have loved every moment.

TABLE OF CONTENTS

PROLOGUE

The first boy disappeared on the day of his birth, on a night when the pale yellow moon that ruled the sky turned red and bathed the heavens in the ghastly color of blood, the same night the Kingdom of Cokyri abruptly ceased its merciless attack.

Across the land of Hytanica, in the villages, infant boys continued to vanish. The King turned a blind eye somewhat foolishly, seeking no explanation, needing to refortify his Kingdom's defenses for fear that Cokyri would resume its brutal onslaught. He was finally forced to take notice when children inside the city's walls began to disappear. A count was made of the number missing, but before he could determine what action should be taken, the disappearances stopped as suddenly as they had begun. The last Hytanican child to vanish was the newborn son of a wealthy baron and baroness.

Within the week, as the bleeding moon waned, the decomposing bodies of the infants were found outside the gates of the city, a final word from the greatest enemy Hytanica had ever known. Grieving parents collected the rotting bodies of their sons, but there was one mystery that would for many years remain unsolved. Forty-nine babies were taken, but only forty-eight bodies were returned.

No one knew why the Cokyrians had withdrawn from the land or why they had not been able to destroy Hytanica and her people. The Cokyrians were superior to the Hytanicans as fighters and strategists, and did not adhere to any code of honor in war, but still Hytanica had not fallen. Some thought they had abandoned the effort out of frustration, for they had many times been poised to win; others thought the Cokyrian rulers had finally accepted the ancient story of Hytanica's conception.

According to lore, the first King of Hytanica, seeking to protect his foundling home, had been advised by his priests that a sacrifice of blood both royal and innocent would hallow the ground and make his Kingdom invincible. After much soul-searching, the King had taken the life of his own infant son and placed drops of the boy's blood at each corner of the land to forever shield the people he loved.

I was born shortly before the end of the war, a Princess of Hytanica, my parents' first heir. As my people settled into a long-awaited time of peace and learned again how to lead normal lives, I was brought before them and grew to be a young woman, living in freedom such as the war-torn generations before me had never known. All such things must come to an end, however, and that is where my story begins.

I

THE OBVIOUS CHOICE

think I'm going to vomit."

I paced in front of the cold stone fireplace that spanned most of one wall in my parlor, clasping and unclasping my hands in front of me. My younger sister, Princess Miranna, had retired to her quarters after giving me a hug and assuring me I would have a lovely evening. Fair and rosy-cheeked at the age of fifteen, with strawberry blond hair that flipped in waves and curls down her back, she was much more enamored with the man I would be meeting for dinner tonight than was I. In fact, it had undoubtedly been notions of romance that had motivated her to dismiss my personal maid so that she could attend to me herself. The shimmering gray gown that adorned my body had been of her choosing, as had the delicate silver locket that graced my neck. Although my dark brown hair usually fell about my shoulders, she had gathered it into a loose bun, with wispy strands framing my nearly black eyes and softening my angular features. Now it was only London, my bodyguard and a member of the King's Elite Guard, who waited with me in the richly furnished room.

"You're not going to vomit, Alera. Just try to relax," London advised, one eyebrow raised in bemusement. He moved toward the sofa and picked up one of my books from the side table, then began to leaf through it absentmindedly.

"How can I possibly eat?" I asked, my voice sounding shrill even to my own ears. "I don't think I can go through with this."

"It's going to be fine. He's just another suitor, and like all the rest of them, he has to impress *you*, not the other way around. Besides, as far as I can tell, you have no real interest in him, so I don't know why you're working yourself into such a state."

"You don't understand," I said frantically. "If something goes wrong tonight, Father is going to be so disappointed."

"Well, unless you've made plans to marry Steldor that I don't know about, you're going to disappoint your father in the long run no matter what."

I stopped pacing and faced London, who had set the book back onto the table and was now leaning against the tapestried wall by the door, arms crossed over his muscular frame. Unruly silver bangs fell across his forehead, contrasting sharply with his deep-set indigo eyes, which were fixed upon me as he waited for a response.

"But I can't stand him! How can I spend the whole evening with him?"

"It's just one evening. You can survive one evening." London hesitated, then added, "Although I hope you're up for a little after-dinner romance —— the weather is ideal for a moonlit stroll in the garden."

"He won't expect that of me, will he, London?" Although I knew London was teasing, I was unable to find humor in such an awful possibility, and he promptly tried to allay the new worry he had inadvertently created.

"If he does, tell him you're feeling ill and that you must return to your quarters at once. He can't argue with that."

I sank into one of the elaborately carved armchairs near the hearth, buried my head in my hands, and moaned. My father, King Adrik, had arranged for this dinner between Lord Steldor and me, as Steldor was the young man he favored to be my husband. He trusted Steldor and felt he was better suited to be King than anyone else in the Kingdom. As heir to the Throne, I was to marry on that basis alone, for it was my husband, and not I, who would come to rule Hytanica.

Even I had to admit that Steldor was the obvious choice. Three and a half years older than me, he was the son of Cannan, the Captain of the Guard, and had one year ago become a military Field Commander at the age of nineteen. He was charming, intelligent, and strong, with stunning good looks, but I had disliked him from the moment we had met.

A sharp rap on the door interrupted my thoughts, and I rose as London stepped into the corridor to speak with the servant who had been sent to summon me.

"We'd better be going," he said upon reentering. "Steldor has arrived and is waiting for you in the Grand Entry."

London opened the door for me and we walked through the second-floor corridors of the Royal Residence toward my family's private staircase at the rear of the Palace. In addition to my quarters and those of my sister and parents, the Residence included a library, a family dining room, a kitchen, and a lesson room that doubled as a parlor. The Royal Ballroom and the King's Dining Hall were the only areas on the second floor that were used for public events.

We descended the tightly spiraling stairs, London offering his arm to escort me down the lantern-lit corridor toward the Palace's main entrance. As we walked, I hardly glanced at the intricate tapestries that adorned the walls, for my attention was drawn to Steldor, who awaited me at the end of the hallway. Idly supporting himself with his left hand on the wall, he was expertly flipping a dagger over and over in his right, looking as though he had purposely positioned himself for maximum visual effect.

"Have fun," London said glibly, coming to a stop midway down the passage, Steldor having noticed my approach.

"You're not going far, are you?" I asked, a bit shakily.

"No, I would wager you'll need more protection tonight than on most occasions. Besides, I'd be a pretty poor chaperone if I did, although I will try to give you two lovebirds some privacy."

"Go ahead and enjoy yourself at my expense, won't you?" I complained, eyes riveted on Steldor, who had returned his dagger to its sheath in one of his knee-high black boots and was striding toward me.

"If you want to know the truth," London confided, "I'm staying back so I don't murder him in your stead."

The abrupt change in my bodyguard's mood caught me by surprise, but I had no time to respond, for my handsome dinner companion was drawing nigh. Although Steldor was dressed more informally than was usual for him, in a white shirt topped by a dark gray vest with red across its shoulders, his deportment made any clothing appear elegant. He was tall, broad-shouldered, and well muscled, with dark brown hair that edged on black and fell in a perfectly careless manner to just below his prominent cheekbones. His eyes, rimmed by long, ebony lashes, were a dark and smoldering brown, guaranteed to make most girls swoon, and his smile was irresistible, given his straight and even white teeth. My skin prickled as I realized that our attire, as well as our dark features, made us a matched pair.

"My Lady," Steldor greeted me, with a bow and a kiss of my hand. As his eyes approvingly swept my form, he added, "Allow me to escort you to the dining room."

With an uncomfortable glance at my bodyguard, Steldor drew me to his side, and I was certain London's demeanor had given warning of how seriously he took his duties. As Steldor guided me through the rest of the corridor, the savory smells emanating from the kitchen aroused my appetite, and I ruefully thought that I would at least be getting a delicious meal out of the evening.

The first-floor dining room was designed to accommodate intimate gatherings. There were double marble fireplaces, one on each side of the room, with an oblong table that could seat forty-five centered in between. Three multitiered, candlelit chandeliers were suspended above the table, and oil-burning lanterns were attached at equal intervals along the walls. A small, round table draped with white linen had been prepared for us at the far end of the room in front of the bay window that afforded a view of the West Courtyard of the Palace. Two flickering candles upon the table provided subtle illumination, aided feebly by the last residue of the day's sun as it filtered through the pane. I sat across from Steldor and he offered me a glass of wine, which I accepted with some trepidation, having no more liking for wine than I did for the man extending the goblet.

"I must say," Steldor observed, "you are exceptionally beautiful tonight, Alera."

He paused as if permitting me an opportunity to extend a similar compliment. When none was forthcoming, he smiled impertinently.

"I am used to my dates dressing well when they accompany me, but few take the extraordinary step of coordinating their clothing with mine."

I paled at his implication, but he continued before I could formulate an appropriately caustic remark.

"You seem a little overwhelmed... perchance from hunger, although I do tend to have that effect on women. Some food may restore you." He indicated to a servant with a flick of his hand that we were ready to receive our meal. "Perhaps some sustenance will enable you to find your voice as well."

I stared at the man my father desired me to wed, feeling ill-equipped to deal with his overly familiar attitude. The arrival of the kitchen staff with vegetable-laden platters, a variety of warm breads, and a full roasted chicken saved me from having to make a reply.

Steldor nodded curtly to dismiss the servants, then sliced the sizzling capon, adding a piece to each of our plates. We ate in silence for a few minutes, although I found it difficult to do more than nibble, for his eyes continued to shamelessly peruse me.

"I hope we shall come to spend a great deal of time together," he finally said, his voice a practiced blend of honey and conceit, velvety smooth but with an undertone of boredom that not even he could conceal. "Although I should caution you that the military demands much of me. Of course, I am well suited for such a life. When I attended the Military Academy, my combat instructors insisted that I was the best in my year, maybe in the history of the school. I was not the largest person in my class, but I was by far the most skilled. As I'm sure you know, everyone was astounded by my progress, and I was allowed to graduate from the Academy a year early."

He pushed his plate forward a few inches so that he could stylistically rest his left forearm on the edge of the table.

"After fifteen months as a foot soldier, I went into officer training and became the youngest Field Commander in Hytanican history. But despite the demands of my position, I find time to help train the students at the Academy in hand-to-hand fighting. The instructors at the Military Academy continue to hold me in high esteem and readily welcome my assistance."

While he was speaking, I became aware that I was paying more attention to his gestures than to his words, for his movements were so fluid they seemed almost rehearsed. Finished with his meal, he settled back in his chair, slowly swirling the wine in his goblet, once more looking perfectly posed.

"It's not as though I did anything special to win such admiration," he blithely continued, an air of condescension creeping into his voice. "I was simply born with enviable talents. It was natural that I would become the favored one. You can understand that, can't you, Alera? It's much the same with you."

"And how is that like me at all?" I said, his arrogance at last goading me to reply.

"She speaks," he gently mocked, then matter-of-factly elaborated. "Well, you didn't ask to be born into the Royal Family, did you? I likewise didn't *ask* to be the most admired man in the Kingdom."

"More admired than my father? Well, then, I suppose I should feel honored just to be here with you."

"Most girls do feel honored, but as you are the Crown Princess, I would say feeling appreciative would be good enough."

The churning in my stomach could no longer be attributed to nervousness. Steldor had achieved a new feat. Just being in his company was making me physically ill.

When I did not converse further, he glanced to the other side of the room, where London was sitting in a chair, booted feet resting on the oblong table.

"It's too bad your bodyguard has to be here, isn't it?"

"Maybe from your point of view," I retorted.

"Don't take offense, Princess," he said with a self-satisfied chuckle. "I only meant that, perhaps if we were alone, we could make things a bit more... intimate."

He leaned closer and reached for my hand, dark eyes lazily scanning me as if I were a gift he was about to unwrap.

"That would be a bit improper, would it not?" I reproached, picking up my napkin to spoil his attempt.

"And have you never done anything improper, Princess?" he drawled, wearing an insufferably indulgent expression. He stood when my only response was a deep blush. "Since you don't seem to be particularly hungry, I suggest we forgo dessert in favor of a stroll in the moonlight."

I tried to think of an excuse, or to remember London's advice, but my brain had stopped working. In combination with my dry mouth, I found myself truly speechless.

"I'll take that as a yes," he said, slipping a hand under my elbow to direct me to my feet. "To the garden, shall we?"

Steldor's arm snaked its way around my waist as he began to escort me from the dining room, and London let his feet drop loudly to the floor, drawing our attention. He rose, and his eyes briefly connected with mine.

"No need to keep such close watch," Steldor told him with a dismissive wave. "She's in good hands."

"That's an interesting assertion, considering your reputation," London coolly replied, not about to let the Captain's son out of his sight.

We walked down the corridor that London and I had earlier traversed, toward the back of the Palace and the heavy double doors that opened onto the garden, which extended from the rear of the Palace to the northern section of the walled city. Beyond the forty-foot-high stone wall of the city stretched the forest that climbed into the foothills of the rugged Niñeyre Mountains.

Steldor acknowledged the Palace Guards who were stationed at the rear entrance, then held one of the double doors open for me, but I vacillated, reluctant to go into the dusky grounds with him, not trusting him at all.

"I'm not sure this is a good idea," I fussed, still struggling for words, uncomfortably aware that my periodic lapses in speech were probably coming across as girlish excitement, when in reality all I wanted was for the evening to be over.

"Of course it is —— it's a beautiful night."

"I am a bit cold, and I did not bring a wrap," I said lamely. The temperature was still comfortable, but since it was the beginning of May, a chill would advance as night settled over the land.

"Just stay near to me, Princess. I assure you I'll be able to keep you warm."

I nodded, and he again draped his arm about my waist to guide me onward, one of the Palace Guards loudly announcing my presence to alert the others who patrolled the area that I had entered the grounds.

Stars were beginning to glimmer in the clear nighttime sky as we strolled along one of the stone footpaths that wove through the walled garden, dividing it into sections. Although torches burned around its perimeter, their flickering light did not penetrate the garden's depths, and the moon served as our only guide. Steldor led me toward one of four double-tiered white marble fountains located on the path, and I was certain he viewed our surroundings as spectacularly romantic; my emotion would have more accurately been described as dread.

Steldor stopped beside a bench that had been placed near the fountain, dragging me down to sit beside him. Taking my hands in his, he gazed deeply into my eyes, silently telling me that he had laid claim to me long before I had been aware of his pursuit, and my heart began to hammer in apprehension of what he might do.

"You enchant me, Alera," he whispered, leaning in close, and my senses reeled from his rich and alluring scent. It was deep and musky, but with the warmth of nutmeg and cinnamon, woven with a wistful hint of violet. As the fragrance washed over me, he played with a strand of my hair, then smoothly slid his hand to the base of my neck and pressed his lips against mine in a firm and entirely unwelcome kiss.

I pulled away, eyes widening, appalled that he would make such a presumptuous move. For an instant he seemed almost angry, but then he dropped his hand with a wicked grin.

"I didn't know that would be your first kiss," he chided, and my cheeks began to burn. "Not that I mind, of course. It's just that you are more inexperienced than I anticipated."

He reached out to touch my necklace, letting his fingertips delicately trace against my collarbone.

"Of course, this does mean many other firsts will follow."

I glared at him in outrage as I floundered for words. Just as it looked as though he might try to kiss me again, a voice cut through my humiliation, disbelief, and dislike, interrupting his advance.

"Princess!" London called, striding into sight. "I'm afraid there's an emergency in the Palace and I must return you to your quarters. You'll have to come with me now."

I sprang up from the bench and almost ran to my guard, warm relief spreading through me. Steldor came to his feet with a scowl, intending to accompany me, but London held up a hand.

"You'll have to go. This is not your business."

Steldor glowered at London as though to intimidate him, but my bodyguard met his stare steadily. Other than the fact that London was slightly shorter than my escort, the two men were a physical match. They even had the same youthful appearance, although, in truth, London was nearly twice Steldor's age, just one of the things that made the man in whose protective shadow I had lived for sixteen years a mystery to me.

Knowing that London, a Deputy Captain in the Elite Guard, held rank, Steldor backed down. I didn't look behind as I hastily left the garden with my bodyguard, but I imagined my jilted dinner companion reentering the Palace shortly after we did and stalking down the corridor.

"You were right about the level of protection I would need tonight," I tentatively admitted as London and I climbed the spiral staircase that was reserved for my family's use.

"Indeed."

London had evidently lost his good humor about the evening, as he seemed to be inwardly fuming, although whether at himself or at Steldor, I couldn't tell.

"And your father expects you to *marry* that pig?" he muttered.

"Apparently."

I was surprised by London's forwardness in expressing his opinion of Steldor. While I knew he did not think highly of my father's top choice of a husband for me, and was grateful that I had someone with whom I could share my feelings, I had only ever known him to listen to my complaints and not articulate his own.

My thoughts returned to Steldor's kiss, and I began wiping at my mouth in disgust. London took note of what I was doing and raised a sardonic eyebrow.

"I don't suppose that was the way you envisioned your first kiss."

"Why does everyone think that was my first kiss?" I demanded, dismayed that my life was so transparent.

"Don't forget you're talking to me," he replied with a knowing smirk.

I briefly averted my eyes, willing myself not to blush.

"Well, in any case," I rejoined, "I'm glad you stepped in. Who knows what else he had in mind."

"What happened to telling him you felt ill if you wanted to make a hasty exit?"

"When we were sitting on the bench, I couldn't think straight. He has this amazing..." I trailed away as I lost the battle to stem the color rushing into my face.

"Amazing what?"

"Scent, amazing scent," I finished defensively, cheeks now aflame.

"He smells good?" London teased, breaking into a laugh. "As if he needs another way to attract women. On top of everything else, he *smells* better than the rest of us!"

Returning to my quarters, I closed the parlor door behind me, murmuring good night to London. I knew he would be headed for the East Wing, to the first-floor rooms where most of the unmarried guards chose to live. As my primary bodyguard, he was on duty from the time I awoke until the time I retired. At night, Palace Guards regularly patrolled the corridors to provide security.

I dragged myself through the parlor toward my bedroom, my limbs heavy with weariness. Upon entering the room that had been my refuge for as long as I could remember, I sank into the chair that stood before my dressing table, removing the pins from my hair and shaking my head so that my thick locks tumbled about my shoulders. I looked into the mirror, letting my eyes wander over the familiar furnishings reflected there: a generously sized canopy bed, topped by a cream-colored spread and deliciously soft, overstuffed feather pillows; a pair of deeply padded, rose velvet lounging chairs that beckoned from in front of the fireplace; a dollhouse and a few other toys from my childhood, including a top and a skipping rope; and several overflowing bookcases.

I stood and crossed the room to pull open one of the double wooden doors that led onto my balcony, my feet sinking into the thick rug that lay on the floor. Though I shivered as a cool breeze touched my skin, I stepped outside to await the arrival of Sahdienne, the golden-haired, round-faced young woman who was my personal maid. From my balcony during daylight hours, I had a clear view of the rolling terrain that spread toward the lake marking the western border of our Kingdom. As it was, I could only see what the moonlight permitted —— the looming shapes of the shadowy buildings in the city.

Hearing the creak of my bedroom door, I retreated inside as Sahdienne entered. She unlaced the back of my gown and drew the drapes across the window to the right of the balcony while I donned my nightdress. Then I slipped under the covers that topped my bed, nestling my head amongst the pillows, and fell asleep before she had finished tidying the room.

II

An Unwelcome
Encounter

t was dusk, my favorite time of day. I cherished the moments when I could stand on the expansive balcony off the Ballroom and gaze beyond the courtyard gates of our Palace into the walled city, watching for the points of light that appeared as its inhabitants lit lanterns to ward off the darkness. Beyond the city, farm fields sloped gradually toward the untamed Recorah River, which flowed out of the mountains and defined our eastern and southern boundaries.

It was the occasion of my seventeenth birthday, and the upper society of several kingdoms had gathered to honor me on this tenth of May. There was an added air of excitement to this celebration, as it was customary for a female heir to marry at eighteen the man who would become the next King, and I was therefore expected to choose a husband within the coming year. I had retreated to the balcony when the whispers and speculations about who was in my favor had at last gotten the best of me, hoping the fresh air would provide relief from the stuffiness of the room as well as the conversation.

Though arguably I should have been allowed to rule, tradition steered my father's and the Kingdom's views on leadership, dictating that they put their trust into the hands of a man, and not those of a woman. As my father had no male heir, I would be crowned Queen, but not ruler, and as such would play no role in the actual governing of the Kingdom. The function of the Queen was to supervise the household, plan and execute social events, and raise the children. While the line of descent would continue to flow through my blood, the man I married would reign in my stead.

Hearing footsteps from behind, I turned, expecting that one of the young men who sought my attention had followed me. Instead, Miranna glided to the railing, absolutely radiant in a sky blue dress. With her porcelain skin and delicately sculpted features, she was destined to break the hearts of many a suitor.

"Are the celebrations too much for you, sister?" she asked, her blue eyes sparkling playfully, for she knew I rarely enjoyed festivities that cast me in a starring role.

"I must confess I find myself struggling to breathe in that Ballroom."

We stood in silence while I took a few deep breaths of the refreshing air, then Miranna lightly touched my hand. "Tell me, has anyone managed to draw your interest this evening?"

"No one who would meet Father's approval," I said, trying to keep from sounding bitter. "And I cannot marry without his approval."

"True, but there are so many intriguing possibilities!" My sister's face shone with enthusiasm, for she had, of late, developed quite an interest in the male population. "I know Father can be a bit demanding, but he is not unreasonable. He has many times proved himself to be a good judge of character."

"He may very well be, but this time he seems to have his sights set on making only one judgment." My half-hearted attempt at humor fell flat, for unlike Miranna, I saw no pleasure in the task before me. "Let's review a few of the candidates: Lord Thane is kind and witty, but he has chosen to study medicine, which disqualifies him, as Father insists a military background is necessary for a King. Then there is Lord Mauston, who is in the Cavalry, but his family has fallen on hard times, so he wouldn't bring enough wealth to the marriage. Baron Galen is a Field Commander who inherited his father's title, lands, and holdings, which ought to make him acceptable, but he is Lord Steldor's best friend and *not* the Captain of the Guard's son, so is relegated to second choice at best. And Father wants me to marry someone at least a few years older than me, someone with the experience and maturity to ascend to the Throne at once, which eliminates all the noblemen of my age." With forced pleasantness, I concluded, "So, you see, the problem is not a lack of interest on my part, but Father's rather extensive list of qualifications."

"And what of Lord Steldor? I don't know if you've spoken with him tonight, but he is looking very fine indeed."

Miranna, like my father, had a preference for the Captain of the Guard's son, although I suspected it was for quite a different reason.

"I have never seen an occasion when he did not look fine. As he has attracted *your* notice, have no misgivings on my account about pursuing him, Mira."

"What is it that makes you dislike him so?"

"If you must know, it's his ego. Steldor doesn't walk; he struts. He doesn't converse with someone; he blesses them with his presence. He doesn't even laugh; it's a haughty and degrading sound that twists my insides until I feel sick. On top of that, he is the most possessive and hot-tempered person I have ever known, and that frightens me more than I care to say."

Miranna distractedly twirled a strand of hair around the fingers of her left hand, and I knew she had understood my point, at least with respect to Steldor's temper. A Hytanican woman was the property of her husband, and he could deal with her as he saw fit. This alone made me a poor match for the Captain's son, for I was, at times, more outspoken than was wise. I suspected that Steldor's reaction to such behavior might prove quite unpleasant.

"Still, he has many exceptional qualities," she finally countered. "And though the issues you've raised may make him less appealing to you as a husband, they hardly detract from his promise as a ruler. Besides, he will be guided by both our father and his. He will make a good King, Alera. Everyone sees it. Why can't you?"

"I think it's time we return to the festivities," I said dismissively. "Father and Mother will be making their entrance soon, and will be expecting me to join them."

I turned from her and reentered the Ballroom, sweeping my long hair over my shoulders and forcing a genial expression. As I walked, the ball gown that had been created especially for this occasion floated airily around my ankles. Made of white silk chiffon that followed the curves of my body, it had lace-accented bell sleeves that almost touched the floor. Upon my head I wore an intricately designed silver tiara, its delicate diamond flowers offset by tiny leaves forming three gentle arches that crested in the middle. Miranna walked at my side, no doubt hoping to resume our discussion, but I prevented her from doing so by greeting everyone we passed.

The voice of Lanek, the Palace Herald and my father's personal secretary, rang out from the front of the Ballroom as he began his traditional announcement. Although he had incredible lung capacity, he was rather short and stocky, and bore a marked resemblance to an overfed and contented cat.

"All hail the King, King Adrik of Hytanica, and his Queen, the Lady Elissia!"

Everyone, including Miranna and me, bowed or curtseyed before my parents as they entered the Ballroom from the Dignitary's Room onto a raised platform. The Dignitary's Room was adjacent to my parents' quarters and served as a waiting area for the King and Queen, and occasionally for special guests, prior to making their formal appearances.

My parents were accompanied by the Captain of the Guard, Cannan, a tall and imposing man with dark hair and eyes who rarely smiled. Close in age to my father, he was a member of the nobility and also the Commander of the Hytanican Military, having assumed that position during the Cokyrian War shortly before my father had become King. In the years since then, he had earned both my father's respect and friendship, and often accompanied the King as an advisor and bodyguard.

My father and mother were dressed in similar colors this evening, as was their habit on formal occasions. My mother wore a golden gown with intricate red stitching on the bodice; a crown set with rubies adorned her upswept honey-blond hair. My father, whose hair and eye color matched my own, was likewise clothed and crowned in gold, and he shouldered a floor-length deep red robe with thick gold cording on the sleeves and at the neckline. While my mother was demure and dignified, my father was very jovial in nature, with laugh lines around his brown eyes and a little extra weight padding his girth.

"Welcome!" my father proclaimed, inclining his head toward the crowd. "This celebration is not to honor me or my Queen, but in honor of our daughter Princess Alera. By the end of her next year, she will marry, and the man who becomes her husband will ascend to the Throne. I trust that you will show the new King the same loyalty and respect you have shown me throughout my reign. Until then, long live Princess Alera!"

My father motioned to me with his hand, beaming broadly, and our guests repeated his petition, shifting as one to gaze upon me. As I curtseyed receptively, I saw my father look directly at Steldor, who had conveniently located himself close to the platform upon which my parents stood. Baron Galen, Steldor's counterpart, was with him, and a few steps away stood the rest of Steldor's entourage —— two burly soldiers of aristocratic birth called Barid and Devant.

A little shorter and less handsome than Steldor, Galen had wavy ash-brown hair, warm brown eyes, and a build that was quite impressive, though not a match to that of my would-be husband. His father had died in the war when Galen was three years old, and Cannan had been as much a father to him as he had been to Steldor. The young men had both become Field Commanders upon graduation from the Military Academy and were practically inseparable, though Galen was noticeably less cocky and more levelheaded than his friend. I sometimes wondered if it was solely Steldor's influence that brought out the reckless side of Galen's personality.

Barid and Devant had become Steldor's tagalongs during military school. They struck me as less intelligent than their leaders, though they had to add value to Steldor in some way or he would never have allowed them to remain among his comrades.

I had not had many encounters with Steldor and his associates, but their rowdy reputation preceded them. They relished making life as unpleasant as possible for the people they viewed as beneath them (which, for Steldor, was just about everyone), though they primarily concentrated on terrorizing the young cadets at the Military Academy. They never did anything truly harmful, but I was sure the students were tired of having their horses untethered, their boots filled with mud or rocks, and their water salted so it was undrinkable.

Steldor and company also had a reputation for making the

rounds of all the taverns in Hytanica in a single night, growing a little louder with each drink and pulling some fairly outrageous stunts. It was both amusing and irritating to me that regardless of how quickly the rumors about Steldor's behavior circulated, as long as he acted the perfect gentleman around my parents, they remained blind to his faults.

My father and mother stepped down from the stage and approached me, accompanied by Cannan, with the King's personal guards falling in behind. The guests went back to their bantering, and Galen good-naturedly shoved his best friend in my direction, though I doubted Steldor needed any such encouragement, accustomed as he was to conquering the ladies. He was clothed this night in black, with silver trim on his form-fitting dress coat, and he moved with a natural grace that subtly gave notice of his physical prowess. Unfortunately for Steldor, any chance he might have had of eliciting a positive reaction from me was squashed by the irritating smirk he also wore.

"Alera," my father said cheerily, as he and my mother arrived before me, "how do you like the décor? Do you find it tasteful for this occasion?"

I scanned the torch-lit hall, noting the large and glorious flower arrangements evenly spaced around its perimeter and the white chiffon and lace that draped the edges of the refreshment tables just as it draped my body.

"Yes, the decorations are splendid, Your Majesty."

"Now, now," my father chortled. "You know I don't stand on ceremony."

"But how can I help myself when you look so majestic?" I teased.

"You are just as deserving of that title as I am, my dear," he said, reaching out a hand to brush my cheek affectionately. "I would like to speak to you later this evening about the selection of your husband. I know you understand the importance of this decision, but all the same..." He trailed off as Steldor, with impeccable timing, came to stand beside me.

"Your Majesty, My Queen," Steldor said with a bow before turning to face me. "Princess Alera."

A self-assured grin replaced his arrogant smirk as he kissed my hand, and my father, looking immensely happy, gave me a wink.

"Lord Steldor." I acknowledged him coolly, and I had the feeling my father would have liked to take back his approving wink.

Steldor crossed his arms, a shadow of a pout tainting his features, and I stole a glance at the Captain of the Guard, who stood as impassively as always. His job was to protect the Royal Family, not to become emotionally involved in its dealings, but I thought I could detect the faintest urge within him to roll his eyes at his son's behavior.

Conversation resumed with surprisingly little input from Steldor, for he was watching me intently, no doubt plotting his next course of action. Displeasure at his manner flared within me, and I moved further away from him as Miranna, clasping the hand of her good friend Semari, floated into our midst.

Semari was the fourteen-year-old daughter of a wealthy landowner, Baron Koranis, and his wife, Baroness Alantonya. Semari's parents were among those who had suffered the loss of a child toward the end of the Cokyrian War. Their lives had always been clouded by tragedy and mystery, for their first-born had been taken in the night from his cradle a week after his birth. His body had not been among those returned by the Cokyrians. The family had moved on as best it could, and two years later, Semari had been born, followed over the next five years by two more daughters and finally an all-important son, for only a male could inherit titles and property.

Now that my effervescent sister and Semari were capturing everyone's interest, I seized the opportunity to exit the Ballroom. With a nod to the Palace Guards in the corridor,

I stepped onto the landing of the open double staircase and peered over the railing to the floor twenty-five feet below. Seeing no signs of movement other than that of the guards stationed by the front doors, I descended the set of stairs to my left and stepped into the Grand Entry Hall, from which one could pass under the Grand Staircase and into the Throne Room, or proceed into either the West or East Wings of the Palace.

I headed into the West Wing, which contained, among other things, the King's Drawing Room, the small dining room that had been the scene of my date with Steldor, the Meeting Hall, and the service areas of the Palace. As I strolled, I listened to the scuffing of my leather-soled slippers against the stone beneath my feet. These floors had not been kind to me in my youth. Running up and down the halls barefoot had made my feet sore, and tripping had resulted in more than a few skinned knees and bloodied noses. My parents had at times been unable to tend to me when I was hurt, for my sister had been very sick as a child and had needed special care. They had also, of course, been trying to put the Kingdom back together in the aftermath of the war. As a result, my personal bodyguard had acted as more of a parental figure to me during my early years than had either of my parents.

I glanced around, but London was nowhere to be seen. A smile crept across my face at the thought that he might not have seen me leave the Ballroom; he had been moving among the crowd, alert for signs of trouble.

Reveling in my unexpected freedom, I turned to walk past the Meeting Hall and toward the rear of the Palace, intent on seeking sanctuary in the garden. When I reached the back entry, the Palace Guards drew open the heavy oak doors and I stepped outside. Following required procedures, one of the guards announced my arrival to his peers who patrolled the area's perimeter.

My father had often warned Miranna and me not to enter these grounds without a bodyguard. He feared the garden was an ideal target for enemy infiltration, as access to the Palace estate could be gained by scaling only one barrier, the wall that the garden had in common with the northernmost wall of the city. This concern was counterbalanced in part by the wildness of the forested and mountainous terrain that lay to the north of the city, and in part by the fact that this portion of the city's barrier rose ten feet higher than the rest. In any event, I had never believed there could be danger amidst such beauty.

It was now fully dark, and only the moon and the torches anchored to the stone walls of the garden provided light. I took a deep breath of the scented air and walked forward into the shadowland, glad for the opportunity to savor the quietude of the evening alone.

"Don't think I didn't see you leave the Ballroom."

I jumped and spun around to find London leaning against the Palace doors, one eyebrow cocked tauntingly. He was dressed, as always, in a brown leather jerkin layered over a long-sleeved white shirt. Leather bracers covered his wrists and forearms, and twin long-knives hung from his belt. He wore tall leather boots folded down below the knee, and I could see the handle of a dagger extending from one of them. A silver ring shone on the first finger of his right hand.

"I was —— I was just going for a walk," I stammered. "I didn't want to bother you with something so trivial."

London smiled in genuine amusement.

"Nice try. It's my job to protect you and make sure you don't go off and do something foolish —— like this. I'd like to see you try that excuse on your father."

"You're not going to tell him, are you, London?" I asked, feeling a rush of panic. Years of war had left my father extremely paranoid, as evidenced by the fact that Miranna and

I were almost constantly accompanied by bodyguards. I knew only too well how displeased he would be if he learned that I'd deliberately slipped away from the man charged with my protection, for I had been bruised by his anger in the past.

"No, I won't tell him," London laughed. "I only said so because I knew you'd lose your nerve if I did."

I fixed him with my most withering glare and turned to stalk down one of the pathways.

"Well, I suppose you'll have to come with me then," I tossed over my shoulder. "Just drop back as far as you're permitted and don't say a word."

"Whatever you say, Princess."

"I mean it, London," I said, catching the mockery in his tone.

"Of course. I can appreciate your desire for some peace." This time he sounded sincere, with a trace of an apology.

I walked along the path, soothed by the rustle of the plants and the trees in the soft breeze. Crickets chirped around me, and I found myself enjoying the sounds of the night as much as I did the garden's fragrance. True to his word, London was completely silent, to the point where I wondered if he was even behind me.

I turned a corner and gasped, barely stifling a scream. Eyes —— luminescent green eyes —— stared at me from the darkness. As I struggled to focus my gaze, fear coursing through my veins, I could discern the sinister outline of a man, clad all in black. He stepped toward me, and a glint of moonlight off metal told me he held a sword in his right hand.

"Princess," he said slyly, in a higher pitch than I had expected.

I backed away, but before I could turn to run, London seemed to fall from the sky and land between the intruder and me, twin double-edged blades drawn and ready. He engaged in combat with the young man, who had been so startled by my bodyguard that he had loosened his grip on his sword. I stood rooted to the spot as the trespasser's weapon flew through the air and landed a few feet away. Dropping his left blade, London twisted one of the intruder's arms behind his back, pressing his other knife against the man's throat.

"Tell me, *Cokyrian*," London spat, as if the name were a bad taste in his mouth. "How many of you are there?"

The Cokyrian made no reply, and I took a small step closer, wanting to get a better look at the assailant, even though my body still tingled with fright. I squinted through the darkness and my mouth fell open in surprise.

"You're... a woman?"

The intruder made no response except to snort at my stupidity for thinking she could be anything *but* a woman.

"Stay back, Alera!" London snapped, and I halted, unaware that I was putting myself in danger. "Call for the guard!"

I hesitated, for the only guard I'd ever had to call was the one right in front of me, but London sharply reminded me of the urgency of the situation.

"Now!"

"Guard!" I shouted, hurrying toward the Palace, repeating the call several times.

By the time I had reached the pathway that formed the perimeter of the garden, three of the men on patrol duty were rushing my way.

"London needs assistance," I sputtered, pointing down the path from which I had come. "There is an intruder!"

I followed as the men hastened to my bodyguard's aid.

"Take her to the dungeon," London barked when the guards reached him, releasing the Cokyrian into their custody. "I will alert the Captain and the King."

London grabbed my wrist and hurried me back inside, and I stumbled along behind him as we climbed the spiral stairway to reach the second floor.

"Where are you taking me?" I demanded when we emerged into the corridor, vainly trying to plant my feet to prevent him from dragging me further.

"To your father. I must tell him what has happened."

"And what exactly did happen?" I asked, hoping I didn't sound completely idiotic.

London swiveled around to face me so suddenly that I almost crashed into him.

"Do you not know who intruded upon your precious garden?"

"N-n-no, I ——"

"Well, perhaps you have heard of her people —— the Cokyrians."

"I have, but what does this mean?"

London did not answer but merely tightened his hold on my wrist and continued down the corridor. I did not fight him but insisted once more that he explain.

"Tell me, London!"

"This may shock you, but it is imperative that you refrain from asking brainless questions! I need to think!"

I hated the tears that welled as a result of London's abrupt and rather rude denunciation. He had never snubbed me in such a manner, and I felt almost as though I had been slapped. Wiping the excess moisture from my eyes, I sped up so I would not hinder him. He stopped outside the door to the Ballroom and faced me.

"I'm not going to haul you in there. It's better if we don't make a scene. Just follow behind and go straight to the King."

His manner invited no response, so I simply nodded, trailing him as he wove through the crowd of revelers. He advanced on my father, who stood beside my mother in a group that included Baron Koranis and Baroness Alantonya, along with Cannan and his wife, Baroness Faramay.

London spoke before anyone had a chance to acknowledge

him. He ignored Cannan, his commanding officer, to whom he should have been reporting, choosing to address my father directly.

"Your Highness, there's been a disturbance. I would advise that your guards escort you and your family to your quarters at once."

My father smiled good-naturedly at London. "This is a little unorthodox, don't you think?" he asked with an unconcerned chuckle.

"Your Majesty, I believe you to be a man of some intelligence; therefore, I expect you are wise enough to follow my suggestion. Please, Sire, do as I say."

Turning to his Captain, London brashly issued an order. "Come with me. We must secure the Palace."

Cannan's brows drew together at London's blatant, though not uncharacteristic, disregard for chain of command, but given the urgency in the Elite Guard's voice, he said nothing. Instead, he glanced around for Kade, the Sergeant at Arms in charge of the Palace Guard, who was "slightly less" than Cannan in every way: slightly younger, slightly shorter, slightly less intimidating, and slightly less serious. Kade was already moving our way, having seen London's hasty advance upon the King. Cannan gave the Sergeant his orders and set off with his Deputy Captain.

As soon as the two men had departed, Kade and the King exchanged a few words, and then my father put a hand around my mother's waist, guiding her toward my sister, who stood nearby with Semari, Steldor, and Galen. After speaking quietly to Miranna, my father motioned to Kade, who assisted the King's personal guards in ushering my family onto the platform and through the door that led to the Dignitary's Room. Just before I left, I glanced back at Steldor to see that he and Galen were quickly heading in the direction the Captain and London had taken, not wanting to be left out of anything related to the military.

III

ENEMIES REVEALED

I once again paced in my parlor, too intrigued and perplexed to sit down or rest. I had been escorted to my quarters for safety, with one guard stationed inside the room with me and two more in the corridor. The guard who had temporarily taken over for London stood by the fireplace, trying not to look uncomfortable in my quarters. He wore the uniform of the Palace Guards —— black breeches and a knee-length royal blue tunic with a gold center panel. The sword that had been issued to him upon completion of the training regimen hung from his belt. He was no more than a few years older than Steldor and clearly had not expected to end up protecting the Crown Princess of Hytanica.

"Do you know what is going on?" I boldly inquired. The young man started as I broke the silence.

"I'm afraid you have a better idea of what this is about than I do, Your Highness." He shrugged apologetically, but I could see curiosity in his eyes. "If you don't mind my asking, Princess Alera... What exactly did happen in the garden?"

I stopped my pacing and relayed the entire story to him, including what London had called the intruder.

"Cokyrian?" he repeated numbly.

"That's what London said."

"What are they doing here?"

"Well, actually, there was only one of them."

"There's never just one of them, Princess."

"But what does this mean?" I grumbled, feeling as though he were spewing gibberish.

A dramatic pause followed, and I would have laughed at his display of histrionics if not for his next words.

"It means the war could begin again."

I felt as though the air had been forced from my lungs and instantly understood London's reaction. I knew enough of the tragedy and the horrors of the war that I had no desire to experience such things firsthand, and most definitely not during the reign of my future husband.

"We haven't seen or heard from the Cokyrians in sixteen years," he continued. "The fighting stopped with no victory for either side and no treaty signed, which means the war could resume just as suddenly as it ended."

"How do you know all this?" I demanded, faintly irritated that this young guard could have grasped the significance of the intruder so much more readily than I.

"When I was in training to be a Palace Guard," he answered, puffing out his chest with pride, "I was taught by some of the greatest men in the military, most of whom are veterans of the war."

I nodded, then resumed my pacing, nervously clenching my fists and pressing my fingernails into my palms. I drew up short at a rap on the door, but it was only a servant to start a fire in the hearth, as a chill was now descending upon the room. Eventually, I sat upon the burgundy velvet sofa and flipped through a book in a vain attempt to distract my mind while the hours slowly passed.

Just when my tolerance for waiting had been exhausted, there was another knock on my door and London entered, dismissing the young man who had been standing in for him. The guard bowed to me and hurriedly departed, for the Elite Guard appeared to be in a rather foul mood.

"Who is she?" I clamored, springing to my feet, the book slipping from my lap onto the sofa.

"I assume you mean the woman in the garden," London said, leaning against the wall by the door. His arms were folded across his chest and he seemed to be scrutinizing the pattern of the rug that covered much of the wood floor, either in deep thought or out of a reluctance to encourage my interest.

"You asked me earlier if I had any idea who had intruded upon my 'precious garden.' I believe those were your exact words. Now I want to know."

London flinched as he became the target of my indignation. "I'm sorry... about how I spoke to you earlier." He raised his eyes to mine, expression sincere, and my irritation slipped away.

"You were dealing with the circumstances at hand," I said, moving closer. "No one can blame you for that. Now, won't you please tell me who she is?"

"Her name is Nantilam," he replied, waving a hand as if I were an irksome fly.

I scrunched up my face in concentration; the name sounded vaguely familiar.

"Who?" I finally said, unable to dredge any details from my memory.

"Nantilam. I'm sure you've heard of her. She's ——" London broke off and shook his head, scowling. "I've said too much already."

He pushed away from the wall and walked to the hearth, where he stooped to add wood to the fire.

"London," I pleaded, pursuing him for a few steps. "If you're worried that telling me will rouse my father's anger, I promise that nothing you say to me will find its way to him. I am well aware that he does not view such matters as appropriate for the ears of a woman, and you would not be the only one with whom he would be displeased. Now, who is she?"

London regarded me for a moment before relenting. "Nantilam is the High Priestess of Cokyri. You might say she's their Queen, except that she bears no marital ties to their Overlord. They are siblings."

"So what exactly is her purpose?"

He sighed, recalling how little I knew of the Cokyrian lifestyle.

"In Cokyri, females are held in higher regard than males, and historically women have ruled the Kingdom. Now, for reasons long since forgotten, the High Priestess and her brother, the Overlord, reign over Cokyri together. The Overlord is a seldom seen and greatly feared entity who protects and defends the High Priestess and the Cokyrian people. Nantilam rules Cokyri in all other respects."

"Why are the people so afraid of the Overlord?" I probed, curiosity roused.

"He is not viewed as a person, like our King. He is a fierce warlord, evil and terrifying, sensationalized by decades of legends and myths. They say he has the power to wield black magic, to call it forth from his wicked soul. That he can kill you or worse with a wave of his hand. And it is not just the Cokyrians who tell these stories; Hytanicans swear by them also —— soldiers who met him on the battlefield and never returned to the way they once were. Few returned at all."

"Did you ever see him?" I asked with trepidation.

I knew little about London's past, other than that he had fought in the war —— he was, first and foremost, a soldier of Hytanica and had been before becoming a member of the King's Elite Guard. I had never asked about his life, and he had never volunteered any information.

London turned to gaze at the crackling fire and did not respond for a long time.

"I did," he finally answered.

My inquisitiveness got the better of me, and I pressed further. "What is he like?"

"We were talking about Nantilam," London said tightly, eyes once more on me, forbidding me to insist he recount more.

I yielded, abandoning my pursuit of information about the warlord and hoping I hadn't quashed his willingness to share what he knew about Nantilam.

"Then please, tell me more about the High Priestess." To my relief, he motioned for me to sit, and I resettled upon the sofa as he continued.

"We don't know much. Despite all his secrecy, we actually know more about the Overlord than the High Priestess. She was not involved in fighting the war, and has not been of particular importance to us... until tonight. Now we need to know what she was doing in the garden of the Hytanican Palace."

"Where was she taken?"

"I sent her to the dungeon, remember?"

"What will be done with her?"

He sighed, clearly tiring of my tenacious interest.

"She'll stay in a cell overnight, and tomorrow she'll be brought to the Throne Room for questioning."

"Will I be allowed to be there?"

"Well, you are a member of the Royal Family." London ran a hand wearily through his silver hair. "However, your father could forbid your attendance."

I frowned, all too familiar with the restrictions brought about by my father's overzealous concern for safety.

"By next year I will be Queen. I must be prepared for that in every way possible, and that means learning about the enemy, doesn't it?"

"Yes, but you will not be *King*. It will not be left to you to make important decisions for the Kingdom, so your knowledge of the enemy, as you call it, is inconsequential."

I was fuming inside, for I knew London was right and that my father in all likelihood would bar me from the interrogation.

"I don't care," I sputtered, rather immaturely. "I will be there, no matter my father's opinions."

London gave an unconcerned shrug. "You should go to bed. Tomorrow will be a notable day, I'm sure."

"Good night, London," I murmured, rising to my feet as he left, for he was now off duty.

I prepared for bed, confident that the Palace Guards outside my door had been posted until morning, for I knew Cannan and Kade well enough to realize that they would view the evening's developments as necessitating extra precautions. I snuffed out my lantern and slid under my comforter, my exhausted body battling my restless mind, for the former sought sleep while the latter wrestled with the best way to approach my father in the morning. My body eventually won out and I fell into oblivion, with no firm plan of action at the ready.

———

"Father!" I called, and my voice echoed throughout the cavernous Throne Room, with its stone walls and floor, and twenty-five-foot-high oak-beamed ceiling. It was just after sunrise, and the weak light that filtered through the windows high in the northern wall did little to dispel the morning's somber atmosphere. I had risen early, determined to be present when the prisoner was brought in for questioning, and had just begun my persuasive assault upon the King.

A spacious marble dais was centered at the far end of the Hall, and my father regarded me from where he sat upon his jewel-encrusted throne. My mother's throne stood to his left but was unoccupied, although whether by her choice or my father's decree I did not know. Two ornate chairs were positioned to the left of her throne, to be used by Miranna and me on those occasions when we attended my parents in the Hall of Kings, as this room was also known.

As I closed the distance between us, with London at my heels, my father stood, his disapproving expression intensified by the austere faces of my ancestors in the portraits that hung to my left and right. The King had been stunned by my unconventional entrance, as had the dozen Elite Guards who stood six to each side of the thrones, their expressions matching my father's exactly. Only Cannan, who stood on the King's right, seemed unperturbed.

"Alera," my father said, dropping his volume but not his scold. "You should not be here."

"I've come to witness the interrogation. I see no reason why I should be confined to my quarters."

"But you must stay in your quarters. I will not have my daughter exposed to the vile creature about to be brought before us."

"I am not a child. I will be Queen in one year. And I have already been exposed to her, for I am the one who was threatened in the garden. Out of all those assembled here, it is I who most deserve to know the significance of this incident."

My father, his mind already focused on the day's business, was at a loss for a response. He moved his mouth to articulate an argument, but no sound came forth. Before he could rally to deny my request, he was distracted by the opening of a door at the far end of the Throne Room, and I knew the prisoner was about to be brought into the Hall.

"Stay," he muttered irritably.

"Thank you," I said, and both he and I took up our seats, London moving to stand behind me.

Kade emerged through the door that led to the dungeon, followed by two guards who held the Cokyrian between them.

The dungeon was a wholly unpleasant place that I had only visited once in my life, thanks to London's willingness to satisfy a ten-year-old's curiosity. There were many cells with stone walls, dirt floors, and thick wooden doors, each with a barred window barely large enough to show a prisoner's full face. It was dark, lit only by dim torches along the corridor walls, and the dampness created a cold that could not be forgotten, even were you fortunate enough to be released.

I did not know how the woman cast before the King had been able to abide her time in our custody. The shadows on her face gave evidence of a rough night, but still she was striking. Her eyes were large and many different shades of green, somehow stormy as the sea and bright as the spring at the same time. Her hair, though unkempt, was a beautiful deep red, falling unevenly to her rounded jaw, and her skin was golden, as if she had spent her life in constant sunlight. She was clothed in black, her shirt and leggings made of a lightweight and fluid fabric. A most unusual silver pendant hung about her neck —— narrow at its gold-tipped base, it widened slightly in a graceful three-inch curve as it flowed upward, banding with six overlapping pieces of silver, reminding me of blades of grass bending before a breeze.

"Tell us who you are," demanded my father, staring down at her and growling out the words with a commanding quality that he saved for criminals and intolerably misbehaving daughters.

The prisoner, whose hands were bound in front of her, did not respond but shifted position, pushing herself more upright so that she crouched on one knee, the other foot planted beneath her. Her head was bowed, although most certainly not out of respect.

"Answer now, Cokyrian," my father again ordered, and I stared at the scene in confusion, for I would have thought it unnecessary to press the woman about her identity.

Still she did not reply but slowly raised her head, meeting the gaze of her enemy evenly, almost challengingly, and there was an unmistakable aura of power about her.

"Need I remind you that you are in our control, and we therefore have the ability to make you talk? You would do well to cooperate."

At last Nantilam spoke, her tone derisive. "And you would do well to let me go, for I am not now, nor will I ever be, in your control, Hytanican cur."

The insult had barely reached my ears when I felt, more than heard, London move forward to jump from the dais and land before the prisoner. With a swift kick to the chest, he knocked her backward off her feet, and I gripped the arms of my chair in alarm, terrified that his hatred of Cokyri had taken control of his senses. I watched in horror as he dropped down beside Nantilam, one of his blades pressed against her throat, his deep indigo eyes boring into her belligerent green ones.

"How did she obtain a weapon?!"

Cannan was striding down the steps of the dais, jaw clenched in rage. He halted next to London and yanked Nantilam to her feet. As my bodyguard stood, I barely registered, above the wild beating of my heart, the clatter of the small dagger the prisoner had been clutching when it landed on the floor.

London reached out with one hand and jerked the silver chain from the prisoner's neck, examining it thoroughly, for the pendant looked broken. Picking up the dagger, he carefully fit it into the portion of the pendant that dangled from the chain.

My father had risen to his feet and was now twisting the Royal Ring he wore upon his right hand in agitation, his expression a mixture of disgust and fear.

"Take her away," he ordered. "Bring her before us again at the end of the week, with a looser tongue."

Kade signaled to his guards, who grabbed the prisoner

by her arms and pulled her away from London and Cannan. She did not resist, but her cool gaze never wavered from my father's face.

While the men conferred, I pondered the question the King had repeatedly posed.

"Father," I asked, when I finally had an opportunity to approach him. "Why did you demand her name when we already know who she is?"

My father's brow creased in bewilderment.

"We do not know who she is, or what she is doing in Hytanica. All we know is that she is a Cokyrian intruding upon our home, and we intend to discover the reason." His frown deepened as he considered me. "Why would you think otherwise?"

"I'm sorry," I mumbled. "I just assumed."

I left the Hall of Kings in a muddled state, wanting to talk to London, who had stayed behind in deep discussion with Cannan. I knew, however, that he would soon return to duty as my bodyguard, providing ample opportunity for me to satisfy my curiosity and clear up my confusion.

IV

TREACHERY AFOOT

hough the interrogation had not yielded any information about Nantilam, the next few days did indeed prove to be notable. Cannan had organized a search of the entire Kingdom for other Cokyrians who might have been aiding our prisoner in her as yet undetermined scheme; he also had put additional security measures in place within the Palace. No member of the Royal Family was to be left unguarded at any time for any reason, which meant that London was now essentially on duty twenty-four hours a day. In addition, Kade, at Cannan's direction, had posted Palace Guards around every corner, and areas that were already under guard were reinforced, so it was impossible to be alone under any circumstance.

As the initial flurry of activity subsided, my father tried several times to talk to me, no doubt about choosing a suitor and how that suitor should be Steldor. While I was confident he would never *force* me to marry Cannan's willful and arrogant son, I also knew he would not understand my resistance to the match. Most people agreed with my father's assessment of Steldor, and it pained me to witness the adoration that was heaped upon him; it seemed every young man wanted to be like him and every young woman wanted to be in his arms. Giggly girls were the worst, inflating his already overblown ego a little more with each compliment they paid him. From their point of view, he was status and wealth wrapped in a very enticing package, and they did not seem to mind that he toyed with them for his own amusement. But I needed neither status nor wealth and had no interest in being used for sport.

Ultimately, my father did manage to confront me about my marriage prospects. I was lounging on the sofa in my parlor in the early evening when there was a knock on the door.

"Should I get that, or do you want to pretend you're not here?" London asked from where he was placidly leaning against the wall in the back of the room.

"You can answer it, if *you* wish to do so," I replied with a shrug.

I tried to disregard his last comment. It was true that I would use that ruse on occasion when I was trying to avoid someone, and London knew I was not looking forward to a conversation with the King. In any case, he went to the door and granted entrance to my father, who swept across the threshold before I had time to mentally prepare.

"Alera," he said cheerfully, "with all that's been going on, I feel as though we've been dodging each other!" He chortled at what he considered to be a joke. "It's good to finally have some time when we can talk."

"Shall I step outside?" London offered from his position by the open door.

"No, no. That's not necessary at all. I'll only be a moment. Besides, you'd probably run afoul of one of your Captain's rules if you did. I wouldn't want to be responsible for getting you in trouble with Cannan!"

London closed the door and rested against the wall, arms crossed in his usual manner, and I straightened my posture as my father settled beside me on the sofa.

"As I was saying, Alera, it's wonderful that we're finally able to spend some time together. I had intended to speak to you on the night of your birthday, but things got a bit chaotic. Thank goodness for Cannan's clear head. If it weren't for him, I don't know what sort of mess we'd be in right now!"

London bristled slightly in an uncommon show of annoyance that my father was giving Cannan credit for dealing with the intruder. All the same, he held his tongue.

"What I would like to discuss with you is the selection of your husband," my father continued, his brown eyes warm and affectionate. "I was delighted to hear from Lord Steldor that he greatly enjoyed the evening he spent with you. Tell me, has any other young man caught your eye?"

While almost any young man would have been better than Steldor from my point of view, I could think of no one whom my father would be willing to seriously evaluate. Steldor was clearly the heir apparent; he had been groomed his entire life to be the successor to the King.

"I'm afraid not, Father."

"I will not conceal my thoughts from you," he responded, a satisfied air settling over him. "I am content that Steldor is the only young man under consideration, and I am quite heartened that he has shown an interest in you."

I suppressed a grimace, having noticed that my father was far more concerned about Steldor's opinion of me than he was about my opinion of Steldor.

"Lord Steldor is... a remarkable person. But I am not convinced he is the man I should marry."

"What can you possibly mean, Alera?" my father asked, genuinely shocked.

"I simply mean..." I was scrambling for a rationale other than the truth, which he would never view as sufficient. "I see

Steldor only as a friend. Perhaps it would be better if he were to marry Mira."

"Oh, don't be ridiculous," he scoffed. "If he married Miranna, he wouldn't become King."

"But she is better suited to his... personality."

"And he is better suited to be King than anyone else in this Kingdom." My father's increasing level of frustration was evidenced by the increasing animation of his hands. "And ability to rule is the primary basis upon which this decision is to be made."

"I understand that, Father," I glumly acknowledged, looking toward the floor.

He cupped my chin to raise my face to his, and his countenance softened.

"It is surely not a big step from friend to husband; I insist you consider Steldor in that capacity."

"Yes, Father," I murmured, deciding it was best at this time to go along with his desires.

"Very good!" he exclaimed, clapping his hands together, his cheerful mood restored. "Then I shall inform him that you are receptive to his advances."

Before I had a chance to protest, my father stood and whooshed out the door.

"No," I whispered, and I could feel the color draining from my cheeks. "What have I done?"

I caught the smirk forming on London's lips and sprang to my feet.

"Don't you dare laugh!"

"I wasn't going to," London insisted, though the smile did not fade from his eyes.

Feeling tense, I sent for Sahdienne to draw a bath for me. My bath chamber served its purposes with a washbasin on a stand and a garderobe built into the sidewall of the castle.

What made it unique, however, was the large tub that was sunk into the tiled floor. Water was supplied to the room by pipes that ran within the walls to one of several wells serving the Palace and was heated by virtue of the double-sided fireplace that served both my bedroom and parlor.

While I bathed and continued my preparations for bed, London waited somewhat uncomfortably in the parlor. Until Cannan's recent orders, his assignment as a bodyguard had not required him to be within my quarters while I attended to such personal tasks. Finally ready to retire, I dismissed Sahdienne and opened my bedroom door a crack to murmur good night to London.

Slumber eluded me as I considered what the morning would bring, for the Cokyrian woman would be dragged before the King and the Captain once more, and I was determined to be in attendance. I had started to sink into sleep, when something from the previous interrogation came rushing back and I hastened into the parlor where London was reclining on the sofa. Before I could speak, he was on his feet, causing me to jump in alarm. His practiced eyes scanned the room for an enemy before coming to rest on me.

"And why are you not in bed?" he asked, irritated at having been disturbed for no good reason.

"How did you know?"

He stared at me in bafflement. "How did I know what?"

"How did you know she was the High Priestess and that her name was Nantilam?"

As he grasped my question, his expression clouded over.

"I was mistaken," he gruffly said. "It was speculation that I unwisely made known to you. Now, can I get some peace or do you want me to read you a bedtime story?"

I rolled my eyes, as London's sarcasm told me quite clearly he was not in a talkative mood, and withdrew to my bed to fall into a fitful slumber. I woke while it was still dark, and, after much tossing and turning, rose to get a drink of water. I poured myself a glass from the pitcher on my nightstand and took a sip, knowing I would not get back to sleep unless I was able to walk around and mull things over. But I also knew I would never be able to get past London and was certain he would not embrace the idea of a stroll.

I decided to chance it. Maybe the Elite Guard had dozed off and would not wake to the sound of quiet footfalls. I slowly opened my bedroom door and tiptoed into the parlor. I was about to go into the corridor, amazed at my luck, when I glanced back to the sofa on which London had been resting. He was not there.

I stepped closer to where he should have been, thinking my vision was distorted by the darkness, but there was still no sign of him.

"London?" I called, knowing that if he were near, he would answer me.

Only silence filled the room. I opened the door to the corridor and peered down its dimly lit length, but he was not in sight.

Suddenly losing the will to wander, I opted to curl up in bed, worrying about where London had gone. Why would he have left me unprotected, against his orders? Had there been some problem that had caused him to run off in the middle of the night? I lay quietly for what felt like hours, at long last falling into a troubled sleep, my dreams haunted by images of the terrible fates that might have befallen my bodyguard.

The following morning, I awoke and went straight to the bath chamber, not wanting to check on London for fear he had not returned. I dressed with Sahdienne's help, electing to wear my silver and diamond tiara so I would have an air of authority for this second interrogation.

After Sahdienne had curtseyed and left, I walked into the

parlor, where, to my relief, London was waiting next to the door into the corridor in his characteristic stance, back against the wall, arms crossed over his chest. We surveyed each other for a short while before either of us spoke.

"What?" London smirked. "Did I put my shirt on backward or something?"

"No!" I blurted, realizing I had been staring at him word-lessly for an inordinate length of time. "I was just wondering where you were last night."

London's smile disappeared. "I don't know what you're talk-ing about," he said, shifting his position, as though uneasy.

"I got up in the dark and you weren't here."

"I didn't go anywhere. I might have stepped into the cor-ridor for a moment, but other than that, I was here all night. Perhaps you were dreaming."

"Pretty vivid dream, I'd say." I bit my lower lip in agitation. "Why are you lying to me, London?"

"I'm not lying to you!" he snapped, pushing away from the wall, his eyes flashing. "Are you accusing me of abandoning my charge?"

"No, of course not," I said, taken aback by his anger.

Abandoning his charge would mean disregarding everything he stood for, all the oaths he had taken as a soldier of Hytanica and a member of the King's Elite Guard. It would mean forfeit-ing his career, perhaps even his life.

"I didn't mean to imply any such thing. I'm sorry if I offended you. I was just... curious."

"If you still want to witness that interrogation, we'd better be going." His manner was brusque and his voice still simmered with indignation.

We walked in silence toward the spiral staircase, a sense of shame resounding within my chest at how I had spoken to London and at how he had reacted, though I knew he would pardon me, for he always did. As we descended the stairs to the first floor, loud and disgruntled voices drifted to us from down the corridor, and my father, the Captain, and four Elite Guards came into view.

"How can this be true?" My father's voice was frantic, and he was almost spinning the Royal Ring upon his finger.

"She must have escaped during the night. When Kade went to retrieve her this morning, she was gone." Cannan's response was calm, but worry lines creased his forehead.

"Is there a problem?" London queried, attracting the attention of the others as we drew near.

My father cut in before Cannan could speak. "It would seem that our prisoner broke out sometime during the night and has fled."

"Has the area been searched? She may still be on the Palace grounds."

"Yes, the search of the Palace and of the grounds has turned up nothing," Cannan replied, rankled by London's tendency to usurp his authority. "I've expanded the search throughout the city and have alerted our border patrols, but so far, we have found no trace of her."

"How could she have escaped?" I blurted, unable to stop myself, though I knew I was not the one who should be asking questions.

Cannan gave me a stern glance but responded nonetheless.

"That is yet to be determined. According to Kade, her cell was locked, exactly as it should have been, except she wasn't in it."

"None of this makes sense!" my father exclaimed, emphasizing his words with gestures so sweeping that the rest of us took a step away from him. "It should be impossible to escape from our dungeon, with or without the surveillance of the guards!"

"I have asked Kade to summon for questioning any guard who was on dungeon duty last night," Cannan replied. "Unless the Cokyrians really are as clever and cunning as myth suggests, the men should be able to provide some answers."

"Blame the traitor!" one of the Elite Guards who had accompanied the Captain and the King cried out.

"Tadark!" Cannan reprimanded the young Lieutenant harshly. "Enough!"

"There is a traitor among us, make no mistake," Tadark continued defiantly. "The prisoner could not have escaped without help, and only someone who was already in the Palace would have been able to gain entry to the dungeon."

Tadark then dramatically addressed my father. "My only request is that you sleep lightly, Your Highness, and be wary even in the presence of your most trusted guards."

"ENOUGH!" Cannan thundered, his voice so severe that I momentarily felt sorry for Steldor if he'd ever had to endure the wrath contained in that one word.

"Yes, sir," Tadark responded, but his sullen tone indicated he believed himself justified in making his point known.

Since there would no longer be an interrogation, I returned to my quarters laden with fresh worries that I desperately wanted someone to alleviate. How could our prisoner have escaped? My father had said it was nigh onto impossible to break out of the Palace's dungeon. Had someone assisted her? But to what end? The more I tried to think things through, the more confused I became, and in the end only succeeded in giving myself a dreadful headache.

———

The next few days were hectic and a little jumbled in my memory. Cannan had again ordered heightened security within the Palace, and Kade had doubled the number of guards stationed at every post and on every assignment. Perhaps more disconcerting, my sister and I were forbidden to leave the Palace at any time, even to visit the garden.

Cannan must have taken to heart the inopportunely expressed conjectures of his young Lieutenant because he ordered that no member of the Royal Family was to be left alone with a single guard. This meant that I was given a second personal bodyguard, and it was my misfortune that the man who received the assignment was none other than Tadark.

Tadark was at least two inches shorter than me, and several inches shorter than London, with well-kept sandy brown hair and brown eyes. He was baby-faced, which gave him an innocent look, although I knew he had to be in his late twenties. Unlike London, he dressed in the uniform of the Elite Guard, a double-breasted royal blue doublet, white shirt, and black breeches, and was obviously proud to have achieved the position. He wore the sword of the Elite Guard on his right hip, from which placement I surmised he was left-handed.

In many ways, Tadark was the opposite of London. He was superstitious and spoke often and at great length. While London tended to blend into the background, Tadark was constantly at my side, always telling me to "Watch out!" for this and "Stay away!" from that. London, of course, found Tadark's methods comical, but I did not. By the end of the week, I was ready to poison the annoying Lieutenant. I began to speculate about how he had become a member of the Elite Guard and resolved to ask London at my earliest opportunity.

Morale inside the Palace dropped throughout the week, and tempers flared as those who worked for the Royal Family started to suspect one another of having betrayed us in some way. Only Cannan, Kade, the members of the Elite Guard, and the King knew the full details of the investigation. While this was probably necessary so as not to compromise the integrity of the inquiry, it also ensured that tension in the Palace remained high.

I was growing increasingly frustrated as London, a Deputy Captain, learned more and more about the state of affairs while

I was left maddeningly in the dark. Although I was a member of the Royal Family, I had no more ability to gather information than did the Palace staff, for Princess or not, I was but a woman and had no need to be involved in military matters. This situation did little to allay my anxiety, and I disliked the feeling that I was a prisoner in my own home, especially when, given the possibility of a traitor, the danger inside was potentially as great as any that lurked outside the Palace walls.

Then one day during the following week, an idea came to me. Steldor, as the Captain's son and a troop commander himself, most likely knew a good deal of information relating to the Cokyrian woman's escape. It was also true that he loved to hear himself talk. As much as I loathed the prospect, it was time for another date with Steldor.

OF STEALTH AND STELDOR

xactly why are you doing this again?" London asked, for the third time in the last half hour.

We were about to leave my parlor, as I was going to be spending the afternoon with Steldor in the Central Courtyard, but I stopped to face him, exasperated by his refusal to drop the subject.

"With all these new rules, the only way I could obtain my father's permission to go outside was to play upon his desire that I spend some time with Steldor."

I wasn't being entirely forthcoming with London —— though the Palace seemed to shrink in on me with each passing day, this was not the reason I had arranged another rendezvous with the Captain of the Guard's son. I needed to know what was going on, and Steldor was going to be my unwitting source.

"So, you're willing to be alone with Steldor for hours just to get a little fresh air?" London said, one raised eyebrow punctuating his skepticism.

"London, you should be jumping at this opportunity, just as Tadark did," I pointed out, trying to distract him from the fact that I would be without a bodyguard for most of the day. "You are free of your duties for once and should be taking advantage of that, not trying to dissuade me from my plans.

And remember, this wasn't my decision. It was the King's. He has somehow acquired the idea that Steldor is a little put off by you and thinks it would be best if the two of us spent some time together outside of your shadow. Besides, Steldor could protect me if the need arose, and there are dozens of guards stationed in the Courtyard. So go into the city! Do… whatever it is you do for entertainment! Be thankful that you finally have a day when you don't have to worry about me or my schedule."

Guilt nipped at me for not being completely honest —— I had been the one to tell my father that Steldor was uncomfortable around London —— but if my bodyguard were allowed to be my chaperone, he would figure out what I was doing and spoil any chance I might have for success.

"I still don't like it," London said morosely. In a rare display of affection, he reached out a hand and brushed the backs of his fingers along my jawline. "And I can no more stop worrying about you than I can stop my heart from beating."

I couldn't restrain my smile, despite my determination to stay firm.

"I know you don't like Steldor or the King's decision, but you must comply with it."

"It isn't just dislike. I don't trust him. Have you forgotten what he tried last time?"

I put my hands on my hips, my patience put to the test.

"He won't try anything out in the open in broad daylight, London. He's not that idiotic. And besides, Madam Matallia has consented to act as our chaperone."

Madam Matallia, plump but nevertheless pinch-faced, was the elderly woman who had been instructing Miranna and me in etiquette for the past twelve years, and in household management for the last five.

"Madam Matallia? She'll be asleep under a shade tree within five minutes. And even if she's not, she adores Steldor. She'll purposefully look the other way in the hope that he kisses you!"

I again fought a smile, for Madam Matallia's infatuation with Steldor was precisely the reason I had requested her.

"And what of his *amazing scent*? How will you ever resist him?" London had moved to lean against the door, as though standing in front of it would make me forget where it was located.

Gnawing on my lower lip in frustration, I made one final attempt to mollify my bodyguard. "I know what I'm up against this time, so if he tries to kiss me, I'll slap him, all right?"

"Well, that would certainly be a new experience for him," London muttered.

As we left my quarters, he crossed his arms and sank into a stony silence. In an effort to dispel the tension, and since Tadark was not with us for once, I decided now was the time to ask about my younger guard.

"London, I've been wondering about something. Tadark doesn't seem to fit the mold of an Elite Guard. Do you know how he came to be one?"

My bodyguard uncrossed his arms and smiled a little despite his somber mood, and the discord between us eased.

"Well, that depends," he said, casually running a hand through his hair.

"On what?"

"On which version you want to hear."

"There's more than one?"

London nodded, his smile broadening into a grin. "Do you want to hear the official version, the one Tadark claims to be true, or an eyewitness account from another guard?"

"Begin with Tadark's, then tell me the other," I eagerly prompted, sensing I was about to hear an interesting story.

We had reached the spiral staircase, but rather than proceeding down it, London settled himself against the wall.

"The incident leading to Tadark's placement in the Elite Guard occurred a few years ago and involved your mother. The Queen had been browsing the merchandise in the market and was about to make a purchase when an imbecilic thief snatched her money pouch from her hands, bumping into her and knocking her to the ground. Her guards ensured she had not suffered injury before pursuing the man, so the cretin was given a head start... and then Tadark showed up on the scene. According to Tadark, he saw the thief assault the Queen, then gave chase, catching him, wrestling him to the ground, and taking him into custody before the others could lend a hand."

I almost laughed out loud at the notion of Tadark acting so heroically. "And the other version?"

"The beginning is very much the same," London said, enjoying the telling of the tale. "It is in the circumstances surrounding Tadark's arrival that the accounts differ greatly. According to one of the Queen's own men, he and another guard pursued the thief. They were gaining ground on the man when Tadark, then a City Guard, stepped out from a side street. It would be correct to say that the thief did not see Tadark in time to avoid a collision, and the two crashed into each other. The criminal was knocked out, presumably from the impact of his head upon the ground, and the other guards arrested him as Tadark struggled to his feet.

"Tadark and the unlucky thief were brought before the Queen, who, naturally enough, assumed some act of bravery on Tadark's part. Upon her return to the Palace, she insisted that he receive recognition for his 'noble deed.' Cannan thereupon placed him into the training program for the Elite Guard. I have always suspected that some other issue was preoccupying the Captain at the time, otherwise he would have come up with a less grand reward."

London moved away from the wall, indicating with his hand

that we should descend the stairs, and I obliged. As we stepped out into the first-floor corridor, he finished his story.

"I would guess Cannan never thought Tadark would complete the training program, as about half of those who enter drop out. But he inexplicably made it through. Personally, I believe someone made an appalling mistake in determining who was to be admitted to the Elite Guard that year, thus cursing us with the constant and aggravating presence of our dear friend Tadark. My only consolation is that he is unlikely to advance up the ranks of the Guard, always and forever remaining a lowly Lieutenant."

I was forced to stifle another laugh as we walked onto the mosaic stone floor of the Grand Entry Hall and saw both Madam Matallia, clutching a basket of embroidery, and Steldor, carelessly flipping his dagger, waiting for me.

Palace Guards pulled open the twin heavy oak doors, and Madam Matallia, her graying hair arranged into a precise bun, stepped over the threshold and out into the sunshine. Steldor sheathed his dagger and stepped forward to bow and kiss my hand, then smiled lazily at me, an unmistakable trace of tedium in his eyes. Despite the simple style of his belted green suede tunic, he was effortlessly stunning, and I actually felt plain in comparison in my sapphire blue gown. I took the arm Steldor was extending, wondering if he counted me as just another task on his schedule, and glanced back to assess London's reaction. My bodyguard, however, refused to meet my gaze.

The Central Courtyard was one of my favorite haunts, second only to the garden. Lilac hedges lined the wide stone path that led from the Palace to the front gates, the point of entry into the grounds, and their profuse blossoms gave off a fragrance that clung to your clothes and hair like mist to the lowlands. Majestic oak trees, white birches, and flowering cherry trees cast cooling shadows over the benches situated throughout the grassy expanse, while doors on both of the fifteen-foot-high side walls of the Courtyard could be opened to provide access to the equally beautiful East and West Courtyards. It was a lovely place to read, think, or simply daydream. Neither the increased number of guards on the grounds nor the company I was keeping could dampen the joy I felt at being able to spend this early June afternoon outside the Palace in such a pleasant setting.

I came out of my reverie, trying to listen to Steldor, who was once more reminding me of how incredible he was.

"So I thought, 'Why not?' and kissed her on the cheek," he said, sounding as though he were speaking by rote. "I wasn't really attracted to her, but she was totally infatuated with me, and I saw no harm in paying her a little attention."

"Yes," I said sweetly, interrupting his monologue. "There are so many who would be pleased to receive a single crumb of your attention."

He looked bemused for a moment, then continued undeterred.

"She, of course, was delighted to be in my company. But then, who wouldn't be, given my extraordinary looks, heritage, and charm."

My first reaction was to gawk, but then it occurred to me he might be teasing, and I managed to disguise my reaction with a girlish giggle. Sensing an opportunity, I glanced around for Madam Matallia, who had perched herself upon a shaded bench and was conveniently out of earshot.

"Not to mention how strong and brave you are," I daringly put forth. "I have no doubt that everyone admires you and, of course, would trust you with important information."

"Well, I do hear about many things," Steldor confirmed. I couldn't believe how easily my scheme was succeeding.

"Oh, do tell me about something... official," I said, moving closer to him.

He put his arm around my waist, and I nervously hoped I hadn't given him the wrong kind of encouragement.

"What do you want to know?"

"Tell me something about Cokyri, perhaps about the Cokyrian woman who was our prisoner."

"You want to know something about Cokyri?" he repeated, and I wondered if he had caught on to what I was doing.

"Yes, I mean, you're so experienced and smart, you must have a theory about how she escaped."

We stopped walking and Steldor faced me, brows drawn slightly together. I reached out flirtatiously to finger the silver wolf's head talisman that he wore around his neck, and he laughed.

"Well, I *am* experienced and smart," he smirked, placing his hand atop my own and pressing it against his chest. "But *really*, Alera, it would be much simpler just to ask me if you want the details of the investigation."

I stared at his pendant, my cheeks turning every conceivable shade of pink.

"Then again, I do generally enjoy flattery, and your attempt to trick me into providing you with confidential information has been amusing." To my mortification, he put his other hand under my chin, raising my deep brown eyes to his own. "But you'll find it difficult to match my wits."

I jerked my hand away from his, stung by his words, horrified and embarrassed that I had been caught. Spurred by the threat of tears, I turned around, not wanting him to know that he had hurt me. Taking several deep breaths, I walked bleary-eyed toward a stone bench that stood beneath the branches of a white birch tree. When I reached it, I sat down with a poor attempt at dignity, gazing away from him and wishing that London would return and rescue me. After a moment, Steldor walked over to sit beside me, but I could not bring myself to acknowledge him.

"Now, now," he said, in an unbearably patronizing tone, as if to a recalcitrant child. "There's no reason to be this upset that your little ploy didn't work."

When I refused to respond, his voice softened, and he sounded as though he were offering me a treat.

"I know my father and the King would be unwilling to talk about military affairs with you, but I actually see no harm in satisfying your curiosity. After all, there is no use to which you could put the information." He began to play with the hair that tumbled down my back. "All you have to do is ask."

My breath caught in my throat at the humiliating position in which he was placing me, but I swallowed my pride and looked at him, seeing no other way to garner what I wanted to know.

"I would appreciate some information about the investigation into the Cokyrian prisoner's escape."

"Very well," he said, far too pleased. He rested his upper arms on the back of the bench, continuing to play with my dark brown tresses.

"We have reached no conclusions as of yet, but I do know my father has redirected the investigation toward finding a traitor. The two dungeon guards who came on duty at midnight have confessed that they fell asleep during their shift. Neither man has ever shown neglect in his duties before, leading my father to suspect treachery. He thinks the guards were drugged.

"A meal was brought to the men about three hours after they reported for duty, and they nodded off right after they ate. Both say they woke just as the sun was rising, shortly before Kade came to retrieve the prisoner. That gives us the timeframe of the escape."

"Does your father suspect anyone in particular?" I probed, my embarrassment forgotten.

"No, but the traitor would have to know the orders that were issued by Kade to the dungeon guards. They vary day to day, and only those on duty at that time and the Elite Guards would have known the schedule for changing posts. If the traitor knew the orders, he could have drugged the food."

"So, our traitor has to be someone in the Elite Guard?" I forced the sentence from my tightening throat, for while I could not conceive of any of the Royal Family's most trusted guards engaging in such an act of betrayal, the very suggestion was disturbing.

"In theory. Hence the doubling up of all the bodyguards. The drugging also seems plausible because there were no signs of a forced breakout. The keys could easily have been used and returned while the guards were unconscious."

"That's frightening," I murmured, and a chill swept through me despite the warmth of the day.

"Ah, never fear, Princess," Steldor said with a self-assured chuckle, putting his arm around my shoulder and drawing me near. "I'll protect you."

"I'm sure you will," I forced myself to say, slipping from beneath his arm to come to my feet, London's lack of trust in Steldor beginning to nag at me.

"Let's walk a bit more, shall we?" I invited.

I spent most of the afternoon with the Captain's son, sharing a bite to eat with him and listening with feigned interest as he returned to making speeches about himself. Eventually, we went back inside the Palace, I, at least, feeling somewhat guilty about leaving Madam Matallia asleep on her bench. Steldor accompanied me to the spiral staircase, and although he offered to escort me further, I latched on to a Palace Guard as a stand-in for London.

Having escaped Steldor without a kiss, I trod lightly up the steps, picturing the faces of the Elite Guards in my mind as I considered the possibility that one of them was a traitor. Most of them had protected the Royal Family for at least half my life, and I knew that in order to be inducted into the Elite Guard, a soldier's loyalty to the Throne had to be proven. What could have prompted one of them to betray the Kingdom he loved?

I heard muffled conversation coming from inside the library as I reached the second floor and moved in the direction of the sound. As I approached the half-open library door, Tadark's unmistakable voice reached my ears, and I sent the Palace Guard who had walked with me on his way. Words were tumbling from the Lieutenant's mouth in rapid succession, and I assumed London was with him, for no one else would have had the patience to put up with such endless chatter.

"When I was nine, I would steal my father's sword to play with. I never hurt anybody, but I got in a lot of trouble, believe you me. For some reason, I kept doing it, though. I don't know why. I guess I was just destined to be a soldier. It was my dream to become part of the Elite Guard. You people inspired me to become what I am today. I made a lot of stupid mistakes when I was just a soldier, so I didn't think I'd make it, but I did! I remember hearing in military school about the training you have to go through to be in the Elite Guard, and I just thought, *Never*. Never would I survive that. But once I was in the training program, I didn't want to drop out, and so somehow I made it through."

There was a pause, and I pictured Tadark surfacing like a swimmer for air, as his speech had surely put a strain on his lungs. Then he continued, more slowly, his enthusiasm now tempered with curiosity.

"How did you survive it?"

Time slipped away as Tadark waited for London to respond. I guessed that the Deputy Captain was reading a book and not paying heed to what the younger man was saying.

"You're the quiet type, aren't you?" It was still Tadark who was speaking.

"Only around you," London replied absently, at last giving his partner his due.

"Why's that? I really can't picture you talking much ever. You strike me as a bit... dull."

I covered my mouth with my hand in order to keep from laughing out loud, drawing many odd stares from the guards and servants who passed by me.

There was a pause, then London gave an explanation. "I just figure you talk enough for the both of us, Tad."

"My name is *Tadark*."

"What, you don't like the name Tad? I think it fits you. Tad."

"Don't call me that!"

"Whatever you say... Tad."

Tadark exhaled huffily several times, and I was certain London had returned to his book, at ease with Tadark's displeasure. After a moment, the Lieutenant collected himself and attempted again to engage London.

"You want to know why I follow you around all the time?"

"Because we're stationed together?" London drolly guessed.

"Well, yes, but I mean other than that."

"Tell me, Tad. Why do you follow me around all the time?"

"Because I respect you. You're everything I strive to become —— everything an Elite Guard should be."

"Oh, now I feel honored."

"I'd hate to think you'd betray your King and Queen for your own profit."

A few moments of silence greeted this outrageous statement.

"What are you talking about?" London finally said, speaking as though Tadark were hopelessly feebleminded.

"Someone has to have done it —— released the Cokyrian prisoner. It could be you just as easily as it could be anyone else."

"There's no proof that anyone helped her escape."

"Oh, please," Tadark said, as though London had made a

joke. "You know there's a traitor. I'm just saying that... *every-one*... is a suspect."

"You're in no position to point fingers, Tadark. More often than not, the accuser is the guilty party." London was riled. I had never before heard him use a deep, warning tone like the one he was using now. "Don't push it with me. I can cause you a lot of problems, boy."

"*Boy*? Who are you to be calling *me* boy? You look younger than I do!" Tadark was almost squealing, his voice rising dramatically in pitch as he became increasingly overwrought.

A book tumbled to the floor, and I knew London had gotten to his feet.

"Attention! Have you forgotten that I am your superior officer?"

"No, sir, I haven't, sir," Tadark mumbled.

"I didn't hear you," London snarled.

"No, sir, I haven't, sir," Tadark repeated, with greater volume and clarity.

I decided to intervene before some horrible punishment befell my younger guard. I knew London, who generally followed no rules but his own, had to be incensed to have called upon military protocol.

Swinging open the library door, I hailed them, deliberately cheerful. "I was heading back to my room when I heard you talking and thought I might join you here."

London, uncharacteristically agitated, stood across from me in front of the library's bay window, the book through which he had been paging forgotten at his feet, while Tadark was frozen at attention before him amidst several scattered armchairs. Along the right wall, near the fireplace, were a sofa and several additional chairs. On the floor, between the seating areas, was a large rug upon which I had frequently lain as a child, often entertained by drawings that London would make for me. Book-filled shelves formed legions of aisles on the left.

"At ease," London muttered upon seeing me, and the rigidity left Tadark's posture even as an embarrassed flush crept up his neck. The two men glanced at each other, and I could almost hear the question that had formed in their minds —— *Did she hear us?*

"Now, gentlemen," I teased, "judging by your faces, you must have been discussing something I'm not supposed to know about."

There was an awkward hush that was finally ended by London.

"Don't be ridiculous."

I decided to stop making them feel self-conscious.

"Well then, please resume your discussion. I'll just browse through the books while we're here."

My father had assembled a substantial book collection over the years and had insisted that both of his daughters be not only *taught* to read but *permitted* to read a wide variety of subjects. The books themselves represented years of painstaking effort by scribes, who copied the original authors' words onto sheets of parchment that were then bound in leather or in elaborately designed metal covers.

As I meandered down one of the aisles, I ran a finger lovingly over some of the volumes. Here were books of science, theology, philosophy, history, and medicine, along with vocabularies and encyclopedias. There were also compilations of short stories and folktales, as well as poetry, romances, and plays. London, in all likelihood, had been reading one of the books of law, as he had a keen mind and knowledge of Latin. I was thankful that my father was a progressive man when it came to the education of his daughters, as we had been taught how to read, write, and do figures, in addition to the traditional feminine subjects of etiquette, movement, household management, embroidery, and music.

I continued to wander among the dusty tomes, not really in the mood to read but needing some time to think without distraction. I was still unwilling to believe there was a traitor among the Elite Guards, or any of the guards for that matter, but, as Tadark had said, there seemed to be no other possibility. But how could I doubt any of them? They were my guardians, and I trusted each of them with my life. At the same time, any of them could have accomplished the act, except perhaps for Tadark, who was too loud and foolish to get away with something as clever as this escape had been.

The only other option, one to which I clung desperately, was something Cannan had said after our prisoner's escape. He had mentioned that the Cokyrians were famous for their stealth and trickery. I hoped that Nantilam's flight was proof of that and not of a traitor within the Royal House.

VI

SECRETS AND REVELATIONS

I needed additional information. Not about the breakout, but about the Cokyrian people. I ran through the list of those who might be able to tell me something but turned up no one whom I would dare to ask. London would be dubious of my motives and Tadark was unlikely to know anything. I had already solicited Steldor and had no desire to do so again. My father, Cannan, and Kade would refuse to tell me anything and would view such a request from a woman as inappropriate. Settling upon a person whose knowledge of the Cokyrian people was uncertain, I walked back to where my bodyguards sat in tense silence —— London perched on the deep padded sill of the library's sun-streaked window and Tadark in a leather armchair.

"I'm going to seek out my mother," I announced. "I have hardly spoken to her in weeks."

While this was not my true reason for wanting to spend time with my mother, it was accurate all the same, as I had seen her only occasionally at dinner since my birthday celebration nearly a month before. Both London and Tadark rose to escort me to the quarters that my mother and father shared. I knew my mother would be there, as the sun was going down and it was her habit to retire early. She jealously guarded her sleep so there would be no circles beneath her sparkling eyes or lines upon her delicate face, for it would be unacceptable for the King to have anything less than a beautiful wife.

My parents' quarters occupied the opposite corner of the second floor from my own and consisted of five luxurious rooms: two primarily for my mother, two primarily for my father, and one large parlor used by both. It was thought unwise for the rulers of the Kingdom to sleep beside each other at night; separation made it more difficult for an enemy to pose a threat.

A servant girl answered my knock. "Is my mother in her bedroom?" I asked.

"Yes, Your Highness," she responded with a curtsey.

I entered the parlor, leaving London and Tadark in the corridor with the Queen's personal guards, and went to rap upon her bedroom door.

"Come in," my mother responded, her voice airy and melodic.

I opened the door to find her sitting before the mirror at her dressing table, brushing her beautiful long, honey-blond hair. She was already in her nightgown, and her personal maid had drawn the heavy drapes across the window that looked out over the garden.

The color predominating my mother's room was a deep plum that drew out the richness of the wood furnishings. Her bed had elaborately carved posts that matched the carvings on the wardrobe that stood nearby, as well as those on her dressing table. Plum velvet armchairs sat in front of the hearth, while woolen tapestries adorned the walls and blanketed most of the floor.

My mother turned with a smile, gazing at me with blue eyes that were identical to Miranna's in every way.

"It's good to see you, my darling. I trust Cannan's restrictions have not been too stifling for you?"

"I'm managing," I said truthfully, electing not to mention

my escapade with Steldor. "I just wish that the mystery of the Cokyrian prisoner's escape would be solved."

My mother nodded sympathetically as she laid the hairbrush on the table.

"Tell me what you wish to know," she said, gliding to sit upon the bed and gesturing for me to join her, and I was surprised by her insight. "Don't look so astounded," she admonished light-heartedly. "I was the same way at your age —— always wanting to know everything. But you mustn't tell your father that it was I who enlightened you."

"I won't, Mother." I went to sit on the bed, scooting close to her. "What can you tell me about Cokyri?"

She studied me for a moment, and I wondered if I had raised a proscribed subject.

"I'm not sure I am the one you should come to for knowledge of Cokyri. There are many who know more than I, London in particular."

I cocked my head, a bit confused. "Why would London know so much about the enemy?"

"Oh," she said, apparently realizing she had made reference to something about which I did not know. "It may not be my place to tell you."

"Tell me what?"

She hesitated, and I feared she would not continue. With a whisper of a sigh, she relented, reaching out to push my hair away from my face.

"Years ago, toward the end of the war, London was a prisoner of the Cokyrians for almost ten months."

My eyes widened in shock, and it was suddenly difficult to breathe.

"There had been a ruthless battle in which our soldiers were greatly outnumbered. London was in command of the troops at the time, and when our soldiers were forced to retreat, he stayed to the end. When we went back to collect the bodies of our fallen, London was not among them, and we were left to assume he had been taken for interrogation. The Cokyrians rarely took prisoners, and he is the only one who ever survived. Most of the information we have about the Overlord and the High Priestess has come from him."

My mother's lilting voice was sharply out of character with the nature of the topic about which she was speaking, making the story she was telling all the more unreal.

"He was a prisoner at the time the Cokyrians were stealing our children. He said they must have found what they were after, as they abruptly withdrew from our lands. All we really know is that they vacated their encampments and took flight. It was during the disarray surrounding the return of the troops to Cokyri that he managed to escape."

"What exactly do you mean when you say he was 'taken for interrogation'?" I asked, anticipating the worst.

"We know little of what London went through while he was away from us," she replied, patting my hand soothingly. "Those details were not something he wanted to share."

"But did they hurt him?"

I felt ill remembering how London had spoken of the Overlord. I did not want to believe that he had incurred the warlord's wrath, but it was inconceivable that a prisoner would not have been mistreated.

"As I said, we know very little about what he endured," my mother repeated.

It was clear she hoped I would cease my inquiries if she refused to satisfactorily address them, but the determination in my eyes told her otherwise.

"He returned to us in a very strange state," she reluctantly continued.

"What do you mean by 'strange'?"

"He had no physical injuries that we could see, but it took months for him to recover."

"Well, of course it would," I reasoned, enormously relieved that my bodyguard and friend had not been tortured by the enemy. "It would take a while to put such an ordeal behind you."

"Yes, it would, but that's not the kind of recovery I'm talking about."

She raised a hand to delicately massage her forehead, as if encouraging the memories to surface, and I waited, bewildered, for her to carry on.

"He was terribly sick, but not from any illness that our doctors could identify. He seemed feverish, but his skin was colder than ice. He was delirious, unable to speak coherently or respond in any way to what was said to him. He screamed as if in terrible pain, but our doctors could not locate a source for the pain. He ate and drank little for weeks. Our doctors bled him several times, but it made no difference, and they advised us he would die."

She sat deep in thought for a moment.

"We can't imagine the willpower it must have taken for him to return to Hytanica in that condition. When he came to his senses, he told us what he could, about his escape and about the Overlord. I'm afraid your father and Cannan quite besieged him, concerned he would slip back into the mysterious illness that had incapacitated him for so long. Then I suppose he needed time to come to terms with the agony he had endured. He was withdrawn for many months but gradually returned to his former self."

I contemplated the pattern of the tapestry that lay on the floor, trying to make sense of the information my mother had provided.

"London has never mentioned any of this to me," I murmured.

"London is a very private person," my mother offered by way of a rationale. "If you ever ask him about Cokyri, don't let your questions become too personal. Some things are better left buried."

I agreed, knowing that bringing up any of this with London would be uncomfortable for us both.

"Good night, Alera," my mother said, giving me a kiss on the cheek before returning to her dressing table to resume brushing her hair. "Do not let your curiosity lead you to err."

"Good night, Mother. And thank you."

I left her bedroom, taking my time crossing the parlor to the door leading to the corridor. I had been so naïve when I had asked London about Cokyri and the Overlord, on the night the Cokyrian woman had been discovered in the Palace garden. I now understood to some extent why London never spoke of fighting in the war or his experiences with the enemy. I very much wanted to know what he had suffered, but I would never raise the subject with him. I had to accept that I might never know.

———

I tossed and turned in bed that night, plagued by disturbing images, with Tadark and London on duty in my parlor. London had claimed the sofa as his, which meant that Tadark would try to catch a few winks, rather gracelessly, in an armchair. Over the past week, the sound of the Lieutenant's moaning and complaining had put me to sleep, but tonight the noise was irritating rather than calming in its familiarity.

I lay in the darkness, imagining the man reclining on my sofa to be starving in a Cokyrian dungeon, not knowing whether he would live or die. Our dungeon was a horrific place, and I dared not consider how the Cokyrians housed their captives.

He had said he'd seen the Overlord. I had been frightened by the reality that such a person existed in this world. London had faced him. He had borne his fury. Or had he?

London had not sustained any physical injuries but had only suffered from an unusual illness. Perhaps it was a Cokyrian illness —— one of which Hytanicans had not heard and to which we had never been exposed. But if that were the case, the disease would have spread like wildfire and the whole Kingdom would have become infected. And London should have died. The doctors had said it. Maybe the illness was unidentified, but surely a doctor would know when someone was going to die.

As I continued to sort details out in my mind, comprehension dawned. London knew Cokyri better than anyone in Hytanica. It was implausible that someone could have seen the Overlord and not also have seen the High Priestess. He had recognized Nantilam in the garden and had later told me who she was, then had tried to claim he was mistaken. Why would he withhold such information from the Captain and the King? And if he was reluctant to reveal what he knew, why had he shared it with me? I could only presume that my pledge to maintain his confidence had made him more willing to speak than he perhaps should have been, and that he had not thought my father would permit me to attend the interrogation.

And why would he lie to me, not once, but twice? London had never lied to me before, but here, with the Cokyrians, came a side of him that I did not know or like. He had left my quarters during the night of Nantilam's escape, and though he had tried to convince me otherwise, I knew it to be true. I wanted to believe there was an explanation, but I had no faith that he would tell me even if I demanded it of him. And then I came to a decision, one that made me anxious and sad, but that I judged to be right. London might lie to me, but he would not lie to his King.

———

The next morning, I sent word to Lanek that I wished to see my father, then visited our family Chapel, which was in the

East Wing just past the Queen's Drawing Room and the Music Room. At this time of day, sunshine filtered through the dramatic stained-glass windows set high into the eastern wall of the Chapel, glinting off the gilded altar and cross at the front of the room. I slid into one of the intricately carved pews and bowed my head in unspoken prayer, soliciting strength and guidance as I carried out the decision I had reached. Then I departed, determined to see my father, with London and Tadark joining me as I reentered the corridor.

I paced in the small antechamber outside the Throne Room, for I needed permission to enter. The antechamber provided a waiting area for formal audiences with the King and was accessed by walking beneath the Grand Staircase. There were three other points of entry into the Throne Room: one through the guard room next to the Captain of the Guard's office, another through the guard room by the Sergeant at Arms' office, and the last through the King's Drawing Room. The King's Drawing Room was in the West Wing across the corridor from our private staircase and therefore gave my father easy access to the Throne Room from his quarters.

London and Tadark were both in unusually good moods, or perhaps it just seemed so in comparison with my own. They remained on their feet, despite the availability of several armchairs, unwilling to sit down while I remained standing, although London, as always, rested his back against a wall.

"So what time is your 'appointment'?" London teased, referencing my father's need for extremely formal arrangements just to meet with his own daughter.

I gave no response but continued pacing, feeling as though the elaborate tapestries on the walls that depicted battle scenes were telling me I ought to retreat.

"It's rather ironic, really," London persisted. "The Princess can't see the King without an appointment. I suspect it would be easier for her to swim the Recorah River than to see her own father on short notice."

Tadark chuckled, then whipped his head around as though worried someone might have seen him act less than dignified while on duty.

London was more relaxed than he had been the previous afternoon, and it pained me to be in his presence in light of what I was about to do. The military was his whole life. Was I prepared to destroy that? I shook my head. London would have a good explanation for everything, and if he didn't... then he had destroyed his life himself.

Deciding I was in no mood to reciprocate his teasing, London moved on to his new pastime —— antagonizing Tadark. While this was entertaining for both London and me, Tadark did not appreciate the pursuit.

Just when my younger guard had finally conceived of a retort to a rather unkind comment of London's, the doors to the Hall of Kings were pulled open, and I was motioned inside by one of the Palace Guards who stood just over the threshold. I felt weak as I entered, aware that this was my last chance to turn from my decision, but no matter how I felt about what I had come to do, I believed I did not have a choice.

London and Tadark remained outside for the second time in two days as I stepped up to speak to one of my parents. I curtseyed to my father where he sat upon his throne, my eyes falling on the Royal Coat of Arms that hung on the wall behind him. Banners in the Kingdom's colors of royal blue and gold framed the imposing shield, which was divided into quadrants. The top section of the shield was red with a golden lion to symbolize courage, a quality I definitely needed right now. The right section was purple with a silver moon for justice, reminding me that I was relying on my father to be fair. A blue tear upon gold in the bottom section encouraged me to trust in my father's usually kind nature. The final section of the shield consisted of a falcon on a blue background for loyalty, a characteristic I had always believed London to possess and that I hoped he would now display.

"To what do I owe the pleasure of this visit?" my father asked, his deep brown eyes warm and bright, and I knew at once what he was expecting me to address, like a rush of cold wind hitting me in the face.

"It has nothing to do with choosing a husband or with Steldor," I told him, not wanting to move into that topic.

His face fell, and he lost a bit of his good humor. "Well then, what can be so pressing as to seek me out at this time of day? You know I have a busy schedule, Alera." A scold had now crept into his voice.

"I think you'll find this of greater importance than today's business, Father," I asserted, twining my fingers anxiously.

His eyebrows drew together in concern. "Is everything all right? You're rather pale, my dear."

I took a steadying breath before abruptly inquiring, "Do you have any leads as to the identity of the traitor?"

"How do you know about that?" my father demanded.

"Word travels. The guards suspect one another."

"Still, this is not your worry. You needn't be afraid within the Palace, and you should not concern yourself with the military's business."

"Father, please. Do you know who he is?"

He exhaled heavily. "No, we do not. But we will find him... if in fact there is a traitor. Do not fret, Alera. Cannan is taking care of everything."

My eyes passed over the Elite Guards who stood in their usual formation, six to each side of the King.

"Could we talk privately, Father?"

"If that is what you wish."

He stood, puzzled, and stepped down from the dais, motioning me through the door to the side of the thrones that led into his study.

My father's study was warm and inviting, but a bit cluttered. On our left, shelves overflowed with books, and a mahogany desk, littered with parchments, was straight ahead. Against the wall to the right was a brown leather sofa, upon which were strewn even more books. The near right corner of the room was occupied by a fireplace, and several armchairs sat haphazardly in front of the hearth. In the far corner, between the sofa and the desk, was a table that currently held my father's prized chess set. Rich tapestries hung on the walls, and furs strewn on the floor provided softness beneath our feet.

I crossed the study and sat on the sofa, my palms moist from nervousness. My father gathered the books and dropped them on the floor with a resounding thud, then sat beside me, waiting for me to speak.

"London left me alone in my quarters on the night of the Cokyrian woman's escape," I began, without any preliminaries.

"What?" he exclaimed in alarm. "Are you certain?"

"I woke up during the night and London was gone. I called for him —— he was not there."

"You have no doubt of this?"

"I am certain, Father," I confirmed, feeling somewhat queasy. "I would not have come to you if I were not."

"He knew he was not to leave you. Why did you not tell me this sooner?"

"Because London is my bodyguard and my friend. I was afraid of what might happen to him if I did."

My father lay a hand upon my own to quiet them, for I had been fussily clasping and unclasping them in my lap.

"And you no longer fear for him?"

"I fear for him," I said, head bowed. "But I could no longer hide this from you."

"And have you spoken of this to London?"

"He lied to me, Father," I said disconsolately, raising my head to gaze upon his troubled countenance. "I know he left, but he claimed he was with me all night. He said I must have been dreaming."

"Perhaps he is right. In any event, it becomes your word against his. Royal or not, you are but a woman, and London is a highly respected soldier of Hytanica."

He stood to pace in front of the cold hearth. I took a heaving breath, regret nipping at me, and then resumed my confession.

"That is not the only reason I came to you. If you remember, on the night the Cokyrian woman invaded our garden, it was London who put her under arrest."

"Yes, I remember," my father said, coming to a halt. "Of what importance is that?"

"London said something strange to me that night. He spoke of the woman as if he knew her. He said she was the High Priestess of Cokyri, and that her name was Nantilam. When you told me her identity was not known, I asked him about it, and he said he had been mistaken. He lied to me again, Father. I know he did."

My father said nothing but stood deep in deliberation, distractedly rubbing the Royal Ring with the fingers of his left hand. I fidgeted, feeling as though I had just disclosed the most important secret of my life, a secret I had promised to keep for someone I dearly loved.

"This cannot be," my father muttered under his breath.

"I know that he was a prisoner of war in Cokyri for ten months. He would know the High Priestess if he saw her."

"Has London told you —— ?"

"No. He hasn't told me of his time as a captive." At his baffled expression, I gave an honest explanation. "I spoke to Mother. I went to her for information and she obliged. Be angry with me if you must be angry with someone."

He said nothing but resumed his pacing.

"I'm sure London has an explanation for why he was gone," I said tentatively, "other than what I know we're both thinking. He will tell you if you ask it of him."

"But nothing can excuse the fact that he left his post while under strict orders not to do so. And any explanation he has will not justify keeping this woman's identity a secret."

He pivoted, then moved to open the door of his study. "Guard! Summon the Captain immediately."

"Yes, Sire," one of the Elite Guards responded before exiting the Throne Room.

"Alera," my father said, coming to sit next to me once more and enfolding my hands in his. "It's very important that you tell Cannan exactly what you told me."

I nodded. As much as it pained me to know that with every word I spoke, I condemned my bodyguard and friend further, I would tell the Captain of the Guard the truth.

After a few minutes, Cannan strode into my father's study.

"What is it, Your Majesty?" he inquired with a touch of urgency. "Your guard made it sound as if the Cokyrians were marching on us as we speak."

My father stood and motioned to me, and I complied with his command, telling Cannan all that I knew. While the Captain's reaction to the information was difficult to discern, his slightly drawn eyebrows told me he too was shaken by this information.

"London and Tadark are in the antechamber?" he finally asked, his dark, perceptive eyes fixed on me.

I inclined my head in confirmation, and he spoke to the

Elite Guard outside the door to the study just as my father had done.

"Bring London and Tadark in, now."

Cannan glanced at my father, who indicated to me that I should accompany them, and the three of us reentered the Hall of Kings to await my bodyguards. My father took the throne, while I sat in one of the ornate chairs to his left, Cannan standing on his right.

The guard did as he had been told, and soon both men were before us, Tadark plainly perplexed, London wary.

"Tadark, escort Princess Alera to her quarters," Cannan ordered.

"Sir?" he said uncertainly, expecting his commanding officer to give London similar orders. None came.

"Now," the Captain prompted.

I rose and went to Tadark. I glanced sideways at London as I passed him, and he shot me a look filled with both fire and quiet resignation, a look that told me he knew exactly what I had done.

VII

No Explanation

I sat stiffly in an armchair in my parlor, too distraught to move. Since leaving the Throne Room, I had tried to eat, to read, and to embroider, but as time passed without news of London, I had become less and less able to concentrate. I longed to think of anything but what was happening in the Hall of Kings, but at the same time I could think of nothing else. It had been almost six hours, and the waiting had become unbearable. I wanted to know what London's fate was going to be, and yet I didn't, because if a punishment befell him, I couldn't help but feel it would be my fault.

Tadark had several times taken a breath as if to say something, but had thought better of it each time. He wanted to ask what I had said to my father that was so confidential London would be trusted with the information but not he. Though he had tossed accusations at London in the library, I knew it would never really enter his mind that my first bodyguard, his partner, could be charged with treason.

London would not be charged with treason, I assured myself. He would be able to explain everything and would return to duty before the day was out. I kept repeating the phrase over and over in my head —— *London is not a traitor* —— until it sounded hollow, and I was ashamed to discover that there was a part of me that doubted its truth.

I did not hear the knock on my door, but Tadark went to open it, granting entry to an Elite Guard I knew at first sight.

"Destari!" I exclaimed, rising from my seat as he advanced a few feet into the room. "What are you doing here?"

Destari bowed, then assumed a less formal stance. He was an unusually tall and muscular individual who made Cannan look short and Tadark even more childlike. He had raven hair, black eyes, a chiseled jaw, and thick eyebrows that gave him an intense and intimidating presence, but I had known him my entire life and he did not frighten me in the least. Like Tadark, and every member of the Elite Guard other than London, he wore the proper uniform, a royal blue doublet, white shirt, and black trousers.

"I have been assigned to be your secondary bodyguard," he said in his deep resonating voice, and the bit of undigested food that remained in my stomach from lunch swirled, making me queasy again.

"Where is London?"

Destari stared at the floor as he struggled to answer my question, for he and London had been friends since attending the Military Academy and had entered the ranks of the Elite Guard together.

"London has been relieved of his duties."

"What?" I whispered, shocked by this news. "Why?"

"You know why," Destari said, throwing a furtive glance at Tadark that cautioned me to monitor what I said.

Tadark was evidently not deemed trustworthy enough to be told all the information in the hands of the Elite Guard, or at least he was not deemed trustworthy enough by Destari. From what I knew of Tadark, I didn't blame the older guard.

"What I said doesn't prove anything!" I retorted recklessly as I absorbed the consequences of my actions.

"It proves enough."

"What does that mean?" My mind was racing, seeking some way to reverse what I had done.

"London would not allow doubts to be cast on your credibility, so he admitted to knowing the identity of the Cokyrian woman. He also admitted leaving your quarters on the night of her escape, and therefore abandoning his post, but he would not speak further. He neither confessed to nor denied assisting her."

"I must see my father," I announced, moving toward the door. I tried to step around my replacement bodyguard, who was blocking my path, but he would not budge.

"Destari, move this instant!" I ordered, with as much authority as I could muster, both my pitch and my volume rising.

"With all due respect, Princess Alera, it is getting late, and it would be better if you waited until morning to meet with the King."

"With all due respect, Destari," I fired back, hands now gripping my hips, "get out of my way."

Tadark, who had been remarkably absent from this entire exchange, could restrain himself no longer.

"I'd have to agree with Destari, Princess," he began, but I cut him off.

"You have no say in this, Tadark! I am sick of hearing your opinions!"

Tadark, brown eyes mournful as a hurt puppy's, shrank back, and I aimed my ire at the towering guard once more.

"Unless you were given orders to keep me here, orders that I would nonetheless refuse to obey, you are overstepping your bounds. So move!"

I pointed in the direction in which I wanted him to shift, willing him to yield. Admitting defeat, Destari stepped aside, and I stormed into the corridor, both guards following. I

descended the Grand Staircase, the hopelessness of my quest
tearing at me, and my anger turned to desperation.

I entered the Hall of Kings, leaving Destari and Tadark in
the antechamber, to see my father upon his throne, no guards
in attendance. The waning afternoon light coming through the
high northern windows resulted in lurking shadows in the corners, giving the room an ominous feel.

"Father, what is going on?"

"Alera," he said wearily. "I knew you would come when I sent
Destari."

My father was rubbing his jaw as I came to stand before
him, the laugh lines upon his forty-nine-year-old face paradoxi-
cally giving him an aged and haggard appearance.

"Cannan and I acted on what you told us. We had to do what
we did —— there was no other option."

"What will be done with him?" I choked, a horrible sinking
feeling in the pit of my stomach.

"He is spending one last night in his quarters under guard.
In the morning, he will be removed from the Palace grounds."

"But Father, London is not a traitor. He must have an
explanation!"

"If he does, he did not share it with us. I cannot allow him
to continue serving as a guard, much less one of the Elite
Guards who protects the Royal Family, when his allegiance is in
question."

"His allegiance lies with Hytanica!" I cried out, for I could
not bear to think that London's loyalty might lie anywhere else.
"He is *not* a traitor."

"Well, someone is!" my father countered, matching my
tone and emphasizing his words with his hands. "Would it be
easier to accuse some other member of the Elite Guard, when
you have known most of them your entire life? One of them is
guilty of treachery. Why could it not be London?" Taking in my

tormented visage, his attitude softened. "I know that you are close to him, but I cannot run the risk of further betrayal."

"I know there is good cause for his behavior of late," I pleaded. "He just hasn't spoken of it yet."

"If he would not explain his actions to his King or his Captain," my father noted coldly, "then to whom will he speak?"

I wilted, sitting down on the steps of the dais. Although the answer was evident to me, I did not want to say it. If London would not explain his actions to his King, he would explain to no one.

"I want to see him again, Father," I finally said, a dull ache in my chest where my heart had once resided. "I need to say goodbye."

I knew this could be the last chance I would have to see London. I had been forbidden to leave the Palace, and London would be forbidden to enter the grounds. I knew not how long this arrangement would last, and if there came a time for me to see or speak with him again, I did not know if he would oblige. I had ruined his entire life in one audience with my father, and I would not have blamed him if he never forgave me.

"Very well," my father agreed, his expression now more sympathetic. "I will have him brought to your parlor in the morning before he is taken from the Palace."

"Thank you," I murmured, rising to curtsey. I departed the Throne Room, returning to my quarters to try to rein in my feelings and bring order to my jumbled thoughts before I had to face London.

———

I awoke early the next morning and sat on the edge of the sofa in my parlor to await London's arrival. I knew he would be brought to my quarters with the rising of the sun, and I could not risk that I would miss him while I slept. Destari and Tadark silently attended me, Tadark standing by the fireplace, and Destari, dark and brooding, near the door to the corridor.

There were so many things I wanted to say to London, but I would not have much time, and I was not sure how to say them. I did not know what his mood would be, or if he would be willing to listen. But I had to try.

There was a knock on the door, and I sprang to my feet as Destari stepped forward. He swung the door open to reveal London, accompanied by a Palace Guard almost as tall as Destari and twice as thick. Apparently Cannan believed that someone of substantial size was needed to control London. While this would have been true if he were set on resisting, it was completely unnecessary in this situation.

"London!" I exclaimed, as though I had experienced qualms about who would be outside my door. "I was afraid you wouldn't come!"

"If it had been my choice, Princess, I would not have." His voice was bitter as he stepped into the room.

I was dismayed by his manner, though I had no right to expect him to greet me warmly. I glanced around the room to see that Tadark was in a snit —— his rounded cheeks were almost a match to my burgundy furniture, and his fists were balled at his sides. Though he appeared to be in an uproar over the way London had spoken to me, I knew that his antagonism really stemmed from the fact that he had borne the brunt of London's wit for weeks.

The guard who had come with London did not seem to care one way or another what London said or how he spoke to me, a Princess of Hytanica, and was likely as thick in his head as he was in his arms. Destari, who had stepped up beside his friend, looked uncomfortable, though he was not surprised or infuriated the way Tadark was. No one said anything, however, and it took me a moment to recover from the hurt I felt at London's harshness and formality before I could continue.

"Would you leave us now?" I said to the three guards. I felt anything London had to say would be justified, and I worried that someone might interfere on my behalf. I needed to talk to him alone.

Tadark was predictably the first to assert an opinion.

"I'm not going to leave you alone with this criminal!"

He pulled himself up to his full and unimposing height, puffing out his chest in a feeble attempt to look menacing, then deflating as he read the deadly glare in London's eyes.

"Oh, be still, Tadark," Destari grumbled, reaching out to grab his best friend's shoulder to hold him in position.

Tadark mumbled something incomprehensible under his breath, and Destari nodded toward the door with his head.

"Get into the hall."

Tadark wavered, then crossed the room to slouch past the older guards into the corridor, not daring to disobey a Deputy Captain.

"Take as long as you need," Destari said, giving me a slight bow. "I will detain Tadark."

I nodded, and Destari lifted his hand from London's shoulder. Stopping only to tap the thickly built guard on the arm to remind him that he also needed to exit, Destari departed, and I turned once more to London. He said nothing but crossed his arms and moved to lean, as always, against the wall, although this time his posture was unusually rigid.

"You must be angry with me," I ventured, taking a couple of steps toward him, not knowing where this conversation would lead.

"And why would I be angry with you, Princess?" he replied coldly.

"You don't need to address me so formally," I faltered. The

way he was referring to me as "Princess" was making him feel distant and increasing my sense of desperation.

"I don't know what you're talking about, Your Highness. I am speaking to you the same way all of your lowly subjects speak to you. That's what I am now, you know."

"London, stop it," I insisted, guilt scorching the inside of my chest.

"Yes, My Lady," he said with mock politeness, as though he were backing off rather than doing exactly what I had just requested that he not do.

"Please, London."

"I'm not sure what you desire of me, Princess."

"London, don't," I finally implored with a stamp of my foot, unwanted tears searing my eyes. "I did what I thought best, and you're furious with me! Shout at me! Tell me I'm foolish and that I meddled in things I shouldn't have! But don't just stand there and ignore what has happened!"

After my outburst, there was a silence in the room that threatened to stretch into eternity. Then London straightened and stepped away from the wall, his jaw clenching in subdued anger, and I stumbled back from him. His indigo eyes were harsh and a chill pulsated from him that was sufficient to rob me of breath. At last he spoke, his words as cutting as a knife.

"It's interesting to me —— it is my life that has been ruined, and yet you act as though you are the one who is suffering. Perhaps you are not entirely convinced that what you did was necessary."

"I did what I believed best," I tremulously repeated, for London had just pinpointed the question upon which I had dwelt since I had spoken to my father —— had I done the right thing? My decision had seemed justified at the time, but now, in the aftermath, nothing was clear. "If I was wrong in my suspicions, you should have explained to my father and Cannan."

"Don't be a fool, Alera," London spat. "There was no way for me to defend leaving your side against my orders. No matter what explanation I might have had, that was inexcusable."

"You could have told them the truth," I said daringly.

"I told them what I could."

"What does that mean? You've been branded a traitor, London! The truth can't be worse than that."

"Perhaps it is."

I was growing more distraught by the second. London was making no sense at all.

"What would you have had me do? I went to my father because I could think of no alternative. If you know of some other action I could have taken so things would not have reached this end, I beg of you to enlighten me."

"You should have come to me," London said, as if that would clearly have been the most logical course.

"I did! You wouldn't tell me anything. In fact, you lied to me twice! What was I to think?"

"If I had known what you were planning to do, I would have... offered you assurances." London sighed heavily and brushed back his silver bangs. "You should have given me that chance."

"Then perhaps you would like to explain to me now," I mercilessly countered.

"It no longer makes a difference what I say." London sounded almost sad, but I would break down if I let myself feel his pain, and right now I wanted him to talk to me.

"Just answer one question, then. Did you help her escape?"

"This isn't —— " London began, but I cut him off.

"Did you help her escape?"

"You don't know —— "

"It's a simple yes or no question, and I wish you would just answer it. Are you the traitor? Did you assist in her escape?" I glared at him, silently compelling him to respond honestly.

"I am not a traitor," he quietly declared. The air thrummed with tension for a moment, then he continued, his heart obviously heavy. "If you truly trust someone, then you trust their words and actions, even without explanation. You apparently don't have that level of trust in me."

I felt for a moment as if I were drowning. The only thing I found harder to endure than London's anger was his disappointment. I looked pleadingly at him, but his expression did not change.

"If there is nothing further you want of me, I will take my leave."

I grudgingly dismissed him, stepping into the corridor after him. As he and the guard assigned to remove him from the Palace strode away, I was gripped by genuine sorrow, instead of guilt, regret, or denial. I did not know when I would next see him, and I felt as though my heart were trying to follow him. With each step he took, it pressed more painfully against my chest, trying to escape. I wanted to run after him and somehow erase the events of the past day, but there was no way to fix what I had done.

VIII

TEA AND TALK

The days that followed London's removal from the Palace brought similar feelings of sorrow and regret, and I wished I could stop wallowing in my grief, his comments about my self-pitying behavior continuing to ring in my ears. I found myself going through the motions of my day, working on embroidery and handwriting, receiving music lessons, visiting the Chapel for afternoon prayer, reading in the evening, without any energy or enthusiasm. Cannan had now lifted some of the restrictions imposed upon Miranna and me, so that we could again go outside the Palace accompanied by our bodyguards, but I had no desire to do so.

London's shoes were impossible to fill, and regardless of how I spent my time, it felt as though something were missing from my life. I longed for someone to whom I could talk, but though Tadark and Destari were constantly around, neither of them made appealing candidates. Destari was probably feeling somewhat the same as I, for he was a good friend of London's, but he was reserved and stoic, and I did not know him well enough to talk openly with him. As for Tadark, he couldn't resist spewing about how he had never really trusted London, how there had been something sinister about him, something that just didn't make sense. It was ironic that the person I really wanted to talk to about this was, in fact, London.

About two weeks after London's dismissal, my mother forced me back to life and out among my friends and acquaintances. For as long as I could remember, she had been holding social gatherings at the Palace for groups of twenty to thirty young Hytanican women of noble birth, and such a function had been planned for the nineteenth of June. The purpose of these gatherings was to continue our etiquette training by testing our social graces. Sometimes the gathering was a picnic, oftentimes it was a tea party, and once a year it was a holiday party. Whether my mother and the older women who helped her evaluate our skills knew it or not, it was also always a gossip party.

This particular event was a tea party that coincided with Miranna's sixteenth birthday. As sixteen was not an age that held special significance in the Kingdom, it was not to be heralded with a Palace celebration as my seventeenth had been. Nevertheless, my mother had decided to take advantage of one of her gatherings to include a small tribute to her younger daughter.

On the appointed afternoon, I strolled into the East Courtyard with my mother and Miranna, accompanied by the Elite Guards who protected the Queen. The East Courtyard had its own distinct attributes, different from both the Central Courtyard and the West Courtyard. While the West Courtyard was relatively unspoiled, with crab apple and cherry trees growing among the wildflowers that spread at will, the East Courtyard was statelier, as it was often used for public functions. Its middle area was paved with multicolored stone that formed concentric circles around a large two-tiered fountain. Oak and elm trees provided shade, and flowers grew riotously toward the exterior walls. Today, the air was thick with perfume, and the water in the fountain sparkled in the sunlight as it splashed into its basin.

Five small tables, each with a white linen tablecloth and five place settings, stood in close proximity upon the paved stones. The young women who had been invited had already gathered and were twittering among themselves like exotically plumed birds. Four older women were also present so that one adult could oversee each table to ensure that our manners were impeccable. The lovely Lady Hauna, mother of Steldor's best friend, Galen, was in attendance with her demure seventeen-year-old daughters, Niani and Nadeja; the sensible Lady Edorra had accompanied her vivacious daughter Kalem, also seventeen; the exceedingly proper Lady Kadia had brought easily excited sixteen-year-old Noralee; and bubbly Semari had come with sedate Baroness Alantonya.

Miranna and I wove our way through the guests with our mother, greeting each in turn. When at last she approached her table and stood behind her chair, all of the women moved to the tables as well, observing proper protocol by remaining on their feet until after the Queen had been seated.

The tea service itself was very formal and somewhat orchestrated. Biscuits and sweet cakes were served along with the hot drink. We were expected to sit up straight, arms in at our sides, no leaning over the dishes or elbows on the table. Gentlewomen took small bites and ate slowly, and did not talk or drink with food in their mouths. In addition, only particular subjects were appropriate for a lady's delicate sensibilities, but given the level of scrutiny we were under, we did not speak unless it was necessary.

It was when the formal tea ended that the real conversation began. Released from the tables, and enormously relieved if we had survived without being chastised, we would walk and talk among ourselves, gossiping freely while the adult women chatted with one another.

I stood with a group of ten acquaintances that included Galen's twin sisters and Steldor's cousin Dahnath, all of whom were dying to discuss the latest developments with me. Today's primary topics were, of course, the discovery of the traitor in the Palace and a review of the young men in the Kingdom who might be suitable as a husband for me.

"Tell us, Alera," began Reveina, a bold and serious brunette who tended to be the leader of our circle. "How was the traitor discovered? Rumor has it that *you* were the one who uncovered him and turned him in to the Captain of the Guard."

I did not know how to answer. It had been information provided by me that had led to London's dismissal, but I, at least, did not regard him as a traitor. This seemed too complicated to explain, so I answered the question as simply as I could.

"I had observed some activities that were relevant to the investigation and, I suppose, played a small part in the decision to dismiss London."

"He was your bodyguard!" blond-haired Noralee blurted, sounding scandalized, for she generally found everything to be shocking. "Doesn't it give you pause to think of all the times you were alone in his company, not knowing he was a threat to the Royal Family?"

A strong urge to defend London rose within me, but at the same time, I wanted this conversation to end.

"I never felt unsafe with him," I said firmly. "And he was never proven to have betrayed the Royal Family. He was dismissed for dereliction of duty."

"So do you believe he aided the Cokyrian prisoner in her escape?" Reveina chose to ignore my explanation for London's dismissal, her eyes dark with a desire for intrigue.

"I don't know what I believe."

Just then Miranna and Semari joined our group, drawing attention away from me, and I hoped my ordeal had ended as the girls extended birthday greetings to my sister. Unfortunately, this reminded several of them of my recent birthday celebration, and the discussion shifted to an examination of the Kingdom's eligible young men and their relative qualifications to be King. After a dozen were discussed and discarded, Reveina gave voice to what everyone was thinking.

"We all know there really is only one candidate. We just don't want to give him up to you."

Amidst a burst of giggles, several eager voices murmured, "Lord Steldor." There were also several sighs as the girls thought longingly of spending time in his company, although Dahnath, an auburn-haired beauty, rolled her eyes, likely tired of the adoration heaped upon her cousin. She was the daughter of Cannan's younger brother, Baelic, and was known for both her kindness and her rather studious nature. She would not be so easily taken in by Steldor's charm.

"He is divine," Reveina gushed, voicing a collective opinion. To my consternation, even Galen's sisters, who were blond like their mother but with the light brown eyes and carefree smile of their brother, were enthusiastically nodding along. "You are so fortunate to have him among your choices... and to have attracted his notice as well. He could marry anyone he wanted, you know."

"The way he looks at you," added Kalem, the most boy-obsessed of the young women, her alabaster skin shining radiantly. "I hope someday a young man looks at me in that way."

Again, many heads bobbed in agreement. This last statement struck me dumb, for I had always viewed Steldor as coveting the Throne, rather than being interested in me.

Kalem laughed at my expression, tossing her coarse dark hair. "Oh, Alera, you really are naïve. He swoons over you the way we swoon over him!"

Although I disliked Steldor intensely, her observation brought a satisfied smile to my face. At that moment, Lady

Edorra, Kalem's mother, approached, interrupting us and drawing several dismayed sighs.

"The Queen is preparing to depart," she said, glaring knowingly down her narrow nose at us.

Feeling that my life was not in need of further examination, I glanced at Miranna to convey my desire to leave, and she and I departed shortly after our mother. As we passed the guard room to the right of the Grand Staircase, our bodyguards fell into step with us, and Miranna caught my hand.

"How are you, really? London's absence must be hard to bear."

"It is hard to bear. Every time I turn a corner, I expect to hear a sarcastic comment about something but only encounter silence. He's been with me most of my life, and I feel adrift without him. I guess I relied on him for many things other than protection."

"I can understand how terrible you must feel. Halias has always been my bodyguard. Part of my life would be lost if he weren't with me anymore. But I'm sure it will get better with time. And you will see London again, someday."

Halias had become Miranna's personal bodyguard on the day of her birth. He, London, and now Destari shared similar styles in that they liked to keep their distance from their charges to give them privacy. Tadark, on the other hand, hovered much too closely; currently, he was hanging off my elbow. Miranna had also been assigned a second bodyguard, but she had been fortunate enough not to get stuck with a Tadark.

"I suppose I will see him again. But I just don't know how to feel right now. His absence leaves a great void that no one else can fill." Merely saying the words caused me fresh pain.

Tadark, who had a million remarks about London at the ready these days and was always looking for an opportunity to let them spill from his mouth, could no longer restrain himself.

"London left his post, in the middle of the night! *I* would never do such a thing!" he exclaimed, as though his ego had been dealt an enormous insult. "There was always something about him. I saw it the first time I met him, I did!"

"Tadark," I said, mildly irritated. "This phrase is probably meaningless to you since it is so oft repeated, but do be quiet."

"London wasn't half the bodyguard I am!" He said it as though he were trying to convince himself that his statement were true.

"*Now*, please," I said, striving to keep my tone civil.

Tadark stared petulantly at me, then dropped back to fall in step with our other guards. I glanced back in time to catch the glare he received from Destari.

"I don't know how much more of him I can tolerate," I whispered to Miranna, and her face told me that she understood completely.

As we approached the spiral staircase at the back of the Palace, I decided to take a stroll in the garden. Although my sister would have walked with me, I assured her such was not necessary, preferring to be alone and trusting Destari to control Tadark.

The Palace Guards on duty pulled the doors open for me and I stepped through to amble along the garden's paths, letting my mind become still amid the beautiful foliage: the elm, oak, chestnut, and mulberry trees that offered cooling shade; the pear, lime, and orange trees that supplied us with unusual fruit; the abundant lilies, violets, tulips, and roses that plied the air with fragrance; and the herbs that provided seasoning for cooking and for treatment of injuries and illnesses. Of course, the grounds were also home to a multitude of birds, and their music in the softly rustling leaves was often the only sound in the gloriously peaceful setting.

By the end of the afternoon, my mood had improved significantly. Although I continued to ache for London's presence more than I had ever longed for anything before, the beauty of the garden had assuaged my disconsolate feelings, and I slept well that night for the first time since the Elite Guard had been removed from the Palace.

IX

A Good Catch

lera!"

A shrill and exhilarated voice jarred me from sleep, and I sat up, dragging my eyelids open. The drapes on my windows were drawn together, making my bedroom as dark as if the sun had not yet risen, but my noisy intruder saw fit to remedy that, flinging aside the window coverings so that I had to squint to keep from going blind.

"Miranna? What...?" My body demanded sleep, and my brain refused to work hard enough to form a complete sentence.

"Have you heard the news? You won't believe it!"

Miranna sounded elated, so I assumed that the *news* to which she referred was not something bad.

"This early in the morning, I'd believe just about anything," I said, sounding raspy from my deep slumber. "What is it?"

"You simply won't believe it!" my sister repeated, bouncing up and down on her toes in excitement, her strawberry blond curls dancing about her face.

"Yes, we've covered that," I grumped, sitting up so I could more readily examine her.

"Try to guess. You'll never guess! This is *so* exciting!"

"Mira, can't you just tell me?"

Miranna put on a little pout, disappointed that I was not in a mood to play guessing games, but regardless could not contain her secret.

"Listen to this," she bubbled, lying down on her stomach atop my bed, propping her elbows so her hands held her chin. "The servants are whispering about it. Our soldiers have captured another Cokyrian within Hytanican walls! Cannan is bringing him in today!"

Miranna had succeeded in arousing my interest.

"Are you positive?"

"After I heard the rumors, I talked to Halias to find out if they were true." She cleared her throat and dropped her pitch to do a surprisingly accurate imitation of Halias. *"Another one has been arrested within the city, but you didn't learn that from me."*

"Just hope he didn't hear you," I teased, for all four of our bodyguards were likely standing self-consciously in the parlor while we gossiped.

Miranna waved my comment off with a grin. "Are you up for a bit of spying?"

"Me? Sneaking around? Never!"

We both laughed as Miranna went on to explain how she planned to spend the whole day in the Central Courtyard, *inadvertently* being present when the prisoner was brought into the Palace. My curiosity was too great not to join her, though we both recognized that Halias, at least, would know exactly what we were doing.

"He'll be fine about it," Miranna assured me, swinging her legs off the bed to sit up straight. "It's not like a sword fight is going to break out in the middle of the Courtyard. Halias knows there will be no danger. Though he'll probably expect us to hide to save his skin. If Cannan sees we're there, he'll have Halias's head!"

"Destari's, too," I agreed, knowing Cannan would assign the blame to the older and more experienced of his Elite Guards.

I found myself feeling almost jealous of Miranna's good fortune in a bodyguard, as I had on a few other occasions. Halias was similar in height to London, but with twinkling blue eyes, a broad face, a ready smile, and soft ash-blond hair that fell to his shoulders when not pulled back at the nape of his neck. While he was irreproachable when it came to protecting my sister, he made even someone as relaxed as London look tense. He had always given Miranna a lot of freedom, asserting that his job was to keep her safe and not to raise her. This easygoing attitude made him very approachable and immensely popular as an escort. Like Destari and London, he was a veteran of the Cokyrian War, having served as a Palace Guard, and was credited with uncovering a plot to kill the King.

Tired of my sluggishness, Miranna jumped up and yanked my blankets off me.

"Come on," she said, tugging at my hand. "I haven't the faintest idea what time Cannan will be bringing the prisoner in. For all we know, we may have already missed it!"

Deciding not to call for my personal maid, I scrambled to my feet and dressed with my sister's help. Skipping breakfast, we rushed from my quarters and into the corridor, followed by Destari, Tadark, Halias, and Miranna's secondary bodyguard, a reserved Elite Guard a few years older than Tadark named Orsiett.

As we hurried toward the Courtyard, I felt vaguely unsettled about our enthusiasm. I knew we should not be this enthralled about finding our worst enemy within our homeland. We were acting like children, with no appreciation whatsoever for what this incident might mean. But when I remembered the few but intriguing facts I had learned about Cokyri in the previous weeks, and what a stir the capture and escape of our other prisoner had caused, I could not contain my inquisitiveness. The only Cokyrian I had ever seen was Nantilam, the High Priestess, and this new person would be of a completely different status. For one thing, this time our prisoner was, according to Miranna and her informants, a man. London had told me that men were inferior to women in Cokyrian culture, and I wanted to know how he would act and the manner of his speech; what he would look like and the style of his clothing; if he were a soldier, or perhaps a servant or even a master.

A warm breeze caressed my cheeks as we stepped into the Central Courtyard, a welcome reminder that summer had arrived. It was late June, and though just yesterday it had been cool and refreshing outdoors, this morning it was sultry, with a promise of blazing hot weather as the day wore on.

Hytanican summers were notorious for sweltering days, with light rain often falling in the evenings. The weather was predictable in a most uncanny way, which was good for the crops grown by the farmers in the villages surrounding the walled city, and ensured that the rolling hills that marked our western border lay draped in green.

We stayed outside for hours, until I felt faint from the heat and ready to abandon our mission, but Miranna wouldn't hear of it.

"The minute you leave, Cannan will come marching up to those gates with the prisoner, and you will miss it."

She was referring to the exterior gates that permitted entry into the Courtyard. The gates were locked to commoners most hours of the day, open only for a short amount of time during which anyone who had not been banished from the Palace grounds or the Kingdom itself could seek counsel from the King.

All at once, Halias spoke up. "They're approaching now. If you don't want to be seen, you'd better hide —— and not behind that cherry tree."

He motioned to the thin trunk of a young tree that Miranna was moving toward as though it would conceal her.

My sister changed course, and she and I maladroitly crouched behind the lilac hedges, peering through the irregular gaps in the branches to where the stone path leading from the gates to the steps of the Palace lay, dirt-free and so white from the sun that it was almost painful to view. Our bodyguards seemed to vanish, as I supposed they had been trained to do.

Drawn by shouts and the sounds of milling horses, our heads snapped toward the gates and we impatiently waited for them to open. Within a few minutes, they swung inward and Cannan strode between them, looking extraordinarily grim. He turned to wait for his troops to dismount, for no animals were permitted in the Courtyard; a single spooked horse could seriously damage its beauty. The mounts would be taken to the Royal Stables, where they would be fed and groomed while their riders attended to business.

My eyes roved over the scene before me until the movement of a particular soldier caught my notice. He was roughly pulling a man whose hands were tied behind his back off one of the horses. This soldier and another then approached Cannan, holding the bound man by his arms between them.

"That's him!" Miranna whispered to me. She gripped my wrist in anticipation.

I could not see the prisoner's face from where we were hidden, but he was wearing the white shirt and sleeveless brown tunic typically donned by a Hytanican villager, and had I not known he was Cokyrian, I never would have guessed it. Nothing about him that I could see would have set him apart from all the other villagers frequenting the streets and shops of our Kingdom.

I slipped behind Miranna and, continuing to stoop, moved down the line of bushes to the far end so I could get a better glimpse of the man held captive between the large guards. As the gates closed and Cannan turned to lead his troops onward, I gained a more distinct view of the prisoner's face and stifled a gasp, for our prisoner was not a man, but a teenage boy. He held his head high, as though unafraid, but the way his eyes flitted between the guards at his sides and Cannan before him gave away his unease. His hair was thick and many shades of gold, the sun's rays having unevenly bleached it. It was cut about an inch below his ears, and his bangs, which were slightly shorter, fell haphazardly over his forehead.

Miranna, plainly as astounded as I, moved to crouch next to me.

"He can't be any older than I am!" she exclaimed.

My eyes swept the rest of the soldiers, and all thoughts of the Cokyrian youth left my mind as I caught the light but confident stride, the muscular frame, the twin double-edged blades sheathed at the hips, the untidy silver hair partially obscuring mysterious indigo eyes —— London was there, walking at the forefront of a half dozen soldiers as if he were one of them.

"What is *he* doing here?" I asked aloud, more to myself than to my sister.

"Who?" Miranna queried, too spellbound by the young Cokyrian to notice anything else.

"London," I responded, pointing.

Miranna's gaze followed the invisible line stretching from my finger and landed on my former bodyguard, and astonishment broke over her face as well.

"What is he doing here?" She sounded equally confused.

With no available answer, we returned our attention to the approaching soldiers, and it was then, as I studied the captive, that I noticed his eyes. They were steel blue, sharp, and intense. Despite the youthful glow of his suntanned face, his eyes were cold and unfriendly, suggesting he had great experience in the world and was now expecting the worst.

I stooped lower as the troops passed, watching London stride toward the Palace, oblivious to my presence, and an unexpected flood of emotions threatened to overwhelm me —— regret, guilt, sorrow, shame, and love for the man before me. The urge to run to him once again surfaced, and I had to look away, though Miranna continued to watch, entranced, until the soldiers had passed between the thick wooden Palace doors.

"Curious about London?" Destari's deep, resonating voice startled us, and we wheeled around to see the pair of Deputy Captains crouching behind us.

As booted feet scraped against bark, I turned my head to see Tadark tumble out of an oak tree, gracelessly landing on his rear end. He let out a wounded groan and was shushed by Orsiett, who was walking toward him.

"Making furry friends up in the tree, were you?" Halias jibed, his blue eyes alight.

"No," Tadark sulked. "I wanted to see what was going on."

"Oh, now I understand!" Halias laughed. "You're a *scenery* guard, not a bodyguard!"

"Halias, we've been mistaken all this time," Destari added, unable to pass up the fun. "It's not the Royal Family we're supposed to protect, it's the Royal Foliage!"

Tadark's cheeks burned and he bitterly muttered, "Leave me alone. You've made your point."

I watched the three guards in amusement, surprised to see Destari, who was usually quite serious, teasing the Lieutenant much like London would have done, and it struck me that Tadark drew jests from people like a flower drew bees.

Destari returned his attention to me, and I suppressed my mirth in order to repeat my question.

"What is London doing here? Isn't he banished from the Palace grounds?" I forced out the words, on some level believing they would cease to be true if I refused to say them.

Destari opened his mouth to speak but was interrupted by

Tadark's moans as he inched closer to where the four of us sat, agonizingly pulling himself along the ground.

"Are you trying to make that inchworm feel good about itself?" Halias ridiculed, pointing to a slow-moving specimen that was nonetheless crawling faster than Tadark across the grass.

Tadark made a noise that sounded like *humph* and continued to scoot along.

"I think I broke something," he mumbled.

Reaching another tree, he sat up and leaned against its trunk, then plucked a blade of grass, fiddling with it between his fingers. Orsiett stopped and sat down by Tadark, presumably too intimidated by the older guards to join us.

Destari chuckled, noticing, as we all were, that Tadark was monitoring the greenery rather than his charge, more or less proving Halias's statement to be true.

"You wanted to know about London, right?" Destari finally said.

I nodded earnestly.

"He's here because he is the one who discovered the Cokyrian in the city. He went to the Captain at his home and asked that in exchange for handing over the prisoner he be allowed an audience with the King."

I made some noise of affirmation, for everything suddenly made sense to me, but Miranna was bewildered and pursued the subject.

"But how did he find that boy when no one else could, when the search of the Kingdom by all of Cannan's soldiers turned up nothing?"

Halias and Destari glanced at each other, as if they were trying to judge how much they should tell us. At last Destari spoke.

"During the war, London saw much of the Cokyrians. I suppose he developed a keener eye for their mannerisms than the average foot soldier."

Miranna nodded, satisfied with this explanation. Unbeknownst to the guards, however, and thanks to my mother, I was mindful of the real reason London had greater knowledge of Cokyri than did anyone else.

———

Suspicion and apprehension rippled through the Palace that afternoon like the swift rapids of the river, but I cared not. I waited nervously outside the doors to the Throne Room, faint, inarticulate voices barely reaching my ears.

Miranna and I had lunched together, then she had left, as the day was getting late and she had other tasks to undertake. After we had parted ways, I had entered the antechamber and now paced ceaselessly, too anxious to sit down and too agitated to stand still. Destari leaned against the wall next to the door to the Grand Entry in London's characteristic posture, while Tadark stood uncomfortably in the middle of the room, shifting his weight from foot to foot. Every time he winced in pain, I remembered with some sympathy his fall from the tree, or, more to the point, his not-so-gentle landing.

Though neither spoke, I wished I could be alone. Even the dull sound of Tadark's fidgeting in the otherwise quiet room was a distraction to me. While I very much needed to think, I seemed to have lost the ability to do so.

The time I might have had for reflection was cut short by the creaking of the Throne Room doors as they were pulled open from the inside. London stepped between them and immediately took note of me. If he had any reaction to my presence, however, it was difficult to discern.

"Princess," he formally greeted me, halting and tilting his head in respect.

"Please, let's not start where we left off," I beseeched, wanting to avoid the pattern of our earlier quarrel.

An awkward pause followed, the only sound the breathing of

the others in the antechamber, but I gratefully realized that the lack of a heated reply meant London's hurt had eased somewhat.

"You spoke with my father?" I finally chanced.

London's only answer was a nod.

"I hear you made a good catch," I timidly continued. "Is he pleased?"

"He is."

"And?"

"Your father is not a forgiving man."

I cast my eyes to the stone floor. I knew it had been a fool's hope that London might be given his life back based on this one deed, but against my will, my heart had become set upon it. It was the only thing that could possibly heal the rift between us, but any such hope had now been shattered by my father's obstinacy and mistrust. There was only one thing I could think to say.

"And you, London? Are you a forgiving man?"

"Some might say so." He said this in a way that was very near lighthearted, as if he meant to make me feel better. Then his tone darkened almost imperceptibly. "But some things are not so easily forgiven."

I managed to hold his gaze, though my head felt heavy with shame, and I searched his familiar face for something more.

"London... I'm sorry." I did not elaborate, hoping my simple words would suffice.

"I know," he said dispassionately, and an uneasy silence fell between us.

His eyes flicked to Destari, who was no longer leaning against the wall, probably having straightened the moment my former bodyguard had come into the room.

"I must take my leave now," London said, then he crossed to his friend to say a few words before stepping into the Grand Entry Hall.

A sinking feeling of uncertainty as to when I would next see London overwhelmed me, and I waited for a chance to talk to Destari. He knew London better than anyone, and I desperately wanted some reassurance from him.

"Will he ever forgive me?" I moaned when Destari looked at me.

"I cannot say," he said, black eyes murky and unrevealing. "London does not trust easily, and he does not forgive easily when his trust has been betrayed."

I pondered Destari's words for a moment, convinced he was hiding something.

"You speak as though you know of some other betrayal. Help me to understand him so that I can learn how best to seek his pardon."

Destari glanced warily at Tadark, not wanting to discuss London in his presence.

"Tadark," I said sharply. "Remove yourself to the Entry Hall. We will be but a minute."

Tadark hobbled from the room without comment, shooting the Deputy Captain a sullen look on his way out.

Destari cautiously assessed me, trying to decide whether he should confide in me.

"I already know London was a prisoner of the Cokyrians during the war," I disclosed, hoping to persuade him. "If this relates to that time, you needn't keep anything from me."

Destari's heavy eyebrows rose slightly, and I knew he had expected me to be ignorant of London's history. After a few more moments of deliberation, he capitulated.

"The incident of which I am about to speak is related to that period in his life."

"Go on, Destari," I urged.

"Before London was imprisoned by the Cokyrians, he was betrothed to a young woman of noble birth."

Destari halted at my stunned expression. While I knew London had never married, I had always assumed the reason was that his devotion to the military had left little time for a personal life. Destari's revelation reconfirmed how paltry was my knowledge of the man, and a crushing sense of remorse hit me at the thought that I had always been too self-absorbed to even be curious. I took a deep, steadying breath, waiting for my bodyguard to elaborate. With a measure of concern, he stepped forward and lightly gripped my elbow, directing me to an armchair. When I had seated myself, he resumed his tale, voice strangely hollow.

"A couple of months into his captivity, the parents of his betrothed determined to have her marry another, as London was believed dead. She had already been pledged to him for a year and a half, and her parents worried that at age twenty-two, her marriage prospects were becoming limited. She at first refused, for she was very much in love with London, but in the end, acquiesced to her parents' wishes. She was married to a much older man about two months before London's escape.

"As I assume you know, London was deathly ill upon his return to Hytanica, and so he did not immediately learn of any of this. When he was well enough to communicate, he began to ask for her, and it fell to me to tell him of her circumstances."

Destari rubbed the back of his neck as though he were reliving the unhappy memory.

"He did not take the news well, and I feared he might not be strong enough to survive this second trial. He was withdrawn for a long time, and in truth never came fully back to himself, becoming more guarded than he once was."

Destari sounded weary, as if just telling the story were exhausting.

"He has not, since that time, permitted himself to form deep attachments. Or at least, he has tried not to form strong attachments, but he did not count on the bond he would develop with you due to being your lifelong bodyguard." Destari paused, sighing heavily before he finished. "London never really forgave his betrothed for doubting his return, and I don't know that he will ever really forgive you for doubting his loyalty."

I stared numbly at Destari, momentarily too overwhelmed by London's tragic past to respond. Finally regaining the ability to speak, I softly asked, "Who was she?"

Destari frowned, then shook his head. "That is not for me to say. Perhaps someday London will be inclined to tell you."

I continued to stare at him, biting my lip as I debated whether to ask him the question upon which I had unendingly dwelt since London's dismissal from the military. Finally, I risked his anger.

"We both know London recognized the High Priestess. Do you think he released her?"

As I had expected, Destari glowered at me.

"I don't know whether he released her or not, nor do I care. London has always acted in Hytanica's best interests, and if he did release her, he had good cause. He is not and never has been a traitor, and I would follow him without hesitation, even to my death."

I shrank under his glare, feeling unbearably pitiful, for I did not have the same ability to simply take things on faith.

Destari and I left the antechamber in weighty silence, to be rejoined by Tadark in the Grand Entry. I could tell by Tadark's sulky expression that he was unhappy about having been excluded from our conversation, but he simply fell into step with us. I returned to my quarters to eat dinner, then prepared for bed, emotionally drained. As I lay in the darkness, beginning to drift toward sleep, I heard Destari and Tadark's faint bickering. The only thing I could make out was Destari saying, "*My* sofa, *your* armchair."

X

CLANDESTINE MEETING

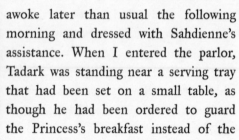

awoke later than usual the following morning and dressed with Sahdienne's assistance. When I entered the parlor, Tadark was standing near a serving tray that had been set on a small table, as though he had been ordered to guard the Princess's breakfast instead of the Princess herself. Destari's looming form, however, was absent. As Sahdienne departed, I took the tray and went to sit in one of the burgundy velvet armchairs.

"Where is Destari?" I asked, removing the cloth that covered my food to keep it warm, the delicious aroma of fresh-baked bread and scrambled eggs wafting up to greet me.

"He was sent for by the Captain of the Guard early this morning," Tadark responded, still lingering by the table.

"For what purpose was he summoned?" I pressed, justifiably concerned in light of recent happenings.

"I don't know —— I wasn't told anything," he said, trying to act nonchalant, although I could tell he was bothered by the fact that he had once again been left out of a meeting.

I shrugged and continued to eat my breakfast, hoping to conceal that my insatiable hunger for Palace politics was building.

Just as I put my utensils down upon my empty plate, there was a knock and Tadark opened the door. Destari entered and I could contain my curiosity no more.

"The last time I awoke to find one of my bodyguards missing, the outcome was disastrous," I said, managing to make a small joke out of London's dismissal. "I would like to know what's going on."

I stood and walked toward him, placing my tray back upon the table it had originally occupied.

"I am to inform you that I will no longer be your bodyguard," Destari answered, giving me a slight bow.

"And are you to inform me as to the reason you have been removed?"

I had grown tired of Cannan and my father making decisions that directly affected me without even bothering to offer an explanation.

"I was not instructed to tell you anything further," he rumbled, "but the explanation is straightforward. I have simply been given a new assignment."

An involuntary shudder rippled through my body as it came to me that with London gone and Destari reassigned, I might end up with a single bodyguard by the name of Tadark.

"Couldn't *someone else* —— " I tipped my head toward Tadark " —— be given this new task?"

Destari shook his head as he caught my meaning. "I'm afraid this is much too important to be entrusted to *someone else*."

I frowned in annoyance. "What is this new assignment?"

"Perhaps you should raise that question with the Captain or the King."

"I'm asking you," I said pointedly. "I will learn what this is about one way or another. You may as well save me the trouble and tell me now."

He briefly grappled with the decision, for he was unwilling to relent yet knew there was truth in my assertion. In the end, he acceded.

"Have you not wondered where we are holding the Cokyrian prisoner?"

I heard Tadark shuffling around by the door and saw his eyes shift to Destari's face, his interest also captured by the Deputy Captain's words.

"In the dungeon, I presume," I said, already unsure of my statement based on Destari's expression.

"Do you see your father as the type of man who would imprison in such a place a boy of the same age as his youngest child?"

"No," I said, considering his words carefully. "Is it safe then to assume he is being housed in the Palace proper?"

"That would be a fair assumption."

"And can I also assume that he will be guarded by someone with great experience?"

"That also is a reasonable conclusion."

I nodded gratefully. "One last thing, then."

Destari scowled at me, wondering what else I could possibly demand of him.

"Will I be assigned a new secondary bodyguard?"

"I'm afraid not," Destari responded with a knowing smile. "The Captain has decided that the measure of security we've been maintaining within the Palace is no longer necessary as the traitor has been identified. The members of the Royal Family will once again have only one bodyguard and he will return to a normal daily routine. Tadark will be your permanent guard."

I contained my groan of misery with some effort. I was relieved, however, that Tadark would no longer be protecting me twenty-four hours a day, as he was a bit more tolerable when taken in smaller doses.

"Well," I said, trying to sound lighthearted. "I appreciate

that you took the time to tell me of your change in duty."

Destari inclined his head slightly and turned to leave.

"Wait!" Tadark cried. "Aren't you going to tell us about your new assignment?"

Destari stared at him as though no expression he could form upon his face would quite convey what he was feeling, then walked out the door without another word.

———

I saw nothing of Destari or the Cokyrian prisoner over the next few days, which led me to believe that the boy was being held in one of the guest rooms on the third floor, away from the areas the Royal Family frequented. My father and Cannan could often be seen in deep discussion, most likely about their unexpectedly young captive, but they never said anything in my presence about what they intended to do with him. If not for Destari, I would have believed the boy to be starving in the dungeon like our other prisoners, though it should have occurred to me that my father would not allow a child to be confined within those dank walls. The captive needed to be interrogated, but my father would not want him subjected to torture.

As I considered these things, I felt relieved that I, unlike my father, did not have to make judgments as to the prisoner. He was young, yes, but also a Cokyrian, and though they would not treat him unkindly for the first reason, neither could they trust him. Hytanicans had only ever encountered Cokyrian adults, and no one could imagine what this boy was doing here, if he had been sent as a spy or a messenger, or if he had for some reason fled his homeland. I was, of course, also frustrated by the lack of information I had been able to gather, but I supposed this situation was held in stricter confidence than even the investigation of the Elite Guard had been. It was unlikely Steldor would know about this, I had been thankful to deduce, not wanting to suffer through another afternoon with him.

On the morning of the fourth day after Destari had been assigned to be the young Cokyrian's guard, I headed to the library, desirous of a location to think, where Tadark might hold his tongue. I was brimming with questions, yet could not concentrate, as the Lieutenant was still bent on talking about London's incompetence. In fact, he was in the middle of a tirade when I pushed the library doors open.

"Once in a while I would see a glint in his eyes almost as though he were taunting me... "

I fought the urge to tell Tadark outright that London had actually *been* taunting him, when I saw my sister. She was sitting on the padded window seat across the room with her best friend, Semari, whom I had not known was visiting us. They were clearly gossiping about something, because their voices were low and occasionally one of them would clap a hand over her mouth, aghast at what the other had said. Aware that someone had entered the library, they stopped talking and looked in my direction.

"Come here, Alera!" Miranna said delightedly, springing to her feet. "We were just discussing the latest scandals!"

I smiled and moved toward the window, ready to contribute heartily to their conversation. When Tadark began to follow, I waved him off, and he instead joined Halias by the fireplace.

"Miranna has just been telling me about the Cokyrian prisoner," Semari said, her clear blue eyes glistening. "She says he is very handsome."

She and Miranna giggled, and I readily concurred, sitting in a chair opposite them. The prisoner was undeniably attractive, though in a much different way from Steldor. Steldor had a polished style, with classic good looks and sophisticated taste. The Cokyrian was unique, with eyes that entranced in a moment, and a young but extraordinarily worldly face. While I had seen him only once, I sensed a deepness within him that Steldor would never possess. Not wanting to share any of these thoughts, I attempted to redirect the discussion to something of greater appeal to me.

"What do you think he's doing here?"

"I don't care much about that," Semari scoffed, not sharing my interest in the least. "But I do so want to meet him and ask him about his homeland. I've never been into the desert lands of the east or into the mountains, and can't imagine what it must be like to live in such a forbidding place."

"He can't be as dangerous as the adults of his kind, so it would be safe to talk with him, wouldn't it?" Miranna agreed. "He may well be our only chance to learn firsthand about the Cokyrians!"

Semari sat quietly, gnawing distractedly on a fingernail. Although she was almost a year and a half younger than my sister, her bubbly nature and love of all things feminine had made them an ideal match.

"What are you thinking?" Miranna asked.

Semari sighed in frustration, having discovered a fault in whatever she had been working through in her mind.

"We could never get to him in the dungeon. With all the guards down there, it would be impossible!"

I laughed to myself, as I knew something they did not. I leaned closer, motioning for them to do the same, and whispered in their ears.

"Are you certain?" Miranna asked incredulously when I had finished.

I gave a self-assured nod.

Semari was gleeful. "This is perfect! I know exactly what to do."

We huddled together so that our foreheads almost touched and began to plot our strategy.

Semari, as had been planned for her visit, spent the night with Miranna, and the next morning we put our scheme into action. In order to discover where the prisoner was being kept, I chanced a visit to the Guest Wing that comprised the eastern half of the Palace's third floor. As I thought it probable that the Cokyrian was being housed in one of the rooms at the rear of the Palace, I avoided using my family's stairway, instead using the stairwell located just off the Grand Staircase to gain access to the upper floor. Although there were generally no guards posted on the third floor unless guests were occupying the rooms, I did not want to emerge into the corridor and blunder into Destari.

My mission was to lurk in the Guest Wing for as long as it took to locate the prisoner's room, then return to the library where Miranna and Semari would be passing the time. The only disquiet I felt about my task was due to Tadark's constant and clinging company, but he became a potential obstacle only once.

"I don't understand what we're doing here," he said, bored with my chosen activity, or more precisely, lack thereof.

"You don't have to understand, Tadark. You just need to leave me be."

"Are you doing something you're not supposed to be doing? Destari said something about guest rooms —— "

"I implore you to be quiet... Tad," I needled, remembering how much he despised the moniker.

"Don't call me that." Tadark's brown eyes narrowed resentfully.

"If you stop talking right now, I'll never call you Tad again."

He nodded, then stood back from me, and no further sounds escaped from his tightly compressed lips.

"Now, stay here. I will be back momentarily."

Tadark shrugged, for once content to do as he was told.

The Guest Wing contained seven rooms, five of which were located along exterior walls, and two of which were windowless interior rooms. A corridor led all the way through the wing, so I could start where I now stood and travel past all of the rooms, arriving back at my point of origin.

I walked to the west, then turned north into the corridor

that divided the Guest Wing from the Servant's Quarters. Coming to the end of the hall, I stealthily leaned around the corner to the right to peer down its length, looking for Destari. He stood with his back to me outside the nearest of the two interior rooms, seemingly large enough to block the entire corridor. Though there was no sign of his charge, I had to assume I had discovered where the Cokyrian was being held. I considered the location, realizing that it made sense to house our captive in one of the windowless rooms.

I retreated to the front stairwell and descended the steps to return to the second floor, Tadark trotting obediently behind. I hastened past the King's Dining Hall, then continued toward the library at the rear of the Palace, where I was to collect Miranna and Semari. They were seated together on the wide sill of the bay window when I entered, with Halias in front of them in an armchair, indulging their desire to braid pieces of his long blond hair.

"Miranna, Semari, come with me!" I called eagerly. "I have something to show you!" They knew by my words that I had located Destari and the prisoner.

Semari and Halias stood, but Miranna remained seated for a moment longer, the brightness of her smile fading.

"Are you all right?" Halias asked as he moved his chair off to the side of the window.

"Yes, I'm fine," she murmured. "Just a bit dizzy."

She got to her feet and began to cross the room with her friend.

"Now, what is it you have to show —— "

Without warning, Miranna collapsed, falling like a rag doll in the middle of the large rug on the library floor, her sentence left unfinished. I rushed to her, dropping to my knees beside her.

"Mira!" I cried, panic in my voice.

She lay on her side and her limbs began to quake, violent

shivers soon consuming her whole body. Nonsense tumbled from her lips in the same way it had when she had suffered similar attacks as a little girl. Semari was standing with her back to the library wall, her face stricken. Halias was at Miranna's other side in an instant, his blue eyes darting between me and my sister, as this was not a danger from which he could provide protection. It had been twelve years since Miranna's last attack, and none of us were any more prepared to handle the situation today than we had been more than a decade ago.

"Tadark!" I called to my horrified bodyguard, who was frozen by the door. "Fetch Bhadran! Tell him it's Miranna!"

Tadark raced from the room, off to find the doctor who attended the Royal Family.

"Quickly," I said to Halias, my words catching in my throat. "Find my mother."

Halias followed Tadark out the door without a backward glance, and Semari scurried after him to peek into the corridor.

"They're gone!" she whispered, turning to face me.

Miranna stayed her spasms and sat up, whereupon I helped her to her feet.

"We don't have long," I reminded them. "So we have to hurry."

Semari rushed out the door, her face flushed with excitement. Miranna and I followed, having successfully eluded our bodyguards, and the three of us hastened south through the corridor toward the front of the Palace, then up the stairs to the third floor. I led our trio out of the stairwell, and turned east, then crept north until we could peer to our left around the far corner to observe the prisoner's room.

Semari retreated to the southern end of the corridor as Miranna and I ducked into a vacant guest room. It wasn't long before she let out an ear-piercing scream. A few seconds passed and then we heard another.

Destari came hurtling around the corner to investigate, going past the room in which my sister and I were hiding and giving us a chance to slip out undiscovered. As he searched for the source of the screams, I clasped Miranna's hand and we went directly to the door Destari had been guarding. I turned the handle, stepping quickly inside, followed by my sister, who gave the door a push so that it swung shut.

The Cokyrian was sitting cross-legged atop the bed in the sparsely furnished room, one of his hands shackled to the bedpost, but despite this, he looked more relaxed than the last time I had seen him. He had bathed and changed into different clothing, black trousers and a loose white shirt, both too big for him, the cumulative effect of which was to make him appear even younger. The only items on his person that were probably his own were the belt about his hips and the well-worn boots on his feet.

He looked up when we entered, his deep blue eyes appraising us, the lift in his eyebrows his only reaction to our unorthodox arrival. In that instant, my tongue failed me. I had been concentrating so heavily on executing our plan that I had not given a single thought to what I would say should it prove successful.

For a long and agonizing moment, Miranna and I stared at him, and he stared back at us. Finally, I introduced myself the way I would have to anyone else.

"Excuse our intrusion," I said, trying my best to sound confident. "I am Princess Alera of Hytanica, and this is my sister, Princess Miranna." I motioned to Miranna, who was standing beside me. "We deemed it time to greet our guest."

He continued to dispassionately assess us. Just as I was beginning to wonder if he were mute, he spoke, his voice smooth and polite.

"Forgive me for being forward, Your Highnesses, but I was under the impression that I am more of a prisoner than a guest." He raised his arm and shook his shackled wrist.

I fought back the blush that threatened my cheeks, for this was not the answer I had expected. Rallying my dignity, I tried again.

"Prisoner or otherwise, you cannot deny that you are being treated kindly. Since we have already introduced ourselves, common courtesy would dictate that you do the same."

He continued to watch us warily, as if determining whether we represented some new interrogation technique.

"I am called Narian," he finally answered, a hint of suspicion in his voice.

"It's nice to meet you, Narian."

Miranna had not yet uttered a word, apparently too stupefied that our strategy had worked to enter the conversation. She was not to be given the chance to speak, for at that moment, the door swung open, and she and I just managed to avoid being hit. Destari stood in the corridor, face livid, black eyes glittering like shards of glass, grasping Semari's wrist in his left hand. He tugged her into the room behind him, glaring fiercely at everyone present, excluding Narian, who had played no role in creating the present circumstances.

"What were you *thinking*?" Destari boomed. "I would never have expected such rash behavior from any of you —— especially you two!" he said, aiming his tirade at Miranna and me. "Princesses! Whatever made you think to try something this brainless? And just how were you planning to slip back out once you were inside? Did you actually think you would get away with something as childish and irresponsible as this? You should be ashamed!"

He continued his rant for a moment longer, then stopped, realizing no one was listening to him. My sister and I were gaping at Semari and Narian, who were staring transfixed at each other. Though Semari's blond hair was lighter and her skin fairer, their faces were strikingly similar, with full lips, straight noses, and softly arching eyebrows. Their eyes, too, were a similar shade of blue, though Narian's were cold and aloof in contrast to Semari's, which were bright and innocent. The resemblance was so strong, in fact, that once I saw them together, I couldn't believe his features had not immediately brought her to mind.

"Kyenn?" Semari said tentatively.

"I'm taking you to the Captain of the Guard," Destari interjected, taking control of the situation. "All of you."

He unshackled Narian from the bedpost, then marched us out of the room and west through the corridor toward the spiral staircase, keeping a distrustful hand on Narian's shoulder the entire way. As we approached the landing, we ran into Halias, who had caught on to some of our plan and was not the least bit amused, and Tadark, who was quite perplexed, as he had not yet figured out what was happening.

"Destari!" Halias exclaimed in unmistakable relief when he saw us in the company of his fellow Deputy Captain. He approached, his relief instantly suffused by an unusual display of temper. "Where did you find them?" he growled, glaring at Miranna, Semari, and me.

"In the prisoner's room," Destari fumed, his black hair and heavy brows making him especially formidable. "They took it upon themselves to meet him."

Halias gave Miranna a look that would have made me tremble, but which she met with a sheepish grin, peering up at him through lowered lashes.

At last realizing what we had done, Tadark gasped, then glared at me in an attempt to match Halias's look of disapproval, but it did not have nearly the same effect. I smiled serenely at him, and he widened his light brown eyes as if to intensify his glower, but with his boyish face, he only succeeded in making himself look all the more ridiculous.

Halias continued to hold Miranna in his severe glare as he informed Destari of the details of our grand scheme.

"Bhadran and the Queen are in the library, waiting for us to return," he finished.

"Then we should go to them at once." Destari's statement left no room for argument.

Halias moved to Miranna's side, and Tadark to mine, as we descended the stairway and proceeded toward the library, Destari following with Narian. I was glad that, after my mother and father, it was Tadark to whom I would have to answer and not London. I didn't even want to consider what London's reaction to our scheme would have been.

We arrived in the library far too quickly for my liking. The Queen and the Royal Physician rose from armchairs by the window the moment we entered but did not speak. My mother was shaking her head at Miranna and me in disapproval, and I could not meet her gaze for shame.

Destari remained by the door, not relinquishing his grip on Narian's shoulder, and motioned for Halias to join him. The two guards had a hushed exchange, and several times Halias glanced from Narian to Semari, who was standing quietly beside me, examining the floor. As they finished, Halias seized Narian's upper arm and guided him toward the window seat. Dragging an armchair several feet away from where my mother and the doctor stood, he roughly pushed the young man into it.

"Sit," he commanded.

After Destari had departed to find Cannan, my mother walked over to where Semari, Miranna, and I were clustered in the middle of the rug. Although she was as composed as ever, I couldn't help dreading what she would say.

"Miranna, tell me that you did not fake this entire thing," she said reprovingly, referring to my sister's seizure.

Miranna hung her head, her coppery-blond hair falling forward like a veil.

"I'm sorry, Mother, but I cannot tell you that," she almost inaudibly confessed.

"I do not understand the three of you," my mother continued, although she did not raise her voice. "What could possibly have possessed you?"

"We only wanted to see what he was like," Miranna replied, her face still obscured by her hair.

"We... weren't really thinking at all," I conceded, hoping my mother, who had recently told me of her own irrepressible girlhood curiosity, might sympathize with us.

"You're right. You didn't think this through at all." Her voice was devoid of its usual lyrical quality, and her blue eyes sparked with rare anger. "We know *nothing* about this boy! You marched into his room without a single guard to protect you. Do you not see how reckless you were?"

"He's my age, Mother!" Miranna protested. "What could he have done?"

"Foolish child!" she admonished, sounding incredibly formidable while keeping her voice low so that no one could hear except we three. "If he were a Hytanican boy, he would be in his third year at the Military Academy! We do not know how they train their soldiers in Cokyri, but if he had intended to do you harm, I believe he could have done so. You haven't the faintest idea with whom you are dealing. He is *Cokyrian*! None of you were alive during the war, but perhaps if you had been you would comprehend how brashly you acted today. If you had seen the death, the agony —— if you had lost your entire family to those cold-blooded creatures as I did when I was young, then maybe you would have thought twice before entering that room."

Semari, Miranna, and I stood still as death, barely daring to breathe, my mother's lecture somehow more painful than a physical form of punishment would have been.

"Your behavior calls for apologies to your bodyguards," she finished primly. "And I would strongly suggest that you seek forgiveness in the Chapel and say a prayer for better judgment in the future."

She turned from us and approached the physician to tell him he had been called unnecessarily. After hearing her account, Bhadran bowed and took his leave, shaking his graying head reproachfully at us. My mother reseated herself, and we moved to stand beside her, heads bowed in penitence. Time passed in strained silence, until Narian spoke, and I became aware for the first time that he had a subtle accent.

"Why did you address me in that way before? Who is Kyenn?"

Semari tore her eyes away from her hands and stared at him, hope illuminating her face, which was so uncannily similar to his own. I could draw no other conclusion than the one I knew was spinning in the minds of everyone around me. Semari opened her mouth to reply, but Halias stopped her.

"Don't say anything, Semari. There will be no conversing with the prisoner until the Captain arrives."

As if on cue, the library door swung open and Cannan strode in, followed closely by Destari, the dark and imposing bearing of the two men casting a further pall over the room. All attention shifted to the Captain of the Guard, but he said nothing. Instead, he stood in the center of the rug, first studying Semari, then shifting his eyes to Narian, then back to Semari, and again to Narian, his expression ponderous.

Destari, who had stepped up beside him, gravely asked, "What do you make of this, sir?"

"There is a clear likeness between them," Cannan allowed.

"Can it be?" Halias echoed, momentarily too distracted to use proper military protocol, but finally adding, "Captain?"

"I cannot think of another explanation. The King must be notified."

XI

BACK FROM THE DEAD

Rumors quickly circulated in the Palace, stirring up questions and speculations that became my only source of information. My father was furious with both Miranna and me, but he was preoccupied with settling the issue of the Cokyrian boy's possible identity and had not yet taken the time to discipline us. I was grateful for this small mercy.

The day after we had executed our plan, Semari had returned to the Palace with her parents. Neither Miranna nor I had been in attendance when they had met with Cannan and my father, and I had not since then been able to discover exactly what had transpired.

Miranna longed to speak with Semari once more, but she was afraid to ask Father's permission to pay her friend a visit, lest she remind him that he had not yet dealt with us. I wanted to know as well what had been determined about Narian, but the only people from whom I could receive accurate information were in the military, and none among them would be willing to enlighten me.

My thirst for knowledge was likewise not to be quenched by my father, who finally broke away from his duties to deal with his errant daughters. He came to my quarters during the early hours of the morning, before undertaking his duties as King.

Tadark had reported to his post and was waiting in the corridor to learn of my schedule for the day. He rapped upon my door and then opened it to announce the King, who entered looking unusually grim. I had just emerged from my bedroom and was sitting upon the sofa, brushing my dark brown hair. The humid morning air already had a stifling quality, which I felt even more keenly upon my father's arrival. I put down the brush and stood, but he bade me sit with his hand.

"Your actions of this past week have greatly disappointed me, Alera," he said with little emotion. "I have lost much confidence in your decision-making ability."

"I know, Father," I said remorsefully, not dropping my head as I had done with my mother, but meeting his gaze earnestly. "I'm sorry."

"I'm afraid 'sorry' simply isn't good enough this time. You endangered not only yourself but also your sister and her best friend. You made a very foolish choice, and I am not certain I can trust you to act less rashly in the future.

"What am I to do, Alera? You are seventeen years old, and yet you continue to play these childish games! You are to be Queen in less than a year. Given your age and upbringing, I should not have to be telling you to behave more sensibly."

He began to talk with his hands as his agitation increased, while I sat in wretched silence, letting his criticism rain down upon me.

"Who is to govern beside such an unpromising Queen? Would she enable her husband to rule the Kingdom with a steady hand or distract him with her silly ploys?"

He looked sternly at me as though daring me to respond, but I knew there was nothing I could say. My throat had constricted, and I was incapable of thinking about anything other than my own incompetence, which my father had just brought rather painfully out into the open.

"A suitor must be chosen, Alera," he continued, beginning to pace in front of me, his brow dampening with sweat. "You know whom I want to succeed me. If another young man of quality does not soon present himself, then you will marry Lord Steldor, under my last order as King of Hytanica."

"But I cannot marry Steldor," I gasped, my brain finally jarred into action.

"Then perhaps you have another suitor in mind?"

My father stopped and turned toward me, his tone telling me he thought it unlikely he would approve of anyone of my choosing.

"There is no one else, Father," I murmured, vague echoes of a previous conversation rebounding in my head.

"As I expected," he said unpleasantly, and I could not help but feel inept. "I have taken the liberty of inviting Steldor to accompany you on a picnic outside the city walls. I have given him my permission to court you and insist that you honestly evaluate him in terms of his qualities and not based merely on your whims."

My father swung around to go, but I hastily stood to call him back.

"Wait! Miranna would also enjoy such an outing. I pray you to permit her to come with us."

My father did not appear to be in a mood to compromise, but I was compelled to plead my case by the thought of how stressful such an outing would be.

"A young man could be chosen to accompany her as well. Such an arrangement would place less pressure upon Steldor and me. And it would help me to be at ease in his company."

My father thought for a moment, and as usual, began to toy with his ring.

"Amidst all of your terrible ideas, there is occasionally one of value," he finally conceded. "I will inform Miranna that she will be joining you and Steldor on your outing ten days hence."

He left the room without another word, and I sank down on

the sofa, the morning heat and my misery depleting my energy. After many minutes, it dawned on me that my father might have paid a visit to Miranna, too. Even if he had not, my sister was someone who would empathize with my feelings.

Leaving my parlor, I hastened down the hallway toward Miranna's quarters, which also consisted of a trio of rooms, although she did not have a balcony as I did. Her parlor was similar to mine, with tapestries decorating the walls, rugs padding the floor, and a sofa and several armchairs providing seating. The primary difference was in color; she favored blues while I preferred burgundy.

Halias knocked on Miranna's parlor door, then opened it to grant me entry. My sister was sitting in a deep blue velvet armchair doing some handwork but stood to usher me into her bedroom at sight of my gloomy countenance.

Unlike the parlor, her bedroom was in sharp contrast to mine, for hers was decorated more playfully, with a lacy spread and pale blue velvet draperies. The walls were not hung with tapestries but with silks in the softest hues of blue, yellow, green, and pink. Ribbons in the same colors hung in streamers from the four posts of her bed and decorated the edges of its canopy. A large number of lovingly kept dolls sat atop her bookshelf and dressing table.

She plopped down on her bed and motioned for me to do the same.

"Is it Father?" she asked.

"Of course." I sank gloomily onto the bed beside her.

"He spoke with me this morning about the need for me to act more prudently and to set a good example," she said, hugging a pillow to her chest. "While it wasn't a pleasant conversation, he at least didn't strike me. How did he treat you?"

"He didn't hit me either, although that might have been easier to bear. No, he lectured me on my shortcomings as a daughter." I hesitated, then gushed, "He told me he fears I will be an incompetent Queen. He said that I am too old to be playing childish games and that he can no longer trust my judgment."

My eyes welled with tears, though I was determined not to let them fall, for that would have somehow been an admission that his assessment was correct.

"He doesn't know what he's talking about," Miranna simpered, shifting to take my hands in hers. "You will be an exceptional Queen. He should not base his opinion on this one incident."

"Father rules this Kingdom, Mira. He, better than anyone, knows the qualities that are necessary in a Queen."

"What we did was very unwise, but Father has overreacted. He has never before doubted your suitability as the heir, and I'm sure in his heart he truly doesn't now."

"He also said that unless I soon find another 'man of quality' to be my husband, he will order me to marry Steldor." I removed my hands from hers and began to fiddle with the lace of her bedspread.

This Miranna had not expected. "Order you?" she repeated.

"Yes! What am I going to do? I cannot marry Steldor!"

"That doesn't sound like Father," she said, dismayed. She regarded me sympathetically for a moment. "He is just... under a lot of stress right now. I'm certain in time he will rethink his position... and regain his sense of humor."

Her attempt to reassure me fell short, for her tone was not very convincing.

"And if he doesn't? Then what am I to do? I had hoped to marry for love —— an intelligent and compassionate man —— someone with the potential to become the greatest King in Hytanican history! How much time will Father give me before he forces me to marry the man I detest?"

"Calm down, Alera!" Miranna insisted. "While I do not

share your negative opinion of Steldor, I do agree that you should marry for love. Just give Father some time and he will come around."

We sat in abject silence for a few minutes, then she scrambled to her feet.

"A change of scenery would do us both some good. Why don't we go out for a while? Leave both the Palace and our troubles behind?"

"A change couldn't hurt," I wretchedly agreed.

She twisted a strand of her hair over and over with her left hand as she reviewed our options, then flashed me a smile.

"I think today is Market Day —— let's get some fresh air and take in the sights." She grabbed my hand and pulled me to my feet. "And we can scout for alternative suitors!"

I couldn't keep from smiling at her suggestion, although I did not see my predicament as the least bit comical.

————

Two hours later, Tadark and Halias followed us out of the Palace, through the Central Courtyard, and into the city. We proceeded for a short while down the thirty-five-foot-wide main thoroughfare that cut the city in half, then turned west into the Market District. Here, storefronts opened onto narrow streets, with similar types of businesses clustered together. As we strolled along, we perused the offerings of the bakers, the spice grocers, the apothecaries, and the jewelers. Their wares were displayed on counters that doubled as the bottom halves of the shutters that closed the shopfronts at the end of the day. The top halves of the shutters were propped up to provide the merchandise with some protection from the elements. Down one of the many side streets we could see the signboards for the shoemakers, saddle and harness makers, and tanners. Down another were the fish merchants, butchers, and chandlers.

As we came to the last of the shops, the cobblestone street opened into a large grassy area atop a hill that sloped down into the training field just south of Hytanica's Military Complex. Here, temporary tents and stalls had been erected to accommodate the various vendors who had brought items for sale or trade.

Market Day was held once a week and attracted a teeming crowd. In addition to farm products, the craftsmen from the villages surrounding the walled city would come to sell their handmade goods. As traveling merchants would also offer wares for sale, there was an ever-changing assortment of items available. Furniture, tools, furs, glassware, exotic spices, rare oils and perfumes, pots and pans, laces, and unusual fabrics were all part of the hodgepodge that was Market Day.

Miranna and I were wearing simple frocks, for Cannan had long ago decreed that we should dress in the style of villagers when we visited the market. The Captain was a cautious man and did not want the manner of our dress to announce who we were. Of course, no disguise in the world would have worked when our uniformed bodyguards were conspicuously present, so Tadark and Halias were clad more plainly as well. To my great relief, and Tadark's chagrin, the Deputy Captain was also willing to give us a bit more freedom to roam and was refusing to permit the Lieutenant to hang off my elbow. As Halias outranked him, Tadark had no choice but to comply.

As we joined the throng of people surrounding the tents and stalls, we were bombarded by the sounds of vendors hawking their wares, customers arguing and negotiating, little children playing, and animals complaining in their various ways. My spirits immediately lifted as I absorbed the energy that hung in the air in this fascinating place.

"Oh, look over there!" Miranna said, touching my arm and pointing over the heads of the milling crowd to a young man in his mid-twenties who stood beside one of the many vegetable stands.

"He's handsome —— you could marry him!"

"I'm sure that would improve Father's opinion of me," I replied, playing along. *"Sire, I would like to marry a vegetable merchant... or perhaps the servant of a vegetable merchant,"* I said with exaggerated formality.

"While he would not approve the match, it would be interesting to see his face when you asked him," Miranna laughed.

We continued to work our way through the shoppers, scanning the items on sale this week. Miranna was replacing a scarf she had been examining at one of the stands when a familiar voice rang out from behind us.

"Mira!" Semari was making her way toward us through the bustling swarm of people, her cheeks flushed and her blue eyes dancing with excitement.

"Semari!" Miranna cheerfully returned, moving forward to greet her friend with a hug. "How are you?"

"Papa was furious when he was told what we had done, but I'm hardly even sore anymore," Semari said, the smile on her face broadening, though it hardly fit her words. "And he's forgotten all about it now."

"Because of Narian?" Miranna pressed, jumping to the topic that had been foremost in our minds of late —— the shocking resemblance between Semari and the Cokyrian youth.

Semari nodded and we moved off to the side of one of the tents so we could converse without being jostled by the milling shoppers.

"When the Captain of the Guard and the King met with us, they asked if my parents could identify him as their son in some manner other than his looks and his age. My mother recalled that Kyenn had been born with an unusual mark behind his left ear, a mark in the shape of a jagged crescent moon. The Captain examined Narian and discovered the mark exactly as my mother had described it! How likely is it that two people would have the exact same birthmark, let alone such an unusual one?"

"Not likely at all," I said, captivated by her tale.

"The King and the Captain then concluded that he is the long-missing member of our family, my older brother."

"What are they going to do with him?" Miranna asked, equally intrigued.

"Well, my parents want him to live at home, but he can't be completely trusted, so for now he stays under guard at the Palace. The Captain wants to slowly introduce him to Hytanican life, at the same time watching over him, in case the Cokyrians did send him here for a purpose."

"Have you spoken with him?" Miranna persisted.

"Of course I have! The Captain has arranged for him to visit us each week. On the appointed days, Destari transports him to our home in the morning and returns him to the Palace in the evening. The men keep a close eye on him when he is with us, but there have been no real problems."

"What is he like?" I breathlessly asked.

"It's so thrilling to meet him, my long-lost older brother, but the situation is also very strange." Semari had become contemplative. "I have always been the oldest child in my family. It feels odd to be someone's younger sister. And from my parents' standpoint, it's as though he's come back from the dead."

I reflected on this for a moment. Semari's older brother, Kyenn, had been abducted just a week after his birth and was believed to have been murdered, though his body had not been among those returned by the Cokyrians. The trauma Semari's parents, Baron Koranis and Baroness Alantonya, had suffered had been so devastating that they still felt its pain sixteen years later, and they had always been haunted by the uncertainty of their son's true fate. It was almost inconceivable that the Cokyrian youth arrested by London could be their missing child. But their joy at his return had to be tempered by the knowledge that he had been raised in the land of Hytanica's greatest enemy.

"He is very quiet." Semari's voice drew me from my thoughts. "He doesn't talk much at all; he just observes everything."

"Well, Hytanica must be interesting to him," Miranna speculated. "The way we live is no doubt different from life in Cokyri."

"I don't know if 'interesting' is the right description. He acts almost condescending about the way we live... like he's disappointed, as if he expected more from us."

"What do you mean?" I queried.

"He's not exactly conceited. To give you an example —— he was surprised, irritated almost, when he learned that I did not know how to handle a weapon, that the focus of my education and that of my sisters has been on etiquette and not Hytanica's history or its politics. He seemed to think our educations insufficient."

"Does he ever mention Cokyri?" Miranna asked, managing to divert us to the subject she'd been dying to discuss since we had begun chatting.

"As I said, he's not very forthcoming. The only thing we know is that while he was in Cokyri, he discovered he was Hytanican, and that's why he left to come here. He hasn't said how he found out or anything else about his life, and we haven't pressured him to tell us. My parents believe that he was raised among the upper class, though, as he is quite well spoken and well mannered."

Just then, another aspect of the situation occurred to me. "How are you addressing him? He apparently has two names."

"That is somewhat undetermined," Semari answered ruefully. "My parents want to call him Kyenn —— he was born to them and that is what they christened him —— but he insists that they call him Narian. My mother, though it dismays her, understands his preference and is willing to use his Cokyrian name, but Papa refuses. My father went to him and told him that he can introduce himself as Narian, or whatever he wants to be called, when he is elsewhere, but while he is under his father's roof, his name will be Kyenn. My brother replied that he would respond to no name except Narian, regardless of whose roof he was under.

"So as not to anger my father, the rest of us have been calling him Kyenn, which only increases the tension for he will respond to my mother's use of the name, but not my father's. He also directs any questions he might have, though they are few indeed, to her and glares at Papa as if he were a simpleton should he deign to answer on her behalf."

"London told me once that Cokyrian women, rather than men, occupy positions of power," I mused. "Perhaps that is why he is willing to obey your mother but not your father."

"I suppose that could be the reason."

Semari glanced down the street when someone called her name.

"I'm coming, Mother!" she responded, and then continued. "It's just that neither of my parents knows quite how to deal with him. My mother is not accustomed to being the center of attention, and she knows little about some of what he asks her. My father is the head of the house and deserves to be treated as such, but at the same time, he does not want to be angry with Narian —— Kyenn. My father's oldest son has come back to life, and all Papa wants is to get to know him. Kyenn's attitude is difficult for all of us, but especially for my father, as he is not used to being someone's second choice."

This was an attitude with which no one in Hytanica would be familiar. I could not imagine someone showing more respect for women than men or treating their father as inferior to their mother. Both would be completely unacceptable in Hytanica, and I wondered how Narian would ever fit into our world.

"I'm coming, Mother!" Semari repeated, her name once again reaching our ears over the crowd. "I have to go, but maybe you can come for a visit to our country estate. There is a good chance that Kyenn will be there." She hugged us each in turn and then ran off to join her family.

"She's incredibly lucky," Miranna sulked in the aftermath of her friend's departure. "The plan was for us to meet him and ask about Cokyri, and now he's practically living in her home."

"Life just isn't fair sometimes, even for Princesses," I teased, though feelings of envy were twisting my stomach also, for it was unlikely that we would be allowed to visit Semari at home while Narian was there. My father would insist upon giving the Baron and his family privacy so that Koranis and Alantonya could get reacquainted with their son, and their children could get to know their brother.

"We'd better return to the Palace," I said, noticing that the sky was clouding over in preparation for an evening shower. We were walking back through the cobblestone streets, Tadark and Halias in tow, when a different issue sprang to mind.

"Father wants me to see Steldor again," I said drearily.

"Really? When?"

"Next week. I unfortunately had to use you to avoid being trapped alone with him. Father is going to find an escort for you, and then the four of us will go on a picnic."

"Oh, that sounds splendid! We haven't been out of the city in such a long time."

"So you're not upset with me?"

"Not in the least! I rather welcome Steldor's company. And I can help by drawing some of his attention away from you."

I still did not understand how Miranna could look forward to spending time with Steldor, but I wasn't about to argue with her. The more diversions there were, the less time would be available for the Captain of the Guard's son to brag about himself.

XII

THE PICNIC

hat had started as a simple picnic soon became an event requiring as much meticulous planning as a grand festival. First, there came the problem of finding a suitable escort for Miranna. My father spoke with most of the upper-class young men in Hytanica but had difficulty finding one whom he viewed as responsible enough to attend his youngest daughter.

Next, the King gave due consideration to how we would be transported and where we would eat. I had assumed we would spontaneously pick a site, but he was insistent on knowing exactly where we were going to be at all times, and I slowly realized that his desire for oversight had less to do with fatherly interest and more to do with paranoia over potential Cokyrian danger.

And what about our bodyguards? Should both accompany us? My father concluded that only one was necessary since we would be in Steldor's very capable hands, although I suspected Cannan would have the place where we were heading under surveillance. Tadark, who was closer to the rest of us in age, staunchly refused to be left behind, and so became the favored one, despite Halias's superior rank. Neither Halias nor I was happy about this particular decision, but as long as the King was satisfied, there was nothing either of us could do about it.

At my father's direction, my mother spoke with the cooks to have them prepare and deliver a list of foods from which we could choose our picnic lunch. The resulting menu was pages long, and I picked the first few items that caught my eye, not having the willpower to review all the options.

By the time the day of the outing arrived, I was so tired of hearing about it that I was eager for it to be over. Miranna's enthusiasm, on the other hand, continued to run high, due more to her infatuation with Steldor, I was sure, than with anything else.

It was the third week in July, and the day was destined to be hot. Miranna and I had thus chosen to wear long, full-cut skirts with short-sleeved white blouses. I had also braided my hair into a single plait down my back, while Miranna's was tied at the nape of her neck in the manner in which Halias often wore his.

We left the Palace grounds mid-morning, riding in a buggy that had been furnished by the Royal Stables and was pulled by a magnificent pair of black Friesian horses. The buggy had a high wooden seat over the front wheels upon which the driver would sit, with a double front-facing seat over the back wheels that was padded for comfort. The floor of the buggy was relatively low to the ground for ease of entry.

As Steldor would be handling the reins, it was assumed that I would sit beside him, and a pad had been laid on the normally bare wooden seat in recognition of this arrangement. My escort was informally but elegantly dressed in a double-breasted white shirt with gold buttons and trim, and black breeches. He wore his showy black boots with the half dozen buckles running up the tall shafts. His shirt sharply contrasted with his dark hair and eyes, and had no doubt been calculated to increase the intensity of their effect and raise the pulse rate of any woman within range. Even I had caught myself staring when he'd strapped our picnic supplies to the rear-facing jump seat at the back of the buggy.

Miranna's companion was a stocky young man named Temerson, whose height and eye color matched my own but whose hair was cinnamon brown. He was clad in the Military Academy's standard-issue brown tunic and sash, and looked terribly out of place next to Steldor, although in truth he would have been rather cute if not subjected to such a comparison.

Miranna and Temerson occupied the backseat, while Tadark rode alongside on his own mount, the horses' hooves clacking pleasantly against the cobblestones of the main thoroughfare as we passed through the walled city. To the west of the thoroughfare lay the Market District, while to the east was the Business District, where money changers and lenders, tavern owners, innkeepers, doctors, and barbers did a lively business. Further away from the wide street, we could see church spires, the granary, and innumerable residences. Ahead of us rose the thirty-foot-high turreted stone wall that surrounded the city, with guard towers on each side of the gate as well as spaced evenly along its length. The city was home to about fifteen thousand people, with another twenty-five hundred living on farms and in villages scattered throughout the Hytanican countryside.

As we left the city, the stone thoroughfare turned into a dirt highway that wound its way through the terrain to the only bridge spanning the Recorah River. Our route soon took us east onto a much narrower and less traveled country road, for we were headed toward a protected setting in the bend of the river, where trees promised shade and the wide, rapidly flowing water would ensure a cool breeze. Even at a brisk trot, it would take well over two hours to reach our destination.

The outing had begun smoothly enough, but it did not take me long to discover that the mind-numbing planning for the picnic had made me even less tolerant of Steldor's ego. It helped that Miranna was present, but Steldor was flirting with me, not my sister. I tried my best to silently dissuade him by concentrating on the passing landscape.

Hytanica's rolling terrain was lush and green at this time of year, and the fields of flax that would soon be harvested were dotted with beautiful pale blue flowers. As the horses trotted onward, we saw many farmhands hard at work in the fields, and my suitor would wave magnanimously to them on occasion.

Undaunted by my reluctance to interact with him, Steldor proved quite capable of carrying an entire conversation by himself. After another tedious monologue similar in content to the one he had delivered on the night we had dined together, he leaned toward me.

"So what's the name of your sister's friend?"

Temerson had shyly introduced himself to us all, but Steldor had been too busy being Steldor to pay attention.

"Lord Temerson," I supplied, his arrogance rapidly depleting my patience. "I assume you know his father, Lieutenant Garreck, as he is a veteran Battalion Commander who has been teaching at the Military Academy for the past fifteen years, and his mother, Lady Tanda, is a friend of my mother's, and I presume, of your mother's."

"Ah," he replied, then he glanced back at the young man with whom my sister had been unsuccessfully attempting to converse. "So, Temerson, are you a student at the Military Academy?"

The inquiry was unnecessary, given Temerson's age and apparel, but I suspected the military might be the only subject they would have in common.

I scrutinized Miranna's escort while waiting for him to respond and saw the look of a cornered animal settle upon his face. He opened his mouth but no sound came forth, and he instead opted for nodding his head twice. It struck me that for someone with a naturally reticent nature, Steldor could be exceptionally intimidating, and probably doubly so to a young cadet over whom he held rank. It was also possible that Temerson had at some time been the object of Steldor's and Galen's razzing.

"The quiet type," Steldor remarked to me, as if Temerson weren't there. "Reminds me of another his age."

"And whom would that be?" I asked, social graces winning out despite my determination to discourage him from talking.

"That Cokyrian boy."

"You mean Hytanican boy," I corrected, assuming he knew the young man's true identity.

Steldor brushed my comment off. "He was raised Cokyrian. He thinks like them and behaves like them. That's all I need to know."

"Yes, but he was *born* Hytanican," I argued, hardly believing that Steldor would be so quick to judge Narian. "That's all *I* need to know."

"That's beside the point, anyway. All I was going to say is that he has barely spoken a word since we brought him to the Palace, and I find it rather odd."

"Perhaps he is just overwhelmed by all that has happened to him. He was captured by the people he undoubtedly fears the most and now has been reunited with the family he's never known. I don't think I would be talking much either."

"Or perhaps he doesn't speak because there is nothing going on in his head."

"Just because he is not about to divulge his life story at the merest implication that he should does not mean he is unintelligent, Steldor." I could tell my keenness to debate was beginning to annoy him, but I was enjoying his discomfort too much to drop the matter.

"Why are you defending him? You know no more about him than I do."

"Then why are you deriding him?"

"We clearly aren't going to agree on anything here."

"That's the one opinion of yours with which I will agree."

The rest of the trip passed without much discussion. Steldor and I did not converse further, and though Miranna tried several times to elicit a response from Temerson, nothing came of her attempts.

Steldor halted the horses beside a large oak tree near the river, leaving Tadark to secure them. Temerson helped Miranna from the buggy, and I grudgingly permitted Steldor to lift me to the ground. His hands were upon my waist as he set me down, but he did not immediately release me. Instead, his eyes bore into my own, and the blood drained from my face at the thought that he might kiss me. Then he smiled rakishly and dropped his hands, leaving me with the distinct impression that he had wanted to elicit such a reaction from me.

Tadark and Temerson began to remove the picnic supplies from the buggy while Steldor supervised, unmistakably of the opinion that he was exempt from the work. He did, however, give directions as to where everything should be located, treating the picnic like some sort of military drill. When he directed Tadark to a specific spot to lay our quilt, I could restrain myself no longer.

"I would like the quilt to go over there," I called genially to the men, motioning to a grassy area closer to the river where several large willow trees stood, their tendrils trailing across the ground in the breeze.

"No," Steldor said with an unbearably commanding air. "The quilt should be here."

Tadark, who was standing with two corners of the quilt in his hands, ready to lay it on the ground, stopped to watch us bicker.

"This ground is smoother," I contended, walking over to my chosen location, remarkably willing to spend the entire afternoon arguing about this insignificant decision.

"We will have better shade here."

"But I'm standing *over here*, and if we put the quilt *over there*, I will have to move." I gave Steldor a sickeningly sweet smile.

"Tadark already has the quilt halfway on the ground," he tried once more.

"Surely it will take minimal effort to pick it up and bring it to me. If Tadark does not wish to exert himself, I expect you could manage without undue strain."

Steldor studied me for a moment, aware that he and I were engaging in some form of power struggle. Concluding he could afford to lose this skirmish, he surrendered.

"As you wish. We will put the quilt wherever you direct, Princess."

"Thank you," I said, trying to conceal my smugness.

Tadark huffed as though moving the quilt were the most unreasonable thing I could have asked of him, but he nevertheless picked it up and brought it to where I stood. Temerson, who had been holding a large basket of food during our entire exchange, set it down appreciatively but did not say a word.

The men returned to the buggy, Tadark and Temerson to retrieve whatever drinks the cooks had supplied, and Steldor to again supervise the task. Miranna and I settled ourselves on the quilt, whereupon my sister turned to me with an exasperated sigh.

"Why can't you treat Steldor with some decency?"

"I simply am not in the mood to put up with his pretentious behavior," I replied defensively.

"Give him a chance, Alera," Miranna pleaded. "Has he really done anything so terrible today? And don't say he's egotistical. He's *Steldor*. That's a given with him."

"I suppose he really hasn't behaved too badly," I said, a bit more petulantly than I had intended. "If it will make the day more pleasant for you, I'll try to assume his intentions are for the best."

"See that you do."

Steldor was the first to return, strutting along in front of Temerson and Tadark, who were carrying wine flasks and goblets.

"I propose that we go for a stroll along the riverbank before we dine," he said, his manner once again authoritative and, to me at least, grating.

"I think we should eat first," I disagreed, in blatant disregard of the promise I had just made to my sister.

"If we walk now, we will build up an appetite."

"I am hungry already. If we walk, I may faint."

Steldor seemed to know what I was doing, and his amused visage only rankled me more. Unable to abide my obduracy, Miranna took control, rising to her feet to accompany him. She gave me a chilling look that told me to yield, and I exhaled in resignation.

"On second thought, a walk sounds lovely," I managed, though my tone was insincere.

I stood and gripped Miranna's hand, pulling her next to me so I would not be forced to stroll alongside Steldor.

The two military officers joined us without delay, Tadark's duty and Steldor's pride not allowing either of them to let us get far ahead. Temerson trailed the four of us, too daunted by the company he was keeping to walk in step with us.

The ground sloped gently toward the Recorah, flattening as it reached the river's bank, thus permitting us to walk within a few feet of the racing water. Here, where the Recorah changed course, no longer flowing south but curving toward the western hills in the distance, its wide expanse narrowed, increasing the speed of its flow and creating a white froth against the far bank.

The one bridge that spanned the river to permit entry into our Kingdom was several miles to our west and was heavily guarded by Hytanican soldiers. Even though the threat from Cokyri that had been felt after the High Priestess's capture had seemingly abated, my father and Cannan had not relaxed their vigilance, and patrols continued to monitor Hytanica's borders while sentries kept twenty-four-hour watch over the bridge.

Miranna and I followed the bend in the river, talking softly. Steldor attempted to slide in next to me, but I was walking close to the water's edge with Miranna planted on my other side so he had no way to position himself. He chose not to try again, as that might have cast him in a foolish light, instead drifting over to Tadark, with whom he began to talk just loudly enough for us to hear.

"So, you've become Alera's new bodyguard, have you?" he asked, a sly connotation to his words that I did not like.

"I have indeed," Tadark replied proudly.

"Here's hoping you prove better than the last one."

"I most definitely am better!" Tadark squeaked. "London was not a good bodyguard. He couldn't keep track of Alera for a minute. I don't know how he came to be a member of the Elite Guard. He clearly wasn't fit to handle such important responsibilities."

"I agree," Steldor said with mock indignation. "I was never much impressed with him, unlike my father. The Captain was in such an uproar when we learned that London was the traitor. Personally, I don't understand why no one saw it coming, especially since he has always been a bit of a renegade."

"I saw it coming!" Tadark exclaimed, sounding like an excited five-year-old. "I knew there was something suspicious about him from the very first moment I met him. I never quite trusted him, for his mind was often elsewhere, as if the Princess were not his first priority."

Unable to suffer more, I opened my mouth to defend London, but Miranna's soothing voice cut me off.

"Just ignore them," she advised. "They don't know what they're talking about. Besides, Steldor is doing this on purpose. He wants to needle you. Don't give him the satisfaction of knowing he has succeeded."

With some effort, I regained my composure, recognizing that my sister had spoken wisely. Steldor and Tadark continued to talk, but I did my best to shut them out, for their words hurt me and only increased the level of dislike I held for the Captain's son.

We circled around and returned to our picnic site, the baskets waiting for us upon the quilt. Tadark withdrew toward the buggy, while Temerson finally came to join the rest of us, and we sat down to unpack the provisions. Our picnic fare of hearty breads, cheeses, cold soup, fruit, and wine looked delicious, but Steldor's presence had once again robbed me of my appetite. Even so, I was thankful we were eating, for it brought all talk to an end.

As the meal drew to a close, Miranna turned to Temerson with a sweet smile.

"Would you go with me to the river? I would like to rinse my hands in the water."

Temerson nodded, his eyes growing large at having received such a request. Then he stood to accompany her, leaving me alone with my escort.

I thought there would be a very long, very tense silence, but Steldor had other plans. He sidled over to me and, placing one hand about my waist, swept me into his arms. I tried to resist, but he was strong and assured in his actions, and his intoxicating scent addled my brain.

"Don't be afraid of me, Alera," he murmured. "I appreciate a little spirit in a woman." His lips brushed my cheek, and he added, "At least this time we have a bodyguard who won't interfere."

"What do you mean by that?" I snipped, leaning away from him, his reference to London jarring me to my senses.

"The last time we had a chance to be alone, London rudely interrupted us, claiming there was some *emergency* in the Palace."

He was now whisking the strands of hair that had escaped my braid over my shoulders, lightly caressing my neck with his fingers.

"I would deem rescuing me from your unwanted advances to be an emergency," I said emphatically, pushing against him.

Steldor froze. I was certain no one had ever before even intimated that his advances might be unwanted, and I had just bluntly told him I had no desire to be close to him at all. I could almost feel the heat rising inside of him as he got to his feet, knocking me off balance so that I tumbled uncomfortably onto my side.

"Here I am, alone with you, as affectionate and charming as anyone could ever be, and you want none of it!" His voice had lost its honeyed quality, sounding lower, rougher. "There are many young women in Hytanica who would, without hesitation, give everything they have to win the attention I freely give to you, Alera."

After giving the picnic basket a swift kick, he stormed off to the river's edge, where Miranna and Temerson were sitting side by side on a rock outcropping. Miranna had finally encouraged some conversation from the timid young man, but as the Field Commander approached, Temerson fell silent.

Steldor situated himself close to my sister, unsheathing his dagger and placing one foot upon a boulder. I was too far away to hear him, but his body language as he flipped the knife back and forth between his hands, and the way Miranna was blushing, told me enough about what he was doing. With every giggle he elicited from her, my dislike for the Captain of the Guard's son grew stronger. I was positive Steldor was trifling with Miranna in an attempt to make me jealous, but while I was feeling many things at that moment, jealousy was not in the mix.

Steldor's flirtations continued for many minutes, until Miranna glanced over toward me and understood what his motivations truly were. She abruptly stood and pointed over his shoulder.

"Look, an apple tree!" she exclaimed.

Steldor seemed momentarily taken aback that my sister would have the presence of mind to notice an apple tree while under his spell. Then he shrugged and pivoted to face in the direction she was indicating, presumably deciding that, in her youth, she simply did not know how to respond to such a show of interest from someone as attractive as he.

"Alera!" Miranna called. "Come pick apples with me!"

My sister walked toward me, followed by Temerson and Steldor, who had returned his dagger to its sheath. Steldor stopped beside me, wearing a smug expression, confident that his attempts to make me jealous had succeeded.

"Yes, Alera, come pick apples with us."

I motioned to Miranna and Temerson to go on ahead and turned to the suitor of my father's choosing.

"Perhaps you and Tadark should ready the horses for our departure," I suggested, trying to limit the amount of time I was being forced to spend in his company.

"Oh, hoping to leave so soon?" he asked acerbically. "The King won't look for our return until late afternoon. We really shouldn't disappoint him." He moved closer, his eyes locked on mine.

"The horses do need tending, though," I repeated, nervously giving ground. "You and Tadark should lead them to the river for some water."

For a moment, I feared he was going to seize hold of me, and my pulse quickened in recognition of how easy it would be for him to assert his will. Then he stepped past, the glint in his eyes revealing he had once again achieved his intended effect.

"As you wish," he said flippantly over his shoulder. "Tadark and I will water the horses."

He strode toward my befuddled bodyguard and gave him a push in the direction of the buggy.

Shaken, I trailed after Miranna and Temerson, knowing I should not oppose Steldor so boldly, for women in Hytanica were expected to obey the men in their lives without question, or suffer the consequences. While Steldor was not yet my husband, he had my father's ear, and I did not doubt that the King would permit him considerable latitude in dealing with me.

I crested a small hill, pleased to find that there were, in fact, several apple trees. My sister was standing beneath one of them, staring up into its branches. I began to wonder where Temerson was, then heard a *snap* and a startled yelp from high up in the tree. Miranna's mouth opened in alarm as the young man fell from above, landing right on top of her. They tumbled to the ground, and Temerson scrambled to his feet.

"Are you h-hurt?" he asked as I rushed forward, his face turning scarlet with embarrassment.

"No, no, I'm fine," my sister reassured him, but she winced and had not yet attempted to stand.

"Well, c-can I get you anything?"

"A sip of water might be helpful," Miranna replied, not really needing a drink but wanting Temerson to feel like he was aiding her in some small way.

"Are you sure you're not hurt?" I dubiously asked after the young man had gone, afraid she might be downplaying her injuries so as not to worry anyone.

"Yes, I'm all right, really," she maintained. "Just a little stiff."

"What was Temerson doing in that tree?"

"He was trying to get that big apple for me —— the ripe red one on that upper branch —— and he fell. Just help me up. I don't want to be a burden to anyone."

I reached for her hand and had her halfway to her feet when she cried out in pain and fell back again.

"What's wrong?" I asked anxiously. "Where are you hurt?"

"I —— I don't know," she said, as though every word cost her dearly. "I can't breathe."

"I'm calling for help." Turning to face the buggy, I shouted, "TADARK!"

The Elite Guard was at my side in an instant, accompanied by Steldor, who had likewise heard my urgent call.

"What's wrong?" Steldor said worriedly, as though I had called for him and not my bodyguard.

I set my eyes on Tadark as I explained, "Miranna is hurt —— we must return to the Palace with haste."

"I've seen something like this before," Tadark said, looking at Steldor.

"Are you that desperate to get away from me, Alera?" There was a definite edge to Steldor's voice, and it was clear he had heard of the attack Miranna had faked in the library, which no doubt had generated talk among the guards.

I, in turn, was furious. "Though this may come as a revelation, not everything is about *you*, Steldor! My sister is hurt, and I demand that you transport us back to the Palace."

Miranna's ragged breathing had become more regular, and Steldor interpreted this to mean she had grown tired of pretending.

"See," he said, motioning to her where she lay on the ground with her eyes shut. "Her condition has improved. The game is up, Alera. Your little tricks will not work on me. We will not return to the Palace until the appointed hour."

"Fine! I will take the buggy and bring her back myself! But I would start creating excuses, Steldor, because you're going to need something spectacular to explain this to my father!"

I bent down beside Miranna with my back to my bodyguard and my escort. "Try again to stand and I will help you to the buggy."

I guided her into a sitting position, although she gasped with the effort. As she attempted to rise, a sharp cry escaped her lips and she collapsed, fainting from the pain. I barely managed to put my arm under her back and catch her, thus saving her from further collision with the ground.

After easing her down, I glared at the men with whom I was growing ever more enraged, willing them to do something. At last Steldor knelt beside my sister's limp form and pressed a hand against her ashen cheek.

"Her skin does feel clammy," he acknowledged, his forehead furrowed with worry.

"What do we do?" Tadark asked, shifting his weight from foot to foot as if he wanted to run somewhere but was uncertain in which direction to flee.

"Gather whatever you can in the next few minutes and pack it into the buggy," Steldor commanded. Then he turned to me. "How was she injured?"

"She fell," I lied, hoping to save Temerson from Steldor's wrath. Fortunately, he did not press me further.

"Go to the buggy," he directed. "I can carry Miranna."

I watched as Steldor lifted my sister, then he and I strode after Tadark. Temerson was standing beside the picnic quilt, holding the cup of water he had retrieved, shock upon his face as he watched the Field Commander bearing the incapacitated Princess.

I stopped Steldor as he was about to try to position Miranna upright in the back of the buggy.

"Don't! She needs to lie down." I hurried to tug the quilt

out from under the remaining picnic items, then carried it to where Steldor stood with my sister in his arms, moving past him to fold the quilt and provide Miranna with a pillow.

"There isn't going to be enough space for the rest of us," Steldor pointed out.

"I can kneel on the floor and watch over her."

Steldor frowned, then laid Miranna smoothly down.

"You will ride up front with me. Temerson can kneel and tend to Miranna. The floor is no place for a lady, and I fear you would tumble from the buggy. One injured Princess is quite enough."

He called to Temerson to take up his place and assisted me onto the front bench seat.

"Abandon anything that cannot be transported with you on your horse," he told Tadark, climbing up beside me. With a snap of the reins, he sent the horses off at a gallop, and I silently prayed that Miranna had not suffered serious harm.

The enormous stone walls surrounding the city looked forbidding and cold against the steadily darkening sky as we neared our destination, and the first rumble of thunder reached our ears as Steldor pulled the horses down to a trot. The heavy gates of iron that controlled access to the city were raised at this hour of the day, and though we passed unhindered beneath their spikes, the City Guards on either side regarded us quizzically, having witnessed our somewhat reckless return.

We continued down the thoroughfare toward the Palace at a slow but steady trot, for it was Market Day again and the streets were packed with people. Steldor halted before the gates to the Courtyard, and he and Temerson leapt from the buggy. As the Captain's son lifted me to the ground, he barked an order to the worried young man.

"Run ahead and tell the Palace Guards to summon the doctor. I will bring Miranna to her quarters."

I went to my sister, laying a hand upon her damp forehead, meeting her agonized blue eyes.

"We'll have you in your bedroom in a few minutes," I murmured.

She gave a slight nod but did not otherwise respond. Steldor brushed me aside and scooped her into his arms, then proceeded through the Courtyard gates and up the hedge-lined pathway that led to the Palace. By this time, Tadark had arrived, and he and I followed behind. As we approached the entry, I could see Palace Guards holding the double doors wide open for us.

"This way," I said, moving past Steldor as we stepped into the entryway, leading him up the Grand Staircase and on to Miranna's quarters. I opened the door into her parlor, and we went straight through to her bedroom, where he ducked beneath the pastel ribbons that streamed from the canopy over her bed to gently lay her down.

"I'll wait in the parlor," he said, glancing uncomfortably about at the frilly and feminine decor.

The Royal Physician arrived a short time later, along with my mother. Temerson, flushed and frightened, followed behind them, but he remained in the parlor with Steldor and Tadark.

As Bhadran examined Miranna, he asked me to explain how she had been hurt.

"She tripped and fell when we were gathering apples," I said circumspectly, attempting to make eye contact with my sister. I hoped she was alert enough to understand what I was doing.

The man who had treated every injury and illness we had suffered throughout our lives looked skeptically at me but did not comment, and I exited the room, for Miranna was now in highly qualified hands.

As soon as I joined the others in the parlor, Temerson turned his terrified eyes upon me, and I was filled with sympathy as I thought about the unfortunate circumstances in which he found himself. He had never before escorted a Princess, likely felt at fault for causing her some irreparable injury, and was anticipating that Steldor and perhaps the entire Royal Family would be furious with him. I wholeheartedly admired him for the simple fact that he had not fled. I smiled kindly at him but then addressed Steldor, who was likewise worried, although whether about Miranna or his own skin, I could not tell.

"Thank you for your assistance," I said, as rain began to patter against the window. Unable to help myself, I added, "It would appear our picnic was ill-fated for a number of reasons."

He studied me carefully, no doubt trying to ascertain whether or not I would tell my father that he had delayed our return to the Palace by questioning our honesty, but he did not make the inquiry.

"How is she?" he asked instead.

"The doctor has not yet determined the nature of her injury, but she is awake and some rosiness has returned to her cheeks."

"Tell me again how she came to harm," he said, dissatisfied with my earlier explanation.

"She tripped and fell. She must have landed on top of something, perhaps a stone or a branch."

Steldor looked askance at me, then whirled on Temerson. "You were with her. Is that how she was hurt?" The color drained from the young man's face, and I deftly intercepted the question.

"The injury is what it is. It is not really relevant how it was inflicted."

Just then Halias rushed through the door, his hair falling loosely about his shoulders rather than pulled back in its customary manner.

"What is going on?" he demanded. "Is Miranna safe?"

"She fell and was injured," I told him. "Bhadran and my mother are with her."

"This is the last time she goes anywhere without me by her side," he declared, with a reproving look at Tadark. "She does not come to harm when I am there to protect her."

Tadark glared at him, having taken offense to Halias's implied criticism of his ability as a bodyguard. Before he could reply, however, the bedroom door opened, and my mother glided into our midst.

"Our physician has given Miranna something to relieve the pain, and she is sleeping now," she informed us in her genteel manner. "She has bruised or broken several ribs, but will recover." She smiled gratefully at Steldor and Temerson. "Thank you for bringing her back to the Palace so quickly, and for your kind ministrations."

Although my mother's voice was gentle, they understood that they were being dismissed. They bowed respectfully and turned to leave.

"Temerson, a moment," I called to him. As both he and Steldor hesitated, I categorically said, "I only need a word with Temerson. *You* are free to go."

Steldor looked irked but departed nonetheless.

I approached the fidgety youth and quietly explained, "Miranna's injury was an accident, and I will not put you in a position of blame. As she and I remember it, she fell."

His cheeks dimpled into their first smile of the day, then he bowed and left the room.

———

Later that afternoon, after I had returned to my parlor and Tadark had resumed his duties, I informed him that I wanted to speak with him, and he entered my quarters.

"I believe the King would be desirous to know of the poor judgment you exercised earlier today at the time of Miranna's accident," I informed him, a devious twinkle in my eyes.

Tadark's posture became more rigid, but he remained mute.

"Perhaps you are not fit to handle such *important respon-sibilities*," I continued, maliciously repeating his earlier criticism of London.

His sullen expression told me that he realized his assignment as a bodyguard might be in jeopardy.

"Relax," I said, savoring the power I now wielded over him. "If you don't cause me trouble, I won't cause you trouble. Understand?"

He stared at me, brown eyes wide with indignation, hating the fact that I had acquired some leverage over him.

"That will be all. You are dismissed."

As he departed, I turned and walked into my bedroom, feeling that my day had just improved immensely.

XIII

THE DIGNITARY'S ROOM

ne week later, my mother called Miranna and me to the Queen's Drawing Room. This was the room in which she received visitors, met with household staff, and planned all of Hytanica's royal functions. I could not anticipate what she wanted from us, for we were rarely needed when she was meeting with visitors or staff, and I did not know of any upcoming events that would require the personal touch of the Queen and her daughters.

Miranna and I were not forced to wait before entering our mother's Drawing Room as we were when going to see our father in the Hall of Kings, so we simply walked through the doorway. The Drawing Room was similar in size to our parlors, with two small cream brocade sofas and several rose velvet armchairs grouped together on the right side beside a wide bay window. An abundance of fresh cut flowers stood in vases on the tables and in large pots on the floor to create a fragrant and heady ambience.

"Oh, good," our mother said pleasantly. She was sitting at a desk to our left, fussing with some correspondence. "We have many things of which to speak."

She came to her feet to guide us to the seating area, settling on one of the sofas. Miranna gingerly sat down next to her, while I chose an adjacent armchair.

"How are you feeling today?" Mother asked, helping Miranna to get settled more comfortably upon the cushions.

Miranna shrugged, wincing in pain. "I'm feeling better, but not as well as I would like."

"I'm sorry, dear, but I still can't quite see how you managed to injure your rib cage in this way just by tripping."

A sly look passed between my sister and me, for we had agreed we would not tell anyone the true story of her injury, lest we condemn Temerson to some horrible fate that he did not deserve.

Remembering something, our mother stood, then moved to retrieve a bouquet of long-stemmed yellow roses from her desk.

"These are for you, dear. Lord Steldor stopped by earlier to ask after you and left these to brighten your day." She handed the flowers to Miranna before training her clear blue eyes upon me. "And how is the courtship proceeding?"

At my averted gaze, she gave a gentle reminder: "Disagreeable women rarely make desirable wives... or Queens."

I glanced contritely at her, for she and Steldor must have conferred about the attitude I had adopted toward him at the picnic, but internally I seethed at his presumptuous attempt to use my mother to his advantage.

"If one gives in to fate, life can become much more pleasurable," she added in her lyrical voice. "Removing the thorns from a rose does not change the nature of the flower, but it does permit one to more easily enjoy its delicate scent."

I nodded once, acknowledging her subtle advice, wondering if Steldor had also spoken with my father. If he had, the King would make his opinion known in a far less tactful way, and his disappointment with me would deepen.

"There is another reason why I called you here today," Mother continued, satisfied with my acceptance of her criticism. "Your father and I have decided to host a gathering in honor of Baron Koranis and Baroness Alantonya, and in celebration of the return of their son, Lord Kyenn. Since you are to be Queen, Alera, I want you to make the arrangements, although I will review everything before it is finalized. Miranna, of course, may assist you."

While I had known that upon becoming Queen I would have to take on all of the responsibilities that my mother carried, I had not expected them to be given to me in such an abrupt fashion. I didn't even know where to begin when planning an affair such as this one, and I was glad that I would have my sister's help.

"The event is scheduled for the third week in August, which gives you just under a month to make the necessary preparations," Mother resumed, smoothing her upswept golden hair. "The most pressing item is writing up a guest list and sending out the invitations. They ought to be delivered by the end of the week."

"Who is to be invited?" I harbored hope that she would have some list of names prepared to show us, but she did not.

"That is for you to establish. Keep in mind that this celebration is to introduce Kyenn to the Hytanican aristocracy, so everyone of noble birth should be included. He has been adjusting remarkably well to Hytanican life thus far —— Cannan returned him to his family last week, and everything is going favorably. This is the final step to restoring him to the life into which he was born."

My mother continued her instructions, detailing what needed to be done and by when. I felt that arranging this event was a blessing in disguise. As I had said to Miranna earlier, marrying the Captain's son was, for me, out of the realm of possibility. This celebration presented the ideal opportunity to seriously seek another suitor, one of whom my father would approve and with whom I could at least have a civil exchange.

Although Steldor would unfortunately be in attendance, as Cannan and Faramay were a given on the guest list, I hoped that in a gathering of more than six hundred nobles, I would be able to avoid him altogether.

Miranna and I were extremely busy during the next few weeks, and I found myself attending to the smallest of details. My father had made no attempt to talk with me about the picnic, and I thought perhaps neither Steldor nor my mother had discussed the outing with him. I even dared to believe that a well-executed Palace function would redeem me somewhat in his eyes.

My duties included planning the food and décor. This event would not include a formal dinner, but all the same, refreshments were a necessity. Accommodations also had to be arranged for guests traveling long distances, some of whom would be staying in the Palace, while others would be placed in guesthouses within the city. Koranis and his family would not be among those staying in our third-floor rooms, however, as his wealth enabled him to own not only a country estate but also a house within the city proper.

It also fell to me to ensure a thorough cleaning of the Palace, and servants could be seen at all hours sweeping floors, whisking away cobwebs from corners, polishing serving dishes, and readying a large number of oil lamps, torches, and candles.

The most tedious task as I prepared for the gala was the design and fitting of the gown I would wear. Miranna loved choosing new fabrics and styles for her clothing, but I viewed it as a rather tiresome process, not having much of an interest in fashion.

Our finished dresses naturally reflected our different personalities. My gown was fitted through the bust and waist, flaring out into a full skirt. The sleeves echoed the cut of the dress —— fitted above the elbows, then flaring out to fall liberally over the wrists. Made of crushed silk in a light wine color, it was simple but pleasing to the eye. Miranna's gown, on the other hand, was fun and flirty. It was made of silk in a shimmering mint green that flowed loosely to the floor. Its empire waist was accented with colorful ribbons that hung freely, rippling when she moved, and that would be matched by ribbons woven into her hair.

On the evening of the event, once Miranna and I were impeccably groomed and attired, we made our way to the Dignitary's Room, the small room off the Ballroom where the King and Queen waited prior to making their formal entrances. While we walked, a swirling sensation pervaded my stomach —— I had organized this affair and planned every aspect of the evening, and if the event did not go well, my father's assessment that I was an "unpromising Queen" would be confirmed.

Halias knocked on the door of the Dignitary's Room, and when it was opened from the inside by a Palace aide, I could see that Koranis and his family had already arrived. As the guests of honor, they would walk behind the Royal Family when we made our entrance into the Ballroom. Miranna and I stepped inside, but Tadark and Halias departed, for they would patrol among the gathering guests, alert for signs of trouble.

"All rise for Lady Alera and Lady Miranna, Princesses of Hytanica," proclaimed the aide, announcing us to the Baron and his family.

Baroness Alantonya and her daughters came to their feet from where they had been sitting on the gold brocade sofa across the room from us. The Baroness was attired in a turquoise gown that had the effect of shading her blue eyes toward green, and her white-blond hair was pulled up off her shoulders. Semari's beautiful pale gold dress was similar in design to her mother's but was cut more simply as was befitting a girl of fourteen. Her hair, which was the same color as her mother's, was also drawn up off her shoulders, with small pastel flowers adding a playful touch. Her younger sisters, Charisa, twelve, and Adalan, ten, wore simple blue frocks, their ash-blond hair falling halfway down their backs.

Baron Koranis stood to the right, just behind the three steps that led up to the double doors that would be opened when it was time to enter the Ballroom. One heavily ringed hand hung by his side, and the other held the inside edge of his ostentatious cream-colored dress coat, the sleeves and sides of which were decorated with elaborate gold embroidery. Nine-year-old Zayle, as blond as the rest of his family, had sprung up from his sitting position on the edge of the platform in the far left corner, upon which were placed a pair of massive armchairs.

Narian stood on the opposite side of the room from his father, facing us with arms crossed over his chest, shoulder resting against the wall, an occasional shift in his stance suggesting he was discontented with his circumstances. He was handsomely clad in a dark gold fitted coat that fastened off to one side rather than down the center as Hytanican garments did, suggesting he had dictated the design himself. Only the state of his well-worn boots seemed out of character with the rest of his attire. Made of leather with a deep cuff below the knee, they had a higher heel and thicker sole than was typical of the boots worn by Hytanican men.

While I knew Narian's identity had been confirmed by the mark he bore upon his neck, the blue of his eyes, along with his straight nose and strong jawline, also offered proof that he was the Baron's son. His thick and untidy hair connected him to the Baron as well, but only by its golden color, for Koranis's hairline was receding and every inch of him was fastidiously groomed.

Alantonya and her daughters curtseyed before us, while Zayle gave a slight, but very endearing, bow. Narian stepped away from the wall to bow in the same way his father did, bent at the waist with head lowered in respect.

"Your Highnesses," Koranis said, walking forward to greet us. "Allow me to introduce my son, Lord Kyenn."

He held his hand out toward Narian to invite him over, but the young man did not move, looking as if he were choosing whether or not he would comply. Just when we all began to feel self-conscious, he came to meet us.

"Pardon my father," he said, inclining his head, his keen eyes momentarily obscured by his thick hair, "but my name is Narian."

Koranis's focus abruptly shifted to his son, while Alantonya, who was just behind her husband, put her hand over her heart as though the one thing she had been dreading had just occurred.

"I'm *not* under your roof," Narian added, meeting his father's harsh gaze. His voice contained no trace of disrespect, sounding instead as though he were stating fact.

The silence that followed was unsettling for everyone except Narian, who was completely unperturbed despite the affronted look on Koranis's face. It was Semari who broke the awkward hush.

"Your gowns are gorgeous this evening," she complimented, stepping around the Baron. "Are they new?"

We began to converse, the rather peculiar exchange we had witnessed between father and son temporarily forgotten. A few minutes later, Koranis, having regained his tongue and his poise, approached Narian, who had resumed his earlier stance against the wall. As Miranna and Semari were now talking primarily to each other, I was able to overhear the Baron's words.

"This event is in celebration of your return to Hytanica," Koranis stated in an unassailable tone. "Therefore, it will be your Hytanican name that is used tonight, and to which you will respond."

Narian unflinchingly met his father's gaze, neither an acquiescence nor an objection upon his lips, and my attention was drawn to his deep blue eyes. Piercing yet guarded, they lacked the childish light everything else about him suggested should be there. While he was lean and obviously strong, his body had not yet matured into the well-muscled physique of Steldor or any of the bodyguards protecting my sister and me. And Koranis physically overshadowed his son, standing several inches taller and weighing half as much again. If not for those intense eyes and his inscrutable expression, he would have passed for a normal Hytanican youth, not yet fully grown, enjoying carefree days with his friends and creating terrible worry lines upon his parents' faces.

The King and Queen, wearing robes of royal blue that were banded and stitched in gold, joined us shortly thereafter. They were accompanied by Cannan and their personal guards, although the latter took up posts in the corridor. Lanek preceded them into the room to make his usual introduction.

"All rise —— " He paused momentarily as he realized everyone was already on their feet " —— for his Highness, King Adrik of Hytanica, and his Queen, the Lady Elissia."

Once more Alantonya and her daughters, as well as Miranna and I, curtseyed, while Koranis and his sons bowed. Just as he had upon my arrival with my sister, the Baron stepped forward and addressed my parents.

"Your Majesty, My Queen. It is my pleasure to introduce to you my son, Lord *Kyenn*."

He said the name with an emphasis that was lost on my parents and followed it with a warning look in Narian's direction. Narian came away from the wall to bow his head respectfully to the King and Queen.

"Your Highnesses," he murmured as he came before them. Though he had seemed insolent to me moments before, he now sounded awed by the grand company among whom he stood.

"It is delightful to finally meet you under such amicable circumstances. I am afraid our previous encounters were a bit less civil," my father said with his typical cheeriness, and the slight rise in Narian's eyebrows implied that the King's jovial nature had not been made known on the other occasions when they had met.

"Indeed, Your Majesty, I am honored you feel that way," Narian replied, his words and manner befitting a gentleman. There was not a trace of his earlier attitude toward his father, and I was unsettled by his chameleon-like ability to adjust his personality to his interlocutor.

My father's smile broadened, for he was favorably impressed by the young man's comportment. Most Hytanicans viewed Cokyrians as ruthless thieves and murderers; therefore, a boy who had grown up among them was not to be expected to have such a respectful manner. While my father did not easily succumb to closed-minded notions, some part of him believed Cokyrians to be so insufferable that even he expected less of Narian because of where he had been raised.

I did not share these prejudices, perhaps because I knew very little of Cokyri and the horrors of the war, but still I was perplexed by Koranis's son. While we knew nothing of his upbringing, his pattern of speech and impeccable manners provided proof that he had been well bred, and yet his demeanor suggested a harsher childhood. I glanced at Cannan, whose dark eyes seemed to be taking stock of Narian, and realized he, too, was struggling to figure out the mysterious boy.

Lanek departed, as it would be his role to inform the King when all of the guests had arrived, and my father and mother took up their seats on the raised platform in the corner of the room, conversing with the Baron and Baroness. Semari, Miranna, and I resumed our small talk while the younger children claimed the sofa. Cannan stayed by the door, his interest held by Narian, who once more stood with his shoulder against the wall.

I wanted to ask Semari about her older brother just as I had that day in the marketplace. Had anything changed now that he was actually living with them? Had he spoken further about his past? But I refrained, for doing so might seem rude, especially with Narian nearby.

After about half an hour, Lanek returned, and the aide who granted him entry swung the door fully open so that the Elite Guards in the corridor could follow after us when it came time to enter the Ballroom.

"Sire, the nobility have arrived and await your pleasure," Lanek reported with a deep bow.

"Very well," my father said, coming to his feet. He motioned toward the doors across the room from him. "It is time to greet our guests."

My mother stood, and after smoothing her gown and her hair, linked arms with my father as she always did when they made public appearances. They stepped down from the platform and crossed the room, while Cannan pushed open the doors that led into the Ballroom and proceeded through them to make way for Lanek. The stocky, small-statured man marched up the steps onto the stagelike platform and took a deep breath so he could generate sufficient volume to be heard throughout the Hall.

"All hail the King, King Adrik of Hytanica, and his Queen, the Lady Elissia," he boomed, and hundreds of eyes turned toward us and then were lowered in respect, as those gathered bowed or curtseyed to their Sovereign.

My parents stepped forward, and Miranna and I followed, moving to stand beside our mother. We would not be receiving a formal introduction as had the King and Queen, for the event was not in our honor, but all the same, the people knew who we were and were showing respect to us as well.

"Welcome," my father proclaimed, starting his introduction in his usual way. "On this occasion, we honor a family that has, for many years, served this Kingdom well, and in so doing has earned my friendship as well as that of my Queen and our daughters. I present to you the Baron Koranis and his wife, the Baroness Alantonya; their daughters, Lady Semari, Lady Charisa, and Lady Adalan; their youngest son, Lord Zayle; and the young man whose startling return has provided the impetus for this gathering —— their oldest son and firstborn child, Lord Kyenn."

Koranis and his family stepped forward on my father's right as they were introduced, and the guests gave a vigorous round of applause at the end of the King's speech.

Cannan led my parents down the set of stairs on the Ballroom side of the stage, and the rest of us followed, the guards who protected the King and Queen bringing up the rear. A seating area with two thrones had been readied to the right of the platform, and my parents would spend most of the evening there, greeting guests and speaking to those who sought an audience with them. Ornate chairs had been set in the same area for Miranna and me, though we were unlikely to use them. While my father would no doubt expect me to wait for Steldor, I was dead set on avoiding the young man who had permission to court me, intending to mingle with the crowd in an earnest effort to find a different suitor. Narian and his family would also move among the aristocracy, making less formal introductions and engaging in small talk, although the younger children would run off to find their friends.

Tonight the Ballroom was arranged so that two long refreshment tables lined its sides, with the area in the middle occupied in part by a dance floor. The remaining space was left open, providing an area for people to meet and chat. As the purpose of the gathering was to welcome Narian into Hytanican society, the colors that dominated the décor in the room were Hytanica's royal blue and gold.

Walking with Miranna through the vast Hall, I scoured the crowd for what my sister kept referring to as "a good catch." It wasn't long before young men were coming up to me every-where I turned, having taken my glance in their direction as an invitation to approach. While I needed to find a suitor other than Steldor who would be acceptable to my father, I soon tired of the monotonous interactions. Every gentleman to whom I spoke had apparently been taught to greet me in the same way: "Good evening, Princess Alera. You look beautiful tonight... And what lovely weather we are having."

Even Miranna, who was far more boy-obsessed than I, was growing weary of these clumsy flirtations. She seized the oppor-tunity to escape the boredom when she spotted someone she knew across the room close to one of the refreshment tables.

"Oh, look!" she exclaimed, taking my hand in hers and tug-ging it excitedly. "There's Temerson! I must go speak with him."

After pinching her cheeks to raise their color and fluffing her curly hair, she sashayed toward the bashful sixteen-year-old. As she approached, his eyes widened in panic, and I wondered if he knew he was fast becoming her favored escort.

Unfortunately for me, my sister's departure meant that I would now have to brave the guests on my own. I moved toward my parents, desiring a break from the males swarming around me, noticing Steldor halfway across the room as I did so. Galen was, of course, at his side, and the two friends were surrounded by a group of girls who were giggling and blush-ing at every utterance that came forth from their mouths. Although Steldor was likely toying with the affections of the other girls in an effort to make me jealous, I was very content with this tactic. I did not care with whom he flirted as long as he kept his distance from me.

I looked ahead at the large group of people surrounding my parents, then rethought my destination, opting instead to visit the dance floor on the other side of the Ballroom. While I had no desire to dance this evening, I appreciated the music and was curious about who was courting whom.

My eyes were on the musicians as I approached, for they seemed to be enjoying themselves right along with the dancers. They performed using a variety of instruments, including mandolins, lutes, a dulcimer, the flute, and various types of recorders and drums. Depending on the instruments used, the sound ranged from beautiful and haunting to fast and wild.

Standing at the edge of the dance floor, I couldn't help but smile at the absolute delight on the faces of every individual spinning in the arms of another. As the couples moved around the crowded floor, my gaze came to rest upon Miranna and Temerson. They were by no means the most refined couple present, and at times it was difficult to tell who was leading and who was following, but they were laughing and smiling and having more fun than anyone else I could see.

My spirits lifted while I listened to the music and beheld the movement. My good mood evaporated, however, when I glanced behind and saw Steldor making his way toward me.

I scanned the room for an escape route, some way I could flee without making my intent to avoid him obvious. I moved away, hoping he did not know that I had seen him. When his progress was impeded by several parents keen on introducing him to their daughters, I hastened to the back of the Ballroom, where the wide-open balcony doors beckoned. I stepped out into the warm late-August air, looking over my shoulder to confirm that Steldor's progress was still hindered. Satisfied that I had eluded him, I turned, expecting to be alone. I was not.

XIV

CONFRONTATION

y heart began to thump much too loudly as I saw Narian leaning back against the railing, his hands resting on either side of him on the dark wood, barely visible in the sudden change from the brightness of the Ballroom to the moonlit balcony. A slight smirk curled his lips, belying his otherwise serious countenance.

"I didn't mean to startle you, Princess," he said, straightening to give me a respectful bow, his face smooth and unreadable now that his smile had vanished. His speech was refined, with a faint but pleasing accent, and his tone was rehearsed, as if he had been taught precisely how to speak to people of status.

"You are forgiven, Lord Narian," I said, addressing him formally while I endeavored to regain my composure.

Trying to mask my unease, I glided to the railing a discreet distance from where he stood and rested my forearms upon its surface. He casually moved closer to me, turning to face the railing and assuming a posture similar to my own.

"Think me impudent if you will, but I must inquire as to what a Princess is doing out here on this balcony in the middle of such a grand gala."

I tossed my hair over my shoulders and gazed at him, drawn to his intense blue eyes. Unable to pull away, I stared into them as though I might break through the floor beneath my feet if I looked anywhere else.

"I have my reasons," I answered, acutely aware of his proximity. "On occasion I come out here to avoid the crowd."

My skin was prickling, and I felt disconcerted, although I could not have identified good cause for my reaction. Irritated at myself, I posed an inquiry of my own.

"Now I must ask what the guest of honor is doing out here on this balcony with so many people inside clamoring to meet him?"

"Avoiding the crowds or avoiding that dark-haired gentleman?"

Narian had lightly sidestepped my question and I was unnerved by both the intrusive nature of his query and the astuteness of his observation. How could he have known Steldor had designs on me? For what purpose had he been watching me? Despite the warning now flashing through my brain, I could not bring myself to move away from him, for I was as enticed by him as I was flustered.

"Lord Steldor might have something to do with it. He is the son of Cannan, the Captain of the Guard." I half expected some sort of reaction at the mention of the man who had arrested him, but there was none. "He wishes to take my hand in marriage."

"And you do not return his affections." He turned toward me, one hand now resting on the railing.

"No," I admitted, pivoting so that my posture was the mirror image of his.

Although I felt I had said too much already, I was compelled to continue by his unwavering show of interest. Here was someone other than London who was listening to me, rather than brushing me aside because I was a woman.

"It is what my father desires, not I. Steldor is hot-tempered and spoiled, and I do not see him making a good King, now or in the future. But my father will see to it that Steldor becomes King, no matter my feelings."

I stopped, embarrassed that I was pouring out my deepest secrets to someone I barely knew, and perturbed that he had so easily inspired me to share such confidences. This was not a topic about which I readily spoke, and I had not voiced my opinions about Steldor and my father's edict that we be wed to anyone other than London and Miranna.

"I'm sorry," I fumbled. "I should not be saying this to you."

"There is no need to seek my pardon. I, too, despise having my life laid out for me."

Although Narian had pinpointed my feelings with his presumably casual statement, I was not about to acknowledge it.

"If my words have implied that I am dissatisfied with my obligations as Crown Princess of Hytanica, I certainly meant no such thing," I said defensively.

"I understood no such thing," he responded with a hint of a smile, as though he knew something I did not. "Duty is important. But at some point the choice you will face is whether to carry out your duties or live your life."

"And what would you know of such matters?" I pressed, ruffled by his uncanny ability to distill the truth. I waited as he stared for a moment at the flickering lights coming from the lanterns in the city.

"We should go back inside," he advised, once more disregarding my question. "I'm sure someone has noted the absence of the Crown Princess and the guest of honor."

I nodded, not foolish enough to be disappointed by his reluctance to provide answers.

"Shall I escort you back to your parents?"

"Perhaps it would be best if we went in separately," I suggested, my thoughts flying to Steldor and his temper.

Narian, as if reading my mind, asked, "Are you afraid of Steldor?"

"No!" I exclaimed, not willing to admit that the man I detested was the reason I dared not be seen with him. "I do not fear Steldor."

"Then are you fearful of what people will think?"

"Of course not."

"Then it will be my honor to escort you."

Having no further basis for objection, I accepted his arm and together we walked through the balcony doors to rejoin the celebration.

As soon as we entered the Ballroom, my eyes connected with Steldor's and I halted, knowing there would be no escaping this time. He had evidently seen me move toward the balcony and had come looking for me, and now stood but fifteen feet away. I could almost feel the anger simmering inside him as he took note of my hand nestled in the crook of another man's arm. He strode to where we stood, then abruptly put his arm around my waist, twisting me forcefully away from Narian.

"I can take it from here, thank you very *much*," he spat, holding me at his side.

"Steldor, let me go!" I demanded, straining against him.

He did not comply, instead wrapping his arm more tightly about me, which meant he'd had too much to drink this evening, as he would normally have had the good sense to release me.

Despite how practiced he was at hiding his emotions, Narian could not disguise his disdain in the face of Steldor's behavior.

"It would seem that Princess Alera does not welcome your advances," he said grimly.

"And who are you to speak for the Princess?" Steldor retorted, pushing me behind him so I would be out of the way.

"She spoke quite clearly for herself, though you did not heed her."

"Stay out of this, Cokyrian," Steldor growled, his eyes dark with menace.

The heads of the people around us had begun to turn, and the surrounding area had stilled. Pleasant banter had ceased, for everyone's attention was now riveted upon Steldor and Narian.

"Was that supposed to be an insult?" Narian asked, having taken no offense whatsoever to having been called a Cokyrian.

"No, that was a warning."

"Then consider me warned."

Steldor stepped toward Narian, fists clenched, but Narian did not yield. I cast about for someone who could intervene and prevent the clash between the two young men from becoming more heated. I saw no one in the immediate crowd who would be of help, as the guests were too busy watching the altercation unfold to think about putting a stop to it. While Steldor's friends, Galen, Barid, and Devant, had joined the circle, they had no interest in interfering. To the contrary, their faces showed they were relishing the action. For the first time since he had become my bodyguard, I desperately longed for Tadark, but then just as desperately hoped he would stay away, knowing he would be ineffectual at best and might make the situation worse.

Narian and Steldor were now standing less than two feet apart, and the unsettling thought that Steldor might strike Narian flashed through my brain. Steldor was almost four inches taller and more heavily muscled than his challenger, leading me to believe Narian might actually be in danger. The fact that Steldor was capable of overpowering almost anyone in Hytanica was an additional reason for me to fear for the younger man's safety.

"Steldor, that's enough," I implored, coming up beside him and grabbing his arm to no avail. "Come with me, my Lord, and we can talk," I persisted, now tugging on his arm to get his attention. "This really isn't necessary."

He jerked away from me, and I stumbled back in alarm.

"What?" he scorned, nodding his head in Narian's direction. "Your pretty boy can't take care of himself? He needs to be saved by a woman?"

"You will not speak to the Princess in such a manner," Narian interjected, authoritative in a fashion I would not have thought possible. "If your fight is with me, then you will address *me*."

Steldor rounded on Narian, his rage rising to the point where it was almost an audible rumble.

"Perhaps you should run off to Mama and Papa before you get hurt," he taunted.

Steldor shoved his challenger in the chest, trying to push him backward, but Narian shifted his weight to absorb the prod. As Narian stood his ground, Steldor's eyes burned, and I knew he was dangerously close to exploding.

"Did you hear what I said?" he demanded, jabbing Narian with increasing force.

"I heard what you said, but perhaps you should be more concerned about your father than about mine."

Steldor faltered and his eyes flicked over the crowd, as if he worried Cannan might be among the spectators, then returned to rest on Narian's face. A flush crept up his neck, for the younger man had somehow deduced one of his only vulnerabilities.

I felt ill, knowing that Narian was too brave, or perhaps too foolish, for his own good. I feverishly searched the vicinity and finally caught sight of several guards conversing near the western wall. In the midst of them I saw Destari, and I frantically willed him to notice my plight.

After a moment, he glanced in my direction, then stepped away from the other guards to stride toward me. Tall enough to peer over the heads of the guests, he assessed the situation and quickened his pace. He had no idea how anything had started or exactly what was taking place, but all the same, Steldor was involved, and everyone in the military knew of the youthful Commander's fiery temper.

"I said, MOVE!" Steldor thundered, and Narian assumed a fighting stance with his forearms in front of his chest and his left foot slightly ahead of his right. As Steldor employed his full weight to drive him back, Narian deflected his lunge with ease.

For an instant, Steldor looked stunned, then he balled up his fists to strike his challenger. Fortunately, Destari stepped between the two of them at that moment, putting a hand on Steldor's chest to restrain him.

"This is not the place for such conduct," he admonished in his deep and powerful voice.

Steldor forcefully thrust Destari's hand away in another attempt to get at Narian, but the Elite Guard gripped him firmly by the arm.

"Get out of my way!" Steldor demanded, fixing Destari with a glare that contained all the loathing he could rally and unwisely landing one great shove upon his superior officer's shoulder.

"If you are a wise man, you will not try that again," Destari warned, his black eyes glistening.

Steldor took a step back, and as he did so, glanced past Destari, whereupon I saw his resolve weaken. Though his anger did not diminish, his face paled, and I followed his gaze to where Cannan, composed yet dangerous, stood just outside the circle of people surrounding us. The Captain must have seen that trouble was brewing and had come to deal with whatever the problem might be. I suspected that by the time he had drawn near, Destari had arrived on the scene, and Cannan had decided to let him handle things so Steldor did not have to suffer the indignity of being reprimanded by his father in front of all these people.

"You need to cool off," Destari said to Steldor through gritted teeth, not raising his volume. "Go. And that's an order."

With one final vindictive glower at the Elite Guard, my hotheaded suitor turned and, motioning to his friends to join him, stormed off, to where I knew not.

I thought about Steldor's reaction to his father, and knowing what I did about Cannan's status and temperament, I could understand Steldor's reluctance to cross him. Cannan was a confident and decisive man of action who was known to have a formidable temper, although it was much better controlled than that of his son. I did not know of a single person who was not, to some extent, intimidated by the Captain of the Guard, and Steldor had grown up answering to him. As Cannan had an uncanny ability to see right through people, it was inconceivable that he was taken in by his son's charm. Steldor also had to deal with the fact that Cannan was not only his father but his military leader, and in that role would tolerate no disrespect.

For a brief moment following Steldor's ignominious exit, Destari and Cannan locked eyes, then both of them scrutinized Narian, attempting to sort out what they had just seen. What manner of sixteen-year-old boy would challenge Steldor, much less do so without a sign of trepidation?

Narian did not acknowledge the military men but simply held out his arm once more to me.

"Shall we?"

I clutched at him, feeling weak in the knees, and for a moment leaned against him.

"Are you all right?" he asked, and I could feel his breath upon my cheek.

"Yes, of course," I murmured, then I straightened, giving him a feeble smile. "Let's just move on."

As we walked toward the front of the Ballroom, people continued to gawk, although they resumed their activities upon our passing. The entertainment was over, and there was no need to waste such a delectable evening.

Having recovered my poise, I thanked Narian when we reached the sitting area where my parents were holding court. Koranis and Alantonya were nearby and immediately motioned their son over for additional introductions. As he joined them, I wondered who he truly was, for I knew his name and little else. How could he, a boy one year my junior, be so courageous? Grown men quaked in the face of Steldor's temper, but Narian had not even flinched. Perhaps he had underestimated Steldor's skill, or overestimated his own, and all in my defense.

I was flattered, though I supposed his actions had nothing to do with me personally. Semari had told Miranna and me in the market that Narian had an unusual amount of respect for women, and he had no doubt been offended by Steldor's treatment of me on that basis alone. Mulling this over, I realized how unaccustomed I was to being taken seriously. I had been taught all my life how to be a lady, a submissive being (though my actions were sometimes viewed as less than appropriate), and the rapt attention Narian had paid to my opinions out on the balcony had made me feel credible and important in an entirely new way.

I looked around and saw my sister pushing through the crowd of people, coming in my direction. I nodded my head toward the door to the corridor and informed my parents that I had developed a headache and would be returning to my quarters. After meeting with me, Miranna would return to the Ballroom, but I was beginning to feel as though I would drown in its heavy air.

A guard opened one of the double doors for me, and I stepped into the corridor, noticing for the first time how stifling the gala had become with so many people in attendance. Where I now stood, it was cool and open, and, more important, quiet. All I could hear was the faint hum of conversation through the thick Ballroom doors.

Miranna joined me a few seconds later, the babble of the guests momentarily loud as she stepped out beside me.

"What happened?" she asked, her voice trembling with barely contained curiosity. She clasped my hand and led me onto the landing of the Grand Staircase. "All I saw was Steldor as he stormed off, and you taking Narian's arm, but judging from the muttering around me, the three of you created quite a stir."

I relayed the story to her, beginning with my hasty escape to the balcony and my interlude with Narian, and finishing with our courteous goodbyes once we had reached the front of the Ballroom.

Miranna laughed, playfully tugging at her strawberry blond hair.

"What?" I asked, unable to see the humor in the evening's events.

"Well, sister, it appears that *you* are being fought over," she said with a grin.

"Oh, nonsense."

"It's true! Perhaps Narian could be the man of your dreams, standing up to your enemy to defend your honor."

"You're ridiculously infatuated with romance," I said flippantly.

"Perhaps, but all the same, I'm going to arrange an outing to Semari's country home for us. Perhaps we'll get another glimpse of your champion."

I shook my head, believing it better to let Miranna poke fun than to waste my breath arguing.

"And how about *your* suitor?" I said, expertly changing the subject.

"Who, Temerson?"

I flashed a mischievous grin of my own. "You two were quite a sight on the dance floor."

Miranna's blue eyes shone. "I may have lost a few toes tonight, Alera, but nothing you say can put a damper on my mood."

"Is there something you're not telling me?"

"No," she replied with a shy smile. "But he blushed horribly when I kissed him on the cheek."

"Mira!" I exclaimed in feigned disapproval as she giggled. "It seems you are having quite an enjoyable evening."

"Yes indeed, and I will continue to do so if I ever get back inside. I'll speak to Mother in the morning to make arrangements to visit Semari."

Her face lit up in anticipation of rejoining the festivities. She did a graceful pirouette as she said good night, then reentered the Ballroom, brushing her fingertips through her hair as the doors closed behind her.

Just after Miranna's departure, Tadark tumbled through the doors to see if I desired an escort. He would be off duty after I retired, so I gave him leave to enjoy the rest of the celebration. I walked alone through the corridors, savoring the tranquility, my mind returning to Narian. I had formed several new impressions of the young man over the course of the evening, many of which were contradictory, and none of which shed light on his obscure past. While I did not live in Miranna's romantic fantasy world, the idea of seeing him again was more appealing than it should have been.

ENIGMA

he buggy jostled us uncomfortably as we made our way to the country home of the Baron Koranis and his family, for the road had become pitted from the rain the night before. Miranna sat beside me, surveying the passing landscape as the black Friesians trotted onward under the guidance of a Palace Guard, our bodyguards traveling with us on their own horses. I stared straight ahead, excitement stirring within me, mixed with a hint of annoyance at how closely Tadark rode to my side of the buggy. I supposed his zealousness was due to the fact that Koranis's estate lay along the eastern border of our Kingdom, in the direction of Cokyri.

Miranna had arranged everything so that our mother and father were under the impression that we were making this journey to visit Semari. If either of our parents had known our true purpose, we would not have been allowed to go. I felt slightly guilty, not about permitting Miranna to mislead our parents, but about causing Alantonya the effort of preparing for and fussing over our arrival, just so that we could get another look at her eldest son, whose privacy we would indisputably be invading.

In spite of Miranna's encouragement, it was impossible for me to think of Narian as a suitor. One year younger than me, he was not even an adult by Hytanican standards. Age was not, however, my only concern.

Narian was an enigma, a complete and total mystery to me, to my father, to his family, and to Cannan. There was simply too little known about him for me to put much faith in him. And after the incident at the celebration in his honor... though it had happened five days previously, it was as fresh in my mind as though it had occurred moments ago. I could see his youth plainly, but I could sense no youthful innocence within him, and that confused and disturbed me.

After another hour, our driver brought the horses to a halt in front of Koranis's home. Halias and Tadark dismounted and helped us to the ground as my eyes roamed over the property. I had only been to this country estate a few times in my life, for although I was compatible with all members of Koranis's family, I was not especially good friends with any of them as Miranna was with Semari. My sister had come here often during our childhood, but I had rarely accompanied her.

The house itself was large and well crafted, standing two stories tall upon a stone foundation. It was wood-framed, filled in with wattle and daub, and had costly glass windows in every room. The cream-colored exterior was partially covered with vines and topped with a dark brown tile roof, and the grass surrounding the multicolored stone path leading to the door was lush and green.

I barely had time to acclimate to my surroundings when Semari rushed through the front door and over to Miranna and me. She curtseyed to us, then discarded all formality as she jabbered to my sister. A few moments later, Alantonya more sedately came out of the dwelling, followed by Charisa and Adalan, who stood behind her while she waited patiently for us to approach.

"Your Highnesses," she said in greeting, dropping into a low curtsey, her younger daughters imitating her movement.

She invited us into the house, where we took up seats in a

tastefully decorated parlor and began to engage in idle conversation. Less than an hour later, a servant entered to announce that tea was ready to be served, and Alantonya informed us that we would be taking our refreshment in the backyard. As she ushered us through her home, we passed several lavishly furnished rooms that shamelessly gave notice of Koranis's wealth. I looked over my shoulder for Narian one final time as we stepped out the rear door of the dwelling but was again disappointed. I had hoped to catch sight of him, but was forced to conclude he was not at home.

Before us on the soft, green grass was a small circular table set for six, obligingly shaded from the mid-afternoon sun by a large maple tree. Although the days were still hot, they were becoming less humid now that the end of August neared, and the evenings had a definite chill. As we seated ourselves around the table, I looked out across the Baron's property. To my right under the cloudless sky lay vast fields, while to my left and before me the land sloped toward the forest, and I marveled at the unsurpassed beauty of this property.

The small talk continued, although Charisa and Adalan said not a word, probably afraid they would make some glaring error in etiquette. I complimented Alantonya on the loveliness of her home, then inquired about the property itself.

"Does the Baron own all the land reaching from here to the forest?"

"Yes," Alantonya replied, sipping her tea. "Lord Koranis owns in excess of a hundred acres, most of it cleared for farming. He inherited some of the land, received some as a gift from the King, and purchased the rest. But he also claims part of the forest. When he first took over the property, he hired some villagers to cut trails through the woods for safer passage on horseback. That's where he is now —— out riding with Kyenn and Zayle."

I nodded, now understanding Narian's absence, though I could not help but be dismayed by it. We had primarily come, after all, to see *him*. We finished our tea, then Alantonya made a suggestion.

"Semari, perhaps you and the Princesses would like to walk along the riverbank. It is a lovely afternoon, and a stroll will put a blush into your cheeks."

"Yes!" Semari happily agreed, tugging at my sister's hand and pulling her to her feet. "It's not far into the trees, and it's so pretty there!"

Miranna and Semari skipped away from the house, Halias following, as I remained a moment longer to thank our hostess.

"It was my pleasure," Alantonya responded, rising to give me a small curtsey, then she beckoned her younger daughters to accompany her into the house.

I hastened after the other girls, Tadark as always at my heels, and though I was not dressed for such an excursion, I soon caught up with them, for they were dillydallying. I was wearing two skirts over a white chemise, the topmost layer in blush pink, and a matching panel bodice that laced up both sides, and was already feeling the exertion. On my feet were soft thin-soled goatskin leather shoes. Miranna was similarly attired, except her dress was pale yellow.

The three of us, bodyguards trailing, ambled down the hill together and into the woods, taking care to follow the winding, leaf-strewn, tree-rooted path where water still puddled, for the sun could not easily reach the forest floor. The dampened foliage and earth emitted a slightly musty fragrance, a smell I always associated with the earthworms that rose to the surface in the Palace garden after it rained.

A short while later, Semari led us to the right on a rockier trail that soon opened directly into a narrow clearing that bordered the Recorah River. Trees hung over the edges of the clearing, their trunks obeying the invisible boundary, but their leaves and branches unable to be restrained. The open space between the woods and the river was only about twelve feet; although the closeness of the trees ensured refreshing shade, it also seemed to magnify the sound of the water.

I looked into the splashing and tumbling torrent and saw that it was deep here, even along the water's rocky edge, so deep that it would have risen above my head had I stepped forward a few paces. The sound of Semari's giggling drew me from my reverie, and I looked up to see the younger girls skipping away, following the Recorah downstream. Sighing, I once more followed.

The two friends stopped by a cluster of rocks and boulders that stood sentinel next to the river, the craggy tops of the stones rising above the rapids. Semari perched atop one of the boulders and Miranna joined her, but I chose to stand a few feet away, too wary of the roiling water to move closer.

The trees grew even nearer to the river here, giving the area an ominous feel. I gazed further upstream and could see the remains of the old bridge that had once provided passage to the east. It had been burned during the war and had never been rebuilt. Across the Recorah from where we stood, the terrain became rocky and the foliage more intermittent as the land stretched into the foothills of the Niñeyre Mountains. This inhospitable area was sparsely populated, primarily by nomads, for it became windy and dry as one moved away from the water. This was the land the Cokyrians had to cross to enter our Kingdom, for they claimed the high desert area of the mountains as their own.

Miranna, growing restless atop the boulder, rose to her feet and took a step forward, peering downward.

"What are you doing, Mira?" Semari asked, shifting to get a better view of her friend.

"I'm seeing if I can spot any fish. Temerson told me they sparkle when the sun shines off their scales."

"You won't see any fish in this part of the river," Semari giggled. "The water is moving too fast."

"You may as well come down," I called apprehensively to them. The last thing I wanted was for my sister to plunge into the Recorah.

I glanced over at Halias and Tadark, who had moved along the tree line with us and were talking at the edge of the clearing. Tadark was sitting on his heels near a large willow tree, but Halias had remained on his feet, eyes fixed on his charge.

"As you wish," Miranna said grudgingly, dropping her hands to the rough stone surface to make the short descent less arduous. I heard the *chink* of something metal as it ricocheted off the rock and splashed into the water, and Miranna looked at me in dismay.

"Oh no!" she exclaimed, leaning forward. "My bracelet! It's fallen into the river!" She dropped to her knees, preparing to reach for it.

"Get down from there now!" I scolded, my overprotectiveness as her elder sibling kicking in full force.

Miranna looked at me petulantly, but then eased her way to the ground.

"But what about my bracelet? I can see it —— it's right there, caught between two of the rocks."

She and Semari approached, a definite pout upon my sister's face. I again glanced at Halias, whose stance had relaxed now that Miranna's feet were securely on the ground. I deliberated calling him over to retrieve my sister's lost jewelry, then settled against it. While the younger girls deemed this incredibly important, I thought it rather trivial, and would have been embarrassed to make anyone attempt this ridiculous retrieval task, especially a member of Hytanica's Elite Guard.

"I'll try to reach it," I finally groaned.

I pulled myself, with a distinct lack of grace, up on top of the rock outcropping, crouching down on its jagged surface. I could see Miranna's bracelet directly below me, shimmering with sunlight between the last of the bleak gray rocks that tumbled into the water, and I cautiously advanced toward it. As I could not reach it from my current position, I sat and continued to move forward, using the uneven edges of the stones as footholds. When it looked to be within my grasp, I seized the best handhold I could find and stretched toward it, straightening my arms as I attempted to rescue the bracelet from the clutches of the Recorah.

I wasn't close enough. Grimacing with frustration, I released my handhold very slightly, trying to gain another inch.

Things happened quickly then. My fingers were vainly grasping air and my arm was waving about as if independent from my body, desperately groping for something to keep me in place, but there was nothing to which I could cling to prevent myself from plummeting into the frothing water. As the river consumed first my left shoulder and then my hips and legs, I vaguely heard the sound of a high-pitched shriek, either from Miranna or Semari, but the water splashing into my mouth prevented me from uttering any similar cry of distress.

The raw torrent swirled around me, threatening to drag me under, and I sputtered and flailed in panic, certain I would drown. Just as the current was about to sweep me away from the boulders, I was half dragged onto the rock by a pair of strong arms. My dress, which was now soaked and extraordinarily heavy, seemed reluctant to leave the river behind, but this did not hinder my rescuer. My first coherent thought, strangely, as I coughed and fought to draw air into my burning lungs, was that London had somehow materialized to save me. When my breathing eased, I looked into the face of the man upon whom

I was leaning heavily for support and felt a shock as intense as the one the cold water had just dealt me.

Narian. Narian had pulled me from the river. I hadn't known he was there, yet somehow he had been near enough to reach me, and agile enough to save me, without falling into the water himself.

"Where did you... ?" I muttered in bewilderment.

"I came down the path," he said as he nimbly jumped off the rock pile. "I saw you falling."

He turned to offer me a hand, but Halias brushed him aside and lifted me to the ground. The Elite Guard had evidently seen me plunge into the water but had not been close enough to help. Narian must have been very close indeed to have grabbed me before I had yielded to the river's strength —— much closer than either of the bodyguards and definitely closer than the path.

"Are you all right, Princess?" Halias asked urgently. "Are you hurt?"

"I'm fine," I assured him, although my heart continued to pound in recognition of the danger in which I had placed myself, and I shook from the chill of the water.

Miranna and Semari, who had been hanging on to each other as though afraid they might fall into the river as well, now rushed to me. Miranna impulsively hugged me, having concluded that I would live, and then she and Semari began to laugh in relief. Even I had to chuckle a little bit at what had undeniably been an ungainly entry into the water.

Miranna wrung the water out of my long hair, and Halias removed the royal blue doublet he wore as a member of the Elite Guard, insisting that I put the garment on for warmth. As I did so, I stared down at my skirt. It was rumpled and dripping, and grime from the rocks had collected among its thick folds. I looked at Narian and saw that his dark shirt and breeches were also wet where he had held me against him.

Halias, too, was now gazing at Narian, although there was a much edgier look upon his face than on mine. I realized that this must be confounding for both him and Tadark, who had stopped a few feet away, too shaken to step forward (I was, after all, his responsibility). They had been trained to notice and react the moment a disloyal eye flickered in the direction of a Royal, and yet they had been effortlessly skirted by a sixteen-year-old boy. And, on top of it, this boy had just saved the dignity, if not the life, of one of their charges.

"What is going on over here?" A man's voice hailed us, and a breathless Koranis, followed by Zayle, emerged from among the trees, the two having come down the path. Koranis's eyes widened as he passed Tadark and took in the entire scene.

"My goodness, Princess Alera," he exclaimed. "What has happened to your gown?"

He looked at the others gathered around me, then a frown creased his brow as he noted the condition of his older son's clothing.

"I fell in," I quickly said, motioning toward the river with my hand. "Nar —— Kyenn rescued me." I glanced at Narian to see his reaction to the name I used for him, but his face was inscrutable. "I am quite grateful to him."

"You should return to the house without delay," Koranis decreed, rather needlessly, given my sodden appearance. "We are certain to have something into which you can change." He gazed at Narian, then finished in his somewhat overbearing manner, "Kyenn and I will accompany you. He could benefit from a change of clothing as well."

"Thank you for your ministrations, but please don't let this ruin the afternoon for everyone else," I politely, but firmly, stated. "I am completely unharmed, and there is no need for you to escort me to the house. The Baroness will be there to provide whatever assistance I need. I would much prefer that you take some respite from your day rather than trouble yourself further."

"Oh, please, Papa!" Semari implored. "Won't you stay for a little while? You and Zayle have only just come."

Koranis paused indecisively, and I recalled what Semari had said about her father having been told to keep an eye on Narian. Most likely concerned that letting his son walk through the woods with the Crown Princess of Hytanica would be unwise, Koranis turned to Halias, seeking his opinion. At the Elite Guard's permissive nod, he smiled indulgently at his daughter.

"I suppose I could stay for a short while," the Baron pronounced. "Kyenn, you will return to the house with Princess Alera and her bodyguard."

I could tell from Narian's expression that he detested his father's dictatorial air, just as I could tell from Tadark's wide brown eyes that the prospect of being my only defense against Narian was making him feel ill. It was obvious from my bodyguard's reaction that talk of the recent confrontation between Steldor and Narian had circulated among the Palace force.

"You're not truly frightened of a teenager, are you?" I heard Halias mutter irritably to Tadark.

"No," the younger guard said, puffing out his chest like a small and very offended owl.

Halias saw right through him and added, his words barely audible, "My God, Tadark, he's not even armed! How did you get into the Elite Guard anyway, with such a core of cowardice?"

I was once again amazed at Tadark's ability to provoke even the most tolerant of people. It was practically impossible to anger the good-natured Deputy Captain, and here Tadark had done it as effortlessly as a bird taking wing.

"Come, Tadark," I interposed, before their exchange could

become more heated. "I would like to return with some measure of haste."

My bodyguard's cheeks colored as he stepped forward to lead the way. I followed behind, wondering where Narian had gone, for he had departed the moment Koranis had told him to do so, although I was sure he hadn't acted out of obedience. Perhaps he did not like the company gathered in the clearing, or perhaps accompanying me didn't appeal to him in the least. But when Tadark and I came to the end of the narrow trail that connected to the main path, I saw Narian resting his back against a tree, waiting for us. Tadark shot the young man a distrustful glare when he came to walk beside me, then dropped behind us in order to better monitor Narian's conduct, his left hand gripping the hilt of his sword.

We made our way through the trees without speaking. I was eager to say something to Narian —— I had never been so intrigued by a person in my life —— but he seemed content to maintain the silence between us, the only sounds the incessant sloshing of my gown and squishing of my shoes.

I grabbed fistfuls of my skirt in an attempt to make my movement less hindered as Narian lithely moved ahead of me, but with no success. It continued to cling to my skin and my undergarments, causing me to stumble over and over. I moaned, longing to break free of the woods. I knew from the sunlight that filtered through onto the path that the trees were finally becoming less dense and could only hope I didn't fall before we came to the trail's end.

"Do you always dress like that?" Narian had halted fifteen paces in front of me to check on my progress.

I stared at him as if a stream of profanities had come from his mouth rather than the simple question he had actually posed, astounded that he had spoken.

"I'm generally tidier," I said, eyes shifting to my disheveled clothing as I pushed my damp, limp hair away from my face.

"I mean, do you always wear those impractical skirts?" he clarified, scrutinizing me while I labored to move toward him without tripping over the heavy tent that hung around my legs.

"Impractical?" I frowned at him, unsure whether he had meant to insult me.

"Well, yes. You no doubt would have drowned from the weight of your gown had I not been there to prevent it."

Stopping a few feet in front of him, I scoffed, "I'm afraid I didn't consider the risk of falling into a river and nearly drowning when I chose my wardrobe."

"Well, what did you consider?"

"I don't know!" I said, bridling at the subtle criticism in his tone. I uttered the first thing that came to mind. "The weather!"

"The weather?" he repeated, raising a derisive eyebrow.

"What would *you* have had me take into account?"

"Self-defense. Cokyrian women only wear dresses at formal functions, and even then they bear weapons. You have no ability to carry a weapon at all."

"That's what *he's* for," I countered, waving in Tadark's general direction.

"He is your only protection?"

"Yes, on an outing such as this," I confirmed, perplexed by his interest but certain I was about to put an end to this debate. "At larger affairs, multiple guards watch over me."

"Tell me," he murmured, taking a step closer. "How would your guard protect you now?"

Narian's nearness was disturbing, and I began to worry that Tadark was daydreaming.

"From what would I need protection?" I asked slowly, unable to look away from his keen blue eyes, which were boring into my suspicious brown ones.

A flash of light, a glint of metal in the sun, told me before he readied it to strike that he held a dagger in his right hand. In stunned disbelief, I saw the blade come toward me. Terror flitted through my brain as I grasped that I might actually again be in mortal peril. Then Narian stooped and slashed off the front of my skirt below the knee so that my leggings were exposed rather indecently to the air.

I stood frozen, too horrified to move. Tadark was at my side in an instant, his sword drawn, but I knew he would have arrived too late had Narian actually intended to do me harm.

"Step away from the Princess," Tadark commanded.

Narian stared unflinchingly down the length of the cold metal, then relented and moved backward so that I was beyond his reach. Skillfully flipping the dagger so that he held the blade, he extended the weapon to my bodyguard.

"I assume you're going to demand that I relinquish my weapon," he calmly explained.

Tadark said nothing but snatched the proffered knife from Narian's hand.

"It is of no great loss to me," the young man continued, as Tadark tucked the dagger away in his belt. "A Cokyrian is never without a weapon."

I wasted no time puzzling over this last statement, for anger was rapidly rising.

"Look what you've done!" I railed, frustration emanating from the very pores of my skin. "My dress is ruined!"

Narian surveyed me, unaffected by my outburst.

"You'll find walking to be much easier now. And I must say, Princess, that there wasn't much hope for your gown anyway."

I opened my mouth, expecting a suitable comeback to emerge, but none came. Before I could gather my wits, he started once more down the path, and I followed, shaking my head in awe of his nerve. But, I grudgingly had to admit to myself, I didn't stumble once.

XVI

UNAPPEALING PROPOSALS

y Lady, Lord Steldor awaits you in the garden."

"Thank you," I said to the Palace Guard who had been sent to the library to find me. I had been lounging, scanning a book, and simply letting my thoughts wander. As the guard hurried away, I groaned inwardly, though my feelings were no doubt written upon my face. Steldor was not the person I wanted to see.

In fact, there was just one person on my mind. I could not escape the image of Narian's knife drawing near my flesh, or erase the knowledge of how easily he could have harmed me before Tadark had arrived to stand between us. Narian was correct regarding my protection —— in a scenario such as the one I had faced two days previously, the only person who could have defended me was me, and I barely possessed the ability to flee with some semblance of coordination.

I thought back to how he had rescued me from the river. I could have drowned —— my own bodyguards had been too far away to help me. But Narian had been there, somehow having bypassed Tadark and, more impressively, Halias. How could he have gotten close enough to reach me without anyone noticing? How long had he been there, and would he have revealed himself to us if my clumsiness had not made it necessary? These questions haunted me, despite my efforts to divert my attention elsewhere.

Tadark had ignored my strangely introverted attitude of late, too humiliated by his own blunder in underestimating Narian to bring up the incident. I, too, kept silent about it, preferring to ponder the mystery that the young man presented on my own.

I stood and made my way to the garden to meet with the man of my nightmares. I had not seen Steldor since the evening of the event held in honor of Narian's family and still had no inclination to do so. Narian was almost the converse of Steldor, and having spent time recently with the former, I suspected that I would have a harder time than usual abiding the latter's ego.

I ambled through the corridor, in no rush to get to my destination, and walked down the family staircase, Tadark beside me this time rather than behind. My last visit with Narian had substantially increased my bodyguard's vigilance, inside as well as outside the Palace. He would not accompany me within the garden, however, as Steldor was viewed by my father and Cannan as fully qualified to protect me.

I saw Steldor as I entered the grounds, a short way down the path from me. Given his attire —— black leather military jerkin with deeply etched scrolling over the shoulders and front, sword at his side —— he must have come from the Military Base. As I approached, I saw that he held in his left hand a bouquet of flowers, which I recognized as having come from the garden in which we stood, obviously an impromptu addition to whatever he had planned for me.

"You're especially radiant today, Princess Alera," he said, bowing and kissing my hand in his customary way, apparently hoping that the cheap flattery he used on other girls would have a softening effect upon me. He extended the hand in which he held the bouquet. "These flowers pale in comparison."

I wanted to roll my eyes, but I suppressed the urge and half-heartedly accepted his gift.

"What do you want, Steldor?" I bluntly inquired, his outrageous behavior of a week ago uppermost in my mind.

"Perhaps we should walk." He made a sweeping motion with his hand toward the garden pathway.

"I'd rather not."

A shadow of displeasure fell upon his features at my outright refusal, and I knew his thoughts had tracked my own. "You're not making this easy for me."

"And why should I make things easy?"

"Really, Alera," he scoffed, voice thick with condescension. "You can't honestly believe my actions at the Palace celebration were unjustified. I admit I may have overreacted *somewhat*, but you can hardly claim my anger was unprovoked."

"And what exactly did I do to provoke you?" I asked, my jaw set, not willing to let him get away with blaming that fiasco on me.

"You must get past these childish games!" he admonished, running a hand through his dark hair. "You know very well we are courting. Could you have possibly thought I would react in any other way? Being seen with another man will not change the fact that we are to marry. It's time you accepted that and began acting in an appropriate manner."

I was momentarily at a loss, for this was the first time marriage had come up in conversation between us. Both of us knew the expectations held by our parents and the Kingdom, so we had never felt the need to discuss the matter specifically. It was assumed, by Steldor at least, that we would in the future be wed. I had a different opinion.

"That wasn't quite the proposal I envisioned," I said, giving him a withering look.

He sighed in frustration. "Do you want me to get down on

one knee, Alera? Is that it? If that will cause you to see things as they are, then I will gladly do it."

"That will hardly be necessary, as you would only dirty your knee to hear an answer you would not welcome." With no thought to the consequences, I forged ahead. "I believe *you* need to get past the childish assumption that everything will fall neatly into place for you, because the truth is, the expectations of my father, of my mother and sister, of the *Kingdom* cannot force me to marry you. In order for you to marry me, my Lord Steldor, I would have to say 'I do,' and quite frankly, I don't!"

I brandished the bouquet he had given me in his face.

"My only regret is that my flowers had to die in vain!"

I hurled the bouquet at his chest, then turned and stalked down the path, a triumphant smile pulling at the corners of my mouth.

As I reentered the Palace, the same guard who had informed me of Steldor's desire to meet with me was talking with Tadark.

"Your Highness," he said, giving a slight bow. "The Captain of the Guard requests to see you and your bodyguard in his office. He said it was of some importance."

I nodded to the guard, dismissing him, and my victorious feeling was eradicated by dread. Cannan had never before sent for me, and I could think of no reason for him to want to speak with me now. Did this have something to do with the courtship between his son and me? Should I add Cannan's name to the growing list of people I had disappointed? The list that included London, my father, my mother, and Steldor?

Tadark and I walked through the King's Drawing Room to gain entry into the Throne Room, continuing across its floor to the Captain of the Guard's office, which was located near the antechamber. As we entered Cannan's domain, I saw Halias standing in the back of the room, though Miranna was nowhere to be seen.

The furnishings in Cannan's office were dark and imposing, much like the man himself. Weapons of every kind hung on the walls or were confined in glass-fronted cabinets. A map of Hytanica hung on one wall, next to a map of the entire Recorah River Valley that identified neighboring kingdoms as well as our own. The Kingdoms of Gourhan and Emotana lay to the south, across the Recorah River. West of us, Lake Resare, fed by a tributary of the mighty river, marked our boundary with the Kingdom of Sarterad. I shuddered involuntarily as I noted the identification of the Kingdom of Cokyri in the high desert area of the Niñeyre Mountains to the north and east of our borders.

Cannan, as Commander of Hytanica's military, had to be the busiest man in the Kingdom, for the heads of each of the Military's five divisions reported directly to him: the Major in charge of the Reconnaissance Unit; Kade as Sergeant at Arms in command of the Palace Guard; the Master at Arms who headed the City Guard; the Colonel who was the Headmaster at the Military Academy; and the various Battalion Commanders who led the Armed Forces. In addition, the King's Elite Guard, charged most specifically with defense of the King and the Royal Family, was under Cannan's direct control. London, Halias, Destari, and the others who held the rank of Deputy Captain were the highest-ranking officers in the military next to the Captain of the Guard.

Cannan sat behind his austere heavy oak desk, studying several sheets of parchment. Behind and to his left, the door to the armory stood ajar, revealing an even wider variety of weaponry. A second door that led into the guard room by the Grand Staircase was closed. Cannan raised his head as I entered but did not rise.

"Please be seated, Princess Alera," he said, motioning to the plain wooden chairs across from him on the other side of the desk.

As I complied, Tadark moved to stand on my right, Halias taking up a similar position on my left, neither sitting while in their Captain's office, although there were several chairs available.

Cannan did not waste time with small talk.

"Tadark has reported on the events that occurred during your visit to Baron Koranis's country estate two days ago. He has informed me that you had a conversation with Narian. What was the nature of your interaction with him?"

I was startled by his interest, but nonetheless answered his question, albeit somewhat hesitantly.

"We discussed what he called the impracticality of my clothing."

"Tell me more."

"He said that I should be able to protect myself, that he thought Tadark's protection was —— " I glanced uncertainly at my bodyguard. " —— insufficient." Tadark bristled but remained mute. "He told me Cokyrian women wear dresses only on formal occasions and that they always bear weapons."

Cannan mulled over my words for a moment, then changed the topic slightly.

"Tell me about the dagger. Did you see where he had it concealed?"

"No," I said with remorse, for I could provide very little useful information. "It was just there in his hand."

Cannan did not seem disappointed by my answer. "Can you think of anything else that would be important for me to know?" His words gave me hope that this inquisition was about to end.

I concentrated for a moment and then recalled something I had not fully appreciated at the time, but which now gave me great pause.

"He did say something rather odd to Tadark when he offered

him his knife," I said, recognizing halfway through my sentence that I was likely contradicting whatever story Tadark had woven as to how he had managed to disarm Narian. "He said, 'Cokyrians are never without weapons.'"

Cannan nodded and directed a question to Halias.

"And do you have any explanation for how this boy managed to get to the Princess without alerting you to his presence?"

Halias's light blue eyes flicked in irritation in Tadark's direction, as he apparently had not known before this moment that the younger guard had informed their Captain of this aspect of the incident.

"I have no explanation, sir," Halias said, automatically coming to attention. "But I can assure you we were vigilant in our protection of the Princesses. I know of only one other person who could have accomplished this, and he ought to be standing in Tadark's place."

The silence that followed was deafening. Tadark gave an offended huff, and Cannan shot him a silencing glare before turning back to Halias, his countenance stony.

I was dazed by the boldness of the bodyguard's statement. Halias, unlike London, had never been one to challenge authority. He did his job in protecting my sister but was generally content to trust his Captain and the King to make important decisions. Now, as he looked staunchly at Cannan, I realized that Destari and I were not the only ones who still trusted London, regardless of how damaging the evidence against him might be.

Cannan had not broken eye contact with his Deputy Captain, and I slowly became conscious of the fact that Halias's assertion could be viewed as insubordination. But just as I began to fret, the Captain again scrutinized me, letting his Elite Guard's defiance pass unaddressed.

"You had an exchange with Lord Narian on the balcony at

the Palace celebration last month," he said, and I felt as though I were once more under interrogation. "What did you discuss at that time?"

I shifted uncomfortably, unsure of what information he was hoping to obtain from me. I thought back to the evening when I had stood beside Narian on the balcony, all the while feeling that none of this was Cannan's business but too in awe of him to say so. Just as I concluded it would be best to tell him what I could, I remembered that I had confessed to Narian my disapproval of, and extreme dislike for, Steldor.

"Well...," I said, trying to phrase the information in such a way that I would not be forced to share my opinion of Steldor with his father, "we talked about the importance of duty."

A frown briefly creased Cannan's forehead, as though he were contemplating what would have prompted us to confer on such a topic.

"I see. Go on."

"He told me that he despised having his life laid out for him." I looked downward, examining my shoes, knowing, though no one else did, that my complaints about my obligations as Crown Princess had inspired this declaration from him.

If Cannan was aware of my discomfort, he ignored it.

"Interesting. Did he say anything else?"

"Yes... that at some point I would have to choose between carrying out my duties and living my life." I winced at Cannan's penetrating look and quickly finished. "After that he offered to escort me back inside." I did not elaborate, knowing everyone in the room was aware of what had happened after that.

A long silence followed as Cannan sank into thought, unperturbed by what I might be feeling. In truth, I found myself humbled and humiliated. Did the Captain somehow view my encounters with Narian as inappropriate? Perhaps he shared

Steldor's opinion of my conduct, that I should be approaching my responsibilities more seriously and not be wasting my time speaking to sixteen-year-old boys. I fidgeted with the folds of my skirt, desperate for this line of questioning to end, until Cannan spoke once more.

"I want you to return to Baron Koranis's estate to visit Narian and his family several times during the next month. You will report to me on anything Narian tells you about Cokyri and his upbringing there."

His candid request, or more accurately, his outright order, disturbed me.

"Are you suggesting that I spy for you?" I inquired, my stomach tightening.

"No," he replied, unfazed by my response. "I simply want you to interact with him and relate to me any information he volunteers."

I still was not happy with the idea.

"I don't want to betray his trust," I ventured, though I sensed my attempt to dissuade Cannan would be futile.

The Captain was silent for a moment, as though deciding whether he owed me an explanation. When next he spoke, his voice was placating.

"You must understand that what Narian has told you of his past in your two brief meetings exceeds what he has revealed to any other person. In order for *us* to trust *him*, we need to learn about his life in Cokyri. Who raised him? What has been his training? How did he learn of his true identity?"

Cannan's tone now became insistent, and his eyes held mine.

"It is imperative that we discover what we can about his background. He seems to be more open with you than with anyone else, and it behooves us to take advantage of that fact."

I nodded, feeling rather childish for attempting to argue with him.

Cannan stood and planted his hands on the wood surface before him, brushing the sheets of parchment aside. He then spoke to the three of us, his voice unassailable.

"No one other than those in this room and the King has knowledge of this plan, and no other is to learn of it." Addressing me, he continued, "You may choose to invite Princess Miranna on your return visits to see Narian. In fact, to avoid scrutiny, I would strongly suggest that you do so. But she must remain ignorant as to your true purpose."

Cannan's eyes shifted to Halias's face, and he allowed a transitory pause to emphasize his point.

"That is all," he finished, straightening to his full height. "You may go now."

I rose as Tadark and Halias turned to escort me back to my quarters. Having had very few dealings with the Captain of the Guard in the past, I was impressed by the measure of authority he had exhibited, even toward a member of the Royal Family. He was confident in a much different way from his son —— Steldor was conceited, whereas Cannan was decisive. The deep respect I had for him made me feel as if *I* should have bowed prior to leaving his office.

———

It was early September, and this time my mother was hosting a recital in the Music Room of the Palace. She had invited two dozen young noblewomen, accompanied by their mothers, to share their vocal abilities, as well as their accomplishments on the harp and flute. Miranna was to be one of the young women demonstrating her talents on the harp, but my mother had not approached me with a similar request, perhaps thinking I had endured enough stress over the past month as a result of the Palace function I had successfully orchestrated.

I was thankful that this gathering had such a specific aim, for it would allow little time for gossip. I dreaded the questions that would be flung at me with respect to the altercation between Narian and Steldor that had taken place just ten days previously.

The Music Room was adjacent to the Queen's Drawing Room, and likewise had a bay window that yielded a view of the East Courtyard. Two rows of benches had been arranged so that they faced away from the window toward the front of the room where the performers would sit or stand. I glanced outside as I selected a bench and could see that summer was rapidly giving way to fall, for the flowers in the Courtyard were beginning to forlornly wither and die, while the leaves on the trees were taking on vibrant hues. As I seated myself, dark-eyed Reveina, ever the leader, slid in on one side of me, boy-obsessed Kalem on the other.

"So tell us," said Reveina, brushing back her sleek brown tresses and leaning toward me. "What exactly happened between Lord Steldor and the Cokyrian?"

"Yes, we were in the Ballroom that evening but did not witness the quarrel. We've heard so many conflicting versions of it that we want to know the truth from you," Kalem added, her glistening gray eyes framed by her coal-black hair.

"His name is Lord Narian," I said tersely. "And he is Hytanican, not Cokyrian."

Neither my comments nor my argumentative manner dampened their enthusiasm.

"Did Steldor strike him? Did he strike Steldor?" Reveina was persistent. "We've heard both versions and tend to believe the first, but the second would be so —— "

"Worthy of gossip?" I finished.

"Yes, of course," laughed Kalem.

I looked toward the front of the room, longing for the performances to begin. As Miranna, who was to play first, was not yet ready, I attempted to put a stop to the speculations as tactfully as possible.

"There was no fight at all. Steldor had just consumed more ale than he perhaps should have and became a little jealous. He did not like me speaking with Narian, although it was to be expected I would converse with the guest of honor. Sorry to disappoint, but no one hit anyone."

Their faces dropped, and their lips formed pouts, as if they had at least expected I would make a good story out of it. Before they could say anything further, the first notes of the harp caught my ear, and I was saved by the start of Miranna's solo.

The recital continued for another two hours, alternating between singers and instrumentalists. Right before the last vocalist of the day, I excused myself, exiting the room so I would not have to deal with any further inquiries. I knew my mother would view my behavior as rude, and that I would suffer a reprimand later, but that was a price I was definitely willing to pay.

XVII

ABHORRENT DEEDS AND
SUCCESSFUL MISSIONS

B y the time Miranna and I paid another visit to Koranis's country estate, harvest time was upon us. From mid-September through October, crops such as wheat, barley, rye, and oats were gathered and stored, grapes were harvested for wine, honey was collected, and fruit, including the apples in the Royal Orchards, was picked. It was the most anticipated time of the year, culminating in a week of celebrations at the end of October that included feasting and dancing, along with a Tournament and Faire.

As we crossed the countryside in our buggy, I idly considered what Narian would think of the upcoming festivities. Based on what Semari had told us, I doubted he would be much enthused. After all, if he had been disappointed by almost everything else he had seen in Hytanica, I supposed he would also look askance at the Harvest Festival. Even so, I could not help but hope that after partaking of the most thrilling of the year's celebrations, he would prove to be more impressed with Hytanica than he had been thus far.

Miranna and I chatted with Koranis and Alantonya upon our arrival at the Baron's estate until we were interrupted by Semari's enthusiastic greeting as she bounded out of the house. Alantonya took advantage of her daughter's appearance to retreat into the home, suggesting before she did so that we take another constitutional, though she reminded us to stay far away from the river. Koranis also chose to take his leave, apparently overwhelmed by the chattering of the two younger girls, but was intercepted by Tadark as he began to walk toward the stables. Curious as to what business my bodyguard would have with the Baron, I stepped away from my sister and her friend to position myself for eavesdropping.

"I believe this belongs to you," Tadark was saying, sounding very self-important and extending the dagger Narian had wielded after my fall into the river.

"Yes, that is mine," Koranis affirmed, bewildered. "I assumed I had lost it. How ever did you come by it?"

"It wasn't lost, sir," explained a gleeful Tadark, knowing he was about to cause trouble for Narian and enjoying the bit of revenge he could exact for the embarrassment the young man had dealt him. "I took it from Lord Kyenn the last time we were here. I brought it to the Captain of the Guard as I did not know it was yours."

Koranis looked blankly at Tadark for a moment.

"I remember having it when we were out riding and thought I must have dropped it. But if Kyenn had it..." A flush crept over his double chins as comprehension dawned.

"Kyenn!" he called angrily, turning to face the house.

After several minutes, and another urgent call, Narian sauntered out the front door, not feeling the need to hurry in spite of the insistent quality of his father's voice.

"In what manner did you come by my dagger?" Koranis demanded when his son stood before him.

"I removed it from its sheath," Narian coolly answered.

"Then you are a thief, boy, and I will not tolerate a thief in my home!"

Koranis, who had assumed a stern posture, recoiled almost imperceptibly as Narian's piercing blue eyes locked upon his own. Tadark, who was smaller in stature than the other two men, now looked cherubic, undisguised joy shining upon his boyish face.

"Perhaps a good whipping is in order to teach you respect for other people's possessions." Strangely enough, Koranis's words came out sounding more like a proposal than the imposition of a punishment.

There was silence in the aftermath of the Baron's statement. Even Semari and Miranna's prattling had died away, and they watched father and son with interest. I could not tear my attention from the scene, as the golden-haired pair stared at each other, Narian's lean and muscular build in sharp contrast to Koranis's overfed and overfussed appearance.

Narian appraised his father with disdain in his eyes, showing no sign of remorse or concern in the face of Koranis's threat.

"I wouldn't try that if I were you," he cautioned, his voice barely audible.

Koranis took a small step back from his son, realizing as he did that the two of them had attracted our attention.

"Get back into the house," he blustered. "I will deal with you later."

Narian shrugged, then unhurriedly reentered the home.

Plainly perturbed by Narian's attitude, Koranis turned to my bodyguard and said curtly, "Thank you for returning my weapon." He then huffed off to the stables, leaving an extremely dejected Tadark behind.

Miranna and Semari soon resumed their chattering, but I was staggered by what I had just witnessed. In Hytanica, the father was the undisputed head of the family, with absolute dominion over his wife, his children, and their lands and possessions. Yet I could not shake the feeling that Narian had been the one in charge. This was all the more disconcerting as Narian had shown signs of neither anger nor aggression. Rather, he had seemed to be coldly sizing up a foe, and the shocking notion that Narian held power over the Baron entered my head.

It wasn't long before Semari, Miranna, and I took Alantonya's suggestion and again traipsed through the trees along the path to the river, Halias and Tadark in our wake. To my dismay, Narian was not with us. I had taken advantage of his presence in the house to invite him to accompany us, but he had merely raised his eyebrows, giving no other response, leading me to the frustrating conclusion that I would not see him further this day. I had hoped that simple curiosity would entice him on our walk, although part of me suspected that he thought us tedious and uninteresting.

Upon reaching the clearing near the bank of the Recorah, Miranna and Semari rushed ahead, their giggling becoming fainter as they approached the water. Halias went after them, but I hung back, preferring to enjoy the view from a safe distance.

I examined my surroundings, searching for a shady spot where I might sit, and spied the gnarled, exposed root of an ancient oak. As I moved toward it, I was amazed to see Narian leaning against another, but a few feet to my left. He was clad in a black shirt, this time topped by a leather vest, and black breeches, colors that enabled him to fade into the shadows cast by the dense trees. It occurred to me as I contemplated him that the High Priestess at the time of her capture had likewise been dressed all in black.

Tadark had seen Narian as well and now clung annoyingly to my side, and I knew something had to be done. I stopped and turned to him, struggling to repress my irritation.

"If Lord Narian is to be relaxed enough to talk to me, you are going to have to give me some breathing room."

My bodyguard looked torn, but then motioned forward with his hand to indicate that I should proceed without him. After glancing toward the younger girls, who were being entertained by Halias's demonstration of the proper way to skip rocks, I changed course and walked slowly toward Narian, knowing that there was no way to conceal that I desired to speak with him. He examined me as I came closer but made no indication of a desire to converse when I reached him. I decided to cut straight to the point.

"I've been thinking about what you said to me on my last visit —— about protecting myself."

I felt enormously self-conscious due to the lack of the usual niceties preceding my words but tried not to let my discomfort show.

"You were right. There may come a time when my body-guards will be unable to defend me. It would seem wise that I learn to defend myself."

I waited to see what his reaction would be, but he continued to survey me, and I cleared my throat.

"I can think of no one to teach me these things, except... you," I finished clumsily.

He nodded, as if understanding how I had reached this con-clusion, but his reply was not what I expected.

"I can't do that," he said matter-of-factly.

"Why not?" I demanded, planting my hands on my hips in mild annoyance. "First you tell me that I must be able to pro-tect myself, then you refuse to teach me the necessary skills? Women in Cokyri know how to defend themselves. You said so yourself!"

He smirked, the same smirk I'd seen on the balcony. "Women in Cokyri wear breeches."

I was silent for a moment, slowly grasping his implication. "You want me to... wear breeches?"

"Only if you wish to learn self-defense," he replied, raising an eyebrow ever so slightly, and I had the impression he was issuing a challenge.

"Then I will do so."

I waited for him to offer a pair to me, but he said nothing, the gleam in his startlingly blue eyes telling me he knew exactly what was on my mind, but that he would not give me anything unless I requested it. And that I was not about to do.

"When next I come," I said obstinately, "I will bring breeches."

How I was going to accomplish this was beyond me at that moment, but I cared not. I would not give Narian the satisfaction of having a Princess of Hytanica ask to borrow a pair of his trousers.

————

We returned to the Palace as the pale shades of evening began to brush the sky and slowly walked up the Courtyard path and through the large front doors into the Grand Entry Hall. I began to climb the left side of the winding double staircase, expecting Miranna to follow, but she made a comment about wanting to stroll in the garden, as she was feeling stiff from the buggy ride.

I wavered, debating whether I should join her, when the sound of a door opening and closing, and footfalls other than my sister's, reached my ears. I glanced down and saw Steldor emerge from the guard room to the right of the staircase, from which one could gain access to Cannan's office. Not wanting to be seen, I hurried up the stairs to where Tadark was waiting on the landing. Steldor stood in the entryway for a moment, then headed in the same direction as Miranna, settling the question of whether I should follow after her. I instead elected to go on to the library.

"You're not actually going to wear breeches, are you?" Tadark asked when we reached my destination.

It was obvious he had overheard at least part of my talk with Narian, and I feared he might mention my plan to the Captain of the Guard when next he reported, and that Cannan would relay the information to my father. That would put an end to any possibility of acquiring a pair, which in turn would paint me as foolish in front of Narian when I returned empty-handed, not to mention that it would leave me with no one to teach me self-defense. The time had come to refresh Tadark's memory as to something I had not mentioned since the day of the picnic.

"Yes, I am," I said with assurance. "And you are not to say a word about it... to anyone."

"It is hardly appropriate for a Princess to wear a man's clothing," he grumbled.

"Your opinion isn't relevant, Tadark, and this will not get back to the Captain or my father," I declared, preparing to deliver my final blow. "Or I will be forced to inform them of your errors in judgment when Miranna was injured at the picnic."

Tadark's face paled, and I felt a twinge of pleasure in knowing that I had secured his cooperation.

"Fine," he mumbled, crossing his arms.

Feeling rather proud of myself, I began to ponder the problem of how to obtain the trousers. Concluding that I needed a coconspirator, I decided to find Miranna in the garden after all.

I left the library and descended the spiral staircase, making my way to the rear entrance of the Palace. Tadark held the doors open for me, and I stepped out into the waning sunlight. I looked down the row of unlit torches, and saw Halias, in a posture that brought London to mind, resting against the wall not far from where I stood.

"Where is Mira?" I asked, for he normally would have been walking with her.

"She is by that fountain," he said, smiling in greeting and pointing down the path directly in front of me.

I turned to approach the fountain he had indicated, leaving Tadark in his company, and, as I did so, saw that Miranna was not alone.

Her back was to me, but over her shoulder, I could clearly see Steldor's arrogant, but incredibly handsome, face. He was almost six inches taller than my sister, and based on his expression, took note of me before my sister had any idea that I was present. He was quite openly flirting with her just as he had done during our picnic; on that day, he had been attempting to settle the score with me for refusing his advances. Now, as his dark eyes burned into mine over my sister's back, a sneer curved his lips, and he did something even I would never have believed him capable of doing. Wrapping an arm around my sister's waist, and placing his other hand upon her upper back, he pulled her to him and gave her a long and lingering kiss on the lips.

I was too thunderstruck to react as Steldor stepped back from her. She swayed on her feet, overcome by his romantic gesture, but he moved around her without further consideration.

"Princess," he murmured, swaggering past me, his tone in that single word revealing how infuriatingly satisfied he was with himself.

Miranna turned in confusion when he sauntered away, not understanding his abrupt change in attitude, and I knew the moment she saw me, for her eyes widened in distress. She could no doubt sense my cold fury, though it was directed at Steldor and not at her. I walked toward her without speaking and with no design to be vindictive, but the darting of her eyes and her backward step told me she believed otherwise.

"Alera," she squeaked, her hands flying to her face. "When did you...?"

"I saw the kiss," I said simply, saving her from having to stutter out the rest of her question. I was not angry with her —— there was little she could have done to prevent Steldor's deplorable action. She was also, like most of the girls in the Kingdom, infatuated with him, and to have her first kiss come from someone over whom she swooned had probably been thrilling. But now she was on the verge of tears.

"I'm sorry! So sorry! It was childish of me to be flirting with him. I'm sure I gave him the wrong impression. Steldor is yours —— I had no right to kiss him, and you have every right to be upset with me."

My sister seemed oblivious to Steldor's true motivation for kissing her and was blaming herself entirely.

"It's all right, Mira." I tried to cut her off before she could continue with her unnecessary apologies. "Steldor is not mine, nor have I ever desired that he be mine. He can kiss whomever he wants, as can you. You have no reason to feel guilty."

She shook her head. "I feel so dreadful, Alera. Is there anything I can do to make it up to you?"

"Once again, I am *not* upset with you," I told her sincerely. "But..." I trailed off, determining how best to say what I had in mind. "There is something you can do."

"What? I'll do anything. Just find it in your heart to forgive me."

"Mira, I forgive you," I said, growing impatient, then announced, "I need breeches."

"Breeches?" she repeated, baffled enough to momentarily forget her guilt over the incident with Steldor. "Whatever for?"

"Narian is going to teach me basic self-defense," I said, deciding that honesty was the best course of action. "He said he'd only do so if I wore breeches. That's where I need your help."

"He's teaching you... to defend yourself? But isn't that what our bodyguards are for?"

I almost chuckled at how similar my sister's observation was to what I had told Narian on our first visit to Koranis's estate.

"Do you want to help me or not?" I asked, knowing that delving into the details of my request's origin was not relevant to her decision and would only delay her answer.

"Of course I'll help," she said right away, just as I had known she would.

"Good."

I glanced toward our bodyguards to check that they had not moved within earshot, then pulled her down to sit beside me on one of the garden benches.

"Now, the issue is how to obtain them. We could try the laundry, but I doubt any of the guards' or servants' trousers would fit me, and I *know* Father's wouldn't."

"Perhaps we could take Tadark's," Miranna innocently suggested. "I think his breeches would come closest to fitting you."

"But how would we remove them?" I blurted, the heat rising quickly in my face as I realized how scandalously I had spoken.

Miranna stared at me for a moment, joining me in my deep blush. Then we were both seized with the giggles, and any vestiges of tension dissipated.

"I think, sister," Miranna finally gasped, "that it would be wise just to purchase a pair."

"Yes, that would be a better method. But how will we do it? No one will think it's proper to sell trousers to a Princess, and I don't think we could fool Halias and Tadark as to our activities for long."

Miranna absently twisted a curly lock of hair as she ruminated over my question, then she smiled.

"We'll commission someone to buy them for us!"

"Like whom?"

"I don't know —— but there are plenty of young boys in

the marketplace who would be more than willing to earn some extra money by making a purchase for us. Market Day is only three days away —— how is that for perfect planning?"

I nodded, impressed by the simplicity and yet utter brilliance of my sister's idea, and a bit embarrassed that I had been unable to come up with it myself.

The following days crept past. Miranna was exceedingly attentive toward me, despite my constant declarations that I was not angry with her, and together we created a plan to acquire a pair of breeches without raising anyone's suspicions as to what we were doing. By the time Market Day arrived, we were ready to put our strategy into action. As usual, we dressed like villagers so that we would not stand out amongst the crowd and left the Palace before midday. Our bodyguards were again out of uniform and walking unobtrusively behind us, thanks to Halias, who was in all likelihood restraining Tadark.

Miranna, having an uncanny ability to spot young men across great distances, was scanning the crowd for the boy who would play the most important part in our scheme —— the buyer of the breeches. We needed someone to whom we could talk without our bodyguards becoming suspicious. Unfortunately, we did not generally socialize with those outside of our immediate circle of upper-class young men and women. Two Princesses chatting with a market boy might seem rather odd.

Strolling beside me, Miranna let out a gasp, then grabbed my lower arm to bring me to a standstill.

"What is it?" I eagerly inquired, thinking she had located our quarry.

"Look," she said, indicating where I should glance with a jerk of her head. "It's Steldor and his friends."

I peered in the direction of her nod, and my gaze came to

rest upon Steldor, who was the tallest and most handsome of the group and had a particular quality that called all eyes to him. As I took in his three friends, I realized that Barid and Devant were standing on either side of a cringing young man who wore the gold tunic of the City Guard. Steldor and Galen, clad in the black leather military jerkins that marked their rank as Field Commanders, were particularly imposing figures, and the young guard was struggling to present a brave front. Steldor, wearing a nasty grin, stood in front of his prey, jabbing him in the shoulder in a way that told me whatever was coming out of his mouth was less than kind. After a moment, the four friends burst out laughing, and Galen clapped Steldor on the shoulder as if congratulating him on a well-spoken insult, while the guard's face turned red with resentment and humiliation.

Taking Miranna's hand, I moved us out of the flow of shoppers, and we watched in morbid fascination from twenty feet away as Galen lightly pushed Steldor aside and stepped forward to drape an arm around the young man's shoulders in insincere amicability. He said something that elicited a few chortles from his cronies, going so far as to pat the guard's flaming cheek in mockery. After that, he began to point at the dagger hanging from the young man's belt, presumably criticizing it in some way, then had the nerve to unsheathe it, fluidly disarming him and adding to his embarrassment.

The guard at once tried to snatch back his knife, but Galen tossed it to Steldor, who caught it and flipped it around once in his hand. Jerking free of Galen, the young man made an ineffectual lunge in another attempt to reclaim his weapon. Steldor held it away, laughing at his victim's plight.

It was then that the Captain's son became aware of Miranna and me, as well as of Halias, who had begun to walk purposefully toward the group of friends to break up their fun. Without a word, Steldor extended the dagger to the City Guard, his sadistic grin gradually becoming smug, an expression with which I was all too familiar. The guard hastily reclaimed and sheathed his weapon, glancing distrustfully between the two Field Commanders. Steldor then signaled to his three friends, and the four of them began to walk away from the young man they had shamed. As they did so, Steldor turned to me and bowed, a sardonic gesture that unmistakably indicated I should be applauding the show.

"Oh, he is unbelievable!" I exclaimed, beginning a potentially lengthy rant.

"Yes, he is," Miranna cut in. "But I think I see the exact person we need."

She pointed in the direction of the four friends whom I had just gone from disliking to despising, and I saw Temerson dart around them. He seemed particularly jittery, as if he expected to be their next target, but the tension left his body when the group passed him by.

Miranna fluffed her hair, then clasped my hand and pulled me forward. I cast Halias a grateful smile as we brushed past him, and he tilted his head in acknowledgment.

Temerson's back was toward us, and he jumped when Miranna tapped him on the shoulder.

"P-Princess," he stuttered, then seeing me, added "ce-es. What are you doing here?"

Miranna smiled at his flustered reaction.

"We're shopping," she teased.

His face reddened at the absurdity of his question.

"Well, yes —— of course, what-what else would you be doing? I only meant, that, well, why are you *here*, talk-talking to *me*?" he stammered, tripping over his tongue as he tried to clarify himself.

"Because we're friends, aren't we?" Miranna answered, her tone so sweet and gentle that I had to look away lest I laugh.

Temerson's brown eyes widened and his eyebrows shot upward, indicating both his delight and astonishment at her suggestion.

"I, uh, I, um, er, I mean... okay."

I could tell Miranna was now also trying not to laugh, for she did not want to embarrass our potential ally.

"I'm glad that's straightened out," she said. "I'm afraid we don't have much time to talk, but could I ask you for a favor?"

Temerson's head bobbed up and down vigorously.

"Yes, anything!" he said, at last smoothly delivering a sentence.

Miranna placed her hand upon his arm and leaned forward to whisper to him, just in case there was a chance Halias or Tadark might overhear. As she finished, he stepped back from her, cocking his head to the side.

"Really?"

"Really."

While Miranna's request was a bit unorthodox, I was positive Temerson would undertake it, if for no other reason than the gratitude he felt toward us for never disclosing the true cause of her injury at the picnic.

"If that's what you want," he said in confusion.

"Yes, thank you. We would appreciate it if you didn't tell anyone about this," Miranna stressed, stealthily slipping a small pouch of money into his hand. "The breeches are for a friend of ours, who is about your height but very slight in build. We have to go, but if you'd bring them to the Palace later today or tomorrow —— "

"To the P-P-Palace? Me? By myself?" Temerson was alarmed.

"You'll be fine," Miranna assured him. "Ask to see me —— I'll tell the guards I'm expecting you."

Temerson nodded tentatively. "I can do it," he murmured, though whether he was speaking to us or himself was unclear.

————

However fretful he had been about completing his task, Temerson managed it in the end. Less than two hours later, as I sat upon the sofa in my parlor, Tadark in an armchair across from me, and a chessboard on a small table between us, Miranna rushed through the door without knocking. She held a brown parcel in her hands and was beaming mischievously. Halias entered a step behind her, plainly perplexed by her mood.

I scrambled to my feet, ignoring Tadark's miserable moan of defeat when he realized my last move had made me the victor in the game he had been reluctant to play in the first place, and Miranna and I entered my bedroom. We perched upon my bed, and she untied the cords that crossed over each other to encircle the package from both directions. As she hastily tore the wrapping away, our eyes fell on a long-stemmed pink rose lying atop the package's contents. Miranna's cheeks took on the hue of the rose's petals as she carefully lifted it toward her face, breathing in its delicate fragrance.

"I guess 'okay' wasn't enough of an indicator that he wants to be your friend," I said lightheartedly, knowing how much Temerson's simple gesture would mean to my sister. It was sweet and romantic, and I knew Miranna would be gushing about it to Semari for weeks.

I reached into the package and lifted out the remaining item —— the breeches. They were made of lightweight wool, dark brown in color, and felt rough and coarse in my hands.

I got to my feet and held them up to my waist; they fell almost to my ankles.

"The length is workable," Miranna observed. "But we may have to pull in the waist somehow." She smiled widely at me. "Well, do you want to try them on?"

I nodded eagerly, and Miranna assisted by unlacing the back of my dress.

XVIII

SELF-DEFENSE

ere, see? I have them," I said, lifting my breeches up for Narian's inspection. "Now you have no basis upon which to object to teaching me self-defense."

"I can object as long as you're not wearing them," he stated dryly.

My cheeks colored slightly, and I hoped he could not see my embarrassment.

"I'll need to change."

I glanced around, and the pink of my cheeks deepened. We were standing in a clearing in the woods that we had reached by virtue of a fifteen-minute hike on another narrow path. We had left Miranna and Semari at the river, Halias having distracted the two of them so that we could make our departure. While I would have preferred a shorter walk, we had to be far enough from the Recorah so that neither our sisters nor Halias might stumble upon us. The worst part of our site was that there was no place for me to change with the exception of the woods surrounding us.

Tadark, who stood not three feet from my side, absurdly close in light of the admonition I had given him on our last visit, had begun to glare alternately at me and at Narian, already not liking the way this afternoon was going. I was not particularly enamored with the situation myself. My discomfort increased dramatically at the thought that without my sister or my personal maid, I would have to ask either Tadark or Narian to unlace the back of my gown. Opting for the lesser of the two evils, I directed my request to Narian. At his nod, I turned around and he gathered my long brown hair together, draping it over my left shoulder.

"You should put your hair up or braid it in the future," he critiqued as he loosened my laces. "Or better yet, cut it."

I glanced at him but was unable to determine if he was serious, then walked toward the woods in as dignified a fashion as I could muster.

"I insist that both of you turn your backs!" I called over my shoulder.

I dodged behind some trees, and after glancing toward the clearing to make sure Narian and Tadark had obeyed my wishes, removed my dress. I hurriedly pulled the breeches on, not wanting to have an encounter with someone while only half clad. Having brought no shirt to wear with the trousers, I tucked in my chemise. While this was somewhat bulky, it had the benefit of taking up some of the extra space in the overly large garment. Despite this, the breeches would have fallen to my ankles had it not been for Miranna's inspired thinking in giving me some of her hair ribbons to tightly cinch the waist.

Regardless of the ease with which I could move while wearing men's clothing, I found the breeches to be extremely uncomfortable. The rough fabric against my legs made me desperate to shed them in favor of my usual garb; further, the thought of emerging in such an outfit in front of my bodyguard and a young man I barely knew was distressing. The absence of a heavy skirt covering my legs made me feel exposed.

Knowing I was too far committed to change my mind and retain any self-respect, I walked back into the clearing and over to face Narian and Tadark, who were standing side by side. Tadark shifted self-consciously, not wanting to look directly at me as though I were dressed indecently, yet unable to look elsewhere because of the utter ludicrousness of my appearance. Narian did not seem bothered in the least, although in truth it was probably stranger to him to see a woman in the garments we wore on a daily basis than it was to see me clothed as I now was.

Narian stepped forward and to my right so that he stood between Tadark and me, and I could see the distrustful eyes of my bodyguard over his shoulder. Gripping my right elbow, he pulled me across the front of his body so my back was to his chest. I stiffened at his proximity, for although he was only an inch taller than me, I was keenly conscious of his lean and muscular build, and of my own vulnerability.

"No need to be so tense," he said, near enough to whisper in my ear. I could feel his breath pass over my cheek, and a shiver swept through me.

He pulled my forearms up so they were in front of my chest, and I balled my fists, recognizing the fighting position he had assumed when he'd been forced to defend himself against Steldor.

"Plant your feet shoulder-width apart," he instructed, his voice brisk. "Move your left foot forward, just a little."

He turned my body away from him, then moved back almost on top of Tadark to examine my posture, and I released the breath I hadn't known I'd been holding.

"This is the basic fighting stance. Hold your left arm up a little higher, and relax your muscles. The stiffer you are, the slower you'll move. Now, the first thing you must learn is to always be aware of your surroundings. When you enter a room, you must take note of all who are present, and you must register every exit through which you could make an escape. The opportune moment for an enemy is the moment you let your guard down."

Without warning, he twisted to seize Tadark and, with great force, pulled my bodyguard toward him so that the Elite Guard was thrust across his hip and thrown to the ground. With a grunt of pain, Tadark landed on his back at my feet, head toward Narian, his usually well-kept sandy brown hair in disarray.

"Any questions?" Narian asked, without extending a hand to help Tadark to his feet, as if my bodyguard were merely a prop to be used for demonstrations.

Tadark sat up and glared at Narian, face ablaze with furious embarrassment. I was astounded at the young man's audacity and couldn't help but conclude that he had been letting my guard know who was really in control. In any case, I had to concede that he had emphatically made his point.

Narian strode toward a large tree at the edge of the clearing. He stepped behind it and reappeared a moment later with a sheathed half-sword in his hand that was similar to the long-knives London had carried, only more elaborately styled.

Tadark was on his feet by the time Narian returned, ready to charge full speed at him, a battle cry upon his lips. He resisted, recognizing that the young man was not posing a threat, for which I was quite thankful, more for Tadark's sake than anyone else's. But however grateful I was for my guard's self-restraint, I was troubled by the fact that, for the second time, Narian had acquired a weapon.

"Where did you get that?" I asked, seeing how firmly Tadark was clutching the hilt of his sword.

"I borrowed it," Narian said, unsheathing it and holding it out to me.

"From whom?" I persisted, grasping the sword rather clumsily for I had never before held one.

"Koranis."

"And does Koranis *know* that you borrowed his sword?"

Narian cocked his head and cast his eyes upward, as if picturing what his father might have been doing at that exact moment.

"He may by now. So I suggest we not waste our time." He stepped around me to adjust the position of the sword in my hand, no remorse in his voice.

Now that I was gripping the weapon correctly, he began to teach me some basic movements. I groaned in frustration as I struggled to follow his directions, for I made mistake after mistake. After a time, he permitted me to take a break, and I rested, perspiration dampening my forehead despite the coolness of the mid-September day.

"Why is this so easy for you?" I asked, then blushed at my own idiocy. A typical Hytanican boy of Narian's age would have had sufficient military training to instruct me, if so inclined, in the same things Narian was endeavoring to teach.

Narian, unlike me, didn't think my inquiry irrelevant. "I've been taught to handle a variety of weapons."

"I suppose your training has been similar to that of our boys," I said, thinking out loud. I waited for him to confirm my statement, then realized he would have little knowledge of the way we schooled our young men.

"Hytanican boys enter the Military Academy at fourteen, so you would be in your third year had you grown up here."

He gave me an odd look, uncertain as to my interest, then seemed to perceive my curiosity as simply that —— curiosity.

"By the time I was fourteen, I'd already been in training for eight years."

I gave no response, hoping that none was necessary, as I was unable to formulate one. If he were telling the truth, he would have begun his training at age six. *Six years old*. I could not imagine what fighting skills one could teach a six-year-old, and the only clear thought I processed was that his answer explained why Cokyrians made such fearsome warriors.

"You were sent to military school when you were six?" I finally ventured. Our Military Academy housed its students during the training year, and I tried to imagine being separated from my family at such an age.

"Not exactly."

"Were you taught by your father, then?"

I mentioned the only alternative a Hytanican boy would have had for learning such skills.

Narian gave a short and mirthless laugh. "Father is not a fitting name for the one who trained me."

His words were vague, and I could tell he did not wish to discuss this further. Declaring my break at an end, he proceeded to demonstrate several defensive moves, and by the time my sister and I returned to the Palace that evening, my arms were too sore to lift a cup of tea.

———

A week later Miranna and I climbed into the buggy to begin another journey to Koranis's estate. As we traversed the countryside, I could see villagers hard at work in the fields bringing in the crops. I myself did little to assist with the preparations for winter, but all the same, their activities were a sign of the approaching Faire and Tournament that celebrated the end of the harvest —— an event that was a source of excitement for me as well as everybody else.

We arrived at Koranis's home, and I knew by the way Tadark's jaw locked that he remained adamantly opposed to the idea of Narian instructing me in self-defense. I, on the other hand, was looking forward to Narian's teaching and had been practicing the movements he had shown me with the half-sword using the only tools available to me —— a hairbrush and a fireplace poker. I again had my breeches with me, having debated wearing the trousers underneath my regular clothing, but ultimately deciding I did not want their roughness against my legs as we traveled. To simplify changing, however, I was wearing a basic skirt and blouse, and my hair hung down my back in a long plait so it would not draw Narian's criticism.

After greeting Koranis and Alantonya, my sister and I, accompanied by Semari, Narian, and our bodyguards, went off to enjoy the day. The weather was continuing to cool, and Alantonya had suggested that instead of visiting the river, we pick berries down at the forest's edge. We took several willow baskets to fill as the fruit would be plentiful at this time of year.

To save ourselves from having to haul the filled baskets back to the house, we concluded it would be wise to make use of the buggy. Halias handled the reins to spare our poor driver the boredom of watching while we picked the fruit, and I sat in front with him. Miranna and Semari were in the seat behind with the baskets at their feet, and Tadark rode his own mount. Narian received permission to ride Halias's sorrel gelding and was thus saved the effort of saddling one of his father's horses. And with that, the six of us were on our way.

The berry bushes were not far from the beginning of the path through the woods that we followed to reach the river, perhaps less than a quarter mile. The leaves on the trees and bushes were now transforming their colors, painting Koranis's estate in gorgeous tones of deep gold, orange, and russet. I had not thought the Baron's land could be any more beautiful, but the mixed palette of the forest was breathtaking.

Upon reaching our destination, Halias tied the horses to the trunk of a tree and helped me down from the buggy, but before he could extend the same courtesy to Miranna or Semari, they had jumped to the ground, each carrying a basket, and had run toward the tree line.

I glanced under the backseat of the buggy, where I had hidden the package containing my breeches prior to leaving the city. As Narian had not attempted to speak with me, I did not know if he was in the mood to give instruction this day. Thinking he perhaps was not, I picked up a basket, intending to join the younger girls, but froze as I saw Halias approach the young man where he had dismounted.

"I am to check you for weapons," he informed Narian. "Captain of the Guard's orders."

Without objection, Narian rolled up his left shirtsleeve and extracted a dagger from a sheath strapped to the inside of his forearm.

"You will find no others," he said as he handed it to Halias.

Halias gazed steadily into his eyes for a moment, then tucked the blade into a saddlebag and went to monitor the younger girls. Narian nonchalantly approached me, and I fought the urge to ask if the weapon he had just surrendered to Halias had been "borrowed" from Koranis.

"Retrieve your package from under the seat and tell your guard to bring his horse," he murmured in my ear as he brushed past.

I nodded, marveling at how observant he was, then retrieved the package and surreptitiously tucked it into my basket.

"Take your horse with you," I said to Tadark, who was standing nearby.

At the inquisitive lift of his eyebrows, I shrugged, indicating I knew no more about the request for the horse than did he. He scowled, surmising that this had been Narian's idea, then trudged over to his mount to untie it, startling the animal in the process.

Narian was standing fifteen feet from where Miranna and Semari were picking berries. Halias was between him and the girls, with his back to me. As I moseyed toward our sisters, not wanting to draw notice, Narian disappeared into the woods. I peered into the trees to see where he had gone and discerned a narrow trail that gradually widened the further it reached into the forest. With one final fleeting look at the people to my right, I entered the woods and began to follow the path. A few moments later, Tadark approached from the left, leading his horse, having ducked into the trees some distance away from the others to avoid attracting attention. Ahead, down the trail, I could see Narian waiting for me.

"Where are we going?" I asked as I approached.

"To the clearing," he replied, his tone revealing that he thought my question superfluous. "You'll need to wear those breeches again."

He turned and hiked on. Beginning to feel the weight of my skirt as we climbed a small slope, I called to him, panting from exertion.

"Perhaps I should change now. It would make all this walking much easier."

He stopped and turned to face me, silently consenting. I moved into the cover of the trees and hastily pulled on the breeches, emerging this time without a moment of indecision. After I had placed my skirt into the basket and surrendered both to Tadark, I began to follow Narian once more.

When we reached the clearing, Narian walked behind the same tree from whence he had previously obtained the half-sword, but when he emerged this time, he held a long, coiled rope. He gave the rope to me and went to Tadark's horse.

"We're not going to be fighting today, if that's what you wish to ask," Narian volunteered, guessing my thoughts, and managing with his simple statement to fill me with dread.

"Then what *are* we doing?" I queried apprehensively as he stripped the saddle and pad from the horse's back.

Tadark's body went rigid and his eyebrows dove toward his nose in a scowl, which Narian ignored. After putting the saddle on the ground, Narian grabbed the reins, pulling them from my bodyguard's grasp, and led the horse toward me.

"Surely women in Cokyri don't ride horses," I hedged, hoping I was wrong about his intentions.

"The woman who raised me is one of the best riders in our Kingdom," he told me, and I noted that this was only the second time he had referred to someone who had been present during his childhood. I was too absorbed in my own predicament, however, to give his statement further consideration.

"You don't expect me to get on that creature, do you?" I sputtered, ready to refuse with all my strength of will.

"Do you expect me to continue teaching you?" he countered, taking the rope from my hand and attaching it to the horse's bridle.

I frowned, not liking where this was heading.

"I... do."

"Then I suggest you get on the horse." There was the slightest trace of humor in his voice.

He tied the reins together and slipped them over the animal's neck, laying them upon its withers. The horse was a dark bay, with a black mane and tail, and although it stood calmly enough, I was certain there was an evil gleam in its large brown eyes. It snorted and pawed the ground as if to substantiate my belief.

"I don't particularly like horses," I said, though I sensed there was nothing I could do to deter him.

I gazed at him almost pleadingly, but he simply stood beside the bay, absentmindedly patting its neck, his steely eyes commanding me. With a deep breath, I reluctantly acquiesced and stepped up to the beast, then waited for him to lift me onto its back.

He did no such thing. He simply bent his knee toward me while holding the reins under the horse's chin, offering his leg as a step so that I could mount by myself. Even though it seemed to me that the animal had grown incredibly large in the last few seconds my pride would not let me back down. If Narian thought I could mount this beast by myself, then I would not prove him wrong. I put my left foot on his leg and hoisted myself upward, balancing a moment before proceeding.

"Take hold of the mane," he instructed, and I did as I was told, wrapping my fingers into my mount's coarse hair. Surprisingly, I managed to jump up on the first try, though I landed on my stomach across the horse's back. I fought to avoid sliding downward, employing my full strength so that I was finally able to swing my right leg over the beast and sit upright.

I beamed triumphantly at my accomplishment, even though Tadark, who was standing at the edge of the clearing near the saddle, gazed askance at me. I ignored him, looking instead at Narian, who was shaking his head in mild amusement.

He began to lead the horse, and before I knew it had extended the rope so that the bay was walking briskly around him in large circles.

"Sit up straight, but don't stiffen," Narian said to me, his voice light and calming. "You can let go of the mane. I promise you won't fall."

I relinquished the mane, which I had been clinging to quite tightly, and rested my hands on my thighs. I began to think myself silly for having been so fearful of riding, feeling more secure now that I had mounted on my own and was sitting on the back of the moving animal without having suffered injury.

"Now let your legs stretch down," Narian directed, falling silent when I obeyed.

As I relaxed, my hips moved with the horse's gait, and I began to think riding was an improvement over walking. Although I hated to admit it, I was actually enjoying myself and couldn't keep from smiling.

"You're doing well," Narian said to me. "You may yet become a rider."

"What else do I need to know?"

"Hold on to the mane again, and I'll show you," he said, and my anxiety reemerged.

I latched on to the horse's thick locks, but before I could question his instruction, he urged my mount into a slow trot with a soft *cluck* of his tongue.

Instinctively, I leaned forward into the animal's neck, clinging to its flowing black mane, certain I would fall. As I flopped about like a fish trapped on shore, I wanted nothing more than for my riding lesson to end.

"Sit up," Narian called. "You have to sit up straight and move with the horse, just like before."

"But that's impossible!" I cried, my voice breaking every time one of my mount's hooves connected with the ground.

"It's not impossible. You simply have to try. Now use your hands to push yourself upright."

His words might have been reassuring had I still been paying attention, but I was too petrified to comprehend, certain I would go crashing to the ground. My pride and my determination not to disappoint Narian had long since deserted me, and now surviving was the only thing upon which I concentrated.

"Alera, you're not listening to me," he said, and I was beginning to think he found me rather entertaining.

"I can't!"

Narian brought the horse to a halt and sauntered toward me, casually coiling the rope around his hand. I sat up shakily as he approached. *Maybe he's given up on me,* I thought feverishly, silently begging him to help me dismount.

He untied the end of the rope from the bit and tossed it to the side.

"Move forward," he said.

"What?"

"Move toward the neck," he repeated, speaking slowly as if he thought my awkward riding had jostled my brain.

I slid forward, disappointed that the lesson was not coming to an end. Before I could venture a guess about what he was planning, he had grabbed the mane and swung effortlessly onto the horse's back, landing behind me. Placing a hand on my waist, he pressured me to shift toward him so I would be correctly positioned on the animal's back.

He reached around me and took the reins in both hands, clucking so that the bay moved back into a trot. I was tense now for more than one reason —— the gait was no more comfortable the second time around, plus Narian was sitting so close to me that I was almost forced to rest against him.

If I was feeling flustered before, however, what he did next put me into shock. He dropped the reins, which were still tied together so they would not fall to the ground, and placed his hands upon my hips.

"You are too stiff," he said, his tone calming. "Just sink into the horse's gait and let your body move with it."

With his hands he began to guide my hips into following the rhythm of the horse's legs, and warmth spread from his palms throughout my entire body.

The trot now felt much smoother and was easier to ride, and I once again had to work to suppress a smile of accomplishment. We rode in circles just as I had while Narian had been on the ground, the horse responding simply to the pressure he applied to its sides with his legs. He turned our mount around to trot in the other direction, the quickness of the animal's motion startling me, but with his hands resting steadily on my hips, I was not frightened.

"This isn't so tricky after all," I announced, proud of my new abilities.

"I'm glad you feel that way because we have one last lesson today."

I didn't know whether to be pleased or apprehensive. "And what lesson is that?"

He gave a short laugh and then released my hips to wrap his right arm around my waist. Without warning, he pulled me sharply to the left so that we toppled off the horse, and I shrieked in alarm as the ground came up to meet us.

Narian twisted so that I landed mostly on top of him, my cry stuck in my throat due to the jolt of the impact. I was too dazed to react for a moment, then scrambled to my feet, horrified, for my position on top of him was hardly proper.

"What sort of lesson was that?" I shrilly demanded.

I could scarcely believe that after he had *promised* me I wouldn't fall, he had deliberately made me do so. I was too flabbergasted to be angry, though that emotion would likely emerge soon enough.

Narian had propped himself up on his elbow and, to my astonishment, he began to laugh. His face was alight, and he looked like a different person altogether, his cheeks slightly flushed with happiness, his blue eyes bright and unguarded. My anger and incredulity were shut out for an instant as I saw a genuine smile grace his features for the first time since I had known him.

"You're... laughing," I said, strangely not offended by the fact that he was clearly laughing at me. Instead, I was curiously touched. He had always hidden his feelings, and I felt privileged that I was the one around whom he felt he could drop his cold pretenses.

The smile faded, and he came to his feet. He regarded me almost fondly for a moment before his countenance became shielded, as if his sudden display of emotion had been a mistake.

"Now that you know you can handle a fall," he said simply, "you'll be less worried about it in the future."

My attention was drawn by Tadark's outraged stomping. He advanced on Narian, stopping directly in front of him, his left hand resting on the hilt of his sword.

"Get away from the Princess!" he barked, though the distance I had created between myself and Narian when I had leapt up was several feet, and no attempt had been made to close that gap.

Narian's face did not change, except that his eyebrows went up in amusement, as Tadark, posturing like a child in the throes of a temper tantrum, began to berate him fiercely.

"This is so vastly improper I can barely stand it! Women in breeches, women on horseback! And a Princess, no less! I don't know what you were thinking —— she could have been injured! She could have died! Your behavior is reprehensible." Rounding on me, he added, "Both of you! I don't care what you say, Princess, and I no longer care whether I lose my post over this or not —— no more of these *lessons*! You could have been hurt! Not to mention how horribly unbecoming it is for a Lady of the Royal Family to be... to be..."

He gestured violently with his hand to indicate my appearance, his face red, jaw clenched and eyes bulging, unable to find the correct descriptive words.

"And you," he said, pointing an accusatory finger at Narian, "were sitting much too close to her!"

Tadark marched over to his not-so-lively steed, which was contentedly munching grass, and roughly snatched its reins. He led it over to where I had mounted and tossed on the saddle, fastening it with a vengeance.

"We're going back," he pronounced, leaving no room for argument.

I shot Narian a rueful look, hoping Tadark had not offended him, but he showed no reaction, simply following my blatantly antagonistic bodyguard and his horse. I knew that I should be outraged by Narian's conduct, but instead I resented Tadark for interrupting us and ending the lesson.

We stopped halfway back so that I could change clothes,

then continued on our way. We reached the edge of the forest just as Miranna and Semari, bored with berry picking, were beginning to look for us.

"Oh, there you are," Miranna said, her eyes flitting from me to Narian suggestively. "Where were you?"

"We went for a walk," I explained smoothly.

"With Tadark's horse?"

I motioned toward my guard, implying he was the reason the horse had accompanied us.

We sat in the shade to eat some of the delicious raspberries and blackberries that Miranna and Semari had picked, then the younger girls scrambled into the buggy and we packed the baskets around their feet. I winced as I climbed up to sit next to Halias on the hard wooden front seat. Horseback riding, or perhaps falling, had made me quite sore.

"Is anything wrong, Princess?" Halias asked at my sharp intake of breath, a hint of concern in his eyes.

"No, I'm fine. Picking berries was just more strenuous than I expected it would be." The dubious glance he gave me was a reminder that he was well aware of my failure to participate in the activity.

XIX

Sees All and Tells All

e stayed a short while at Koranis's home before beginning what, for me, was a wholly unpleasant trip back to the Palace, as the jostling inherent in the buggy ride did nothing for my aches. Miranna looked inquisitively at me several times but did not dare press me for information given the proximity of our bodyguards and with a Palace Guard as our driver. Upon our arrival, I retreated, exhausted, to my rooms, instructing Sahdienne to prepare my bath. I was taking a soothing soak in the warm water when there was a faint knock on the door to my quarters.

I would have sent my maid to answer, but I had dismissed her after she had readied my bath, and Tadark was off duty. I waited, hoping my would-be visitor would simply leave, but the knock was repeated with more insistence. I hurriedly slipped on my nightgown to pad through the parlor and open the door myself, certain of whom I would find on the other side.

Miranna sprang across the threshold, seized my hand, and dragged me into my bedroom, settling herself upon the bed. I laboriously lowered myself to sit beside her, my muscles stiff and sore, knowing what she wished to discuss.

"So tell me what you were *really* doing today," she said with a grin.

"You probably wouldn't believe me if I did," I replied with a quiet laugh.

"Try me."

"All right, I was given my first horseback riding lesson."

Miranna gasped, wide-eyed. "Well, that's unexpected."

"It was for me as well."

She smiled slyly, romance obviously on her mind. "Well, is Lord Narian a good teacher?"

My cheeks pinked as I recalled the unexplainable pleasure I had felt when Narian had been sitting behind me on the horse's back.

"Can I assume then that you've been enjoying your lessons?" she teased, reading me with ease.

Hoping to save myself from further embarrassment, I said lightly, "They're quite unlike anything I've experienced before."

"Sounds to me like Steldor may have acquired some competition."

Miranna's smile faded and her face fell, for she knew Steldor was not a good topic to broach around me, but she could not take back the words.

"With or without competition, Steldor has no chance of winning my affections," I crossly declared, my detestation for my suitor gaining control of my tongue.

"Have you spoken to him since... we were together in the garden?"

"No, nor do I have any desire to speak with him. I'd prefer he keep his distance."

If possible, Miranna's face fell even further, her eyes dropping to the cream-colored spread atop my bed. I understood then that she viewed herself as at least partly responsible for my negative feelings toward Steldor, perhaps thinking she had come between us. I immediately regretted having entered into the subject, not only for my sake, but for hers as well.

"My objections to Steldor originated long before the incident in the garden. You are not responsible for the way I feel about him," I gently reminded her.

She raised her head, and I patted her hand encouragingly, which was enough to reawaken her playful mood.

"And do you have objections to Narian?" she cajoled.

I mentally revisited my rationale for why Narian could not be counted among my suitors —— he was too young, although in truth the youthfulness of his face was belied by the lack of childishness in his manner. I could not fathom what kind of upbringing would compel someone to act so much older than his years. And then there was the fact that we had learned next to nothing about his past. I had a difficult time placing my trust in someone about whom so little was known.

But today I had seen a different side of Narian. I had glimpsed within him someone to whom I could relate, perhaps someone I could befriend. But just as quickly as that part of him had emerged, it had vanished. I sighed as I tried to figure out how best to express my thoughts.

"I don't know how to feel when I'm around him. I've spent quite some time with him now, but yet he won't let me see who he really is. He is always so serious, so aloof and distant. Today was the first time he truly relaxed, and it was only for a fleeting moment."

"What happened today?" Miranna queried, and I realized I had not shared any details of the day's visit.

"I fell off the horse," I said, knowing there was no way to make that particular event sound more dignified. "And he actually laughed."

For some reason, I did not want to tell Miranna that Narian had been on the horse with me and had, in reality, pulled me from its back.

"You weren't hurt, were you?"

"No, just my pride. But in that moment, Narian seemed so open —— I had never seen him like that before. I couldn't help but feel something for him."

"Feel what?" Miranna asked, for once genuinely curious and with no implication of romance.

"I don't know," I said, the truth gnawing at my insides. "It's all so confusing."

My sister's sly tone returned. "Do you find any other young man likewise confusing?"

"No, he's very unique."

She smiled sweetly.

"What?" I demanded, irked by the way that smile suggested she knew more than I did.

"I've never heard you talk about anyone this way before," she giggled, and I could not contradict her. "You may as well accept it, Alera —— you have another suitor."

Before I could respond, Miranna hopped off the bed to bid me a cheerful good night, then pranced from the room. A moment later, I heard her exit my quarters, noisily closing the parlor door, leaving me alone with my tangled thoughts.

————

The following morning when Tadark came on duty, he brought with him a message that we were to report to the Captain of the Guard's office. I knew that Cannan would demand to hear about my visits with Narian, and as we walked the corridors, I tried frantically to decide what details I could relate. I was unwilling to divulge most of what I had told Miranna, for the information was either too personal or too objectionable.

We arrived at Cannan's office much sooner than I would have liked, my mind still in turmoil. The last time I had been in this office I had felt as though I were under interrogation, and I was not looking forward to another round of questions. All such worries flew from me, however, when I saw Destari standing in Cannan's office near his desk. Destari had not been involved in any of my visits, so I did not think the Captain could be planning to discuss Narian.

Cannan bade me to sit in the same chair I had occupied during our previous meeting, and I felt a twinge of unease. Tadark did not follow me all the way into the room but faltered by the door as if he were not permitted to cross the threshold.

"You are dismissed, Lieutenant," the Captain said, and Tadark departed.

My brows knit together, then Cannan turned his attention to me.

"Destari is replacing Tadark as your personal bodyguard. I assume this will be a satisfactory arrangement?"

I nodded, but could not stifle my curiosity. "Why is Tadark being replaced?"

I had known that problems would result if the Lieutenant carried out his threat to put a stop to my "lessons" but had never seriously believed he might be dismissed from his post due to my activities.

"He asked to be reassigned. He informed me that personal conflicts had arisen that were compromising his ability to protect you."

A sinking feeling seemed to push me further into the seat of the hard chair, and my pulse hammered painfully in my temples. Tadark had spoken to his Captain. How much did Cannan actually know? Was he aware of the things Narian had been teaching me? And if I withheld that information, would I be caught lying to the Captain of the Guard?

I swallowed painfully but said nothing, hoping neither Cannan nor Destari would notice how overwrought I had become. Thankfully, the Captain did not leave me waiting for long.

"You've been to Koranis's estate several times over the past few weeks," he proceeded in his businesslike manner. "What can you tell me?"

I stalled before replying for as long as I dared, knowing I was risking a rebuke, then said, "Narian doesn't say much, especially about Cokyri. I've learned very little."

"I asked you *what* you have learned, not *how much* you have learned. I will judge the importance of the information myself."

I did not think Cannan was angry —— he just did not allow anyone to evade him. Clearly, I was going to have to tell him something.

"Narian talked a little about his military background," I reported, nervously entwining my fingers. "He told me he began training when he was six."

The Captain said nothing. I had expected some reaction from him, but his commanding expression told me that he knew there was more information to be garnered. I squirmed inside, as his unmistakable power, coupled with his dark hair and eyes, made him tremendously intimidating.

"I don't know the nature of his training," I continued, hoping to satisfy Cannan without having to reveal too much. "But he gave the impression that he was not sent to a school, at least not at that age. He spoke of one teacher, but the man was not his Cokyrian father. He also made reference to a woman having raised him, but he did not call her mother." As I relayed this information, something else came to mind. "In fact, he has never mentioned a mother, a father, or a family in Cokyri."

Cannan nodded. When I did not speak further, he stood to dismiss me.

"Very well then. You will no longer meet with Narian as you have been these past weeks, although more *conventional* visits are, of course, permitted."

I froze, momentarily staggered. There was no denying that Tadark had told his Captain *everything*. My reaction was not only due to Tadark's tattling, however. It was actually, to a much greater extent, due to Cannan's lack of disapproval. The fact that he had not thought it necessary to specifically address my unorthodox excursions gave me hope that he had also considered it unnecessary for my father to be informed of them. He simply intended to make the point that nothing escaped his knowledge, and in that he had succeeded.

"Thank you," I said humbly as I rose to my feet, knowing Cannan would catch my true meaning.

———

Later that afternoon, Miranna sought me out in a state of poorly restrained excitement. She rushed into the tearoom on the main floor, where I was sitting by the bay window, warming my hands on my cup and watching the rain fall in the expansive West Courtyard, my pensive mood perfectly complemented by the weather.

"We've received an invitation to Semari's birthday celebration! And it's just two weeks away!" Miranna announced, waving a scroll of parchment beneath my nose.

My expression mirrored her enthusiasm, but for an entirely different reason. I had been more disappointed than I had cared to admit that my meetings with Narian had effectively ended. Though I knew an occasional visit would be permitted, Cannan had deprived me of the only available justification to see the young man that would not draw questions from my father. Not to mention I would now have to deal with Destari's much more assertive presence. I knew that I would be permitted no latitude while he was my bodyguard, whether or not he had been informed of my recent activities. This celebration, as I saw it, would provide me with a chance to see Narian in a different but completely legitimate context, one that would arouse no one's suspicion.

I took the invitation from Miranna and unrolled it, glancing over the details. The event was to be held on October twelfth, with activities and games such as tag, footraces, and apple-bobbing in the afternoon, followed by an evening of feasting and dancing. As Semari was reaching the age of fifteen, this would be an elaborate affair. At fifteen, young women in Hytanica came of courting age, although marriage before the age of eighteen was generally discouraged.

Miranna gleefully snatched the invitation from my hand when I had finished and skipped out the door.

"I simply can't wait!" she called as she disappeared from sight.

———

The two weeks until Semari's party flew by, as preparations for the upcoming Harvest Festival generated a maelstrom of frenzied activities throughout Hytanica. It was exhilarating to simply roam through the city and observe the changes as merchants and businessmen positioned themselves to earn a sizable profit off the large number of visitors that were certain to attend.

The site for the Faire was the grassy area that was the location for Market Day. Here, additional tents for vendors had been set up and small stages were being erected at intervals among the tents for use by performers. The shopfronts in the Market District were being cleaned, and I noted several freshly painted signboards identifying some of the establishments. The taverns, inns, and public bathhouses in the Business District were also being readied for a large influx of guests.

The land just west of the Faire sloped down to the flat military training field that would be the locus of the Tournament. The field was south of the sprawling Military Complex that lay to the west of the Palace. Both the Military Academy and the Military Base that made up the Complex used the field for maneuvers, although it was being marked out at this time to serve the needs of the upcoming competitions.

When the day of Semari's birthday was upon us, Miranna and I traveled in luxury in an enclosed carriage to Koranis's estate as part of a large contingent from the Palace. My parents led our caravan in their private Royal Coach, thinking it probable they would return to the Palace at an earlier time than their daughters, and a third carriage bore the King's and Queen's personal assistants. A dozen Elite Guards, including Destari and Halias, rode alongside our caravan on horseback, while twenty-some Palace Guards brought up the rear. As my parents were not particularly interested in the games mentioned in the invitation, we left the Palace so that we would reach our destination in the late afternoon, just before the feasting was to begin.

The weather had become noticeably cooler and the days noticeably shorter, which encouraged the leaves to fall from the trees and put additional spring into the horses' trots. Given these seasonal changes, the carriages had been stocked with fur throws and lanterns for use during the journey home.

Upon our arrival, grooms came to take charge of our horses, and servants escorted us to the grounds behind the house, where a large, multicolored, open-sided tent in which the feast would be served had been erected, and a planked floor had been laid for dancing. As we ambled toward the tent, I could see that long rows of tables had been arranged inside, with one raised table at the far side, perpendicular to the rest, at which the Royal Family and the hosts would sit. The high table was draped in royal blue cloth, and several of the Kingdom's royal-blue-and-gold flags fluttered behind. Cooks were busy setting out dishes laden with food on a table draped in white linen at the near end that would be used for serving. While some guests were milling about the area, most had strolled down the gentle slope to watch or participate in the variety of games taking place at the forest's edge.

Koranis, resplendent in all his finery, and Alantonya, a more understated match, came to greet us. I glanced around as my parents talked with their hosts, but I could not find Narian. I did not dare ask Koranis and Alantonya about his whereabouts, lest the inquiry be considered rude in light of the fact that this occasion was in Semari's honor. Such an inquiry might also have piqued my father's interest.

As Miranna and I walked the grounds in search of her best friend, I continued to sweep the crowd for her older brother. As it turned out, Semari located us and came bounding our way with a large and inviting grin upon her face.

"I'm so glad you could come!" she exclaimed, clutching Miranna's hands. Before my sister could return her greeting, Semari had begun to drag her down the hill toward the place where another round of horseshoe toss was beginning. "You'll never guess who's here!"

I looked toward the group of boys and girls surrounding the area designated for the game and saw among them the young man with reddish-brown hair whom my sister had come to favor. Clinging to his arm was a boy about half his size and half his age, presumably his brother.

Semari and Miranna joined the group, Miranna smoothing the skirt of her dark green gown in anticipation of talking with Temerson. She also attempted unsuccessfully to capture the curly strands of hair that fell across her cheeks, having escaped the ribbon that loosely gathered her locks at the nape of her neck.

I was attired in a flared deep blue velvet gown with a square-necked white satin brocade stomacher. The shoulders were puffed and slashed, and the sleeves were tightly laced from elbow to wrist, extending over the back of my hands to a point. My dark hair had been swept up off my shoulders and was encircled by a delicate tiara consisting of two parallel silver bands set with alternating sapphires and diamonds. Although I knew Narian did not necessarily appreciate the way Hytanican women adorned themselves, I had taken special care with my appearance this evening.

I had not gone with Semari and Miranna, for I knew their chattering would center on the male species, a subject I did not want to discuss. Looking back toward the house, I saw that Cannan and Faramay had arrived and were approaching my parents, evidently having elected to forgo the games just as we had. I had already determined that the man I reviled was not currently on the grounds, and his absence from his parents' side gave me reason to believe he had chosen not to attend.

Most of the guests had gathered at the bottom of the hill, and I went to join them, my parents and their friends following soon after. I did not spend much time greeting those around me, for I wanted to find Narian. I scanned the area and saw Cannan break away from my father and mother to walk in my direction, leaving Faramay behind. Confused as to what he could possibly want with me, I glanced over my shoulder and realized he had made eye contact with Destari, who stood approximately ten feet away.

Destari did not move when his Captain arrived. Judging from their serious demeanors and hushed tones, the issue about which they spoke was of some importance. Unfortunately, even though they were not far from me, the incessant prattle of the people in the area made it difficult to distinguish a single word, regardless of how hard I strained my ears.

Their conversation complete, Destari and Cannan walked toward the edge of the forest. While I had not expected my bodyguard to stay at my side all evening, given the vast number

of guards who had accompanied my parents and were now scattered about the estate, the reason for his departure had seemed
official, and therefore worth knowing. My curiosity burning, I
determined to find out where Cannan was going and what was
so important that he needed to have Destari accompany him.

XX

Never Without
a Weapon

I furtively followed Destari and Cannan toward the tree line, weaving my way through the guests. Though they walked purposefully, I was unsure of their destination until I noticed Narian, dressed once more in dark colors, leaning against the trunk of a large maple tree. Narian had an uncanny ability to hide in plain sight and thus pass undetected by almost everyone, including me, but apparently not by the Captain of the Guard. The sixteen-year-old was indifferently observing the celebratory activities but shifted his gaze to Destari and Cannan the moment they began to approach him, as though he had been solely monitoring their movements.

I could see no harm in what Narian was doing and did not understand why Cannan would want to meet with him. I found myself worried for the young man's sake, but he moved away from the forest's edge and toward the two soldiers, no sign of misgiving in his stride. This time, I inched closer so that I was on the fringe of the crowd, enabling me to overhear their discussion.

"I have been informed that you have quite a talent for acquiring weapons," Cannan brusquely stated. "I hear you are never without one. So, tell me, are you now armed?"

"I am," Narian replied without hesitation.

The Captain inclined his head in appreciation of receiving an answer as straightforward as his query, then his eyes flicked toward Narian's hip, where he would have held a sword or dagger, finally moving down to check his boots.

"I see no weapons," he pronounced, with a measure of disbelief that sprang from the fact that Narian had been disarmed by his own men when he had been taken prisoner. Still, it could not be denied that the young man had managed to acquire a weapon on at least three occasions.

"I have them," Narian repeated.

"Is there a problem, gentlemen?" interrupted a self-important voice I recognized as belonging to Koranis. The Baron was panting lightly, his thinning blond hair dampened with perspiration, as he hurried over to the two men confronting Narian.

"Are you aware that your son has been impermissibly obtaining weapons?" Cannan asked, without taking his eyes off the boy standing before him.

"Surely you overstate the situation," Koranis blustered indignantly. "You well know that he took a dagger off my person several weeks ago and was duly punished. There have been no other such instances."

Cannan gave a small shake to his head and Koranis rounded on his son.

"What weapons are these? Where have you been getting them?"

Narian shrugged, decidedly unruffled. "Some are my own. Others are yours."

Koranis's affronted frown deepened, and he looked from Destari to Cannan as if trying to assess their reactions.

"That's impossible," he sputtered, evidently concluding that he needed to defend himself. "I keep all my weapons in a locked trunk in my bedroom."

"Perhaps you need better locks," Narian responded with not-so-subtle disrespect.

"This is absurd!" Koranis blustered, face shading toward maroon, insulted by the fact that Cannan and Destari did not doubt the young man.

Narian ignored the Baron, presumably deeming his father no longer worthy of his time, and addressed Cannan, his tone disdainful.

"You can hardly expect the rabbit to keep up with the fox."

Koranis let out an offended breath, too appalled by his son's audacity to formulate a response. Fortunately for everyone involved, the Baron did not see Cannan's nod toward Narian that indicated he understood his point.

"We will be requiring a location away from your guests," the Captain informed Koranis. "Narian was about to show us the weapons he carries."

Narian's eyebrows lifted, as if he were trying to recall when he had so agreed, but he did not protest.

The Baron huffed a few times, unaccustomed to taking orders while on his own property and unquestionably irked that Cannan had not called his son Kyenn. But he chose not to make his complaints known.

"We can go around to the front of the house," he indicated with some measure of grace, and began to lead the way.

Cannan, Destari, and Narian followed, while I trailed a fair distance behind, praying I would not be discovered. The four men reached the top of the hill, and I allowed a few minutes to pass before pursuing them, knowing that once I left behind the bantering guests, my movements would be easier to detect. When I felt relatively safe, I sidled up to the side of the house and peered around the corner into the front yard.

"Any weapons you may have in the home are of interest to me as well," the Captain was saying. "Go and retrieve them."

Narian stood a few feet in front of the others, facing them. "None of my own weapons are in the house. I could, however, retrieve Koranis's for you."

"That won't be necessary," Cannan said dismissively, ignoring once more the disrespect for his father in the young man's voice. "Well?" he prompted.

"It would be best to demonstrate my weaponry," Narian stated. "I need a target."

Cannan motioned to an oak tree thirty feet from where I was hiding. As the group of men moved toward it, I jerked back to avoid being seen, but to my mortification, did not move fast enough.

"Princess, you may as well come out," Destari called irritably, and my heart began to pound in anticipation of how irate Cannan would be with me.

I stepped out, knowing there was no use in pretending that my presence by the house had been a coincidence, and approached the men, my eyes on the Captain of the Guard, trying to gauge his reaction. To my relief, he turned away without a word, and it occurred to me that he saw no point in issuing an order for me to leave, because he could not ensure I would obey without assigning Destari to escort me.

I stood beside my bodyguard, the house to our backs and the tree on the right, roughly twenty feet away. Narian watched Cannan for an indication he should commence the demonstration, displaying no particular reaction to my unorthodox arrival. At the Captain's nod, he deftly reached into the pouch hanging from his belt and secured a small handful of powder, which he threw to the ground before us.

The flash was blinding. My hands flew to my face as I stumbled backward, and I would have fallen had Destari not seized me and pulled me into the protection of his arms. As I squinted through my fingers at the thick swirling smoke, I began to feel dizzy. The scent of the substance threatened to choke me, though it did not taste or smell exactly like smoke. It was sweeter, and with every breath, my eyes grew more unfocused.

The haze finally began to clear, but my mind remained clouded for a few moments longer. When I could think coherently again, I saw Koranis shaking his head back and forth, and Cannan scanning the area, for Narian had taken advantage of our disoriented state to slip from view. Then we heard a resounding *thunk*, and our heads snapped toward the tree where a knife now protruded at eye level.

Destari loosened his hold on me and we all turned to look at Narian.

"If you want to examine the dagger, I have another," Narian commented, arresting Cannan in midstride on his walk toward the tree to retrieve the weapon. The young man knelt down and adeptly extracted a second knife from one of his boot heels. Cannan, having reversed direction, held out a hand, and Narian extended the grip of the weapon to him. I watched tensely as the Captain checked the blade, which was relatively narrow and only about six inches in length but designed with jagged tines along its edge to tear flesh to shreds. Narian walked to the tree and jerked the other dagger out, slipping it into his boot heel as he waited for Cannan's reaction.

"So the thicker soles on your boots allow for a hidden sheath for the dagger?" he asked, obviously intrigued.

Choosing to let his actions speak for him, Narian took the second knife from Cannan and returned it to its hiding place.

"And this powder —— let me see it," the Captain commanded.

Narian untied the pouch from his belt and passed it to him without objection. Cannan opened it and removed a small amount of powder, rubbing it cautiously between his fingers. The substance sparked dangerously, but there was not enough of it in his hand to create the same effect we had just witnessed.

"Is every soldier in Cokyri equipped with similar weaponry?" Cannan inquired, a lift in his eyebrow the only indication that Hytanica's military was not familiar with weapons such as these.

"Not everyone."

The Captain waited for Narian to elaborate, but when he did not, handed the pouch to Destari for further examination.

"Other than the weapons we took from you when you were arrested and that are in my possession, have we now seen your arms in their entirety?"

"No," Narian replied shamelessly.

For the first time, the Captain of the Guard looked to have lost his patience. Narian was not being particularly forthcoming, and I knew from personal experience that when Cannan asked something of you, he expected you to comply, and to do so without delay.

"Then show us whatever else you have," he ordered, his jaw rigid.

Narian held Cannan's eyes for a moment, then reached toward his belt, lightly brushing the dark stitching with which it was adorned. He pinched the end of one of the stitches between his thumb and forefinger and withdrew a sharp, slender dart. I held my breath, terrified of that tiny needle.

"Poisoned darts," he explained, holding the barb up for all to see. "If I removed this wax from the tip and pierced your flesh, you would be dead within minutes."

A look flashed between Cannan and Destari, and I heard Koranis murmur anxiously, "God save us."

"And is there an antidote?" Cannan asked, holding out his hand to take the dart.

Narian shook his head. "The poison affects the body too swiftly for an antidote to be effective."

"And you wear these next to your own skin?"

"Cokyrian warriors are willing to live dangerously and, if necessary, to die as a result," he confirmed without emotion.

"And are you among them?"

Narian met the Captain's commanding eyes but did not answer.

"I will keep these items for now," Cannan said, passing the dart to Destari. "I would like our alchemists to examine the substances."

The Elite Guard carefully wrapped the dart in Narian's soft leather pouch before tucking both into the shaft of his own boot. The Captain turned on his heel to stride toward the rear of the house, an exceedingly troubled Koranis a pace behind. Stopping abruptly, Cannan once more faced Narian.

"You will report to my office at the Palace in two days. Our military would be well served by learning as much as we can from you about Cokyrian weaponry and fighting techniques. I will return all of your weapons to you at that time, including those taken upon your arrest."

Cannan turned to Koranis in response to the Baron's sharp intake of breath.

"Your son has had the opportunity to kill a number of my guards and your family several times over, not to mention certain members of the Royal Family. As he has shown no inclination to harm anyone, I believe he can be trusted."

Koranis, his face drained of color and his blue eyes wide with alarm, unwisely attempted to challenge the Captain of the Guard's decision.

"That is easy for you to say, as he does not live in your house! I want him off my property, *tonight*!"

Cannan glared at Koranis, and I could see a rage building within him that was entirely out of proportion to the stated demand. He stepped menacingly toward the Baron, who recoiled until he collided with the side wall of the house. Moving directly in front of the cowering man, Cannan leaned toward him, supporting himself with one hand upon the wall.

"You are pathetic, an empty imitation of a father," he spat, glowering down at Koranis with pure loathing in his voice. "It is extraordinary that Narian is alive, a miracle that he somehow returned to Hytanica. There is no justice in the fact that of every grieving father in the Kingdom whose son was stolen by the Cokyrians, it is yours who found a way home. You, who would thrust aside this blessing for which the rest of us would kill. You fail to appreciate the gift you have been given."

Koranis cringed and tried to slide sideways away from the Captain, but Cannan grabbed him by his dress coat, almost lifting him off the ground.

"The sight of you sickens me," he seethed, the controlled quality of his deep voice making him all the more terrifying. "I would give anything for it to have been my son who returned. I would have embraced him regardless of how he had been raised or by whom."

With that, Cannan released the quaking man and stepped back from him, although his deadly glare did not abate. It was a testament to the level of fear that gripped Koranis at the thought of Narian's continued residence within his home that he dared speak again.

"I have a wife and four younger children to protect," he blubbered. "I cannot run the risk that you may be wrong."

When the only discernible reaction Cannan showed to Koranis's statements was a crease in his brow, the Baron slowly straightened.

"Take him with you, enroll him in the Military Academy, do whatever you think best. Just keep him away from me and my family."

Despite his attempt to regain his poise, Koranis was clearly pleading. I inched closer to Destari, concern for the Baron welling within me. I thought it entirely possible from Cannan's threatening posture that he might do the man harm. I glanced skyward in prayerful thanks when the Captain, shaking his head in disgust, took another step away, seeming to recognize that he needed to keep Koranis out of his reach.

Gesturing toward Narian, Cannan admonished, "Like it or not, you have an obligation to the boy. If you won't let him live here, then I will move him into your city residence."

He paused, and when he continued, there was a hint of resignation in his words.

"I know what it is like to have a son who is headstrong, who, like yours, has taken my weapons and horses without permission and who has cost me innumerable sleepless nights. Still, I would not relinquish a single moment of time with him."

I could once again hear anger rising in Cannan, although he did not make a move toward the Baron.

"You, on the other hand, have not even tried to reach out to your son. I feel no compassion for you and have but one regret —— that I ever entrusted him to your custody."

Cannan looked almost yearningly at Narian for a long moment, and I thought I saw a flicker of the same emotion in the young man's eyes.

"You act as though Narian is a disappointment, when it is, in fact, he who has been cheated. Narian deserves a better father than you."

Cannan turned and strode down the hill. Without waiting to see what I would do, Destari took hold of my arm above the elbow and pulled me alongside him to follow the Captain, leaving Koranis alone to face his son. If not for Destari, I would likely have remained rooted in place, reeling from shock. I struggled to comprehend what I could only interpret as a revelation on Cannan's part that he had lost a son to the Cokyrians.

I regained some semblance of my voice as Destari and I joined the guests who had gathered at the top of the hill and were entering the tent for the feast.

"Did Cannan have a second son?"

Destari drew me aside, unhappy with my question, and I didn't know if I would receive a lecture or an answer.

"Yes. Like a number of others in Hytanica, the Captain had an infant son who was abducted and killed by the Cokyrians, and whose body was among those returned for burial by our enemy. Now, let the matter rest." Well acquainted with my persistence when my interest was roused, he added, "Don't ever raise such a question around Baroness Faramay. She never fully recovered from the ordeal."

I nodded but continued to cling to my bodyguard's side for a few moments longer, quietly absorbing this startling information. How different would Steldor's life have been if his brother had survived? I couldn't imagine my life without Miranna. A wave of sympathy crashed over me for Cannan, Faramay, and even Steldor, although he probably had few memories of his younger sibling.

As I thought of the Captain of the Guard's face while he had harangued Koranis, I suddenly understood the reason Cannan had, right from the beginning, treated Narian so well, and so differently, from our other prisoners. Was this also why he had so readily taken Galen, a fatherless boy, into his heart?

And what of Narian? Was he, at the age of sixteen, already a Cokyrian warrior? His words had seemed to suggest as much. I shivered at thought of the weapons I now knew he had carried concealed on his person the entire time he had been in Hytanica. I remembered the first time I had met him, when Miranna, Semari, and I had briefly eluded our bodyguards, and recalled that even then he had been wearing his boots and belt —— the only articles of his clothing that Cannan had let him retain. I once again felt as if I did not know him at all. The only certainty that resonated in my mind was that there were more things in the world of which to be afraid than I had imagined.

As my thoughts continued to whirl, I became conscious that Destari was observing me, a measure of concern upon his face. I smiled feebly at him before venturing away from his side to enter the dining area.

XXI

THE GREATER SIN

y appetite had diminished almost to the point of nonexistence, but I joined the line of people at the serving table and allowed my plate to be filled with food, for it would have been impolite to refuse the elaborate feast. As I exited the serving line, my eyes fell upon Steldor and Galen, and my flickering hope that they would not attend was extinguished. They were standing at the end of one of the long dining tables, their plates of food forgotten in front of them on the wooden tabletop. Galen, wearing a white shirt and black trousers, was flipping a dagger between his right hand and his left, in a manner that I had come to associate with Steldor. Steldor stood by his friend, one booted foot upon the table's bench, resting his elbow upon his knee.

Steldor was wearing a black leather jerkin with split sleeves that showed the white shirt he wore beneath, and black breeches. Given my new curiosity about weapons, I took in the silver sword at his side. The grip of the weapon was wrapped in black leather overlaid with silver wire, and its pommel was set with rubies that might have given it a sophisticated look were it not for the winged and barbed guard that gave notice of its power. His dark apparel suited his dark features and gave him a mysterious and brooding look. In spite of my jaded feelings toward him, and my subdued mood, he took my breath away. Just then he glanced at me, only to avert his eyes. Although I liked to think myself too indifferent toward him to care, his reaction surprised me, and I was pleased to discover that I held some sway over him.

I held my head high and chose a path through the tent toward the front table at which my family would dine. My parents were already seated and were being attended by servants. My route was calculated to take me between the tables that were furthest from Steldor and Galen, so I would not have to risk a conversation with either of them. As I proceeded, however, I saw my strategy spoiled.

Galen moved away from Steldor and began to walk toward me, coming down the same aisle that I had entered, but from the opposite direction, so I would have no way of avoiding him without making blatant that such was my desire. I did not know Galen well, but any friend of Steldor's was not likely to be held in high regard by me. As he approached, he absently played with the hilt of his sword, then bowed respectfully, his wavy ash-brown hair shifting fluidly with his movement.

"Princess Alera, may I guide you to your table?"

I was not inclined to trust him, knowing there had to be a purpose behind his sudden attentiveness. But I consented, permitting him to take the plate from my hands and carry it for me. It was a short walk to the high table, so whatever he intended to say or do, he would have to accomplish it with a measure of haste.

"How are you finding the evening?" Galen asked genially.

"I am glad for the respite from my usual duties." Unable to resist putting forth the insinuation that I was content to maintain my distance from Steldor, I continued, "I have found the festivities to be quite entertaining and the companionship *thus far* to be quite pleasant."

Galen caught my implication, and his tone became more serious as we arrived at the table to stand only a few feet from where my father was seated.

"I'm afraid Lord Steldor has found it quite the opposite, My Lady, for he cannot enjoy himself until he knows he is forgiven."

I could hardly believe what I was hearing. Had Steldor actually been too cowardly to approach me to apologize? Or was such an act of contrition beneath him? Or perhaps he suspected I would refuse to listen to him but would not as readily brush Galen aside. Regardless of Steldor's motives, I knew I was being manipulated and scowled in annoyance.

Galen handed my plate to a servant who set it on the tabletop, then reached into a pouch that hung from the belt at his waist to remove a stunning silver pendant necklace. He laid it across the back of his hand to show how the silver of the pendant swirled around to cradle at its center a teardrop-shaped sapphire. The necklace was beautiful, expensive, and a perfect companion to my gown. I marveled as to how my erstwhile suitor had managed this feat. Perhaps he had purchased several necklaces with different gemstones so he would have one that matched any gown I might have worn. Or perhaps he had an informant. Knowing how infatuated the majority of the female population was with him, I had no doubt that my maid could have been charmed into revealing my planned attire.

"Steldor wishes me to give you this as a token of his affection and as an indication of his longing to mend his relationship with you." Galen proffered the necklace in such a way that anyone watching would certainly see its splendor. "He would be honored if you would wear it tonight, but if you choose otherwise, he will accept your decision with grace and humility."

I understood the real alternatives with which Galen was presenting me. Wear the necklace, and Steldor would assume all was forgiven; refuse, and he would leave me alone for the rest of the evening. Making my choice, I gazed at Steldor for a moment, trying to first tell him that I intended to decline before informing his friend of the same, but I vacillated, temporarily at a loss for words. Steldor had not moved and was atypically alone. One hand was resting on the table beside him, and he was drumming his fingers upon it absentmindedly. His expression was not haughty, nor was his stance. Rather, he looked more vulnerable than I had ever seen him in my life, as if he were actually troubling himself over the nature of the conversation Galen was having with me, and an unexpected sense of compassion swept through me. Steldor did have some fine qualities, a fact that escaped me on most occasions, for I had a difficult time seeing past his intolerable conceit. But now, with that aspect of his personality subdued, I almost wanted to make peace with him. *We might make a good couple after all*, I told myself, picturing us together. *If there were some way to contain his ego.*

As I returned my attention to Galen, my father winked at me, and I came to understand how clever and cunning the two friends could be. They had expertly executed their scheme. It would have been just as simple for Galen to give me the necklace before we'd reached the table, or to do it at a later time in the evening, but instead he had waited to be in the presence of my father, who I knew had heard the essence of our exchange. If I now refused Steldor's gift, I would not only be disappointing Steldor; I would be disappointing the King.

I bit my lower lip, resentment burning in my stomach, then assented, turning my back to Galen to permit him to fasten the pendant around my neck. I glanced once more toward Steldor, whose attention was now upon me, and saw his face brighten as

I accepted the gift. To my dismay, I also witnessed a return of his typical air of condescension.

"Thank you, My Lady," Galen said, and I scoffed internally that he was even expressing gratitude on behalf of his friend. "Steldor will greatly appreciate your gesture." Then he strode off to return to his own table.

I did not track either of the young Field Commanders further but took my seat to my mother's left. My father was beaming at me and my mother turned to admire my necklace.

"He does have exceptionally good taste," she commented in her lilting singsong manner, "and not just in jewelry."

I nodded, picking at the meat and vegetables on my plate. A short time later, I saw an ashen-faced Koranis coming toward our table, but I did not see Narian. What had happened between father and son after they had been left together in the front yard? It looked as though Narian, at least, would not partake of the feast. In truth, I was no longer certain that I wanted to see him, for his display of weapons had been harrowing. I reviewed the past couple of hours in my mind, feeling that the entire evening was spinning out of control.

I excused myself from the table after eating a few more bites and strolled out of the tent to where the musicians were setting up to play. Casting about for Miranna and Semari, I spotted them sitting on a bench along the edge of the dance floor. Judging from their rosy cheeks, they were gossiping about something. The nature of their chitchat became clear when I saw them look longingly toward a group of young men lounging in the shadows, a group that included Temerson. His brother had remained with him, although the boy was now accompanied by Zayle, Semari's younger brother, and from the jostling going on between them, it appeared a friendship had been born.

Dusk was now upon us, and torches were being lit that would, with or without the moon's assistance, bathe the dance floor in a romantic glow. As the musicians started to play, several couples moved onto the wooden planking and began to step in time with the music. I stayed on the sidelines, content to admire the graceful movements of the couples. I saw my mother glide into the midst of the other dancers, escorted by my boisterous father, and wondered whether Temerson would find the courage to ask Miranna to dance, or whether she would have to take the initiative herself. My reverie was interrupted by an altogether too familiar, and definitely unwelcome, voice.

"Would you grant me the honor of a dance, Alera?"

Steldor had stepped into place beside me, and with a slight bow, was now offering me his hand.

I did not extend mine in return but stared fixedly at the scene before me.

"Hardly," I said snippily.

Determined not to look at him, I had to imagine his reaction to my rather indecorous rejection, and tried to envision his face clouded by frustration. Galen had apologized for him, after all, and I had presumably forgiven him. So why was my mood so cold?

"You would accept my generous gift, yet deny me a simple dance?" he asked.

To that I had no answer. The necklace was magnificent and extravagant, and having taken it, I could not with a clear conscience refuse to dance with him. He seemed to read my thoughts, which in truth he had planted, and took my hand without another word.

He was an excellent dancer. He moved with such ease and grace that it was difficult for me to match him. Perhaps we could have more effortlessly moved as one had I been at all content in his arms.

Though at first we danced as would acquaintances, Steldor soon realized that many eyes were upon us and decided to publicly confirm our courtship. He drew me close, and I went rigid. He continued to dance as elegantly as before, but my movements became increasingly ungainly.

"I've learned that you've made several visits here of late," Steldor remarked, and I thought I detected an undertone of jealousy, no doubt stemming from his conjecture that I had been coming to see Narian. He did not know, of course, that his own father had commissioned me to spend so much time with Koranis's elder son.

"Tell me," he continued, maneuvering us around the dance floor, "do you tire of playing nursemaid?"

"Only when I'm with you," I retorted, indignation flaring at his jibe toward Narian.

He cocked his head at me, in neither anger nor amusement, but in some new emotion I could best interpret as consternation. The song ended, and I turned to leave, pleased that I had delivered the final blow, but he slipped his arm around my waist.

"Not so fast. We need to establish some sort of truce."

The musicians began another piece, and once more Steldor and I danced, the elegance of his movements increasingly hindered by my resistance to the pressure his hand was exerting upon my back.

Without further ado, Steldor lamented, "I don't understand you. You seem to be set wholeheartedly against me, and I don't even know what I did to garner such resentment."

I could hardly believe what I was hearing.

"You kissed my sister!"

"Before that!" he exclaimed, as if the point I had raised were irrelevant. He dropped his volume, conscious of the couples surrounding us. "Since the day we met, you've exhibited nothing but contempt toward me. What could I have done so long ago to offend you?"

I distinctly remembered my first impression of Steldor, for my opinion of him had not changed much over the years. I had been ten at the time, and he thirteen, and yet he had already possessed the ego of a young peacock.

"It's nothing you did," I hissed, dying to unleash my anger as I had in the garden in the aftermath of the Palace celebration in Narian's honor. "It's simply... who you are!"

"What does that mean?" Steldor demanded, completely baffled, and I was sure no one had ever dared to tell him there was something wrong with his character.

"It's your attitude," I admonished, the loathing he had inspired within me on numerous occasions quickly surfacing. "The way you walk, the way you talk... even the way you *breathe*."

He raised a sardonic eyebrow to tell me I could do better by way of explanation.

"Honestly, Alera, the way I breathe?"

"Even now, you're unbelievably condescending!" Though I was growing passionate in my speech, I managed to regulate my volume. "You treat everyone as if they are beneath you —— Miranna, the guard in the market, Temerson, Narian, *me*! You can't even deign to apologize for yourself, so forgive me if I'm a little disagreeable."

I tried to pull away, but he held me in place, fuming. I felt trapped, and the deadly glare he fixed upon me was most unsettling. As my discomfort grew, so did my resolve to withdraw from the dance floor, and I remained stiff and unwilling in his arms as he continued to try to dance with me.

"Damn it, Alera, you won't even let me lead!" he snapped, his voice low but heavy with rancor.

He gestured with a hand from my body to his, indicating the distance I insisted on maintaining between us.

"This dance exemplifies our entire relationship! You are more than 'a little disagreeable,' Alera. You can't conceive that anything I do has merit, is good, is right, *has potential*. At least my so-called arrogance is backed up by my actions —— I can do the things of which I claim to be capable, so I do not boast, but rather state fact. You, on the other hand, oppose me without thought or reason! Better to be justifiably arrogant than irrationally contrary. If it were not the case that we must marry in order for me to assume the Throne, as is your father's desire, I would not suffer your company, and I don't think many men would."

The second song ended, but Steldor did not release my hand. With an affectation of pleasure upon his face, he led me away from the other couples.

"Now, won't you join me at the refreshment table?" he said, with forced pleasantness in his voice as well.

Stung by his criticism, and unable to refuse his offer lest I prove his point, I let him guide me to the table, for once not fighting the arm he slid around my waist. I waited for him to bring me a glass of wine, hating that he was at least partially correct about my behavior toward him and racking my brain for a way to escape the circumstances in which I wallowed. As Steldor returned to my side, I noticed Miranna approaching him from behind, and gratitude swept through me when she tapped him on the shoulder.

"Lord Steldor, would you care to dance?" she asked, her tone a touch too sweet.

He glanced between us in annoyance, no doubt aware that Miranna's objective was to rescue me, and I feared he would turn her down.

"By all means, feel free to dance with Mira. It will, after all, give you another basis on which to compare the two of us," I goaded. "Let's see, you have flirted with us both and kissed us both. I would assume dancing with us both would be of interest as well."

His eyes darkened malevolently, then he gulped down his wine and thrust the empty goblet into my hands.

"A gentleman will always satisfy a lady's desires, even should it enable him to make such comparisons," he responded before shifting his attention to Miranna. "I am honored by your request," he said to her, bowing and offering his arm.

While I was relieved to see him walk away, I was dumbfounded by his gall, for he had intimated that both my sister and I sought his attentions. Seized by a desperate desire to leave the gathering, I located Destari and instructed him to inform the grooms that they should prepare one of the three Royal Coaches for departure. I then thanked Koranis and Alantonya for their hospitality, noting as I did so that the Baron had recovered his self-important air. Finally, I sought out my parents to let them know I was returning to the Palace. My father, in particular, looked disappointed, but he ultimately did not object. Shortly thereafter, and due in no small part to Miranna's continued insistence that Steldor dance with her, I was settled into a coach and on my way home, Destari riding his horse alongside the carriage while several additional guards followed behind.

We had not traveled far when I became aware of the sound of an approaching horse, traveling at a leisurely canter. Destari motioned for my carriage driver to halt and rode out to meet whoever had intercepted us. Only an occasional muffled snatch of conversation reached my ears, preventing me from identifying the speakers, and I began to worry that Steldor had pursued me. My disquiet was allayed a few moments later with the return of my bodyguard.

"Lord Narian is here and requests to see you, Princess."

I nodded, puzzled but not displeased, and Destari assisted me to step down from the carriage. I walked toward Narian, who had alighted from his impressive dappled gray steed to stand fifteen feet away, his eyes continually scanning the guards who were with me.

Although I knew I should be wary of him after what I had witnessed only a few hours ago, my reaction was in fact quite different. I was feeling a very pleasant light and tingly sensation at being in his presence.

"Shall we walk?" Narian invited, still holding his horse's reins and seemingly unwilling to speak in front of my guards.

"Yes," I murmured, then I turned to Destari. "Will you bring me one of those lanterns?"

I motioned to the oil lamps hanging from the front of the carriage, and he retrieved the one nearest him.

"We'll return in a short while," I promised when he handed it to me, indicating I did not want him to accompany us.

He did not object, and I could only assume that he was acquiescing due to the amount of trust Cannan had shown in Narian by allowing him to retain possession of his weapons.

"I presume our meetings, and your lessons, are at an end," Narian said when we were out of earshot of the others.

"My permission has been withdrawn," I said, unable to hide my disappointment but realizing his tone had been as heavy as mine.

With a sharp laugh he halted, and his horse shifted restlessly. "I forgot —— you need permission for everything."

I turned toward him, unsure how to respond and unable to read his mood. I held up the lantern so I could see his face, but his expression was inscrutable.

"I know you are not familiar with the types of weapons I carry," he continued, sounding for once ill at ease about the topic he was broaching. "I asked you once if you were afraid of Steldor; perhaps I should ask if you are afraid of me."

It did not take me long to answer. "Reason says I should be, but I am not."

"I would never hurt you, Alera."

His mesmerizing blue eyes held me, then he looked away, as though he'd said something improper.

"Unless you count pulling me off a horse," I jested.

I caught a flicker of amusement in Narian's eyes, and his horse snorted as if offended. He gave it a pat on the neck before indicating with his hand that we should resume our aimless stroll.

"And how are things between you and your father?" I inquired hesitantly after we had walked a few additional paces.

"Koranis fears his own son," Narian said contemptuously. "He wants the Captain of the Guard to enroll me in the Military Academy; until then, I am to move into his manor house in the city. I am to leave with the Captain tonight. Koranis even chose to oversee my packing, not trusting that I will only take those things that are my own." He glanced sideways at me, his countenance less guarded. "Of course, this means I will be living closer to the Palace."

I did not reply, uncertain of his meaning, although my heart quickened at his intimation. I hoped he would elaborate, but he did not, instead changing the subject.

"You didn't appear to enjoy Steldor's company tonight."

I gave little thought to how he had seen me with Steldor, let alone discerned my feelings, for I was growing quite accustomed to his keen observations.

"I don't ever *enjoy* Steldor's company," I said with a laugh.

"Then why do you endure him?" Narian responded to the lightness of my comment with confusion and frustration.

"I really have no choice," I said, confident he would acknowledge the difficulty of my circumstances.

"You always have a choice."

His words were blunt and devoid of sympathy, and I stared at him as we returned to the vicinity of the carriage, without an inkling of what to make of this encounter.

"I'm sure Steldor has noticed my absence by now, so I had better continue to the Palace before he pursues me."

"He may find that rather difficult, as I borrowed his horse."

"Borrowed?" I shook my head in disbelief, watching him mount the powerful animal.

"Good night, Princess," Narian said with a smirk, before galloping into the darkness in the direction of Koranis's estate.

XXII

DIVIDED HEART

o tell me, did Temerson ever work up the courage to ask you to dance?"

This was the first time my sister and I had privately visited since Semari's birthday celebration five days earlier, and we were sitting in my parlor, I upon the sofa and she in an adjacent armchair.

"No," Miranna giggled. "But Perdic, his eight-year-old brother, did."

I laughed along with her, picturing Temerson's face as his own brother asked a Princess to dance, when he could hardly put together a full sentence when he was around her.

Miranna and I were spending the afternoon together, embroidering the handkerchiefs we were to give out before the Tournament. The mid-October sky was gray and overcast, and the logs smoldering in the fireplace were necessary to chase the chill from the air.

It was tradition that each Princess who was of courting age would choose an escort for the Tournament and the dinner the evening before by delivering a personally embroidered handkerchief to the favored young man. While Miranna and I were given leave to stitch whatever design we fancied on the cloth, I had, since the first time I'd been escorted at the age of fifteen, simply sewn my name into the corner.

Miranna's design would be more elaborate and creative, but then embroidery was more to her liking than it was to mine.

"I danced a couple of times with Perdic," Miranna continued, her eyes bright as she thought back to the party. "He's a very sweet boy, though he's much braver than his brother. Zayle, who spent most of the evening with Perdic, also requested a dance, which made Semari laugh. Eventually I asked Temerson!"

"And, of course, he blushed and agreed," I teased.

Our conversation was abruptly ended as my parlor door swung wide and my father bounded across the threshold.

"Ah, both of my daughters, I see! Excellent! Not interrupting anything, I hope?" he asked, bustling into our midst.

"Not at all," I said, returning his smile. "Join us, Father."

The King took in our activity and, grinning from ear to ear, came to sit beside me on the sofa.

"Ah, the handkerchiefs. And who will be so lucky as to receive yours, Miranna? The same boy from last year, perhaps? He was quite charming, if recollection serves."

He winked, and Miranna's cheeks grew warm.

"No," she said, realizing that Father's thoughts had traveled to potential suitors for her, though she would not be of marriageable age until she turned eighteen. "I was planning on sending mine to Lord Temerson."

"Isn't he the boy I chose to accompany you on the picnic?" He chuckled in a self-satisfied way at her nod. "Excellent. Comes from a fine family. I really do have a knack for these things!"

He turned to me, patting my hand affectionately.

"You will be interested to know that Steldor is going to take part in a fighting exhibition at the Tournament. Cannan has arranged a mock battle between his son and Lord Kyenn to show the people some Cokyrian fighting techniques."

"Why Steldor?" I blurted, apprehensive on Narian's behalf.

My father interpreted my words in a way that I had not intended.

"You will only be deprived of your escort's company for a short period of time. What grounds are there to deny such an opportunity to the best fighter in Hytanica, especially when he volunteers for the good of the event?"

I looked at him blankly, and he glanced at Miranna as if begging her to help him allay my anxiety. He was clearly under the impression that the reason for my concern was that I couldn't bear to be apart from Steldor.

When Miranna shrugged but otherwise remained mute, my father spoke again, his spirits slightly dampened by my reaction.

"Well then, there's another item to discuss. I noted that things went quite well between you and Steldor at Semari's birthday. That was quite an extraordinary gift he extended, and I was happy to see you accept it. Your mother and I were also quite heartened to see the two of you dance."

My father's brown eyes seemed to sparkle as his zest for his subject increased.

"I think the time has come to make it known to the Kingdom that you and Steldor are to be wed. I've talked with the Priest about a betrothal ceremony, and I have arranged for it to take place within the next few days so that the engagement can be made known at the Tournament."

My lips parted in shock, unable to believe that he thought I was on good enough terms with Steldor to be betrothed. Steldor would embrace the idea, but I could hardly stand to consider it, as evidenced by my urge to bolt from the room.

"I can't," I faltered, hoping I sounded less distraught than I felt.

My father frowned. "Whatever do you mean, Alera?"

"I mean... that I can't. I can't pledge myself to Steldor. I... am not convinced he is the man I should marry."

A strained silence fell in the room, the only sound an occasional hiss from the fireplace.

"Why not?" my father demanded, exasperated.

I searched for a way to express my feelings, for I knew the simple fact that I abhorred Steldor would not disqualify him. While I knew I was risking my father's anger and jeopardizing his opinion of me, all I could think to do was to tell him something I had only confided to my sister.

"I feel... an attraction... to someone else."

"You are *attracted* to someone else?" he repeated incredulously, playing with his ring in agitation. "Who is this person?"

"I do not wish to say. But the fact that I am drawn to someone else would suggest that Steldor is not the ideal match for me."

I prayed I did not sound disrespectful. Nonetheless, my father did not take this revelation well.

"This is preposterous, Alera. If you will not tell me who this young man is, then I must assume he is someone of whom I would not approve; in which case, you would not be permitted to marry him. Unless this other man possesses the qualities necessary to be my successor, whether you are attracted to him or not is irrelevant. You must marry a *King*."

"I implore you, Father. Just give me a little more time."

He looked at me critically for a moment, then relented with a heavy sigh.

"Granted. But I expect you to use the time wisely. We are six months from your birthday and the day when you will be wed, and a decision must be reached regarding your husband." He then harshly rebuked me. "In fairness to Steldor, it is deceitful to receive such a splendid gift as that necklace with a divided heart."

My father stood to leave, then faced me one last time, his

unusually stern visage making him seem older, and I became cognizant of the extent to which his dark brown hair had been replaced by gray. At that moment, I realized why his sights were so firmly set on my birthday. Eighteen was the traditional age for a female heir to marry; it was also the earliest a successor could be crowned. It appeared that, in my case, my father fully intended to embrace tradition.

"Alera, notwithstanding this other person, you are to bestow upon Steldor the honor of acting as your escort for the Tournament and the dinner preceding it."

My father's steps were noticeably less buoyant when he exited the room. As his footfalls faded, frantic thoughts flashed in my head, but strangely, the one that plagued me most was the fighting exhibition my father had mentioned. Why had Steldor volunteered? His opinion of Narian was no secret to me, and I doubted it was to the Captain. Cannan must have deemed his son trustworthy, but I could not conceive that Steldor's motivations in participating in this simulated fight were completely innocent.

I glanced at Miranna, who was nervously twisting her strawberry blond hair, and knew that she was having similar thoughts.

"Now men really *are* fighting over you," she said.

———

Criers and heralds who had been sent forth several weeks ago to publicize the approach of the weeklong Faire and the Tournament began to return over the next few days, and vendors from surrounding kingdoms arrived to unpack and set up their displays. Everyone intending to offer merchandise for sale was required to check in with the Keeper of the Faire to pay a fee and be assigned a location from which to operate. Inns began to fill, and business at the taverns boomed as excitement reached a fever pitch.

The morning of the first day of the Faire dawned crisp and clear. Miranna and I worked our way through the gathering crowd to the grassy area where Market Day was normally held. Tents spread from here toward the Military Complex and the Palace to the north. A smiling Halias and a grim Destari accompanied us, but this time they remained in uniform and stayed at our sides, in recognition of the increased potential for jostling and thievery amidst such a teeming crowd.

We wandered among the tents, a happy uproar bombarding our ears, as laughing, shouting, and bargaining blended into a cacophony of sound. Above the hubbub, we would occasionally catch an unusual accent or a foreign tongue, or the melodic tones of minstrels and musicians. I cocked my head slightly, believing that I had heard a Cokyrian accent. Was Narian nearby? I thought it possible, for he had been living in the city since the night of Semari's birthday celebration, but I did not catch a glimpse of him.

The sights of the Faire were as overwhelming as the din. There was an astounding variety of merchandise for sale: wool, cotton, silk, and linen cloth were available in a myriad of colors, some interwoven with strands of gold or silver. Hemp for nets, ropes, and bowstrings; furs and skins; and embossed leather were also in abundant supply. Spice vendors busily measured out small amounts of unusual seasonings such as cinnamon, pepper, cardamom, turmeric, and mustard seed for their eager buyers, and purveyors of rare oils and perfumes did the same. As we moved with the flow of people, we saw jewelry, swords and daggers, magnificent tapestries, handcrafted candlesticks and chests, hand-carved ivory and ebony figurines, valuable books, exotic clothing, and rare carpets, all of which were available for purchase.

The inevitable scuffle, and even a brawl or two, would occasionally break out in the pathways between the tents, to be quickly subdued by City Guards who were patrolling the grounds in large numbers. It was important to the success of the Faire that the merchandise be protected from theft and damage, and that the safety of sellers and buyers alike be ensured.

Perhaps our favorite aspect of the Faire was the entertainment, with the large selection of tempting treats for the palate a close second. We laughed at the antics of tumblers and jugglers, and gaped in awe at the magicians who could swallow swords and fire. The smells of stews, meat pies, and other prepared foods whetted our appetites, while unusual sweets, uncommon flavors of cheese, and sumptuous tastes, such as chocolate, fed our souls.

We returned to the Palace that evening quite fatigued but exuberant, our senses battered by the sights, sounds, and smells of the day. We were determined, however, to venture forth again, and our next few days followed the pattern of the first, as it took a good deal of time to fully appreciate the festivities. We would wake in the morning ready to meet the challenge of the day, and fall into our beds utterly exhausted in the evening.

As the week went on, more visitors began to arrive. The inns were now overflowing, and some city residents made extra money by renting out rooms in their homes, while the King permitted travelers to pitch tents on the open ground near the Palace or outside the city walls. Most of these new arrivals were coming to participate in the Tournament that was held on the last day of the Harvest Festival. Young men, lured by the generous prize money and other rewards the King posted for the winners, came from far and wide to participate in the contests that would challenge their skills and, in many cases, their bravery.

On the day before the Tournament, Miranna and I did not attend the Faire, as I was needed to oversee the final preparations that were under way in the Palace for the pre-Tournament dinner. My mother had once again placed the event in my hands, which I understood to be a high honor, for it implied my skills were adequate in this regard. My primary tasks had been planning the menu and the evening's merriment.

The dinner would be held in the King's Dining Hall on the second floor, with approximately four hundred guests in attendance. The guests were those men who had paid their entry fee to participate in the Tournament and their ladies. The King's Dining Hall could seat at least a thousand people, with ten oak tables running the length of the room. Three dozen candlelit chandeliers provided lighting, along with numerous oil lamps that hung by chains from the walls. At the far end of the Hall, a high table was set perpendicular to the rest for the Royal Family and our escorts. Decorations were minimal, as this dinner was less formal than most hosted by the King. Spirits tended to run high, wine flowed freely, bragging was boisterous, and entertainment was plentiful.

On the evening of the feast, Miranna and I awaited the arrival of our escorts in the second-floor lesson room, which doubled as a parlor, with Destari and Halias outside in the corridor. I was wearing a gown of burgundy velvet that laced across the bodice, then fell into a wide circle skirt, the richness of the color complementing my loose dark brown tresses. Miranna's gown of deep blue velvet captured the color of her eyes and was styled with a fitted waist and gently flaring skirt.

It wasn't long before Steldor, self-assured and resplendent in a black doublet with gold stitching, and Temerson, scared and uncomfortable in an ivory doublet, arrived. Tradition dictated that the men honored by the handkerchiefs display them in some way, and Steldor had tied the one he had received from me around the hilt of his sword. Temerson carried no sword, and I could not at first discern how he was displaying Miranna's handkerchief, but then saw it tied about his left wrist.

Steldor took the lead, which seemed to suit Temerson, kissing my hand as he always did. Dispensing with small talk, he extended his arm to me.

"May I have the honor?"

I nodded, uncertain what to expect from him for we had not parted on the best of terms two weeks previously. We left the room to walk down the corridor to the Dining Hall, followed by Miranna and Temerson, and I ruminated over Steldor's atypical behavior —— he had neither flippantly complimented me nor tried to engage me in conversation.

My thoughts flew apart when the door to the Hall opened and the sounds of the raucous guests hit my ears. We walked down the center of the room toward the high table, the noise briefly subsiding when heads were lowered in respect. Wine and ale were being served, but the feast would not begin until the King and Queen arrived. Steldor, at his charming best, held my chair out for me as I took my seat, then poured and offered me a glass of deep red wine.

A trumpet blast from the far end of the Hall told me that my parents were about to enter, preceded as always by Lanek. I laughed softly as I realized even the Palace Herald could not have been heard above this group of revelers, and he had thus been forced to resort to trumpets.

"All rise for King Adrik and his Queen, the Lady Elissia," Lanek shouted.

The room fell silent and everyone stood for the entrance of the King and Queen. My jovial father greeted his guests as he proceeded, while my mother walked serenely at his side. A dozen Elite Guards followed in pairs, moving to stand in a row behind the high table with Halias and Destari, their royal blue uniforms adding vibrant color to the rich, cherry-paneled wall. Cannan, Kade, and a number of Kade's Palace Guards prowled the perimeter of the room, watching for signs of trouble. Stepping onto the platform that held the high table, my father positioned himself behind his chair to open the festivities.

"Let the feast begin!" he lustily proclaimed, holding high a goblet of ale.

A shout went up from the revelers and servants began to bring platters of food to the tables.

The feast went on for hours, stretching through several courses. My father had spared no expense, and legs of mutton and veal, chicken, venison, pork, and beef weighed down the platters amid an array of breads and vegetables. Sugar wafers, oranges, apples, pears, and cheeses were served as dessert. Wine and ale were consumed by the barrel.

As the meal came to an end, the merriment began. Tumblers and acrobats worked their way up and down the aisles, while jugglers and jesters performed at the front of the room, between our table and the others, to be later replaced by singers and musicians.

Throughout it all, Steldor played the part of the solicitous suitor, filling my wineglass, plying me with sweets, pointing out clever tricks and antics, and identifying some of the men who would be the best competitors on the morrow. He did not brag or boast, something I would not have thought possible, but genuinely took pleasure in the available entertainment and in bantering with the guests. Whether due to the wine or his change in approach, I found myself enjoying the evening, and perhaps even his companionship.

Just when it seemed one too many barrels of drink had been opened, as some participants were threatening to start the competitions right in the Dining Hall, my father stood. Trumpets again sounded to call attention to him.

"My good Lords, depart and get some rest, for the sun shall soon rouse you, and the Tournament games will begin," he announced, indicating that the feast had come to its conclusion.

He and my mother left the Hall, followed by Steldor and me, then Miranna and Temerson, with the Elite Guards last. Behind us, I could hear the riotous sounds of our departing guests.

As soon as we were within the lesson room, Temerson bowed and took his leave. I turned to Steldor, hoping he would do the same.

"We must also rise early, so I will bid you good night," I said, rather abruptly.

"Surely you can keep me company a moment longer." His smooth voice and dark eyes contained a touch of amusement, and for the first time since the evening had begun, I grew anxious.

"We should not be together without a chaperone," I argued, twining my fingers.

"I only desire a few minutes, and your bodyguard is outside in the corridor."

I glanced at my sister, hoping for some assistance, but all she gave me was a reassuring smile. With a flip of her bouncy hair, she stepped out of the room, leaving me alone with Steldor. He studied me for a moment, then reached out to still my nervous hands, laughing softly when I jumped at his touch.

"Are you really that terrified of being alone with me?"

When I did not answer, he lightly continued, "It appears you have given some thought to our conversation at Baron Koranis's estate. I'm sure you will agree that our time together is more pleasurable when you do not continually resist me."

I stared at him, his ability to put all blame on me for the problems between us robbing me of speech. As I struggled to formulate a response, he reached out to stroke my long, sleek hair.

"May I kiss you good night?" he asked, once again catching me by surprise, and I knew my face gave full notice of my jumbled feelings.

"Just one kiss, I promise," he teased. "I won't expect anything more."

It came to me then that he thought I was reluctant to be alone with him due to my lack of experience with men. While that was part of the reason, it seemed to have escaped him that I did not like him or trust him. I decided not to correct his misconception. After all, he was at least taking a courteous approach.

I nodded my head and he placed one hand on each side of my face in a gentle caress, his pleasing scent washing over me. Then he sensually joined his lips with mine.

"Sleep well, Princess," he said, removing his hands and stepping away from me. "I will return to escort you to the Tournament field in the morning."

He bowed deeply and departed, leaving me slightly off balance, as I had not anticipated such tenderness from him, and highly unsettled by the knowledge that I had enjoyed both his kiss and his touch.

"Good night, Destari," I murmured, stepping into the corridor where he awaited me.

I drifted toward my quarters, the foreign notion that I had just had a pleasant time with Steldor breaking over me, and I reluctantly admitted to myself that he could, in fact, be good company. Unfortunately, I had no idea how to ensure that the Steldor with whom I had just spent the evening would be the Steldor I would wed if my father had his way.

XXIII

The Legend of the
Bleeding Moon

n the morning of October twenty-ninth, the Royal Family rode in two carriages to the bowl-shaped Tournament site west of the Faire. The King and Queen traveled in one carriage, and Miranna and I, with our escorts, occupied the other. Our bodyguards and numerous other Elite Guards accompanied the carriages on horseback.

The weather was sunny, but cold and breezy, and fur throws had been provided for our use both while we traveled to the event and within the Royal Box. While the spectators would most likely feel the chill as the day wore on, such weather was well suited for the competitions, for it would exhilarate the participants and spur them on to greater feats.

The viewing box that had been constructed for the Royal Family and their guests sat on top of the hill that sloped down to the military training field where the events would be held. It was entered from the rear and had walls with large, open windows and a roof to provide some shelter from the elements. The exterior was draped with royal blue and gold silks, and tapestries that had been hung on the inside provided additional insulation against the cold.

The Royal Box would be full, as it would hold not only my

family, our escorts, and our bodyguards but also visiting royalty from two of our neighboring kingdoms, Sarterad and Gourhan. Emotana's sovereigns had sent regrets and would not be in attendance. Temerson's parents, Lieutenant Garreck and Lady Tanda, would also be our guests, as would Koranis and Alantonya, serving to ratchet up the tension in the Box, although my father seemed oblivious to the strained relationship between the Captain and the Baron. Even though Cannan would be on duty, his wife, Faramay, would join us as well, for she would otherwise have lacked an escort.

It would be clear to anyone who had seen Faramay that she was Steldor's mother; it was equally clear why Steldor was so good-looking. Baroness Faramay was, without dispute, the most beautiful woman I had ever seen. Her chocolate-brown hair fell around her lovely oval face in thick curls that moved when she turned her head, sweeping gracefully across her shoulders and back, drawing attention to her whether she sought it or not. She had blue eyes that were large and striking, and though she was almost forty, her fair skin was smooth and glowing. While Cannan was himself an attractive man, his wife was an arresting beauty, and Steldor had been blessed with many of her features. The only similarities between father and son were their chiseled jawlines, the deep brown of their eyes and hair, and their powerful physiques.

By the time we entered the Royal Box, competitors were already on the field preparing for the contests; Lords and Ladies in colorful raiment of lush velvet and embroidered silk had begun to fill the viewing stand constructed for them on the north side of the field; and the citizenry were gathering on the grassy hillsides. I knew the audience would grow throughout the day, drawn first by the archery, knife-throwing, and axe-throwing competitions, then by the more daring and perilous horse races, culminating in the dangerous fighting events: first hand-to-hand and then with swords and other weapons. The noise level would also continually increase, as the crowd would enthusiastically extol its favorite competitors and be equally vocal in its jeering of those it abhorred, the abundance of wine and ale tending to inspire avid crowd participation.

The field itself had been marked out to meet the needs of the Tournament. An oval track had been established and was roped off on both sides of its twenty-five-foot width, ready for the horse races. On the inside of the near edge of the oval, and slightly to the left of the Royal Box, a large stage had been erected for the one-on-one combat competitions. To the north of the stage, targets were set for the archery tournament and would later be replaced by targets for the knife-throwing and axe-throwing events. To the rear of these areas, but still within the oval, several large tents had been pitched for use by the participants as they readied themselves for the games. Billowing silk banners indicated which tents had been assigned to each kingdom: royal blue and gold for Hytanica, black and silver for Sarterad, crimson and white for Gourhan, and black and forest green for Emotana. Water for drinking and washing had also been provided, and doctors were on hand to treat the injured.

The start of the Tournament was heralded by trumpets and drums, and my father stood to open the event with the traditional speech, deepening the pitch of his voice so that it boomed across the hillside.

"Honored guests, valiant competitors, and loyal citizens of Hytanica, I bid thee welcome to this auspicious Tournament. Competitors, I exalt thee to be brave and daring, yet honorable and true, and I pray you will be safe from injury. To those in attendance, I encourage thee to rejoice with the winners, commiserate with the losers, but above all, to loudly cheer."

My father paused, then exuberantly proclaimed, "Let the Tournament begin!"

The archers, proudly displaying the silks of their respective kingdoms, approached the competition area as the cry of "Let the Tournament begin!" was repeated across the hillside. They eyed their targets and made final adjustments to their bows while waiting for the contest to commence.

I located Lanek, who would be announcing the events, on the field. It would be his responsibility also to provide commentary throughout the day, and he would no doubt be quite hoarse by the time evening fell. As the archery began, Lanek called out the distances to the targets, the marks of the archers' arrows, and the names of those who would be advancing. With each succeeding round, targets would be moved further away to provide an ever-increasing challenge to the competitors' skills.

Steldor's mood had not changed much from the previous evening, and he continued to use his inexhaustible charisma to enchant the King and Queen, as well as the other royals in attendance. If anything, he was even more charming and witty than he had been at the pre-Tournament dinner. While his ability to ingratiate himself with my parents taxed my patience, his mood otherwise suited me perfectly.

From archery, the Tournament proceeded to knife-throwing, followed by axe-throwing, with Lanek continuing to announce distances to targets and accuracy of throws. After a break for lunch, the horse racing began, and by the time the first winner crossed the finish line, the hillside was packed with vocal spectators. The horse racing involved much jostling among the competitors, which sometimes resulted in fallen riders and occasionally downed mounts. While there were some injuries, all of the toppled riders were able to limp off the track amidst shouts from the crowd, most without assistance.

Friendly repartee filled the Royal Box throughout the day's contests, but Koranis was careful to maintain his distance from the Captain of the Guard. Of course, Cannan's reaction to

Koranis's presence was far more difficult to ascertain.

When the fights with weapons began, conversation among those in the Royal Box fell off, although the crowds on the hillside voiced their opinions as vociferously as ever. Competitors would fight one-on-one in several different modes during this part of the Tournament. First would be wrestling, then hand-to-hand combat, followed by combat with swords and other weapons. Although weapons used in the fighting events were blunted in an attempt to prevent harm to participants, injuries were frequent, but rarely fatal.

The men involved in the fourth to last battle, one Hytanican and one clad in the black and silver of the Kingdom of Sarterad, were called forth by Lanek, and they climbed the few steps on either side of the stage, drawing their swords. Steldor had been concentrating on the fights and was startled when Cannan put a hand upon his shoulder and motioned to the exit. He stood, then made a point of offering words of consolation to me before departing.

"I'm afraid that I must leave you now, as the time to fight the *Cokyrian* draws nigh." He bowed and kissed my hand but did not release it, knowing full well he had irked me by the manner in which he had referred to Narian.

"Don't worry, I won't be gone long," he glibly added. "I know you will miss me terribly, but perhaps Miranna will be able to cheer you."

He let go of my hand, bowed to all the Royals, and gave his mother a dutiful kiss on the cheek before leaving to prepare for the exhibition.

After he had departed, talk resumed, centering primarily upon the fight that would soon take place between Steldor and Narian. The Cokyrians were the most feared warriors in the entire Recorah River Valley, and the exhibition we would see offered a rare chance for the public to gauge their skills.

Though it was known by everyone in the Royal Box that the flow of the fight had been plotted from first thrust to final parry, no one except Cannan had witnessed it, and excitement permeated the air. Adding to the sense of danger was the knowledge that, unlike the weapons wielded in the competitions, Steldor's and Narian's would not be blunted. Cannan had wanted to preserve the authenticity of the fight and was willing to trust to the skills of the young men involved to prevent injury. I, too, felt on edge about the upcoming event, though my feeling was not one of anticipation; it was one of trepidation.

Destari's whisper jarred me from my thoughts. "Excuse yourself and come with me."

I looked at him in confusion, but his serious expression discouraged me from raising any questions. I stood, depositing the throw that I had been draping over my legs on the chair, and approached my father, lightly placing a hand on his shoulder to draw his attention.

"I feel a need to move about for a few moments but will return shortly."

He nodded and returned to watching the sword fight taking place on the stage below. As I moved toward Destari, Temerson's mother, Lady Tanda, laid a hand on my bodyguard's arm.

"How is London?" she inquired.

"He is fine," Destari replied, with a hint of what presented itself as disapproval. "He has survived far worse than this."

After glancing at me to ensure I was complying with his directive, Destari slipped out the door. He waited for me outside and extended his hand to assist me down the steps.

"Follow me," he said when my feet touched the ground. Before I could inquire about his strange behavior, he began to walk briskly in the direction of the Faire grounds.

I trailed after him, almost jogging to keep pace. He led me

through the maze of vendors, paths teeming with people, to a heavily draped gold and maroon tent on the outskirts of the Faire near the Market District. The front flaps of the tent were spread open around a long table covered in old and expensive-looking artifacts. I frowned, drawing my cloak securely about me, thinking it unlikely that Destari had brought me here to see ancient relics, but unable to imagine his true purpose.

Behind the table sat a deathly thin, middle-aged man with short scruffy hair and bulbous black eyes. He bobbed his long, crooked nose up and down to motion us into the tent, and I nervously followed Destari, then waited while he pulled aside one of two hanging tapestries that divided the front and rear sections of the tent.

"Destari, what —— " I began, but swallowed my words as my eyes swept the shadowy back section, lit only by a small open flap in the cloth ceiling. Crates that had contained the vendor's merchandise were stacked in the corner, and leaning against them with his arms crossed over his chest was someone I had not seen in many months.

"London!" I exclaimed, delighted to see him.

Only the dust particles wafting through the air in the stream of light from the ceiling flap separated us, and I would have run to him had not my good sense surfaced. London was not a physically demonstrative person and would not appreciate my show of affection under the best of circumstances, which these were definitely not.

I stepped hesitantly forward, aware that he and I had not spoken since the day of Narian's capture, at which time nothing had been resolved between us. While I was elated to see him, he probably did not feel the same pleasure to be with me.

"Princess Alera," he said in greeting. "Glad you could fit me into your busy schedule."

His familiar sarcasm served to remind me of how sorely I

had missed him. I stopped a few feet away while I scrambled for an appropriate response, and Destari stepped through the tapestries to stand behind me.

"You look well," I finally faltered.

"As do you, Princess."

I averted my gaze, disheartened by his continued formality, and stared for a moment at my shoes. Regaining my composure, I tried again, with more sincerity than I had managed before.

"Truly, how are you?"

"Just fine. I always land on my feet." He smirked, then chided, "I hear you've managed to dispose of yet another bodyguard."

I could feel the heat rising in my cheeks, but London did not seem to notice.

"I am sorry for causing you pain," I said, searching his indigo eyes. "But isn't there some way we can put this behind us?"

"Whatever suits the Princess," he responded, and I was relieved to hear a tease in his voice. After a glance at Destari, who had moved up beside me, he more seriously added, "This wasn't intended to be a social gathering anyway."

An awkward hush transpired, during which London ran a finger along the dusty edge of one of the wooden crates. Finally, he broke the silence.

"Destari tells me you've become friendly with Koranis's eldest son."

I should have known Destari would be keeping London informed about my activities —— after sixteen years of monitoring my every movement, it would be difficult for old habits to die —— but I suspected London had pieced together more information about my visits with Narian than even my bodyguard knew. Not wanting to say the wrong thing, I shrugged noncommittally.

"And what is your opinion of him?" London persisted, equally unrevealing as to his purpose in pursuing this topic.

I knew there was no point in trying to deceive him. "He fascinates me, and I enjoy his company."

"You ought to be wary of him," London replied, his tone darkening.

"Why?" I bristled. "Because he was raised in Cokyri?"

"No. Because he is not who he appears to be."

"I could say the same thing about you."

London cocked a cautionary eyebrow at me, and I immediately regretted my words, once again lapsing into silence.

After a moment, he asked, "Have you found no reason to distrust him?"

For some unknown and unwarranted reason, I felt piqued by the way he was speaking about Narian.

"I confess that I do not know as much about him as I would like, but based on what I *do* know, I have no cause for concern."

London shook his head and gave me a disparaging smile. "You see and yet somehow you are blind."

He ran a hand through his untidy silver hair before proceeding, his manner grave.

"At the end of the war, the Cokyrians stole from us forty-nine infants and killed forty-eight, keeping and raising only Narian. Have you not wondered why? How many children do you know who begin their military training at the age of six? And how many have a private teacher?

London stared piercingly at me, but I knew he was not expecting an answer.

"This boy somehow managed to bypass Halias and Tadark without making a sound, moving stealthily enough to escape the notice of two Elite Guards —— well, one and a half." Despite the seriousness of his lecture, he still could not resist a jab at Tadark. "How many sixteen-year-olds would have that ability?"

He pushed away from the crates, his manner more fervent, words hanging, as did his breath, in the chilly air.

"He manages to acquire weapons at will against our best efforts to ensure that he remains unarmed —— you may already know this, but the knife Narian used to cut your dress was taken directly from Koranis's person, apparently before he discovered the ease with which he could break into the locked weapons trunk in the Baron's bedroom."

London let these facts sink into my besieged brain, then continued. "You were witness to the weaponry he carries —— he is armed beyond reason, not only with the weapons of a soldier, but the weapons of an assassin. As you learned at the celebration held in his honor, and as I discovered the day I arrested him, he has no fear of injury or mindfulness of danger."

He glanced at Destari for confirmation. "After a century of war with the Cokyrians, we know what to expect, and this is not it."

A somber silence pervaded the tent. I was certain Destari had heard some of this before, but taken together it made quite an impression. My cheeks burned even as my body shivered, and I snuggled deeper into my cloak. I knew he was correct in that there was something about Narian that did not ring true, but I could not comprehend what he was trying to tell me, nor could I believe that Narian meant harm to anyone in Hytanica.

"If Cokyrians are known for their stealth, how is Narian any different?" I dared to ask, snatching at threads in my desperation to escape the truth.

Destari, who still stood at my side, exhaled in exasperation. "You trust those you barely know, yet have no faith in those who would willingly lay down their lives for you!" His heavy brows drew close to shroud his black eyes, and he moved to stand next to London. It felt as though they were uniting against me.

"I don't need to hear this," I declared. "I'm old enough to make my own judgments."

London scoffed. "Your own judgments, yes. Wise judgments, hardly."

Unable to stand for more, I turned and stalked toward the tapestry behind me, wanting to rip it to shreds rather than to simply pull it open, but London's next words stopped me in my tracks.

"You won't stay long enough to hear the news from Cokyri?"

I peered over my shoulder at him, suddenly uneasy. "What do you mean?"

Destari, who now stood between London and me, likewise stared at him.

"I have just returned from a journey into the eastern mountains. I discovered some remarkable things."

"You've been in Cokyri?!" Destari's angry outburst caught me by surprise, for I had never so much as witnessed a disagreement between the two men. "Have you learned nothing over the years?"

"Alera, have you heard tell of the bleeding moon?" London continued, ignoring his friend and showing no sign of remorse or regret.

I shook my head, unable to articulate a response. London had gone *willingly* to Cokyri? After spending ten harrowing months there as a prisoner, he had returned to the enemy's land of his own accord? The idea was unfathomable to me, but I did not have long to dwell upon it.

"After I captured Narian and his identity was discovered, I became suspicious," London went on, his posture relaxed, although his voice was taut. "Destari kept me apprised of Narian's activities, and I began to ask myself the same questions I posed to you just moments ago. I canvassed Hytanica's records for information on the year of Narian's birth, as much of that time was lost to me."

I realized he was making a rare allusion to his time as a prisoner in Cokyri.

"I read descriptions in scroll after scroll of a 'bleeding moon' that hung in the sky for months, but I could not discern its significance.

"In frustration I traveled to Cokyri and accessed what records I could, just as I had in Hytanica. After several days, I finally came across a single document, written centuries ago, that gave an account of an ancient legend, the Legend of the Bleeding Moon."

London straightened to his full height and planted his feet, no longer relaxed in his stance, for prophecies and legends were not taken lightly in Hytanica, especially since the founding of our Kingdom rested upon one.

"The account held that the Kingdom of Hytanica was built on sacred ground, and that because of this, she would forever be protected from her enemies. We all know Cokyri should have been able to conquer Hytanica during the war, and the Legend confirms our own lore of why they could not do so. But the Legend further held that Hytanica can be defeated by one of her sons who bears the mark of the bleeding moon."

His eyes flicked between Destari and me, assessing our reactions.

"Sixteen years ago, Narian was born a son of Hytanica under a nighttime sky that was ruled by what our own scrolls describe as a bleeding moon, and I'm sure you know of the strange birthmark upon his neck."

My heart lurched in my chest. "But what does this mean?" I asked, almost terrified to hear the answer, suspecting that my face looked as grim as Destari's.

"It means that nothing Narian says can be ignored. It means that whatever Narian's intentions are in Hytanica, he has a destiny to fulfill in Cokyri. It means he is the weapon that can bring Hytanica to ruin."

I reeled as though I had been physically battered by London's words. Nothing made sense, and yet everything made sense. I tried to steady myself, and one clear thought emerged.

"But even if everything you have said about Narian's past is true, he must have a choice!"

I glanced frantically between London and Destari, hearing Narian's own voice echoing in my head. "*You always have a choice*," he had said on the night of Semari's party.

"He can turn from that destiny, can't he?" I urgently repeated, feeling as though I were suffocating in the stale atmosphere of the tent.

"Perhaps." London took a deep breath before continuing. "The Cokyrians are desperate to ensure Narian's return. They are determined to reclaim him, no matter the cost. At the time the High Priestess was captured in the Palace garden, Narian had already been missing for ten days."

"But why would the High Priestess look for him herself?" I needed to concentrate on a different aspect of this implausible scenario, an aspect that was more ordinary, more understandable, and more *real*.

"She was not looking for Narian in the garden."

London hesitated, uncertain he should reveal more. Apparently concluding he had no option but to tell us, he offered an explanation that was just as obscure as his preceding revelation.

"She came to the Palace to find me; she wanted my assistance in locating Narian. I am indebted to her for my life, though it is in a way you would not understand."

Destari cleared his throat, which did little to rid his voice of tension. "Shouldn't this information be brought to the Captain and the King?"

"The information comes from me, so they will not trust it," London said bitterly to Destari. "The time for them to know will present itself, but meanwhile, we keep a watchful eye on Narian."

"And of what do you think he is capable?" Destari pressed, filled with foreboding and concerned that I might continue to spend time with Koranis's son.

"His current capability is not what keeps me up at night. No matter what plans the Cokyrians have for him, he is only sixteen, not fully grown or trained. He has also been treated most kindly here in Hytanica, so I do not believe he poses an immediate threat to anyone. My concern lies in what he may become should he return to Cokyri, whether he goes voluntarily or is taken by force. If he returns, Hytanica's fate may be sealed. We must do all we can to ensure he does not end up back among the enemy." London fixed his gaze upon me. "You would do well to stay away from him, Alera."

I nodded, swaying dizzily on my feet. Taking note of my condition, Destari stepped forward to grip my upper arm, steadying me, as London addressed him.

"It's time you return Alera to the Royal Box. Her continued absence may draw questions."

I made no attempt to move, my mind and body numb, and Destari finally nudged me toward the tapestries with his hand. As I began to pass through them, I stopped and turned halfway around to face London.

"When will I see you again?" I asked, saddened by the knowledge that he could not accompany us.

"I don't know. I'm not exactly welcome at the Palace," he replied, but something in the depths of his eyes told me he felt as I did.

XXIV

THE EXHIBITION

estari and I made our way back to the Royal Box, sorrow at my separation from London now mixed in with the rest of my jumbled emotions. Destari's hand on my upper arm continued to guide me until we came within sight of the guards posted around the entrance; then I moved in front of him to climb up the steps. I tried to act normally as I returned to my seat next to Miranna, picking up the fur throw I had left on the chair and draping it over my lap.

My sister turned to me, and her eyes opened wide. "Are you all right, Alera? You're as pale as a ghost!"

"I'm fine," I assured her, but she reached out to tuck the throw around my legs, concerned that I was ill. When I said nothing further, she went back to talking with Temerson, and I took several deep breaths to calm my nerves.

I wanted to embrace the excuses and rationales I had created in my head for every unknown that surrounded Narian, but none of them could withstand scrutiny. London's information had finally completed the puzzle that Narian represented, but not in a way I wanted to believe.

Realizing that I had been staring at a crack in the wooden floor, I lifted my head to find Cannan observing me. I managed an artificial smile and forced myself to look out across the Tournament field. Just as I did, a young man dressed in crimson and white tumbled off the stage, having been dealt a particularly nasty blow by his opponent, and the King and Queen of Gourhan moaned in defeat. The crowd on the hillside erupted into cheers and applause, apparently favoring the victor, who wore the colors of Emotana.

"Who won?" Miranna asked, breaking from her conversation with Temerson to survey the goings-on. "Oh, I was supporting him!"

I was certain Miranna hadn't the faintest familiarity with either of the competitors and had selected this one to cheer for because he was more handsome than the other. Whatever her reasons, she was now applauding enthusiastically. Since Emotana's royalty was not in attendance, she soon realized she was applauding alone, and her enthusiasm waned.

Lanek announced the victor's name for all to hear, and the fighter on the stage gave a deep bow. When the crowd had quieted, the man hobbled off the stage, having been wounded during this battle or a previous one, while his unfortunate opponent was carried away, presumably to the physician's tent some distance down the field.

The trumpets blared again, drawing attention to Lanek, who had climbed onto the stage in order to be more visible to the crowd despite his small stature. Steldor and Narian mounted the steps on either side of the platform, for the time had come for the exhibition. Both men wore dark trousers, white shirts, and tall leather boots, and each had slipped his arms into a leather breastplate that provided minimal protection for the chest. Heavier armor would have inhibited their movements, and the exhibition, as a feigned fight, posed little risk of injury. Each fighter held a long-sword in his right hand —— Steldor's was his custom-made blade that had a leather grip wrapped in wire and a ruby set into its pommel; Narian's sword had a grip that was likewise covered in leather and wrapped with wire, but was otherwise plain, with a narrower and less unwieldy blade —— and daggers hung at their sides.

I scrutinized Narian but could detect no unease in his carriage, and I fervently wished he would be warier of his opponent. Though I doubted Steldor would intentionally harm the younger man under these circumstances, I could not quell the warning sounding in my head. Narian was noticeably smaller than Steldor, and I still did not trust Steldor's motivations.

"And now, for the climax of this year's Tournament, the much heralded fighting exhibition between Lord Steldor, son of Cannan, the Captain of the Guard, and Lord Narian, son of the Baron Koranis," Lanek bellowed.

Koranis stiffened at the manner of Narian's introduction, although he said nothing. Did he object to the use of the name Narian rather than Kyenn? Or did he simply no longer desire to claim him as a son?

"Lord Steldor will be using his Hytanican weaponry," Lanek continued, "and Lord Narian will be using the weapons of Cokyri."

Excited chattering rippled through the crowd at the mention of the kingdom where Narian had been raised, to be quickly replaced by the usual banter on the hillside and in the stands. His role fulfilled, Lanek marched down the steps to make way for the fighters.

Steldor and Narian nodded to each other from their respective sides of the stage, then advanced, readying their swords. They crossed blades when they met in the center and began some simple combat maneuvers, increasing their speed as they fell into a rhythm.

My tension eased while I viewed the routine fighting upon the stage, content for it to remain as it was, though the crowd shifted restlessly, craving something more. After a time, Steldor pulled back from Narian and tossed aside his sword with an insolent sneer in response to the crowd's discontent. Narian also took a step back but made no move to change his weapon.

Steldor drew his double daggers from the sheaths at his hips and flipped them, catching the handles so that the blades extended from the backs of his fists. Lowering his hands, he advanced on his opponent. Without stopping or breaking eye contact, he raised the weapons, crossing them in front of him and thrusting them toward Narian's chest. Narian reacted faster than I would have thought possible, dropping his sword to catch Steldor's wrists so the blades came to rest threateningly above his shoulders. Steldor leaned into Narian to mutter something, then pushed him backward off his feet, and my apprehension spiraled upward.

Steldor retreated two steps and waited with his hands at his sides, shifting his weight from foot to foot. I glanced around the Royal Box to gauge the feelings of the others but saw only that everyone was focused intently upon the stage.

Gathering his feet beneath him, Narian resolutely rose, eyes boring into Steldor. He drew his own double daggers, which fit around his knuckles so that the blades arched over his hands, then nimbly moved forward. Positioning himself so that he could strike with his left leg, he planted a solid kick against Steldor's chest. Steldor stumbled back a few paces, then gave Narian a nod as though satisfied with his response.

The crowd's attention was now riveted on the stage where the fighters had begun circling each other, Steldor exhibiting a cocky and menacing swagger, while Narian crouched lower, cat-like in his movements. I gnawed on my lower lip, though it *was* conceivable that this change in style had also been planned in order to play well to the crowd.

As the young men completed their circle, Narian's inside shoulder dipped slightly, and Steldor seized the opportunity.

He flipped the dagger in his right hand over again and closed the distance between them to strike Narian in the temple with the butt of the knife. Narian dropped low and turned his head with the blow to avoid its full impact, then spun to his right, slashing Steldor above the knee with his blade. Bleeding from the gash in his leg, Steldor backed off and Narian rose to his feet, blood trickling from his temple.

The crowd had fallen completely silent, no longer sure if what they were seeing was a demonstration.

"I daresay these two are getting a little carried away," my father said with an unconcerned chuckle.

I could not understand his cheerfulness. Steldor's first blow had not been restrained, and Narian had meant to draw blood. I glanced over at Cannan, who was standing and glaring at the stage, jaw clenched, his arms crossed upon his chest. Faramay, expression anxious, was also eyeing Cannan, aware that something was wrong.

I returned my attention to the fight, now sitting on the edge of my seat, gripping the arms of my chair and praying soundlessly for Narian's safety. Steldor had been the victor in every Tournament fighting competition he had entered since coming of age at eighteen and was renowned as the best fighter in the entire Recorah River Valley. It was not a matter of who would emerge triumphant at the end of this battle —— the only uncertainty was how badly Narian would be beaten.

Tiring of their game of cat and mouse, the young men suddenly ran at each other. As they came together, Steldor stabbed at Narian with his right blade, but Narian deflected it, then likewise redirected Steldor's left-handed, follow-up thrust. After pushing both of Steldor's daggers away, Narian circled his right arm down and in, slashing vertically up the center of his opponent's breastplate and nearly cleaving it in two. Steldor drew his arms protectively in to his chest, and Narian immediately brought his left arm across Steldor's body, hooking him by the shoulder with the barbed edge of his blade and jerking him around. As he spun, Steldor extended his right hand, slicing Narian across the shoulder.

Faramay gasped as the two came apart and spatters of blood flew from their weapons. Both of the fighters now had dark stains forming on their white shirts.

Looking down the row of people, I saw Koranis and Alantonya sitting side by side, Alantonya looking mortified, Koranis vindicated. My father was frowning down at the stage, twisting his ring, finally disturbed by what he was seeing, while the faces of the visiting royals registered equal parts confusion and concern. Beside me, Miranna's fingers were pressed against her cheeks, ready to creep up and hide her eyes, and Temerson had tentatively put a hand on her back to reassure her. My mother, Faramay, and Temerson's parents wore appalled expressions. Only Cannan's stance and demeanor had not changed in the least.

As Steldor regained his balance, he turned his left blade over so both of his knives extended from the tops of his hands, and thrust toward Narian, driving the daggers underneath the younger man's arms. Pressuring the base of his fists into the center of Narian's back, between his shoulder blades, Steldor forced him downward until his arms flared out, then brought his right knee up to connect violently with Narian's chin.

Steldor shoved Narian one final time toward the ground before he pulled away. Narian caught himself with his blades so that he managed to stay on his feet, but his head hung forward, heavy bangs hiding his pain. Steldor, unmistakably smug, took one step back and glowered down at him.

"Stay down, Narian," I heard Cannan mutter. "Don't get up."

The disoriented young man took a few deep breaths, then abruptly slid his legs forward between Steldor's and kicked outward, forcing his adversary to splay his legs shoulder-width apart. He then sprang to his feet, and with Steldor now at his eye level, slashed both of Steldor's shoulder straps. With a thud, the already damaged breastplate fell to the ground. Thundering footsteps on the stairs of the Royal Box told me that Cannan had decided it was time to put an end to this fight.

Steldor drew his leg in and shifted his weight onto his left foot, then spun around to plant a solid side kick against Narian's chest with his right leg, once again knocking the younger man off his feet. Absorbing the fall, Narian rolled onto his upper back and sprang forward to land in a crouched position. Steldor faced Narian, settling his weight, right dagger held up, left held low, awaiting his opponent's next move. His smugness had died away to be replaced by intense concentration on the battle at hand.

I could see Cannan pushing his way through the masses, his progress slowed by the excited spectators. Narian caught the disruption in the crowd and thrust his daggers to the side. At first, I thought he was going to concede the fight to Steldor, before the Captain could intervene, but he instead ran at his opponent. He pulled Steldor's arms away from his body, and with surprising agility, used Steldor's thigh as a step, pushing himself off the ground to plant his right heel forcefully against his adversary's chin. Steldor's head whipped back, and he fell hard, the stage shuddering with the impact, his blades flying away from him, as Narian flipped over to land on his feet.

Faramay's hands had gone to her mouth in horror, and mutters filled the box at this strange new development. The air felt thick, making it difficult to breathe, and I prayed that Cannan would soon intercede.

For a moment, Steldor did not move, stunned to be the one flat on his back, then his muscles tensed as a fierce and uncontrollable rage ignited within him. Raising his arms, he slammed his clenched fists against the floor of the stage and rose menacingly to his feet.

Striding toward Narian, Steldor brought his right arm down and back and launched a deadly uppercut at Narian's jaw. Narian grasped Steldor's arm and pushed upward to avoid the blow. Wrapping his right leg around Steldor's, he knocked his opponent's feet out from under him, using the momentum of the punch to send his adversary slamming against the ground for the second time. Pinning Steldor's right arm down with his left hand, Narian pressed his knee into Steldor's chest, rendering his foe helpless against his final move. As Cannan broke through the last line of people and rushed toward the stage, Narian drew back his fist and threw a punch toward Steldor's windpipe that would have taken Steldor's life had he not pulled it back at the last second.

Narian slowly retracted his hand and rose to his feet. His eyes met the Captain's, and his expression was so unfeeling it gave me chills. Glancing around, he seemed to recall that he had been involved in an exhibition and dispassionately examined his defeated opponent, who was struggling onto his elbows, before extending a hand to help him to his feet. Steldor glared at Narian before grudgingly accepting his assistance. As he struggled to stand, the first applause reached my ears, then the sound grew louder until the entire crowd was cheering.

Steldor and Narian gave subdued bows before exiting the stage in opposite directions, doing their best to mask the extent of their injuries. Steldor, limping slightly, walked away with nothing but a fleeting glance at his father, who directed his gaze at the Royal Box as if trying to make a decision, then followed after him. For the first time in memory, the Captain of the Guard had looked pale and somewhat shaken.

A moan captured my attention, and I looked to my right at Faramay, who was on her feet, hanging on to the edge of the viewing window with pallid hands. As my mother turned to offer assistance, she swooned, her legs crumpling beneath her. Tanda and Alantonya went to her aid where she lay on the floor, fanning her face, and my mother dispatched a guard to fetch some water.

With Faramay providing an unexpected diversion, I rushed from the Box without a word to anyone, my head spinning. What had I just witnessed? Steldor, the best fighter the Recorah River Valley had ever seen, defeated by a sixteen-year-old?

Narian's unusual weapons had frightened me, but that was nothing compared with the raw emotions that now clawed at me. I was frustrated and furious at myself for my naïveté —— I had trusted Narian to a large extent and had been at his mercy many times. Now, when I thought of the peril in which I had unwittingly put myself, I was almost traumatized enough to join Faramay on the floor.

I hastened down the slope through the milling crowd, my cloak billowing behind me, frustration building every time my progress was impeded.

"Alera!" Destari called, coming after me.

I did not slow down, but he nonetheless overtook me.

"Where are you going?" he growled, stepping in front of me and putting a hand on my shoulder to force me to stop.

"I need to see him," I said, trying in vain to move past my bodyguard.

"Lord Narian?" His voice was tinged with disbelief.

"Yes!"

Deeming it futile to argue with me, he took me by the arm and forged a path through the spectators, who gave way to the large and powerful man much more quickly than they would have to me, and we crossed the short span of field to where the participants had prepared for the competitions.

We wove our way through the tents, where healers tended

to wounded fighters, but did not see Narian or Steldor among them. Destari intercepted one of the doctors to determine Narian's whereabouts, and we were directed to the medical tent where his injuries were being treated. Destari ducked his head and stepped inside to announce my arrival.

I entered to find Narian sitting on a wooden bench, his blond hair sweat-dampened, and his loose-fitting white shirt tugged down off his shoulder so that his wound could be cleansed, stitched, and bandaged by the physician who was treating him. He rose slowly to his feet when he saw us, pushing the doctor's hand away and returning the sleeve to its rightful place.

The physician bowed to me on his way out, and I directed Destari to likewise leave us.

"If you need me, I'll be right outside," he muttered, eyes narrowed in distrust as he exited the tent.

I was now alone with Narian, and we stared at each other until I found my voice.

"Who are you?" I demanded, advancing upon him.

Narian did not reply but watched me like a hawk watches its prey. My frustration mounted, and I became more insistent.

"Are you the one of whom the Legend speaks? Are you here to destroy Hytanica?"

Though he was adept at hiding his emotions, I could tell that my unexpected knowledge had startled him. Still, he gave me a straightforward response.

"I did not come here for that reason, though it is the Legend that led me here."

I nearly rolled my eyes. "Then, pray tell why you are here, if not to *fulfill your destiny!*"

There was true conviction behind Narian's words when next he spoke, my hostility having spurred him to explanation.

"I did not know of the Legend or that Hytanican blood runs

through my veins until six months ago, when I learned of both through a discussion that was not intended for my ears. I came here only to discover my heritage and perhaps find my family, but that is all. I did not come here to harm anyone."

My racing heart began to calm as I listened to him, and a wave of compassion swept over me for the young man who in age was my sister's equal but who in all else was years beyond.

"Is it your plan to return to Cokyri?" I asked, my anger dissipating, replaced by a strong sense of foreboding.

"No," he said, shaking his head. "There is something that holds me here, something unconnected to my resentment toward the people who raised me and who lied to me." His eyes captured my own, the longing within them achingly clear, then he steadily finished, "But Alera, if ever I do find myself back in Cokyri, the Overlord will be difficult to refuse."

A tremor shook my body as I grasped the reality of Narian's situation and to whom he would have to answer.

"The Overlord?" I murmured, barely able to speak.

Narian stared over my shoulder for a moment, gathering his thoughts.

"The Overlord was and is my teacher. He is the one who trained me, as well as the one I serve."

Nausea broke over me, and it took most of my strength to stay on my feet. London's description of the Overlord sprang unbidden to mind——*"He is a fierce warlord, evil and terrifying. They say he has the power to wield black magic... That he can kill you or worse with a wave of his hand"*—— and I thought of London's condition after having escaped the tyrant's clutches. Narian had faced the Overlord almost every day since he was six, learning his methods and skills, and no doubt, his prejudices and beliefs.

"I did not choose this to be my fate," Narian went on, his countenance softening, the horror upon my face apparently causing him distress. "You need not fear me, Alera."

There was a trace of hopelessness in the short laugh that preceded my next words.

"Needn't I? Perhaps now you mean me no harm, but should Cokyri reclaim you, what then?"

His face shut down, his rare show of emotion disguised and contained. In exasperation, I turned to leave, but his hand caught my upper arm. Before I could react, his other hand was upon my waist, pulling me toward him, and his vivid blue eyes captured mine of deep brown. As my heart raced, his lips met mine, lightly at first, then more insistently, and I succumbed to his embrace. I melted against him, my hands upon his back, all reason having abandoned me. After several moments, our lips reluctantly parted, and he briefly leaned his forehead against mine. Then he stepped back, his hands on my hips to create a little distance between us.

"I will never hurt you," he promised.

My good sense returned, and I stumbled away from him, then turned and fled the tent, unnerved by the passion that had blazed between us.

Destari looked suspiciously at me in light of my hasty exit, but he said nothing, choosing to lead me back to the Royal Box where the awarding of the prizes had begun. It would normally have been my responsibility to assist the King in this ceremony, but my sister had been called upon in my absence. I approached the Box, worried that Father would be angry with me for shirking my duty, but he gave me a knowing look, thinking I had gone to check on Steldor. I climbed the stairs and took up position beside Miranna, who eyed me curiously but was too occupied to say anything. As the names and deeds of the winners were announced by Lanek, I joined in extending congratulations, the King awarding bags of gold, while Miranna and I bestowed elaborate figurines. Ebony falcons went to the winners in archery (including Galen, who was renowned for his skill with the bow), knife-throwing, and axe-throwing; gilded horses to those who had triumphed in the races; and goblets made of gold to the victors in the combat events.

After the Tournament had closed, I returned to the Palace with my family. Sensing my agitated frame of mind, Miranna withheld her questions, for which I was thankful. I begged off from the small dinner my father always hosted for the Tournament winners, claiming fatigue, and retired to my quarters, unable to feign a festive mood.

I prepared for bed and sought sleep, but my mind was plagued with terrible thoughts about Narian and the Legend of the Bleeding Moon. Narian had been raised by the Overlord to destroy my homeland and all that I held dear. He claimed that he did not intend to harm Hytanica, but what choice did he have? Just as it was my destiny as Crown Princess to become Queen, so was it his destiny to fulfill the Legend.

But as I unendingly sorted through all I had learned, I placed two fingers against my lips, recalling the pressure of his kiss. I had felt such extraordinary happiness in his arms. How could someone with such a horrifying fate evoke such tender feelings from me? How could I desire the company of a person who was doomed to become my enemy?

With no answers to these troubling questions, I longed to escape into oblivion, but sleep came slowly and provided no rest when finally it arrived.

XXV

IT'S TOUGH TO BE A KING

The guards pulled open the doors that led into the antechamber and Steldor emerged from between them, magnificent in his long-sleeved, black leather military jerkin, his distinctive longsword sheathed at his left side, a dagger on his right. With a practiced pace, eyes straight ahead, he began the long walk up the center of the Hall of Kings toward the Royal Family, the only sounds his footsteps against the stone of the floor and the crackle of the burning logs in the fireplaces on the eastern and western walls. My parents sat upon their thrones, my father's personal guards in their usual formation, while Miranna and I sat to the left of our mother with Halias and Destari beside us, every person watching Steldor's advance.

Three days had passed since the Tournament, giving him time to recover sufficiently from the injuries he had acquired during the so-called exhibition. The only remaining sign of the fight was the faint bruising along his jawline. Cannan, who stood beside my father's throne, had requested this audience with the Royal Family, presumably at his son's behest, though I, at least, suspected that Steldor had not been informed of the meeting until after it had been arranged. The purpose of the audience had not been divulged, but it took no scholar to ascertain it.

As Steldor arrived before the dais, he fell to one knee, bowing his head before the King.

"Rise," my father said, his aspect for once stern as he confronted the Captain's son.

"Have I permission to speak, Your Majesty?" Steldor asked, coming to his feet.

"Granted."

"I humbly come before you to ask forgiveness for my behavior of late, particularly at the Tournament during the fighting exhibition." Steldor's voice was rich and strong, and his dark eyes were fixed upon my father. "I acted rashly, Sire, and allowed my temper and my competitive nature to overpower my reason. I deserve the disgrace I have brought upon myself, but that I have brought disgrace upon you and your family is inexcusable."

Letting his admission resound for a moment, Steldor switched his attention to me.

"I also ask pardon from Princess Alera, for I was unable to fulfill my duties as her escort following the incident."

His apology did not move me in the least, and I let my scorn show upon my face. He had obviously concluded that as long as his father was forcing him to apologize to the entire Royal Family, he should do so eloquently, and at that he was succeeding. I could already feel my father's resolve breaking down, and I knew Steldor would have been forgiven even if those had been his final words.

After a theatrical pause, the contrite soldier continued, once more addressing the King.

"I would also like to express regret on my father's behalf for administering *unnecessarily* to me when he should have returned at once to His Majesty's side." One eyebrow arched slightly in irreverence as his eyes flicked to Cannan. "While duty to a son is important, duty to the King is supreme."

Cannan looked mildly disgruntled, but not surprised, apparently having expected such a jibe.

Finished, Steldor dropped again to one knee. "In deep remorse, and as an act of contrition, I offer my resignation as a Field Commander to my King."

He hung his head, the very image of penitence, and I wondered how many times he had rehearsed this highly effective performance. Steldor had made an offer my father would never accept, but which portrayed him as the most repentant man who had ever lived. I could scarcely believe his audacity, much less my father's gullibility.

"That's quite unnecessary, young man. Your apology is received without reservation."

"Thank you, Sire," Steldor replied, lifting his head, his tone solemn and a touch too respectful. Anyone who truly knew him would have felt the smugness radiating from his very being.

My father extended his hand so that Steldor could rise and kiss the Royal Ring, pleased with the way Cannan's son had shouldered the blame for the exhibition gone awry. With one final, graceful bow, Steldor pivoted and walked with the same steady cadence away from us and out the antechamber doors.

One week later, at mid-afternoon, my mother, Miranna, and I were having tea in the small room designated for that purpose on the main floor of the Palace. We sat at a quaint table in the room's center, bathed by the rays of sunlight entering through the bay window, and enjoying the West Courtyard in all its late fall splendor.

Our conversation covered a wide variety of topics, from the latest and most unusual raiment we had observed upon the backs of the nobility attending the Tournament, to old friends and acquaintances my mother had encountered at the Faire. Thankfully, Steldor had not been mentioned, nor had my distracted state of mind. I tried to participate in the chitchat between my mother and my sister but had difficulty concentrating, as had been the case ever since the exhibition.

I had not seen nor contacted Narian since we had kissed on that day, and I wondered if he was as confused as I. My response to his kiss had made my feelings for him quite clear to me, but I could not understand why or how these feelings had evolved. And I had departed immediately —— without a word. What if I had given him the opposite impression, that I did not return his affections?

My thoughts were interrupted by a knock on the tearoom door, and Destari granted entrance to Orsiett, the Elite Guard who had been Miranna's secondary bodyguard during the search for the traitor, and who was now working as an aide to Cannan.

"Destari," Orsiett said urgently. "I need a word with you."

Destari exchanged a concerned look with Halias before stepping into the hallway and closing the door behind him. Halias shrugged in reply to our inquisitive stares, then scowled at one of the Palace Guards who accompanied my mother everywhere, for he was inching toward the door in an attempt to overhear the discussion taking place on the other side. The guard was forced to pull away to avoid a collision with the door when Destari reentered the room.

"Halias, we are to escort the Princesses and the Queen to their quarters without delay."

"For what reason?" Halias asked, stepping to Miranna's side.

"A Cokyrian has come to the Palace to speak with the King."

"What?" my mother whispered, reaching distractedly to touch her honey-colored hair, her blue eyes uneasy. She moved closer to Miranna, placing a trembling hand upon my sister's shoulder.

"We do not yet know why she is here," Destari continued. "She arrived under a white flag. The three of you are to return to your quarters until the purpose of her visit has become manifest."

Halias did not speak but stared straight ahead, the clenching of his jaw made particularly apparent by the fact that his hair was pulled back in its customary style. We left the tearoom surrounded by guards, Miranna worriedly watching her bodyguard, then glancing to me for the reassurance she craved. I had none to give. I could hear nothing but the thrum of blood in my ears. Everything I knew about the Cokyrians suggested that they acted, they attacked, they *slaughtered* without warning. Why had they now decided to come and talk? My thoughts flew to Narian. Had they come, as London had predicted they would, to reclaim him? And if that was the case, would we be able to keep him safe?

Miranna and I were allowed to stay together in my rooms, but my mother was taken to her own quarters for security's sake. If the Cokyrians did intend to use some form of trickery to harm the Royal Family, separating us would make it more difficult for them.

Upon the passing of a little more than two painstakingly slow hours, Orsiett returned and informed us that we were to report to my father's study. Accompanied by our bodyguards, we proceeded down the spiral staircase and into the King's Drawing Room, Orsiett breaking off to head down the corridor to our right. From the Drawing Room, we entered the Hall of Kings and crossed its expanse to reach the study through the door to the east of the thrones.

My mother was already seated upon the sofa, and my father's form filled the armchair beside her. He was bent toward her, one of her hands in his, serious expressions on both of their faces. He motioned for us to sit, and Miranna chose the other side of the sofa, while I sat in an armchair opposite him. Destari and Halias remained standing, hands clasped behind their backs.

"I've already informed your mother of this," my father said to my sister and me, his manner uncharacteristically subdued. "But the Cokyrian messenger came with a request. Tomorrow at mid-morning, you must all report to the Throne Room wearing your finest attire. The High Priestess of Cokyri desires an audience with the Royal Family, and I have granted her petition."

I heard Miranna's sharp intake of breath, as did my father.

"There is no need to be afraid," he said at once. "The Cokyrians come under a flag of truce, and there will be no shortage of guards in the Throne Room tomorrow."

"Do you think... Are they here about Narian?" I stammered.

"If they are, Lord Nar —— Kyenn will be safe. Cannan is sending for him as we speak. He will be brought to the Palace and will stay here with us for however long it takes to learn the Cokyrians' intentions and assess the situation."

I nodded, outwardly composed, but inwardly in turmoil. Then I fixated on a small detail and dared to correct my father.

"He chooses to be called Narian."

My father stared at me for a moment, trying to figure out why this was important to me, then returned to the matter at hand.

"You will stay in your quarters until it is time to come to the Hall of Kings tomorrow." Turning to Destari and Halias, he added, "You will remain on duty through the night, as an extra precaution."

Our bodyguards nodded and bowed, and we departed, leaving my father and mother alone in the study.

Destari and I retreated to my quarters, and I sat in the parlor, dazed, while he loitered by the door.

"The King is right, Alera," he said in an attempt to reassure me. "You will be in no danger."

"And Narian?" I asked, wringing my hands.

"The Captain will keep him secure. As for what the future may bring, I cannot say."

———

Palace Guards lined the entire Throne Room, looking eerily identical in their royal blue and gold tunics, with swords at their hips and long spears in their hands. My parents, robed and crowned, sat stiffly upon their thrones. Miranna and I occupied the chairs to our mother's left, attired in gold brocade gowns with gold and pearl tiaras topping our softly falling tresses. Despite the glowing embers in the twin fireplaces, the room was chilled, and I buried my hands in the golden fox-fur throw upon my lap. The twelve Elite Guards who protected my father formed two arcs, one on either side of the Royal Family, while Destari stood directly behind my chair and Halias stood behind Miranna's. Cannan, as always, was to the right of my father, while Kade, the Sergeant at Arms, was next to my mother.

Just like the Palace Guards who lined the walls, every Elite Guard wore his uniform and stood with weapons at hand. The official weaponry of the Elite Guards consisted of a formidable long-sword, a short-sword that strapped across the back, and a double-edged dagger that hung from the belt.

My father rose, looking majestic in his royal blue robes, as the antechamber doors were pulled open. The Palace Guards more firmly gripped their spears, and the tension in the deafeningly quiet room increased. Then the contingent from Cokyri walked forward, led by the woman who had at one time been our prisoner, their measured footfalls resounding in the stillness of the room.

The High Priestess's striking green eyes perused my father's face as she neared the thrones, accompanied by six guards who stood two on either side of her and two behind. She was clad in a black tunic and leggings, a sword sheathed at her side. Red stitching accented the front of the tunic and the black cape that was attached at the shoulders. A ring adorned her right hand, and the silver pendant that I knew concealed a dagger hung around her neck, but she wore no crown upon her head.

Her guards, all women, were likewise dressed in black, but their shirts buttoned asymmetrically off to the side, just like the coat Narian had worn at the Palace celebration in his honor. All of their clothing was loose-fitting, designed for ease of movement, and each carried a sword at her hip, a bow across her back, and a dagger in the shaft of her tall black boots.

The High Priestess halted fifteen feet from the dais, watching the King of her enemy warily, her flaming chin-length hair falling around her bronzed face. She extended no indication of respect or deference to my father —— ruler did not bow to ruler —— but waited in haughty silence.

"State your business," my father commanded when the tension in the room became almost intolerable, his words as frosty as the air.

The High Priestess did not hesitate to speak, and when she did, power seemed to pulse from her, the likes of which I had never before felt.

"I have come to demand the return of a Cokyrian boy who is being held here in Hytanica. Do you know of whom I speak?"

"I know of a boy who was abducted as an infant and raised in Cokyri, but who has now found his true home in Hytanica," my father replied.

The High Priestess did not appreciate the King's disputatious response.

"You know we speak of the same boy," she said, sounding controlled yet impatient.

My father came back with a new tactic. "What reason does the High Priestess of Cokyri have to pursue the return of one runaway child?"

"I would pursue the return of any Cokyrian held within Hytanica," she answered belligerently.

"We have not forced the boy to remain here," my father rejoined, bridling at her insinuation. "He has stayed of his own volition."

"Then you would permit his return to Cokyri if that were his choice?"

After a moment of thought, the King declared, "I would."

The High Priestess's voice grew strong once more as she issued her second demand.

"I insist that I be allowed to speak to Narian."

My father for the first time looked to Cannan, and the imposing Captain of the Guard stepped forward. I saw the High Priestess's perceptive eyes flick between Cannan and the King, no doubt assessing the balance of power between the two men.

"We will send for him," Cannan said through gritted teeth, making the decision the King had silently asked of him. His dark eyes were cold and hard, and I realized how much of a strain it was for those who had fought in the war to keep their words and actions civil.

"My guards will escort you to the Meeting Hall while we await his arrival," my father said, the need to be hospitable masking his abhorrence for the people before him. He then addressed the Sergeant at Arms. "Kade, arrange the necessary escort and notify the kitchens to bring refreshment to our visitors."

Kade quickly implemented my father's orders, and Palace Guards walked in front of and behind the seven Cokyrians, more than doubling their numbers, as they were taken from the Hall of Kings, through the antechamber, and on to the Meeting Hall. With the closing of the Throne Room doors, silence again reigned.

The Royal Family moved into the King's study while Cannan

and an Elite Guard went to collect Narian from the guest room on the third floor where he had spent the night. He had been told to keep to his room so that he could be summoned if he were needed and, of perhaps greater import, so that the Cokyrians would not know of his presence within the Palace.

Destari, Halias, and several of my father's personal guards stood outside the door of the study after we had entered, the rest of the Palace and Elite Guards milling about the Hall of Kings. This room, too, felt agonizingly cold to me, despite the fire snapping in the hearth, and I sank into an armchair near to the blaze. Miranna and my mother sat together on the sofa, holding hands, while my father remained on his feet. Although it was only my family in the study, no one spoke. The hush was broken a few minutes later by a sharp rap on the door, and Cannan entered with Narian. As had been the case with Steldor, Narian's face showed bruising, but his was at the temple in addition to the jaw.

Narian scanned the room, and I recollected the self-defense lesson in which he had told me to always be aware of my surroundings, and to take note of every person present and of every exit. Was such conduct second nature to him? Did he ever relax his vigilance?

"I've informed Narian of the High Priestess's demands," Cannan reported, closing the door.

My father nodded, then addressed the young man standing respectfully before him.

"Do you wish to speak to her?"

Narian's eyes were steely, and he seemed to have detached himself from all emotion.

"No, Your Majesty, I do not."

"Very well. And of her other demand —— do you wish to return to Cokyri?"

Narian's expression did not change, nor did his tone.

"No, I do not."

"Then it is here you shall stay," my father decided, clearly under the impression that Narian's detachment was an attempt to conceal the anxiety he was truly feeling. I doubted that Narian was afraid, but his actual emotions were indiscernible even by me.

Cannan escorted Narian from the study, and my father gave word for the delegation from Cokyri to be brought before us once more. The King and Queen returned to their thrones, and Miranna and I likewise took our seats, with our guards behind us. Cannan emerged from his office, where he had taken Narian, and returned to my father's side just as the antechamber doors swung inward.

The High Priestess and her guards entered exactly as they had before, though this time they were accompanied by Kade and the many Hytanican guards who had been with them in the Meeting Hall. As the Palace Guards resumed their positions on either side of the Hall, and Kade returned to stand beside my mother, the Cokyrians again approached the dais, the High Priestess halting before my father.

"Narian will not be meeting with you," the King announced. "Nor will he be returning to Cokyri."

Sparks danced in the High Priestess's eyes, though the rest of her face remained composed.

"Say what you will, Hytanican King, but Narian must be surrendered into my custody," she retorted with a clear note of animosity. "You can either release him to us voluntarily, or we will take him by force. I advise you to consider carefully, and will know your answer in the morning."

She motioned to her six guards, and they departed in formation, their footsteps and the High Priestess's threat echoing in their wake.

After the antechamber doors had closed behind the Cokyrians, debate broke out among those assembled in the Throne

Room, including the Palace and Elite Guards, as a measure of fear seized almost everyone. What had she meant by *"we will take him by force"*? Did the Cokyrians plan to restart the war? Would protecting Narian put the entire Kingdom at risk? And most pressing, how should the King reply when the High Priestess returned in the morning?

The debate grew strident as suggestions were torn apart and rejected. My father was conferring with both Kade and Cannan, who was the only person in the room who had remained calm.

I was more distraught than ever, and Miranna shot me a glance that told me she felt the same. Narian had stepped out of Cannan's office to observe the commotion, leaning with his shoulder against the wall, his countenance uncharacteristically troubled.

"QUIET!" Cannan suddenly bellowed, and everyone was struck eerily dumb. "That's better," he grumbled, then he pinched the bridge of his nose and closed his eyes, deep in thought.

A resolute voice disturbed the silence. "We should send for London, sir."

For a moment, everyone stared at Halias, who stood steadfast, his glistening blue eyes glued to Cannan's face, then all attention shifted to the Captain of the Guard. Cannan glowered at Halias for several long minutes, making no effort to suppress the heat in his stare. Finally, he turned to Destari.

"Do you know where London is?"

"Yes, sir, I do."

"Find him and bring him here. Make sure he understands the situation."

Destari nodded, then strode from the room through the antechamber doors.

The Throne Room again buzzed with conversation, and I tried several times to catch Narian's eyes. But whenever I glanced toward him, his attention was elsewhere, and I couldn't help but think this was deliberate on his part.

After Destari's departure, my father turned to my mother, Miranna, and me.

"You need not stay. It would be best if you retired to your quarters while we men discuss these developments."

My mother nodded, her face pale, and my father attempted to soothe her.

"We have dealt with the Cokyrians before, and we will deal with this situation as well. There is no need to be afraid."

My mother stood, and she and Miranna left, accompanied by several guards. Halias remained in the Throne Room, however. I made no move to follow them, and my father looked quizzically at me.

"I would like to stay. I will not cause any disruption. I only want to know what decision is reached about Narian."

He acquiesced, too distracted by the matter at hand to argue, and I sank deeper into my chair to make myself both warmer and less conspicuous. Cannan approached my father and they engaged in a muted exchange, at the end of which the Captain beckoned to Narian, who was still observing everyone. Narian straightened and crossed the floor, giving my father a deferential bow as he came to stand before the two men.

Cannan examined the young man for several moments, but Narian looked directly back at him, showing no sign of unease. Finally, Cannan spoke.

"The High Priestess would not personally pursue just any Cokyrian boy. It is time you told us the nature of your relationship to her."

My chest tightened at Cannan's words, and I began to pick at the fox-fur throw upon my lap. At my father's glance, I forced my hands to lie motionless in my lap, for I did not want my nervous habit to draw Cannan's notice, lest he deduce that I knew something relevant to his inquiry. While I wasn't sure how truthful Narian would be, I knew I would never be able to conceal anything from the Captain if he turned to me for information. But Narian said nothing, his expression unreadable.

"Perhaps you are but a runaway," Cannan continued, his commanding eyes set on the sixteen-year-old's face. When Narian still said naught, Cannan turned to the King. "If that is the case, Sire, I see no need to go to war simply to protect a miscreant child from a parent's retribution."

I did not know if Cannan were truly suggesting we return Narian to the High Priestess, but my stomach squirmed at the possibility. I glanced toward the antechamber doors, hoping this conversation would end before London and Destari arrived, for they would certainly give their Captain the information he sought.

"I cannot speak to the reason I was abducted," Narian finally responded, sounding cowed, and I wondered if he were just playing to his audience.

"As I have told you before, I did not know I was Hytanican until last summer. Then I journeyed here only to learn of my heritage. The High Priestess is insistent upon my return because I was raised, as are others, to serve her, and she does not like to lose things she values." He paused, hanging his head, and his golden bangs fell forward to hide his expression. "I will not suffer, as you put it, a mere 'parent's retribution' should I be placed in her custody."

After a brief moment, Narian lifted his tortured blue eyes to my father's kindly brown ones, aware that the King was the weak link.

"I feel no loyalties to Cokyri, Your Majesty. While I will, without argument, comply with any decision you make with regard to my future, I ask you to permit me to claim Hytanica as my home." There was a pleading note in his voice, although I again questioned its sincerity.

My father, in his compassion, could not turn Narian away.

"Cannan, my decision stands. We will provide him with the same protection I would provide to any of our children."

The Captain looked one last time at Narian, measuring him with his eyes, and it seemed to me that he knew the young man was concealing something. He did not, however, pursue the subject.

"You should return to my office," the Captain said.

"Thank you, sir," Narian said to Cannan. Then he bowed again to my father. "Thank you, Your Majesty."

This time the relief I detected seemed genuine. He did as he had been told and retreated toward the Captain's office, although he did not enter, but resumed his earlier stance against the wall.

While we continued to wait for London and Destari to arrive, I reflected upon the deliberately ambiguous nature of Narian's explanation. While he had, strictly speaking, been truthful, his carefully chosen words were capable of more than one meaning. "I cannot speak to the reason I was abducted" would be interpreted as "I don't know the reason" by my father, rather than "I know, but will not reveal it."

It was but a half hour later that Destari and London entered. They strode up the center of the Hall of Kings together, the guards in the room falling silent as they followed the progress of the man most of them had come to call traitor. I knew there were some who believed otherwise, and counted Cannan among them, despite the fact that he had been involved in the decision to discharge my former bodyguard. If Cannan sincerely thought London a traitor, he would not have allowed him into the Palace at all, save to be thrown into the dungeon.

London said nothing but watched the Captain, who found

himself in a rather awkward position. After clenching and unclenching his jaw several times, Cannan posed the relevant question.

"London, you know the Cokyrians better than anyone. What would you suggest we do?"

"What valuable military advice could a commoner offer to the Captain of the Guard?" London parried, raising a mordant eyebrow.

Cannan stared murderously at his former guard for a moment, then cleared his throat.

"With my authority as Commander of Hytanica's military, I reinstate you to your position in the King's Elite Guard and to your former rank of Deputy Captain."

Somehow, impossibly, my horrible deed had been undone. Perhaps now London would find it within himself to forgive me. I was so elated that I struggled to keep myself from running to him. London, for his part, merely tilted his head toward Cannan to show his gratitude, no change in his bearing.

The Captain was unwilling to let London relish the moment for long.

"Now, what action do you propose we take?" he demanded.

"This is really quite simple," London replied, taking control. Turning to my father, he asked, "Do you intend to return the boy, Your Majesty?"

"No," my father replied. "He is Hytanican, and as such is granted the abiding protection of his Kingdom."

"Then this is what we must do." The tone of London's voice indicated he would brook no contradiction. "Inform the Cokyrians that we have prevailed upon Narian to return, but that he needs time to bid farewell to his family. Tell them that we will bring him to the bridge in five days, at which time we will transfer him to their custody.

"During these five days, Hytanica must prepare for whatever

response will be forthcoming from Cokyri when they learn that Narian is not actually going to be turned over to them. Forces must be assembled to defend the city if indeed it comes to that."

"And the meeting?" the King asked. "Are we to ignore it altogether?"

"I will meet the Cokyrians at the appointed time and location to try to forestall their retaliation." London's statement earned a few dubious mutterings, but he did not pay attention. "I will inform the High Priestess that we claim Narian as Hytanican by birth and by choice, and that he will not be delivered into her custody."

Despite the grumbling among those assembled, Cannan and my father nodded their agreement to London's proposed strategy. My father then dismissed all but his personal guards, and Cannan and London moved into the Captain's office to discuss the technicalities of the plan. When they passed Narian, I noticed that his cool blue eyes never for an instant left London's face.

XXVI

The Enemy Without, the Enemy Within

O nce the High Priestess had consented to meet at the bridge five days hence, the city throbbed with activity as it prepared for a potential siege, and Cannan sent patrols to the surrounding villages to instruct their inhabitants to be ready to move inside our walls with little warning if such became necessary. Hunting parties braved the woods to our north, and the villagers slaughtered whatever animals they could sacrifice as part of a plan to stockpile food and other provisions. Hundreds of other supplies were gathered to guard against a potentially long and arduous winter. Weaponry was checked, repaired, and counted, and the armories in the Palace and at the Military Complex were replenished so that not a single soldier would fall short of the required arms.

When the fifth day arrived, I awoke before dawn in order to see London and the thirty soldiers that were to accompany him off on their mission. Destari would also be attending the meeting; as the only soldier of rank other than London, it would be his task to assess how great and immediate a threat the Cokyrians posed to Hytanica while London delivered the King's message.

In Destari's absence, Tadark had been reassigned to be my bodyguard. I had not spoken to the small-statured, baby-faced guard since he had betrayed me to Cannan by confessing the nature of my visits with Narian. He was, therefore, initially on edge around me, but I paid no heed, as I had far more pressing concerns. Unfortunately, it did not take him long to conclude all was forgotten, if not forgiven, and he soon resumed his annoying habits.

With Tadark aggravatingly close to me, I came down the Grand Staircase and went out into the Central Courtyard, where London, Destari, Cannan, and my father stood by the gates at the far end. Destari was in uniform, as was expected of anyone who represented Hytanica, but London, ever the rebel, still wore his leather jerkin and weathered boots. On the other side of the open gates, the troops, in full uniform with plates of armor protecting their chests and backs, waited on horseback for the two Elite Guards to join them.

I approached with Tadark just a few feet behind, the chilly morning air feeling harsh and unfriendly, and I shivered despite my heavy cloak. Though this was supposed to be a simple meeting, no one thought the Cokyrians would receive Hytanica's message with grace. It was probable that fewer soldiers would be returning than were departing.

I stopped a few feet away from the men, knowing I would not be welcomed, at least by my father and Cannan, but wanting London and Destari to know that I wished them well. Although London had returned to duty within the Palace, he had not yet come to see me, and I hoped things were resolved between us.

London glanced at me, then strode to my side before mounting his horse.

"You should not be here," he teased. "But then I've never known anyone who flouts as many rules as you do."

"I believe that can be attributed to your influence," I replied, relieved by his casual manner.

"We will return without injury, but if not, know that what happened between us is in the past, and that you never left my heart."

I nodded, my eyes watery. He and Destari mounted their horses and rode out at the head of the troops. I watched until the somber aftermath became more frigid than the air, then sought the tranquility of the Chapel to say a prayer for the safety of our men before returning to my quarters to wait for news.

Time passed slowly, and with each moment, my sense of doom grew. Our troops would have reached the bridge by now. How many Cokyrians would they have encountered? Had the message been delivered? How had the enemy responded? And, the most terrible question of all, were my two most trusted guards alive?

As the day wore on, I would occasionally stand on my balcony to survey the city and what land I could see beyond its walls, checking for movement. It was not until the weak November sun had begun its plummet toward the horizon, however, that I saw riders approaching in the distance. I stared intently, knowing that London and Destari would lead, then left my quarters to stumble to the Grand Staircase, for I had seen only one horse heading our men.

With a sick feeling in my stomach, I waited on the landing above the first floor. I heard footsteps from below and saw Cannan and my father emerge from the antechamber followed by several guards, obviously having been told that our men were returning.

I stayed put, knowing that my father would not approve of my presence when the Elite Guards entered to make their report. I swallowed several times to try to clear the lump from my throat, and for once Tadark had the courtesy to give me some space by standing against the wall behind me.

The paradoxical tranquility was agonizing, and time slowed to a maddening crawl, although in fact it was only minutes before the doors were yanked open by the Palace Guards. As both London and Destari entered, taking rasping, exhausted breaths, I clutched the banister for support lest I collapse with relief.

London seemed to be unharmed, albeit sweat-drenched and grimy, but Destari's left shirtsleeve was soaked crimson. The wound, however it had been inflicted, had been bleeding profusely for quite some time. I was slightly sickened by the sight of the blood but made no sound nor effort not to see.

"Report," Cannan ordered, startled by the condition of two of his finest soldiers.

"The Cokyrians were not pleased by what I had to say," London said wryly, rubbing the back of his neck as if it were sore. "They attacked us when we were leaving. My horse took an arrow in the neck. Destari came back for me, only to take one in the shoulder."

"The arrow grazed my arm," Destari said, for worried eyes had fallen upon him. "It looks worse than it feels."

"You should have it examined straightaway," my father insisted, gesturing toward the wound, more upset by the sight than I. "You have been bleeding quite heavily —— perhaps the wound needs to be sewn."

"There are many who fared worse, Your Majesty. I am in need of no one's care at this moment."

"How many were injured?" Cannan probed, and I shrank from hearing the answer.

"Twenty-four soldiers returned with us," said London, after glancing at Destari and deciding it was he who would deliver the bad tidings. He sounded strangely distant as he spoke. "Of those, nine were taken to the Infirmary at the Military Base. The six who were left behind are, presumably, dead."

I clenched my jaw so fiercely that my teeth began to ache. I wanted to weep as I thought of the families of the six slain soldiers, and how they would soon learn that their husband, or their father, brother, or son, was dead, killed during a simple and, at first blush, safe mission. Perhaps their wives were waiting dinner for them, not yet knowing that they lay lifeless on the shore of the river, stuck with Cokyrian arrows. I withheld my tears with difficulty, picturing the dignified faces of the Cokyrians who had been inside the Kingdom I called home less than a week ago, no longer seeing the regal figures I had initially judged them to be, but merciless killers.

"Does the enemy have sufficient numbers to pose an immediate threat?" Cannan was asking as I recovered from my shock.

"No, sir, not a threat against the city," Destari answered. "They did not pursue us, seemingly satisfied with the punishment they had inflicted. They also suffered injuries and, perhaps, casualties."

"Go to the Infirmary and see who lives, and Destari, have your wound treated," Cannan instructed, sounding drained as he experienced afresh the pain of war that had been absent for sixteen years. "I will send troops out to collect the bodies and to reinforce our protection of the bridge."

London and Destari gave curt nods, and the small group dispersed, the two guards exiting through the main doors, Cannan and my father heading in the direction of the Captain's office.

———

In the aftermath of the debacle at the bridge, Cannan increased the number of soldiers who patrolled Hytanica's borders by day and by night, and sent scouts into the Niñeyre Mountains to monitor the activities of the Cokyrians. Although our enemy had departed, no one expected this state of affairs to last, and our Kingdom was on high alert for any sign of their return. But there were no incidents. Destari, who had returned to his post less than a week after he had been injured, said it was reminiscent of the end of the war, when the Cokyrians had abandoned their attack and vacated their encampments to remain unseen for sixteen years.

As the days plodded on, the city was restive. An unmistakable sensation of doom hung over it, yet each new day brought another reprieve. It was when we entered the month of December, with the passage of more than two weeks since the meeting at the bridge, that the atmosphere in the city and at the Palace became noticeably less strained. The Christmas season was approaching, and in spite of the unsettled state of affairs with Cokyri, spirits were rising. Though Cannan had not reduced the number of troops on patrol, the Hytanican people began to believe that the Cokyrians did not intend to strike, and many thought it inconceivable that they would start a war over an insignificant sixteen-year-old boy.

During this stressful but uneventful time, I saw very little of Narian, though he continued to reside in our Guest Wing, and I had not yet spoken with him. I could only assume that Cannan had forbidden him access to certain parts of the Palace, probably harboring some concern about Narian's relationship to the High Priestess. I did see more of London, however, as he was often with Destari, and I began to feel as though I once again had two bodyguards. I was not surprised, therefore, when I left my quarters late one afternoon to visit the library and found both men outside my parlor door.

I made my way through the corridors, trailed by both guards, who were speaking to each other in hushed tones, but I was too indescribably happy to have London back to be irked by their manner, whether it was conscious on their part or not. Though it was not yet time for dinner, all the lanterns in the corridors had been lit, as the daylight hours had diminished now that winter was upon us. Despite the fact that fires smoldered in most of the fireplaces within the Palace, the interior temperature was dropping, and I tugged a shawl more closely about my shoulders to ward off the chill.

As we entered the library, my eyes fell on Narian, who was seated in one of the armchairs by the hearth, immersed in a book, light from the flames casting flickering shadows upon his face and adding a touch of red to his blond hair. He raised his head and came to his feet, looking almost hopeful, but his guarded facade emerged when he saw Destari and London with me.

"Princess Alera," he said, giving me a courteous nod.

Now that I had seen him free of his calculated aloofness on several occasions, I hated it when he employed the guise. Nevertheless, I understood the need to observe formalities whenever anyone else was at hand (especially the two guards with whom we were currently keeping company).

"Good evening, Lord Narian," I said, so conscious of the need to act naturally that every word and movement felt awkward. "Does living in the Palace agree with you?"

"I am well accommodated, though I feel a bit constrained."

Mystified as to the constraints to which he alluded, I asked, "Do you miss your family?"

"No, I have not seen my family since before the Tournament. I miss being outdoors; I miss the activity."

An idea came to me, something that might give me a chance to spend some less supervised time with him.

"Perhaps, then, you would like to help us prepare the Palace for Christmas. We will be hanging holly, mistletoe, and ivy throughout the interior of the Palace, and on the exterior —— "

"I don't think that's the sort of activity he is missing, Alera," London interjected, leaning against the wall to the left of the window near the book-filled aisles. "I'm sure he'll tell you if you ask him —— he's used to daily training and drill. You can lose your edge if you go too long without training."

Narian stared coolly at London, though a small crease in his brow had appeared. I closed my eyes, hoping London had finished. Of course, he had not.

"I could continue your training," he calmly offered, though he watched Narian with predatory eyes. "After all, I am well acquainted with your instructor's methods."

I took a quick, involuntary breath. Destari, who had moved to the window seat, looked shocked as well, for his dark eyebrows had risen in disbelief. Narian glanced at us, then returned his stare to London.

"Oh well," London said indifferently, pulling a book from a nearby shelf and riffling through its pages. "Just a thought."

Though everyone in the room was gawking at him, London remained inscrutably nonchalant, and I marveled at his composure. Never before had he mentioned his ordeal in Cokyri, and now he had flippantly implied that he not only had met the Overlord but also knew a great deal about his methods and how Narian had been trained. I was the only one in whom Narian had confided; I alone knew that the Overlord had been his teacher. I should have anticipated, given what London had said to me prior to the exhibition, that he would put the pieces together, but that he would be bold enough to tell Narian how much he had surmised was totally unexpected.

"About Christmas," I said to Narian, my throat having gone so dry that my voice was hoarse. "Would you care to join us?"

Narian appeared not to have heard me. His eyes were fixed on London's hands as they turned the pages of his book.

"That ring does not belong to you," he declared unexpectedly.

London held up his right hand, palm turned in, displaying the wide silver band on his forefinger that was overlaid with two pairs of stacked loops bound together by narrow silver links. I stared at it, the only jewelry that he ever wore and that he was never without.

"Oh, I think it does belong to me," London disagreed, cocking an eyebrow in warning. "I more than paid for it sixteen years ago."

A thunderous silence hung in the room as Narian and London stared distrustfully at each other. Finally, the younger man tore his gaze away, and I repeated my question, hoping to dispel the tension that saturated the air.

"If you want my assistance, then I will be happy to oblige," Narian said.

Though his reply was sincere, I could not hold his attention. I had come to believe that nothing would ever penetrate Narian's defenses, but I was wrong, for London had clearly rattled him.

———

"I need a gift for Ailith, then we will have purchased something for everyone," Miranna said, stopping to peruse the jewelry displayed on the counter in one of the shops.

She and I were visiting the Market District in search of inexpensive yet meaningful Christmas gifts for our personal maids and servants. Every year, we went shopping together for this purpose, though it was seen as improper for us to buy gifts for our bodyguards, who were forced to tolerate us far more extensively than were our maids. While I knew London, Destari, and Halias relished working as they did, I would have liked to have been permitted to show our appreciation by giving them something for Christmas.

Winter had now descended upon Hytanica, but the season was not particularly harsh. While it was rare for it to be cold enough in the river valley for the Recorah to freeze solid, the landscape was nonetheless drab and dismal. Especially in the month of January, skies were gray and cold rain would often fall. At higher elevations, the precipitation would descend as snow, capping the mountains to our north in white.

Miranna left the shop and, weaving her way through the people on the street, made her way to a store where dress fabrics were sold. I continued to scan the display before me, although in truth my attention was captivated by the daggers at the end of the counter rather than by the jewelry. Ever since my self-defense lessons with Narian, I had developed a keener awareness of the weaponry carried by Destari and the other guards who worked in the Palace. I knew little about the daggers this shop was selling, or any other form of weaponry, except that simply taking note of them would be viewed as extremely unladylike. I dragged my attention away from the knives and tried afresh to generate interest in the jewelry, vaguely cognizant of the opening and closing of the shop door.

As I passed my eyes over the merchandise, a strong arm took hold of me from behind, wrapping around my upper chest and pulling me against a well-muscled body. I clawed at the man's forearm, desperate to free myself and frantic that Destari was not coming to my aid. My assailant released me with a chuckle, and I wheeled about to come face-to-face with Steldor.

"What are you doing?" I demanded, cheeks aflame, temper rising. "Do you always pounce upon unsuspecting women from behind?"

Steldor raised an eyebrow in amusement. "Actually, I prefer to pounce from the front," he said, dark eyes lazily scanning my figure. "Besides, I thought you were learning self-defense. It would seem you need a better teacher."

I glared at him, both in response to his subtle criticism of Narian and the fact that he *somehow* had learned of the activities in which I had engaged during my visits to Baron Koranis's estate. I could only assume that Tadark had been overly talkative.

"My teacher is the best fighter in Hytanica," I countered, hoping to strike a nerve.

Steldor smirked, clearly enjoying my reaction, as if he had intentionally baited me.

"You know your way with words, Princess, but just how proficient have you become with weapons?"

I stared speechlessly at him. Was he suggesting that he evaluate my skill and the effectiveness of Narian's teaching? And to what end?

"That is not your concern," I said stiffly, beginning to move away from him to find Miranna at the shop across the street.

"I don't believe your father would view Narian as an appropriate teacher," Steldor commented, following behind me. "Perhaps it would be enlightening to put the question before him."

I turned back to him, distrustful of his motives. His smirk broadened, for he knew he had gained the upper hand.

"If you wish to continue to learn self-defense," he said, reaching out to finger a strand of my hair, "you'll find that I am your only option."

"Well, since you are the person against whom I most need to defend myself, I will decline your gracious offer," I retorted. "If you'll excuse me, I must finish my shopping before the day is out."

I brushed past him to step out of the shop, but to my dismay, he followed right behind, my anger, strangely enough, serving to have encouraged him.

"I am currently off duty, and believe I will accompany you," he informed me, voice brimming with self-assurance and barely disguised humor.

"That won't be necessary." I glowered at him in an attempt to burn a hole through his irritatingly perfect features.

"Not necessary, indeed; but it will certainly make for an interesting afternoon."

Turning my back to him, I made my way through the crowd toward my sister, doing my best to ignore the one person I would rather have seen run over by a buggy than at my side, as he fell into step with me, bent on ruining the rest of my day.

XXVII

A History Lesson

n the days following the encounter in the market, I saw little of Steldor, and frustratingly less of Narian. While I glimpsed Narian at times within the Palace, I was never able to speak openly with him. He seemed especially reluctant to say anything as long as London was with me, and his lack of candor was discouraging.

We were in the Grand Entry Hall when Narian joined Miranna and me to decorate the Palace. While I had pinned my hopes on this occasion, our conversation was fleeting at best. There were so many other people about that we could say nothing of consequence to each other. I returned to my quarters in despair that evening, then released Destari from his post for I intended to stay in my rooms until I retired for the night. Too overwrought to sleep, I picked up a book from the table adjacent to the sofa in the belief that reading might take my mind off my troubles. I sank into one of the armchairs near the hearth, seeking its warmth, and opened to the first page.

A small noise from my bedroom, scarcely louder than the rattling of a shutter, caught my attention. As no other sounds followed, I again concentrated on my book, reading until my eyelids drooped.

Yawning, I stood and tossed the volume onto my chair, feeling pleasantly disoriented. I moved into my bedroom, my eyes flitting to the window beside the balcony doors, and I caught a small movement. I halted, my drowsiness vanquished. The moon was full, shining through the glass and creating a path of light across the floor, and at the edge of it, by the window, I could make out the silhouette of a man approaching me, his silent footfalls terrifying.

Before my paralyzed lungs could draw enough air to scream, the man spoke, his voice gentle and familiar.

"Don't be afraid, Alera. I just wanted to see you."

"Narian!" I exclaimed. "How did you get in here?"

"I came in through the balcony doors."

I stared at him in amazement.

"You can't be serious... How did you get past the guards in the courtyard?"

"It wasn't that difficult." Gesturing to the balcony behind him, he added sardonically, "By the way, you may want to start barring those doors."

We locked eyes for an agonizing moment, both of us unsure what to say, then Narian moved forward. As he drew near, my pulse quickened, but not from fear. While I had been desirous of spending time alone with him, I was wholly unprepared to handle the yearning that now burned within me.

With his compelling blue eyes upon my face, Narian reached out a hand and cupped my chin, then bent down to gently caress my lips with his own. I did not resist, and he put his other hand upon the small of my back, drawing my body to him and pressing his mouth more ardently against mine. I closed my eyes and raised my arms to his shoulders, my fingers playing with his thick golden hair as I returned his kiss.

His lips broke from mine after a few moments and he brushed them across my forehead.

"I was beginning to think I had imagined that," he murmured in my ear.

I nestled against his chest as he held me, his rich, earthy scent of leather and pine and cedar encircling me. Then reason gradually returned, and I grasped the impropriety of my circumstances. Here was a man, in my bedroom after dark, whose lips had been upon mine, and in whose embrace I now stood, with no chaperone to be found. I forced myself to take a step back from him, and Narian slipped his hands down my arms to entwine his fingers in mine.

He did not ask for an explanation as to why I had pulled away, most likely recognizing the unseemliness of my position. Instead, he led me to the balcony doors, whereupon he turned to face me with the hint of a smile.

"Shall we?"

"What do you mean?" I asked, hesitant yet curious.

"I can get you out of here."

Though my common sense told me to refuse, the thought of doing something daring and impulsive was overwhelmingly appealing, especially given the person in whose company I would be, and so I nodded.

Narian retrieved a pack from the floor by the window and opened it, then tossed me some black clothing.

"Go put these on, and bring me one of your simpler dresses so you'll have something to change into later."

I brought a plain linen gown to him, then moved into the bath chamber to don the clothing he had given me. During my self-defense lessons, I had become somewhat accustomed to men's trousers and did not find wearing them now to be strange, though I would no doubt have felt differently if asked to face anyone other than Narian.

As I again approached the doors to the balcony, Narian pushed his dark cloak off his shoulders and removed the long-sleeved black leather jerkin he wore, helping me into it for warmth. He then rearranged the cloak, covering his light hair with the hood so that he became nearly invisible against the night sky. No covering was necessary for my hair; it was already a match to the darkness.

Narian crouched down and opened one of the balcony doors, motioning for me to do the same, and we slipped out into the cold night air. He shut the door behind us and picked up the coiled rope from the floor that he had used to climb up to my room, tying a loop in its end.

"Slide your foot in here," he said, holding it open for me.

I stood and inserted the toe of my shoe. He then tied the rope around my body, fastening the other end to the railing.

"I'm going to lower you down," he informed me, "but first, we must wait."

He pointed to the tower at the corner of the courtyard wall, and I saw that the guard who patrolled the planked walkway extending from the tower in two directions had just turned the corner and was walking north toward us along the wall's western side.

Narian tugged me into the shadows cast by the Palace, and we remained immobile until the sentry reversed direction and began to march south. When he reached the corner, he would pass through the tower, continuing east down the length of the front courtyard wall to the point where it intersected the Central Courtyard, then return.

Easily hoisting me over the railing, Narian lowered me toward the ground. My hands shook and my heart thumped loudly until my feet connected with the earth and I knew that I was safe. I melted into the stone wall as Narian had told me to do, feeling light-headed at the risk I was taking. He climbed down, removed the rope from my body, and tugged it off to the side of the balcony, close to the Palace so it would be less visible.

The sentry was now retracing his steps and would soon pass

through the tower and again turn north. When the man had completed his tour and was once more moving away from us, Narian took my hand and led me stealthily across the Court-yard to stand next to the wall. We then crept toward the ladder leading up to the tower, a few paces behind the guard moving above us on the walkway.

After waiting a few more moments for the guard to prog-ress through the tower, Narian motioned for me to climb the ladder. I obeyed, somewhat fearful of ascending straight sky-ward for fifteen feet upon the rickety contraption, but Narian climbed right behind, hands on the wood on either side of me, providing reassurance.

When we reached the tower, the frosty night breeze tousled my hair and turned the tips of my ears pink, and I shivered both from cold and excitement. Narian did not seem to notice the chill, however. Wasting no time, he pulled a second rope from his pack, fastening it around me as he had on the balcony. Moving to the western side of the tower, away from the sentry, he lifted me over the top of the wall to carefully lower me. To my chagrin, the rope then landed at my feet. I could see noth-ing as I stared upward in confusion, but before my confusion could turn to fright, I heard the swish of a cloak and Narian dropped to the ground.

"Can't leave a rope hanging here," he muttered.

I marveled at our actions —— Narian assisting a Prin-cess disguised in men's garments to escape the Palace in the dead of night, then leaping off walls to join her. I was also a little embarrassed by how effortlessly he had evaded the Palace Guards, both when he had come for me and when we had left.

Narian again took my hand, this time to lead me down the slope into the apple orchard that lay between the Palace and the Military Complex. We walked in silence until we came to the spot where Narian had tethered a horse.

"Care for a midnight ride?" he asked, not really posing a question, for I knew he would not take no for an answer.

I nodded as he untied the steed and moved closer to the large sorrel animal. Thankfully, the horse was saddled, allowing me to mount by the far easier method of a stirrup rather than through use of Narian's knee.

After I was situated, Narian handed me the reins and swung onto the horse's back in the same way he had during my riding lesson. He set the horse off at an easy walk with a *cluck* of his tongue, and I surrendered the leathers to him as he wrapped his arms around my waist.

We approached the darkened city without saying a word, though the silence between us was not uncomfortable. I was happy to be with him, and to be doing something adventurous. The chill I had felt dissipated as we rode, partly from the warmth of the animal and partly from the warmth of Narian's body against mine.

The city was still as I had never before seen it, and in its tranquility seemed almost like a different place. The streets were deserted except for the occasional guard on patrol who did not heed us. I reveled in my newfound freedom, at being out in the open with no need to hide that Narian and I were together, and with no bodyguards to separate us.

We meandered through the city without speaking, the horse's hooves sometimes clacking against cobblestone, other times muffled on a dirt street. The houses as well as their inhabitants seemed to lie in deep slumber. The moon and stars, reflected by the rare dusting of snow upon the ground, were our primary sources of light, occasionally aided by a guard's torch or candle glow from a window. In the almost complete silence, I became much more conscious of the sound of Narian's breathing and automatically matched it with my own. While in truth I knew little about him, I felt more at one with him than

I had ever felt with anyone else; despite London's concerns, I also felt safer.

Time eluded me, but all too soon we had circled around to the Royal Stables just to the east of the Palace, and I smiled when I realized from whence the horse had been obtained. Narian dismounted, then to my delight, for I was not used to his assistance, he told me to swing my right leg over the pommel of the saddle, and I slid into his arms to land beside him.

None of the grooms were working this late at night, and I hovered by the door while Narian put the horse in a stall. The barn was dimly lit by the moonlight that shone through the windows, but though lanterns hung at intervals on the walls, we dared not light one, lest we draw notice.

He came back to me after caring for our mount and led me toward a stack of hay at the rear of the barn. We did not speak, but he motioned to me as he settled upon the hay, inviting me to sit beside him. I did so, and he draped his cloak around us both. Feeling pleasantly tired and warm, I rested my head upon his shoulder, his arm around me, inexpressibly content.

He shifted after a moment to lean against the wall, and I felt his mood change along with his posture.

"Tell me about London," he murmured, after he had repositioned us both.

"What is it you wish to know?" I asked, perplexed by his interest.

"How long has he been your bodyguard?"

"For as long as I can remember. He took up the post when I was a little girl."

"Was he involved in the war?"

"Yes, he was a scout at the beginning of his military career, then sometime during the war began leading troops into battle."

A now familiar pang of guilt hit me over how little I had

bothered to find out about London over the years, as I could dredge up few specifics about his life.

"Then how old is he?"

"He is similar in age to Destari and Halias, perhaps thirty-nine or forty."

Narian made a sound of acknowledgment, but I could tell this was not the answer he had expected, for London looked much younger than his actual years.

"How does he know so much about Cokyri?"

"He was a prisoner for about ten months toward the end of the war," I answered, and his body momentarily tensed.

"Ten months?" he repeated, slowly and incredulously. "The enemy does not usually last ten *days* when the Overlord extends his hospitality."

"We don't know much about what he endured during that time," I said, more subdued, for an image of London suffering as a prisoner of Cokyri had entered my mind.

Narian was puzzled. "But how did London return to Hytanica? How is it that he lived? The Overlord does not release prisoners of war."

"London escaped. After the Cokyrians took you from your home, there must have been great haste to withdraw from our lands, and he was perhaps less heavily guarded. I know nothing else about it, except that he was quite ill when he returned to us. When he had recovered, he was made a member of the Elite Guard in recognition of his bravery and of his service to the Kingdom, and was assigned as my bodyguard."

Narian fell silent, satisfied for the moment with what he had learned. Then the reason for his interest hit me, and I sat up to stare at him.

"Why were you so interested in London's ring?"

"It is Cokyrian," he said, watching me closely. "One of a pair. Its twin sits on the hand of the High Priestess, while the one London wears belongs to the Overlord. It was thought lost in battle."

I stared at him in disbelief. Had London, while a prisoner, managed to steal the Overlord's ring? Though that sounded impossible, it seemed more likely than that he had stumbled across it on a battlefield.

As I absorbed this information, I realized how meager was my knowledge of the history of the animosity between Hytanica and Cokyri.

"Narian," I said, dropping my gaze, aware that he was one of the few people who might be willing to discuss such a subject with me. "Do you know how the war began? I have heard much about the war itself, but never about its beginnings."

Narian laughed, probably aware himself that such an inquiry by a Hytanican woman would be improper, and I raised my head. His expression was so tender and open as he looked at me that I was certain I could see his soul in his eyes.

"I can tell you what Cokyrians believe about the beginning of the war," he responded, a hint of amusement still in his voice.

I gave an eager nod, nestling once more against his shoulder, ready to listen.

"Over a century ago, the King of Hytanica sent his eldest son and heir as an ambassador to Cokyri to arrange for a trade treaty between the two Kingdoms. Hytanica intended to offer a variety of crops to our mountain Kingdom in exchange for some of the jewels and precious metals that we mined. Unfortunately, the ambassador's provincial attitude that men are superior to women was not well received. When he was brought before the Empress of Cokyri, he insulted her by outright refusing to negotiate with a woman. The Empress had him executed for his insolence, and when Hytanica learned of his death, the King was incensed and attacked Cokyri with all his strength. We retaliated in turn, and the fighting escalated from there."

"A hundred years of killing because one person insulted another?" I sat up straight, gaping at him in horror. "Why was the ambassador's action dealt with so ruthlessly?"

Narian bristled at my accusatory tone.

"The Empress of Cokyri was a proud and dignified woman; she commanded respect and obedience, and when it was not forthcoming, no pardon was extended. The King's ambassador should have learned our protocols before approaching our ruler. It was doubly insulting that he felt no need to do so, and his arrogance was dealt with quickly and severely —— with death."

"And has no one tried to negotiate a treaty since that time?" I pressed, both revolted and fascinated by the information Narian was sharing.

"When the Empress died, her children, the Overlord and the High Priestess, came to power, inheriting her hatred of Hytanica. The Overlord will not entertain a treaty, as he is unwaveringly determined to conquer this land."

I could form no reply to this, so I uneasily picked at the hay, listening to the horses snorting and shuffling in their stalls. Then Narian's eyebrows lifted, and I knew he was about to pose a question of his own.

"To where does the tunnel lead?" he inquired.

I gawked at him. "How do you know about the tunnel?"

"Actually, I didn't know for certain it was a tunnel until just now. I discovered some time ago that the floor in one of the unused stalls has greater give than the floor in the rest of the stable and supposed it might conceal an escape tunnel. You just confirmed my hunch."

I fought to maintain my poise, feeling a little insulted that he would use such a ruse to get information from me, but before I could respond, he repeated his question.

"So where in the Palace does the tunnel open?"

My thoughts whirled, as I knew this was something I should not disclose. Very few people knew there were, in fact, two tunnels that led outside the Palace for use by the Royal Family if circumstances warranted a hasty or secretive departure. On the other hand, since Narian had already learned of this tunnel's existence, I had no doubt he would find the entry point within the Palace. As I wrestled with this decision, I became cognizant that he was studying me.

"Alera," he appeased. "You don't have to tell me anything if you feel you shouldn't. Let's just forget I asked."

He smiled reassuringly, then put his arm around me again and I settled against his chest. As my unease evaporated, something else about which I was curious came to mind.

"I have never been in the mountains," I murmured. "Tell me what it is like there."

Narian began to describe the raw beauty of the land in which he had lived, a faint longing behind his words. The steady cadence of his voice and the sweet smell of the hay were comforting, and my eyelids fell like heavy drapes. Just before I drifted off to sleep, secure in his arms, a whisper escaped my lips.

"The tunnel leads into the Chapel."

———

"Alera. Alera, wake up."

Narian's voice gradually penetrated my many layers of slumber, and I groggily opened my eyes. For a moment I was disoriented, but when I saw him gazing out one of the windows of the stable, the evening came rushing back, jolting me awake. We needed to reenter the Palace.

"You should change," Narian instructed, tossing me the gown I had earlier given him to place into his pack. "We need to leave before the stable hands arrive for the day."

I nodded, glancing around for a place where I would not be seen. After finding nothing more fitting, I entered an empty stall and reemerged a few minutes later wearing my simple cream-colored frock. Narian had not moved, and I extended the black clothing to him as I went to his side, watching him tuck the items into his pack.

I could tell from the grayish light filtering through the window that the sun was just rising.

"How are we going to get back into the Palace?" I queried with a touch of panic.

"We'll walk through the front gates."

Unable to think of a better alternative, I nodded, hoping he knew what he was doing. He reached out to pluck a bit of hay from my hair, and my cheeks grew hot with embarrassment.

"I'm afraid I'm not very presentable."

He smiled affectionately, then took my hand and drew me to him.

"I prefer you in breeches," he teased, lifting my chin to give me a light kiss. "But other than that you look just fine."

I shivered, and he draped his cloak around my shoulders, donning the leather jerkin himself. He pulled open the stable door and we walked toward the courtyard gates, the frosty grass crunching beneath our feet.

"Halt! State your purpose!"

One of the Palace Guards on duty hailed us, but before I could answer, he recognized me, and his eyes widened in astonishment.

"Princess Alera! What are you...? How did you...? Where did you...?"

"Pleasant morning for a stroll, don't you think?" Narian calmly interrupted.

"Yes, of course," the sentry replied, eyes flicking back and forth between Narian and me. He pounded on the gate and told the guard on the other side to grant us entry.

As the gates opened, I cast my eyes upward and saw the

tower guards likewise staring at us in confusion. Struck by the incongruity of the situation, I looked down so the soldiers would not see my grin.

We walked up the white stone path through the Central Courtyard to the front doors of the Palace, where we replayed the same scene. Finally gaining admittance, we stepped into the Grand Entry Hall, and I hoped it was early enough so that we would not stumble into any of the Royal Family's personal guards, who would be far more willing to raise questions than the guards on night patrol in the corridors. We climbed the Grand Staircase, and after whispered goodbyes, moved in separate directions, I toward my quarters, Narian toward the rear of the Palace and the stairway that led to the third-floor guest rooms.

I felt giddy as I entered my parlor —— from tiredness, from the happiness I felt with Narian, and from how daring our actions had been. I retired to my bedroom and slipped into bed, not intending to fall asleep, but so that my personal maid and my bodyguards would not detect any change in my daily routine. As long as none of the sentries mentioned the unusual hour of our arrival to Cannan, Kade, or the King, we would go undiscovered, and I smiled to myself, cherishing the memory and wondering if Narian felt as content as I did.

Narian paid one more visit to my balcony before Christmas, but instead of leaving the Palace, we simply talked. It was when we were sitting quietly together in my parlor, warmed by each other's company as well as the glowing embers in the fireplace, that he confided he had turned seventeen, although he was forced to confess that he was unsure of the exact day, only that it was in December. While his parents would know the date, Narian was estranged from his family, by Koranis's decree. A terrible sadness clutched at me as I wished him a happy birthday, for I knew he no longer had a true family in either Hytanica or Cokyri. If he shared any of my feelings, he did not show it, but I thought his eyes as he prepared to leave were a little less bright than usual.

XXVIII

CATASTROPHIC CHRISTMAS

It was Christmas Eve, and the longest holiday of the year had just begun, for the merrymaking would continue until Twelfth Day, on January sixth. The evening would commence with a sumptuous feast provided by the Lords and Ladies of the manor houses on the open land between the Palace and the first buildings of the city. At midnight, most of the celebrants would attend Mass at one of Hytanica's churches and then would resume their carousing until dawn, to disperse until Christmas Day Mass in the afternoon. Following afternoon Mass, the revelry would begin anew.

Miranna and I had prevailed upon Narian to accompany us into the city that night, as he had never participated in holiday rituals of the type practiced in Hytanica. Our bodyguards, as always, accompanied us, as did London, who seemed set on keeping an eye on Narian.

The darkened Courtyard through which we walked was peaceful and starkly beautiful, for the trees were sugared with light snow and the white-tipped hedgerows sparkled in the moonlight. The scene as we passed through the gates into the city was definitely not. Huge bonfires burned and wild boar roasted on spits, to be served alongside stews, breads, and puddings, washed down with ale and mead. Riotously celebrating villagers, peasants, and city residents continually heaped wood upon the fires and nudged one another as they crowded around the serving tables with their own plates and mugs to receive the food and drink.

Virtually every house and shop in the city was decorated with holly, ivy, and mistletoe in the same fashion as the Palace, and many of the celebrants likewise wore greenery in their hair. The exuberant crowd was not to be confined and spilled over into the streets of the Market District and down the thoroughfare as they played games, sang carols, and danced. City Guards were out in force in case spirits ran so high that there was a danger of damage or injury.

Halias and Destari wore royal blue cloaks bearing the King's crest over their uniforms and served as bookends on each side of the three of us. London, in his leather jerkin layered over a thickly quilted white shirt, brought up the rear. Miranna and I were well bundled in furs, and Narian wore the dark cloak that he had of late been sharing with me.

Miranna and I were smiling and relaxed, intent on socializing and sampling the available entertainment, but our bodyguards were unusually tense. They tried to clear some space around us, but it was impossible to avoid the occasional bump or jostle. As for Narian, he was more closed off than usual with me, although I supposed it was due to the company we were keeping, making it difficult to know exactly what he was feeling.

Forgoing the feast for the moment, we watched jugglers and other performers who wended their way through the masses. Much to our bodyguards' consternation, many of the entertainers approached us, bent on eliciting a laugh from Hytanica's Princesses. While we welcomed most of this activity, I was apprehensive about the mummers who would occasionally come near. Ever since my girlhood, I had been frightened by their masked faces, and I found their silence disquieting as they performed plays in pantomime. I did not like the fact that there were no clues to the identities of the people behind the masks. Miranna, on the other hand, would clap enthusiastically to show appreciation for their efforts, and Narian, who seemed likewise fascinated by the mummers, would scrutinize their visages and movements. I lightheartedly asked him if it were possible to mime with a Cokyrian accent and was rewarded with a small smile.

Even as I teased Narian, another group of mummers approached us, their movements eerily fluid in contrast to the constant and erratic bustle of the crowd. Though the others had made me uneasy, these caused me to glance worriedly in Destari's direction, for their masks were dark and grotesque. One mask was black with lines of red streaming from its eyes like tears, its mouth twisted into a cry of misery. Another was gray and hideous like the face of a sickly old man. The third and final mummer wore a blank white mask that revealed only his staring black eyes. This third mummer stepped in front of me and began to bizarrely wave his hands before my face as if casting a spell, and I stepped back in fright. I was greatly relieved when Destari came forward to deal with the man.

"Move away from the Princesses," he ordered. "You'll have to find someone else to amuse."

Destari guided me away from the performer, and I glanced over my shoulder to see that the mummer had now focused his attention on Narian. Still feeling on edge, I walked onward until a strangled cry from behind brought me to an abrupt stop. London, his eyes glazing over, stumbled forward to clutch at Destari's shoulder. Destari pivoted and caught him as he went down to his knees, and my eyes darted around for Narian. I froze when I spotted several men dragging him away into the crowd, one pressing a rag over his nose and mouth.

"Guards!" Destari shouted, easing his friend to the ground. Halias reacted immediately, drawing Miranna to him and likewise shouting for the City Guards. As fear pounded like a drum inside my chest, I turned my attention to London.

With Destari crouching next to him, London reached across his chest to his left shoulder and, with a jerk, extracted a small dart. I gaped at the tiny barb displayed in his palm, terrifyingly identical to the ones concealed in Narian's belt —— the ones soaked with enough poison to end a human life so rapidly that no antidote would be effective. The awful truth also dawned on Destari, and his thick eyebrows drew together in alarm as London struggled to pull himself upright.

"Cokyri... have Narian," London gasped, then his eyes rolled back in his head and he lost consciousness, collapsing against his fellow Elite Guard. I sank to the ground beside him, tears streaming down my cheeks, panicked by his shallow, ragged breathing.

Halias, a Deputy Captain, took charge of the dozen guards who had surrounded us, while Destari forced himself to focus on his obligations as a soldier rather than his commitment as a friend. With tremendous strength of will, he tore his gaze from London.

"I must return to the Palace and sound the signal to close the gates to the city," he told Halias, the shake in his voice bespeaking the cost to him of this decision.

Halias nodded, his face drawn taut. "Go. The City Guards can help me get the Princesses and London back to the Palace."

Destari removed his arm from beneath London, then stood and strode into the crowd.

"You two," Halias commanded, pointing to a pair of brawny guards. "You will carry London. The rest of you will surround the Princesses, and you will *not* let anyone approach them."

Halias dropped to one knee where I sat upon the cold ground. When I did not acknowledge him, he reached out to grip my arm above the elbow and guided me to my feet. I dragged my eyes away from London's limp form to gaze uncomprehendingly at him.

"We must return to the Palace, Alera."

With Halias on my left and Miranna on my right, her arm entwined in mine, we began to walk back to our home, City Guards behind us, before us, and at our sides. The guards bearing London followed. Before we had gone more than three or four paces, a horn sounded, and I knew it was the signal to the keepers of the city gates to shut them down. My mind flew to Narian, and I prayed that the city had been sealed in time to prevent his removal from Hytanica. But the cold fear that rose within me at the thought of Narian was nothing compared to the ache in every fiber of my being for London. I tried to still my mind, not wanting to consider that he could be dead before we reached the Palace.

The noise and activity around us that only moments ago had seemed merry and inviting were now dark and threatening. I was tense, on alert, convinced that every person I glimpsed through the barricade formed by the bodies of the City Guards was a potential enemy.

After minutes that felt like lifetimes, we reached the Courtyard gates and hurried inside, feeling some sense of relief that any danger to us had passed. Our pace increased as we trod the pathway, and we soon walked through the front doors into the Palace. As we entered, Destari, Kade, and a noticeably careworn Cannan were deep in conversation, but all pairs of eyes quickly swung to us.

"Alera, Miranna, are you unharmed?" Cannan asked, stepping toward us.

We nodded, and he shifted his gaze to London, whose arms

were around the shoulders of the two City Guards, head lolling forward.

"Follow Kade to the King's Drawing Room," he said to the soldiers. "I've already summoned the doctor."

As a servant stepped forward to take the furs Miranna and I were wearing, the Captain spoke to Halias and Destari.

"I have sent troops out to canvass the city, and I have others in my command who can coordinate that effort. You will stay with the Princesses... and with your friend."

Cannan was atypically solicitous, and I understood from his words that he knew London's death was imminent.

Kade had already led the guards carrying London down the corridor toward the King's Drawing Room, and the rest of us trailed somberly behind. We entered the room to find Bhadran, the Royal Physician, already examining London where he lay upon the sofa. As Destari stepped forward to engage in an exchange with the gray-haired doctor, Kade departed with the City Guards.

Clearing his throat, our long-standing physician turned to me, his wizened face fraught with worry.

"His pulse is barely detectable, and his breathing is shallow. I'm sorry, but I am not familiar with this Cokyrian poison and know of nothing to counteract its effects. I could try bloodletting, on the chance we could remove some of the poison from his body, but he is already so close to death that I believe it would be pointless."

"Don't," I said, set on sparing London additional discomfort.

"How much time does he have?" Destari asked, voice husky with the struggle to control his emotions.

"Not long," replied Bhadran. "The best you can do for him is to try to keep him comfortable." At my stricken expression, he finished, "I will take my leave, so I do not intrude upon your grief." With a bow, he exited the room.

Halias discreetly moved a leather armchair near London for my use, and I sat down, feeling so weak I would surely have fainted had I kept to my feet. Looking anguished and helpless, the Elite Guards remained standing, one on each end of the sofa.

"I will stay, in case you need me," Miranna whispered, giving me a hug. She went to sit in an armchair along the side of the room, near the gaming tables that the men frequently used for cards, dice, and chess.

As I gazed at London, the memory of the afternoon when Narian had first shown us his unusual weaponry surfaced, and an idea burst into my head.

"Destari," I exclaimed, "Cannan sent one of the darts to the alchemists. Perhaps they have been able to prepare an antidote!"

Destari shook his head sadly. "I already checked with the Captain. Our alchemists have had no success in breaking down the poison so that counteragents can be identified. I'm sorry, Alera."

I nodded, my last hope extinguished, and lapsed into silence. After a few moments, I reached out a hand and touched London's forehead, gently brushing his silver bangs away from his eyes.

"He is so cold," I said, to no one in particular, for despite the fire crackling in the hearth, his skin felt like ice.

Destari and Halias removed their cloaks and spread them over him, their movements so tender that tears again rolled down my cheeks. As sobs racked my body, I heard a door open and looked up to see my father enter.

"Were either of my daughters endangered?" he asked the guards as he came to me, and I stood to let him enfold me in his arms.

"No," Destari replied. "But the Cokyrians have Narian."

I broke from my father's embrace and sank once more into my chair.

"London will suffer a soldier's death," the King said, resting a hand upon my shoulder. "That is the way he would have wanted it. Be at peace with that." Turning to Destari and Halias, he added, "I must go and talk with Cannan. Let me know when there is a change." Patting my shoulder one last time, he withdrew, leaving us to our deathwatch.

As the evening gave way to the early hours of morning, London continued to cling stubbornly to life. Destari and Halias now sat upon the floor, backs against the wall, the strain evident upon their weathered countenances, while Miranna dozed in an armchair. I studied London's face in the dim lantern light, marveling at the strength within him. How could he fight so ferociously against such impossible odds? I held his right hand in my own, wanting him to know someone was with him and that he did not wage his battle alone.

Gradually my head became heavy with stress and fatigue, and I held it in my hands, struggling to ward off sleep. I was about to lose the fight when a slight moan jarred me fully awake, and I saw London move the hand I had earlier been clasping.

"Destari!" I exclaimed. "London is stirring!"

Destari sprang to his feet and came to my side just as the Deputy Captain's eyelids flickered and briefly opened.

"London," I said urgently, placing my hand upon his. "London, can you hear me?"

His eyelids flickered again, but he couldn't yet draw them apart.

"Can it be? Should we summon Bhadran?" There was disbelief in Destari's weary voice as he tried to come to terms with what we were seeing.

The door swung shut, and I knew that Halias had left, returning in a matter of minutes with the Royal Physician. I stood and moved from London's side to enable Bhadran to examine the Elite Guard.

"He has improved," the aging doctor said, perplexed. "I have no explanation, and it is too soon to be assured of a recovery, but he is regaining strength."

Destari shot a quizzical, and for the first time optimistic, look at me.

"Perhaps his thick clothing absorbed most of the poison before the dart pierced his arm," he ventured. Turning to the doctor, he pressed, "Is it possible that not enough of the poison entered his body to take his life?"

"Some poisons are so powerful that even the smallest dose will kill. With others, a small amount will make you ill, while a larger dose will result in death." Then Bhadran added a cautionary note. "However, a significant dose of almost any poison will cause damage to the body, so should he survive, he may never be the same."

"Thank you," I choked, and Halias ushered the baffled physician from the room.

I did not care at that moment in what state London returned to us, simply praying that he would do so.

Miranna moved to stand behind my chair, having been awakened by the commotion, and rested her hands upon my shoulders. Halias rejoined us, and we four kept vigil around the Elite Guard, whose color was definitely improving and whose breathing was more regular. Hope and fresh energy flowed through my veins as I talked to him, murmuring his name. Within a half hour, the indigo eyes that I knew so well opened, and London peered steadily at me, then tried to sit up. Destari put a hand on his shoulder.

"Not so fast. You've been out for several hours."

London collapsed back onto the sofa, then spoke with great effort, sounding as though his throat were swollen.

"Why are you all sitting around?"

I beamed happily at him, although my eyes glistened once

more with tears, and I glanced around to see exuberant expressions throughout the room.

"We thought we had lost you," I said, then with no concern for propriety, I grasped his hand and held it against my cheek.

He made no attempt to withdraw from my show of affection, and a smile played fleetingly upon his features. Always the soldier, he reminded us in the next moment of the seriousness of the situation.

"Has Narian been found?"

"Not yet," Destari answered. "Do you feel up to talking to the Captain? He will want a full report."

London nodded, and both Destari and Halias left the room, Destari to find Cannan, Halias to fetch drink to soothe London's dry throat. Halias returned first, bringing ale, and by the time Cannan and Destari came striding through the doorway, London was swallowing and talking with greater ease. Cannan, his brow furrowed, strode to his wounded man to see the miracle with his own eyes, and the tension left his stance as he confirmed that his Elite Guard was indeed recovering.

"Good to have you back. Now, what can you tell me about the incident?" the Captain asked.

"Three or four men approached Narian, and as I intervened, one of them jabbed me in the shoulder with what must have been a poisoned dart." London paused, his forehead creased in thought. "It is possible that the mummers were also Cokyrian, or at least were working for the enemy to create a diversion."

He struggled to sit up, finally settling for propping himself on his elbows, then began to pummel Destari with questions.

"Were the gates shut down? Did you get a good look at the Cokyrians? Has anyone seen the boy?"

"I promptly raised the alarm, and we're scouring the city," Destari relayed. "I'm confident the Cokyrians could not have moved fast enough to escape before the gates closed."

"I have deployed search parties throughout the countryside just in case," Cannan added. "But so far, neither Narian nor his abductors have been found."

London again tried to push himself upright, and Destari shot him a disapproving look.

"I'm fine," he muttered. "Saddle a horse for me so I can join the hunt."

"London, we can get along without you for a little while," Destari said in exasperation. "You need to regain your strength."

"I'm strong enough. And I'll go on foot if you won't send for a horse."

Reading the determination on London's face, Destari relented with a scowl. "Then I will saddle two horses and accompany you. I'd hate to have you fall with no one to catch you."

Their eyes locked for a moment, and I suddenly understood the depth of their friendship and how much they depended upon each other. After receiving his Captain's nod of approval, Destari departed.

"I will send Tadark to be your bodyguard in Destari's absence," Cannan informed me. "And I will update the King."

After one last assessment of his Deputy Captain, he turned on his heel to exit as well.

By the time Destari returned, London was sitting up, eating the bread and soup that Cannan had requested be brought to him.

"The horses are prepared," Destari announced, monitoring London's movements.

London set the food aside and stood, swaying unsteadily at first, but then gaining his balance.

"I'm strong enough," he said, reading the same question on all of our faces. "Now, let's go."

The two men strode from the room, although London's pace was less brisk than usual, leaving me dumbfounded at his improvement in the past hour. If I had not been with him, I would not have believed he had just come back from the brink of death. I suddenly recalled the evening when my mother had told me of the bizarre illness from which London had suffered upon his return from Cokyri sixteen years previously. The doctors at that time had likewise predicted his death, and it struck me that the Elite Guard had an odd knack for making physicians look ignorant.

Tadark bustled in, and he and Halias escorted Miranna and me to our respective quarters. I entered my parlor and collapsed on the sofa, too tired to prepare for bed, and began to doze. My maid covered me with furs and I fell into a much deeper, and thankfully dreamless, sleep.

———

The next few days passed at an agonizing pace, for Narian had not yet been located. Destari had returned to duty as my bodyguard, but London remained dedicated to the search, knowing better than anyone the threat posed by Narian's return to Cokyri. My feelings continued to alternate between panic and despair. Panic, as London's dire warnings about the Legend rattled around and around in my head; and despair, as I thought of the precariousness of Narian's position were he to be brought back to Cokyri. I was certain the Overlord would harm him if he failed to cooperate with the warlord's plan to destroy Hytanica. London, however, remained steadfast in his conviction that Narian was still within the city, and so I dared hope he would yet be located.

Late in the afternoon on the third day following Narian's abduction, London entered my parlor as Destari was stoking the fire.

"I need to discuss something with you," he said to his fellow Deputy Captain, and Destari stood to follow him into the corridor. I forcefully objected, not about to be left in the dark.

"If this is about Narian, then I, too, want to hear what you have to say."

London considered me for a moment, finally acquiescing with a shrug.

"I think the Cokyrians will try to take Narian over the wall," he asserted, speaking to Destari. "They have no doubt come to recognize the futility of passing through the gates, as we are continuing to search wagons and buggies leaving the city and are checking everyone's identity. And to continue hiding within the city is risky. Cannan has patrols out night and day, and the citizens have been alerted to report anything out of the ordinary."

"You could be right," Destari replied, considering. "Although it would be a struggle to get an uncooperative or unconscious prisoner over the wall. Even so, they might have a stronger chance of success with that method than with passing through the gate." He pondered what London had said, then asked, "And what do you propose we do about it?"

"The Cokyrians are assuredly monitoring our patrol patterns as we speak, trying to decide where to make the attempt. Scaling the east wall would be the best choice; they can obtain cover along the forest's edge and proceed directly toward Cokyri. If we coordinate the placement of the guards who patrol along the turrets, I believe we can dictate where they will try their escape. A gap of ten to fifteen minutes in our sentries is all that would be needed to provide them with enough time to scale the wall. We can keep vigil on the other side and ensnare them should they take the bait."

"It might work," agreed Destari, a gleam in his coal-black eyes. "Have you discussed this with the Captain?"

"No, but I will do so now. If we don't act soon, I fear the enemy will make its own opportunity." He rubbed his left shoulder where he had been pierced by the dart, and I understood there were more lives at stake than just Narian's.

"I will come again when I have Cannan's answer, but you should start to think through the details. You know as well as I what he will say."

Destari returned to tending the fire once London had exited, noticeably more restless. An hour later, London returned with Tadark in tow, and I knew his strategy had met with Cannan's approval. After stationing Tadark outside my door, the two Deputy Captains departed, leaving me to the unending task of waiting.

XXIX

A Sign of the Cokyri

It was two mornings hence when I was abruptly awakened by a loud pounding on my bedroom door.

"Alera, they have him!" Tadark sounded thrilled, and it was clear that he was pleased to be the one announcing the news.

"Who has whom?" I called.

"London and Destari —— they captured the Cokyrians last night! And they have Lord Narian!"

"Is he all right?" I asked, now completely alert. "Are London and Destari all right?"

"London and Destari are tired but unhurt," Tadark jubilantly responded, as if he personally had been involved in the successful mission. "And Lord Narian has been taken to his quarters. I know the Royal Physician has been called, but I think only as a precaution. I didn't hear of any injuries."

"Thank you," I replied, my voice taking on some of the same exhilarated quality. "I will be out shortly and will want to visit Narian." I intended to see for myself that he had suffered no harm.

Sahdienne entered my bedroom and assisted me as I dressed. Forgoing breakfast, I left my quarters, heading toward the third-floor guest room that Narian had been occupying, with Tadark following behind. Reaching Narian's door, which was across the hall from the one in which he had been held prisoner, I rapped sharply upon the wood, waiting to enter until London responded. Both he and Destari were in the room, but neither looked surprised to see me as I crossed to Narian's bedside. He lay upon the double bed in his shirt and trousers, covered with a woolen blanket, his boots on the floor, and his jerkin and cloak tossed across the footboard. His face was gaunter than I remembered, but he otherwise appeared to peacefully slumber. I wanted to reach out and touch his face but knew such a gesture would betray the true nature of my feelings toward him.

"He's been drugged, but the doctor says he'll sleep it off," London explained, moving to stand beside me. "He is too important to Cokyri for them to cause him injury." He paused, then dryly asserted, "I would feel sorry for any Cokyrian who let harm befall Narian."

"Tell me about the rescue," I urged, highly interested now that I knew Narian was safe.

"It went as expected. We ambushed the Cokyrians when they came over the wall and now have three prisoners in our dungeon." London frowned, then continued. "One other escaped, however, and that means the High Priestess and the Overlord may already know that this attempt to recover Narian failed." He glanced at Destari, who was standing at the foot of the bed. "I worry what their reaction will be."

As the two men continued to talk, the door opened and Cannan entered, crossing to his Deputy Captains.

"How is he?" he asked, gazing down at Narian, and London repeated the information he had shared with me. Drawing the Elite Guards a few feet away, Cannan inquired, "What do you think will be the enemy's next move?"

"They will retaliate swiftly and viciously," London said with a note of bitterness. "We need to bring those who live outside the city within the protection of its walls at once."

The Captain stood deep in thought for a moment and then left the room without another word, London and Destari a step behind. "Let us know the moment Narian wakes," London said to Tadark, who had been hanging in the background, as he brushed past.

Alone now with Tadark and Narian, I directed my body-guard to draw a chair near the bed for me, then sat down for the second time in a week to wait for one of the men I loved to rouse.

Hunger finally got the best of me, and I sent Tadark for bread and soup. Although Narian had not stirred, his breathing was strong and steady, and I finally felt safe in showing my affection for him. His face was tipped to the side, away from me, and I whisked a few stray strands of golden hair from his forehead, longing to see his deep blue eyes. As I examined his serene expression, I was seized with curiosity about the "mark of the bleeding moon" to which London had referred. I slid out of my chair onto my knees so I could get a better line of sight, then brushed his hair back from his ear and off his neck. I gasped as my eyes found the birthmark. While it was not particularly large, it was ghastly, for it was indeed in the shape of a jaggedly cut crescent moon, with an irregular line of red that looked very much like blood extending from the bottom point. It was as though someone had ripped through a full moon with a saw-toothed dagger, causing even such a heavenly body to bleed. I pulled the hair back about his neck, for some reason wanting to hide the evidence that he was the one destined to fulfill the Legend.

Old fears having resurfaced, I stood and dawdled about the room, taking in its sparse furnishings. His bed was against the far wall, to the side of a frosty window that opened over the garden, once beautiful but now bleak and barren with winter. There were a couple of padded armchairs in front of the fireplace in which logs snapped and smoldered, and a small table piled with books. Narian's scabbard and sword were slung on one of the posts at the head of the bed, and his daggers lay on a bench near the hearth.

I sifted through the books on the table, marveling at the eclectic mix. There was a volume on Hytanica's history, another on the use of herbs in medicine, and two on weaponry. There was also a philosophy text, a volume on falconry, and, to my delight, a book of poetry. I took up the book of poems and returned to my chair to skim through its pages until Tadark returned with a tray of food. I ate ravenously, but as I lay aside my tableware to pick up the volume again, he cleared his throat, drawing my attention.

"We could play chess," he ventured. "I saw a game board on the bookshelf."

As Narian was sound asleep, I agreed, wanting to alleviate my boredom. Tadark moved the small table and another chair near mine, then set up the game. An hour later, while we were immersed in battle, I was startled by Narian's raspy voice.

"Who is winning?"

"Narian!" I turned to him with an unrestrained smile. "How are you feeling?"

He put a hand to his head and briefly shut his eyes.

"My head is aching and I am thirsty, but other than that, I am well."

"I'll fetch food and drink," Tadark said to me, coming to his feet. "And I'll let the Captain and the others know he is awake."

After Tadark had left, Narian's brow wrinkled in confusion. "How did I come to be here?" he asked.

"Cannan will explain everything when he arrives," I replied, my spirits soaring.

"How long was I gone?"

"Five days."

He nodded, then winced, as if the movement had once more created pain within his head.

"Just rest," I counseled, and he lay motionless with his eyes shut.

Watching him, I suddenly felt awkward, for I longed to embrace him but knew that such a show of affection would be inappropriate for we were alone and he was in bed. Much to my chagrin, I found myself hoping Tadark would return.

Narian continued to lie still, and I wondered if he had fallen back asleep. Before he made any further attempt to speak, the door to his room swung open and Cannan entered, followed by London, Destari, and Tadark, who was bearing bread, stew, and dark ale. Narian opened his eyes and shifted to try to sit upright, then froze as he took in the men approaching him. Without any preliminaries, he addressed London.

"I saw you stabbed with a poisoned dart! How is it that you live?"

"You sound disappointed," London caustically replied, as he and the others came to stand at Narian's bedside.

I impulsively answered the question, knowing of the tension that existed between the two men and not wanting their conversation to become heated.

"We think most of the poison was caught on London's jerkin, and that not enough entered his body to kill him, although he was incapacitated for several hours and gave us quite a scare." I drew a deep breath, aware that I was starting to babble but unable to stop. "London and Destari are the ones responsible for your safe return. They —— "

"This is the military's business," Cannan said to me sternly, damming the stream of words tumbling from my mouth.

He turned to Narian. "Now, what do you remember?"

Narian slowly swung his legs over the side of the bed, clutching again at his head. He accepted the food and drink from Tadark, taking a long swig of ale before he began to speak.

"As you know, I was taken by force at the Christmas Eve celebration. I passed out shortly after I saw London stabbed, then lost track of time. My captors were using a draught in my drink to knock me out, and I tried not to consume much of it, but they could drug me in other ways if needed. I was alert enough, though, to know we were frequently changing locations, usually during the night."

He took a few bites of stew and another long swill of ale before continuing his story.

"My captors were four in number, two men and two women. I would catch snatches of their conversation and knew that they were having trouble getting me out of the city. I also learned that they have known of my whereabouts since the Tournament, but that the High Priestess wanted to give me a chance to willingly return to them."

His brow wrinkled as he tried to remember more, then he exhaled in frustration.

"That's all I remember. Now, I would like to know how I ended up here."

"We set a trap, and when the Cokyrians tried to take you over the wall, London and Destari and others under their command rescued you," Cannan told him. "We now have three of your captors in our custody. One other escaped and is no doubt back in Cokyri."

Narian paused with a piece of stew-soaked bread halfway to his mouth.

"The villagers are in danger," he warned. "Cokyri will not hesitate to strike now that this attempt to take me peacefully has failed."

"London thought the same," Cannan replied. "But wouldn't some attempt be made to secure the release of the prisoners? An attack could lead to their execution."

"They failed in their mission and expect that their lives are lost," Narian stated grimly.

Cannan pondered this information before continuing. "In anticipation of an assault, I have begun to move those who are ready into the city. Temporary housing is being prepared in the churches and meeting halls, and additional shelters will be constructed as well to handle the large influx."

"They have to be brought into the city before nightfall, whether ready or not," London declared.

Cannan glared at him but did not respond, for his orders were inviolable regardless of London's opinion, something I was certain had been asserted once or twice already.

"I assume you had the prisoners change their clothing. Did you confiscate all personal items? Boots, belts, jewelry?" Narian's questions ended the silent battle between London and his Captain, and once again drew Cannan's attention.

"Those were my orders, but I will check that they were fully executed. I have also posted a twenty-four-hour guard outside your door as a precautionary measure and will assign a bodyguard to you when you are well enough to move about the Palace."

Narian nodded but said nothing further.

"You should eat and rest now. The King will visit later today." Settling his gaze upon me, Cannan finished, "Destari will return to service as your bodyguard. You should depart and give Narian some time to recuperate."

He motioned to Tadark and a still incensed London to accompany him, and the three men left together.

As Cannan had given me no choice, I murmured a farewell to Narian and returned with Destari to my quarters. I entered my bedroom and crossed to open the balcony doors, stepping out into the crisp winter air. My eyes took in the activity that was under way outside our courtyard walls to prepare the city to shelter Hytanica's entire population. Beyond the city's gates, villagers were crowding the roads, traveling toward safety in a steady stream. Shivering, I went back into my room, closing the doors behind me.

———

My father came to see me in the late afternoon.

"I am on my way to visit Narian and thought perhaps you would like to accompany me," he said, giving me a kiss on the cheek in greeting.

"Yes, I would," I replied, a tad too eagerly, and a shadow fell upon his face.

"I have come to know that there are... signs of affection... between the two of you," he said, then waited for confirmation.

This was not a topic I had expected him to broach, and I was sure my expression was confirmation enough.

"I am assuming this affection is based on friendship alone. He is too young... and inexperienced... to seriously be considered as a suitor for you."

His words were chosen carefully, but I knew there were unexpressed reservations about Narian hidden within them. I nodded, not trusting to my voice and at a total loss when it came to changing his opinion.

"Very well, then," he said, extending his arm to me, and I knew he viewed the matter as resolved. "Shall we?"

He dismissed Destari, giving him leave to attend to other tasks, and we proceeded to the third floor.

My father and I visited with Narian for half an hour, although in truth I said very little, not trusting in my ability to conceal the true nature of my feelings for the young man. The King, on the other hand, was in high spirits, in spite of the threat from Cokyri that still loomed over our heads, most likely due to the victories that both London's recovery and Narian's return represented.

As my father prepared to depart, he invited me to take tea with him, a subtle reminder that he did not see it as proper for me to stay in Narian's room without a chaperone. We descended the spiral staircase together and turned to walk toward the front of the Palace. Our pleasant stroll through the first-floor corridors was disturbed, however, by the slam of a door and raised, angry voices. The sounds drew our attention to the Grand Entry, where London and Cannan stood glaring at each other, evidently having just exited the Captain's office.

"If you don't get everyone into the city tonight, you will find yourself gathering corpses in the morning!" London's stance was tense, and his fists were clenched at his sides.

My father was distressed by the scene before us, and he disentangled his arm from mine. Indicating with his hand that I was not to follow, he bustled down the hall toward the quarreling pair.

"My patrols have reported no sign of the Cokyri," Cannan said, glowering down at London. He took an additional step toward his vexatious Elite Guard so that naught but a foot was between them. "And you will *not* challenge my authority in this way."

"Then in what way shall I challenge it?" London belligerently responded.

"You will show me proper respect and address me as 'Sir' or 'Captain,' or you will find yourself confined to quarters."

It was clear that Cannan's patience with London's blatant disregard for chain of command, as well as his propensity to issue orders to his commanding officer, was growing thin.

"Then I will catch up on my reading until the next time you need me to deal with a crisis. But when that time comes, you may find me unwilling to..."

London did not finish his sentence, aware of my father's approach. Tossing his Captain one final defiant glare, he turned and stalked through the front doors and out into the Central Courtyard.

My father and Cannan briefly spoke, but they were too far away for me to overhear their conversation. As the Captain glanced in my direction, I shifted self-consciously, wondering if I should continue to wait. I did not have long to ponder the matter, however, for my father returned to my side.

"Forgive me, my dear, but I will have to cancel our tea. More pressing affairs, I am afraid."

"That's quite all right," I assured him, noticing that Cannan had remained in the Grand Entry, waiting for the King.

"Would you like me to request an escort for you?"

"Thank you, Father, but there is no need. I will simply return to my quarters."

I flashed my father a pleasant smile and took his arm to walk down the corridor toward the Grand Staircase. As I left my father's side and walked past Cannan, his troubled expression made me uneasy, and fear began to mushroom inside me at the thought of London's dark prediction.

———

Early the next morning, I was sipping tea at a table in front of the bay window in the first-floor tearoom, passing the time, for the intermittent drizzle falling on the shriveled foliage outside was limiting my options for the day. I planned to visit Narian in the afternoon and had invited Miranna to join me, both for the company she would provide and as a chaperone. Although Destari would have been satisfactory in the latter capacity, I intended to leave him in the corridor, for I knew Narian would not speak freely in his presence.

As I drank, my mind revisited the argument I had witnessed between Cannan and London. I was entertaining the idea that I should ask Destari, who stood near the fireplace, about the incident when London strode into the room.

"No one has entered the city this morning; no patrols have reported to Cannan; no villagers have sought sanctuary —— no one." He sounded anguished as he spoke to his friend. "I do not believe anyone survived the night."

Destari inclined his head in my direction, silently asking whether they should talk in front of me. London merely nodded, too distracted to take much notice.

"Do you know how many were brought into the city yesterday?" Destari inquired.

"Perhaps two thousand, but hundreds were left at risk. I intend to ride out to the countryside to judge the conditions for myself." An undertone of anger had entered London's voice.

"I will ride with you," Destari said automatically.

"No. I suspect it will be dangerous, and there is no need to put both of our lives in jeopardy."

My heart leapt to my throat, but I kept my silence.

"I will see you upon my return."

As London left, fear again enveloped me, and I sought refuge in my bedroom. Every ten to fifteen minutes, I would brave the damp chill of the balcony to watch for movement on the other side of the city's walls, but the landscape was oddly static, no signs even of smoke coming from the distant homes.

Stepping out onto my balcony for the dozenth time, I spied a rider approaching at a gallop. I rushed from my rooms, startling Destari in the process.

"London is coming!"

He caught me by the arm as I turned away to head toward the landing of the Grand Staircase.

"I'm not sure this is your business," he said tersely, and I rounded on him indignantly.

"Everyone in Hytanica, including me, has the right to know what is happening. It is not just the lives of soldiers that are at stake."

He released me, frustrated by his inability to deny my assertion, and we hastened down the corridor.

"Cannan!" London bellowed upon entering the Palace. Pointing to one of the guards stationed by the door, he said curtly, "Find Cannan for me. Now!"

"I am right here." I heard Cannan's dangerously calm voice and saw him emerge from his office through the guard room. I halted on the landing, mesmerized by the confrontation taking place below.

"Are you aware no one has entered the city this morning?" London raged, stalking toward his commanding officer. "Well, I can supply you with the reason! They're dead, all dead! Soldiers, villagers, men, women, and children, even animals, all slaughtered sometime during the night. And the riverbanks are crawling with the enemy." Cannan's dark eyes locked upon London's indigo ones as the Elite Guard scathingly finished, "I would consider *that* to be a sign of the Cokyri."

"We will not discuss this here," Cannan said, in a mighty struggle to control his temper. "You will come with me to report to the King."

"I will take men out to collect the bodies for proper burial while there is still time to do so. *You* can inform the King of how well your strategy is working."

London turned his back on his Captain, but Cannan reached out and grabbed the collar of his leather jerkin, pulling him roughly around.

"You *will* come with me," he declared, having taken umbrage at London's accusatory tone. He signaled to the guards by the door, who took a step forward, and his meaning became clear.

London said nothing, but his hands slowly came to rest on his long-knives. It was then that Destari rushed down the stairs, intent on ending the altercation before someone got hurt.

"London, what our Captain *requests* makes sense," Destari asserted, moving to his friend's side and putting a hand on his shoulder. Then Destari spoke to Cannan. "Sir, I would like to take a detail of men to recover the bodies of the fallen for burial."

A long and agonizing moment passed, as London and Cannan continued to glare at each other.

"Permission granted," Cannan finally said.

Breaking eye contact with the Captain, London shifted his gaze to Destari, and some of the tension left his frame as he deliberately acquiesced to his friend rather than to Cannan. He then marched passed his Captain, heading into the ante-chamber that led to the Throne Room. Waving off his guards, Cannan followed.

Destari returned to my side and gently pried my hands from the railing; it was only then that I realized how fiercely I had been gripping it.

"Let me take you back to your quarters," he prompted, placing a hand on my arm to direct me back down the corridor. I did not object, too horrified at the news to care about where we were going.

Drastic Measures

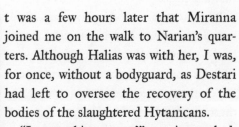t was a few hours later that Miranna joined me on the walk to Narian's quarters. Although Halias was with her, I was, for once, without a bodyguard, as Destari had left to oversee the recovery of the bodies of the slaughtered Hytanicans.

"Is something wrong?" my sister asked, noticing my subdued mood.

"The people who were in the villages last night were murdered," I explained, a wave of anger breaking over me. "Cokyri took its revenge on the defenseless. They slaughtered not just soldiers, but men, women, and *children* as well."

"I did not know," Miranna murmured sorrowfully.

"How can they act so savagely?" I demanded, my anger escalating. "How can they look into a child's eyes and show no mercy? They are no better than animals —— they are *worse*, for even animals don't kill indiscriminately!"

Miranna examined me worriedly, having never before heard such venom in my voice.

By the time we reached Narian's room, I was almost shaking with the effort to suppress my rage. As my eyes fell upon him, the knowledge that he had been raised among the Cokyrians, the people who had committed these unthinkable atrocities, was uppermost in my mind, and I unleashed my wrath upon him.

"Do you know what your countrymen did last night?" I lashed out. "Our people have been massacred —— our men, our women, our innocent children! And all because we thwarted their effort to take you!"

Narian's face clouded over, and he slid off the edge of the bed, a book falling from his lap to the floor with a thump and a rustle of pages.

"They are not my countrymen," he bitterly corrected. "And both London and I advised the Captain of the Guard as to their likely actions." He let his words hang in the air, then finished, "This is war, Alera, and war is neither fair nor pretty."

Another pause ensued, during which he looked straight into my eyes until I could no longer meet his gaze.

"If it is your desire that I leave Hytanica, just tell me, and I will," he added, his voice resolute.

I stared at him for a long moment, a range of emotions churning within me until my anger broke, leaving me weak and trembling.

"I'm sorry," I murmured. "And I do not wish for you to leave."

He searched my face, looking for the truth, then said, "Come sit. Both of you."

Miranna and I took up chairs near him and he returned to his cross-legged position upon the bed, but our conversation was stilted, and the mood in the room remained bleak.

"Maybe we should go," I finally said, after a particularly long and awkward silence.

"I will be up and around the Palace tomorrow," Narian offered, his eyes upon me. "Perhaps we will meet under less strained circumstances."

"Perhaps," I said morosely, and I departed with my sister, Halias falling into step behind us.

"You cannot blame Narian for what the Cokyrians did last

night," Miranna counseled. "Although," she continued, furrowing her brow, "I don't understand why they are so insistent upon his return."

She stopped and faced Halias, the fingers of her left hand entwined in her strawberry blond hair.

"Do you know of a reason for the Cokyrians to be so obsessed with recovering Narian?"

"I do not." Halias shrugged, his answer no doubt honest.

"I'm not sure that is our concern," I interjected, trying to quash my sister's inquisitiveness.

I saw Halias raise his eyebrows skeptically, and I knew he was thinking that I was not one to leave well enough alone. I decided it was time to move on and took Miranna's hand to lead her to her quarters. As we reached the door to her parlor, she unexpectedly tugged me inside, leaving Halias standing in the corridor.

"What is going on between you and Narian?" she queried, without any preliminaries.

"What do you mean?" I answered guardedly, though I knew my reddening cheeks would give me away.

"Come now, sister," she teased, pulling me down to sit next to her on the deep blue velvet sofa. "I know you too well not to recognize the signs." She grew more serious as she continued. "You were much too nervous while he was missing, much too eager to see him upon his return, and your outburst just now was a bit extreme. So, it's time to confess."

My thoughts were scrambled —— I knew I could trust her, yet did not want to tell her some of the secrets Narian and I shared. I felt as though the clandestine time I had spent with him would be spoiled if anyone else knew about our meetings.

"I have come to enjoy his company."

"Have you kissed?" she audaciously demanded.

I once again knew that my rising color would give me away.

"Ye-e-es." I drew the word out as though that would prevent her from pursuing the matter.

"More than once?"

"Yes," I said, slightly irritated that she was clinging to the topic so tenaciously. She waited, a knowing smile upon her lips, and I continued, "He is very warm and considerate, and he treats me differently from the way Steldor or any of the other young men I know treat me."

"Differently in what way?"

"With more respect. He actually listens to me, giving me his full and undivided attention; and he values my knowledge and seeks out my advice."

"Well, that would be a bit different from Steldor," she admitted with a laugh. "So are you going to talk to Father? After all, he has only given Steldor permission to court you; he would be very unhappy to find that someone else is secretly doing the same."

"I would, but just yesterday, Father made his opinion of Narian known."

At her puzzled glance, I elaborated.

"Father came to my quarters so that I might accompany him on a visit to Narian. He said that he has come to know of signs of affection between Narian and me, but that he assumes they are signs of friendship. He said that he would not view Narian as an appropriate suitor." I sighed heavily before continuing. "Even I admit that Narian does not meet any of Father's criteria. He is too young, owns nothing but the shirt on his back, and has a questionable military background."

Miranna again played with a strand of hair, considering how to reply.

"I know you don't want to hear this, but if that is the way Father feels, then you should perhaps limit your contact with Narian. Otherwise, you may just be setting yourself up for heartache." Her manner was gentle, but her aspect was unusually serious.

"You are right, of course. But I'm not sure I'll be able to keep my distance."

"Then at least stop kissing him!" she lightly admonished. "Just try to keep your relationship one of simple friendship. That shouldn't be asking too much, as I doubt you have many opportunities to be alone with him."

I couldn't help but smile, knowing how wrong she was. I quickly changed the subject before she could begin to quiz me about the *where* and *when* of the times Narian and I had kissed.

"So tell me about the romance you seem to have under way with Temerson."

It was finally my sister's turn to blush, and we spent the next half hour pleasantly discussing the young man in her life.

I left Miranna's quarters shortly thereafter, longing to take advantage of my lack of a bodyguard and the freedom it provided with a brief stroll outside, but the rain had started again to drizzle down Miranna's windows while we had been conversing. Nonetheless, I did not want to return to my rooms, and so I chose to visit the library. I wandered aimlessly among the stacks, hardly glancing at the books, trying to sort through the events of the day. Hearing a noise, I cocked my head to listen and began to amble back down the row toward the seating area. As I approached, my ears picked up London's troubled voice and I froze.

"For the moment, Narian wants to remain in Hytanica, but we must contend with the possibility that he will return to Cokyri once he accepts that he cannot be with Alera."

"I take it you do not trust him." It was Destari who had responded.

"No, I don't. I think he stays only because of his interest in her, for he really has no other ties to Hytanica. He is alienated from his family and has turned down Cannan's offer to enroll in the Military Academy."

"And if he tries to leave, what do we do?"

"If he tries to return to Cokyri..." London trailed off, and I strained to hear more, daring to creep close enough to peer at the two guards through a row of books. An ominous silence hung in the room until London continued. "We must be prepared to take drastic measures. Even the most drastic of all. We must be prepared to end his life, if necessary, to preclude his return. Would you be willing to do that, knowing that we could be accused of murder? Knowing that we could be hanged for our actions?"

"My duty is to protect Hytanica, and I will do so even if it means I forfeit my life," Destari avowed without hesitation.

"Good. But let's pray it does not come to that."

The two men clasped arms before going their separate ways, and I sank weakly back against a shelf of books, horror-struck at what I had just overheard. Knowing that Destari would soon learn that I was out and about the Palace, and not wanting him to search for me in the library, I willed my racing blood to slow and attempted to regain some semblance of composure. After several gulps of air, I stumbled to the library door and slipped across the threshold into the corridor, driving my fingernails into my palms in the hope that physical pain would momentarily hold my anger and despair in check. I proceeded, feeling as though my world were awry and saw Destari coming toward me.

"Alera," he said pleasantly, "I was just coming to find you." He took in my ashen complexion, and a peculiar look crossed his face. "Is something wrong?"

"No, I'm fine. My mother just wanted to talk to me for a minute."

I ground out the necessary lie without stopping, continuing

past him with my eyes focused straight ahead. Although he fell into step with me, I chose to ignore him until we reached my quarters.

"I won't be in further need of you tonight." I turned stiffly toward him, my voice brittle. Before he could respond, I entered my parlor, slamming the door in his bewildered face.

I sought the sanctuary of my bedroom, tears stinging my eyes. Too disturbed to sit, I paced around and around the room, frenetic energy coursing through me as I railed against Destari and London in my head. Once my rage subsided, fear for Narian clutched at me, and my breathing became fast and shallow. Certain that my rib cage was attempting to crush my lungs, I sank onto my bed, feeling dizzy and trying to control the panic that threatened to immobilize me. Then anger again blazed white-hot, scorching my insides, as a sense of betrayal stole over me at how callously London and Destari had conceived of their plan. I stood and resumed my pacing, my temples throbbing painfully.

For the first time in my life I wanted to throw and break something, but what I really wanted to break was not an object, but the prejudice that kept London from seeing Narian as he really was. With my anger turning to despair, I sat again on my bed, twining my fingers, the emotional battle within threatening to tear me apart. Just when I thought I could endure no more, my torment poured itself out in a rain of tears, and I fell sobbing against my pillows.

———

I slept fitfully that night, and my efforts in the morning to control my emotions were fruitless, as I obsessed over what I had heard the men discussing in the library. I had sent for London, and by the time he entered my parlor, I was pacing, my feet almost burning a path in the rug that lay in front of the sofa. Before he could open his mouth, I attacked him.

"I was in the library last night and heard every word you said to Destari. How can you possibly suggest taking his life?"

My hands were shaking, and I tottered on the edge of hysterics as I advanced on him.

"Sit down, and calm down, Alera," he said sternly, instinctively taking control.

I defiantly shook my head, then continued, my whole body now atremble.

"He is innocent in all of this! He did not choose his destiny any more than I chose to be Crown Princess. Our situations are but accidents of birth!" I was almost screeching as my emotions stretched taut my vocal cords. "And Narian will *not* return to Cokyri! You do not know him as I do and are grievously misjudging him. He is our friend and wants only the best for me and for Hytanica."

"Perhaps you are right," London said appeasingly, alarmed by my overly excited state. "Now, come and sit down, and we can talk about this."

I took a shuddering breath, somewhat calmer in the aftermath of my outburst, and permitted him to lead me to the sofa. I sat down gingerly, not feeling the least bit friendly toward him, watching with narrowed eyes as he settled beside me.

"Destari and I were discussing an option of last resort if we need to prevent Narian's return to Cokyri. If I am wrong about him, then neither you nor he has anything to fear."

My hysteria subsided at his words, but my hurt did not. We sat in silence while my dark emotions drained away, then he inarguably made his position known.

"You must understand, Alera, that I am a soldier of Hytanica and a member of the King's Elite Guard. I have sworn an oath to protect the King and the people of this Kingdom, and I will take whatever action is necessary to do so."

I gaped at him, feeling as though I no longer knew him.

"We have nothing more to discuss," I said coldly, dismissing him.

London shook his head in frustration, then stood and strode from the room.

———

As news of Cokyri's brutal assault spread, the holiday celebrations abruptly came to an end. The victims of the slaughter had been buried in several mass graves, and panic now permeated the overcrowded city. Panic turned to terror once it became clear over the following few weeks that Cokyri's strategy would be to contain us and starve us into submission, for no one, not even Hytanica's soldiers, could leave the city and safely return. The dreary and often rainy view from my balcony now included Cokyrian soldiers moving about our lands, and at night I could see the fires from their encampments.

In an attempt to make the city's provisions last as long as possible, the King had ordered an inventory of food supplies and had instituted rationing. Cannan, for his part, frequently met with his troop commanders, presumably belaboring strategies to retake the land between the city and the Recorah River. We would be in desperate need of supplies come spring... if we could last that long.

Security at the Palace had, of course, been tightened, and the social activities that would normally have been held at this time of year, including my mother's holiday party for the young nobles, had been cancelled.

During this stressful time, Narian resumed his late-night visits, eluding his guards by climbing out his window and across the roof to drop down onto my balcony. At first, he would stay but a brief time, for it gave us a chance to talk freely. As the weeks passed, he stayed for longer periods of time, and we would often sit together in front of the fireplace in my parlor, watching the flames dance while the cold January rain drummed against the windows.

There was now a persistent voice in my head telling me to put an end to these secret meetings, but I could not bring myself to do so, for I enjoyed Narian's company far more than anyone else's. I also could not deny my feelings and end my physical relationship with him. My resolve melted every time I looked into his dazzling blue eyes. I chose to live purely in the present, refusing to acknowledge the passage of time and its unrelenting march toward my eighteenth birthday.

On a beautifully clear night at the end of the month, Narian helped me escape the Palace just as he had once before. He had again secured a horse for our use, and we rode for a time on the military training field, Narian familiarizing me with the common gaits employed by a horse —— walk, trot, and canter. Then we sat peacefully on the hill that sloped down to the field, gazing at brightly burning stars rather than at smoldering fireplace embers.

While sneaking me out of the Palace had not posed a problem for him, returning me to my quarters did represent a challenge. Given the increased security at the Palace, we could not expect to pass unquestioned through the front gates in the early morning. Narian, of course, had already given this problem due consideration and had fashioned a harness of sorts, which he used to assist me to scale the courtyard wall and climb up to my balcony.

After we had returned to my bedroom, Narian waited while I changed out of the black clothing he had again brought for me. Upon reentering my room from the bath chamber, I brought the garments to him, as I dared not keep them lest my maid discover them and the resulting gossip reach the ears of my mother, my guards, Kade, Cannan, or the King.

"I should go," Narian said, after placing the items in his pack. "The sun will be up soon and then it will be impossible for me to climb unseen over the roof."

I nodded, sinking into his arms. We kissed, and as he ran his hands through my tangled hair and down my back, drawing me against him, a thrill swept through my entire body. It was becoming more difficult to part from him on these nights, and I knew he felt the same. He remained a gentleman, however, and took a step back, opening the balcony doors to depart. I stepped outside with him, and he gave me one last kiss before bending down to pick up the harness and rope.

"My things," he said, bewildered. "They're not here."

I, too, scanned the balcony floor, but the items were gone.

"Looking for these?" said a man from the shadows behind us.

I jumped and whirled about to see London leaning against the Palace wall, Narian's harness and rope in his hand. My heart dropped to my feet, for I knew we were now in serious trouble.

"Inside, both of you," London commanded, and we hastily complied, neither of us daring to speak, for there was really nothing to be said that would excuse our actions.

London followed, forcefully closing the balcony doors, then he brought his eyes to bear upon me.

"Tomorrow we will board shut these doors. They seem to be letting in too much cold night air. I wouldn't want you to catch a chill."

"London, I know what this must look like —— "

"Don't," he said shortly, cutting off my meager attempt to put forth an explanation.

Then he spoke to Narian through gritted teeth. "You will come with me. And we will leave the *proper* way, through the parlor door." With a scowl, he again addressed me, and I cringed in the face of his rage. "You, Alera, will stay here. I will discuss your behavior with you later."

He opened my bedroom door and roughly pushed Narian through it, slamming it shut behind him. I lingered by the threshold to listen, knowing Narian had taken offense to London's handling and certain he would be equally unreceptive to London's reprimand. It was but a minute before I heard a scuffling sound and a thump as someone's back slammed against a wall.

"You will keep away from Alera or you will deal with me," London growled.

"Do you really think I would find you to be a worthy opponent?" Narian's voice was low but steady.

"You will find me to be much more dangerous than anyone else you have met in Hytanica."

There was silence, and I imagined London and Narian staring at each other, each sizing up his adversary.

"Now, we will proceed out the door, and you will return directly to your quarters, and I had better not catch further sight of you today."

London had ended their exchange, and I heard the two of them step into the corridor, leaving me alone and miserable in the unsympathetic darkness.

———

London waited until late afternoon to discuss my early-morning excursion with me. I suspected he had purposefully left me to stew over my actions all day as a small sort of punishment. He entered my quarters with a carpenter, whom he directed to my bedroom with instructions to board shut the balcony doors. As the man undertook the task, London rested his back against the wall that separated the parlor and the bedroom, arms crossed, eyeing me critically. I sat on the edge of the sofa, head pounding in rhythm with the carpenter's hammer, wishing this would all soon be over.

After the craftsman had gone, a most uncomfortable silence reigned until London, still leaning against the wall, opened the subject.

"Explain yourself to me, if you can."

"I don't believe I have to do so," I said, attempting to stand up to him.

"Then perhaps I should take you to your father," he responded, and my bravado deflated.

"London, say what you will to me, but I beg you not to tell my father."

He cocked an eyebrow derisively and I felt compelled to continue.

"I have no excuses," I said miserably. "I simply wanted to spend time with Narian alone, and... these late-night meetings... just developed."

Even as I spoke, I knew my words sounded ludicrous.

"I don't understand you," London scolded, shaking his head in irritation. "Both Destari and I have warned you to stay away from him and yet you do not heed us. You place your faith where it has not been earned. You ignore your upbringing and demonstrate no sense of propriety or respect for tradition. You recklessly endanger your life without thought for those who care about you. In short, you act like a child, and at seventeen that can no longer be tolerated."

London's disapproval cut me deeply, and I examined my clasped hands, unable to bring myself to look at him. Pushing away from the wall, he came to stand in front of me.

"Look at me, Alera."

I raised my eyes, brimming with tears, to his face, and shame burned my cheeks.

"Are you in love with him?" he asked, voice more sympathetic.

"Yes," I replied, tears now tumbling freely.

He dropped to one knee before me, indigo eyes dark with concern.

"We cannot control our hearts, but we must control our

minds and bodies. You cannot marry him, Alera. It is best that you keep away from him, so that these feelings will gradually lessen."

"You don't understand," I choked, feeling as if the air were being sucked from my lungs. "I *must* seek my father's permission to marry Narian. My happiness lies with him."

"Do not bring this to your father, for no good can come of his knowing. Now listen carefully. Hytanica cannot have a King with divided loyalties. We have fought far too long and sacrificed far too much in our effort to prevent Cokyri from conquering our people. We cannot let them conquer us more insidiously, through the domination of our ruler."

"It is not your opinion that counts," I retorted, wiping away my tears, not wanting to concede that he was right.

London stood, wearily running a hand through his untidy hair.

"Then your father will need to have all the facts to make such a decision. I once said that the time would present itself when your father should know about the Legend and Narian's destiny. It would appear that time has come."

"My father will not care about his past. My father will judge him on who he is now, and who he can become in the future."

While I wanted desperately to believe my own words, I did not need London to contradict them, for my father was more paranoid than anyone else about the dangers posed by Cokyri. I felt as though I were drowning, only this time London was not throwing me a rope.

"None of us can completely escape our pasts," he flatly asserted.

"Then perhaps I will give up my claim to the Throne so that I may be with Narian," I dared to put forth.

"Your father still would not permit the marriage."

I stared at London, tears again welling in my eyes, for some part of me knew he spoke the truth. I watched in misery as he moved toward the door, then intercepted him with a question.

"How did you know?"

He frowned, trying to decide whether I deserved to be told, but then gave a candid reply.

"I've been noticing for some time that you and he seem exhausted on the same days, and any fool could see from the way you look at each other that you are more than just friends. I started monitoring Narian's movements and last week discovered his remarkable talent for climbing over the roof. Then I simply waited for him to pay you another visit."

As I listened, I had a new appreciation for London's shrewdness and abilities, and understood to some extent what could make him a dangerous opponent.

"If his actions hadn't been so completely inappropriate, I would have been impressed," he concluded.

I held back my despair until after London's departure, then curled up on the sofa and cried in earnest.

XXXI

AN UNEXPECTED ALLY

did not see Narian at all the next week, as London and Destari had determined to keep us apart, and had even taken to guarding my door at night. But our forced separation only made me more acutely aware that, in many ways, the young man held my life in his hands.

I had begun to marshal arguments in Narian's favor: He was young, yes, but mature beyond his years; he was estranged from his family, but Koranis would certainly provide him with an inheritance were he to marry the Crown Princess; he may not have attended Hytanica's military school, but he undeniably had extensive military training. But the one objection I could not counter was the only one that mattered: that his loyalties might be divided. Although my heart did not want to admit it, reason told me that London's assessment of the situation was correct, for it would be foolish, and entirely unnecessary, to run any such risk when the son of the Captain of the Guard was prepared to assume the Throne. Even London, who probably disliked Steldor as much as I, would see Steldor crowned before he would put Narian in a position of power.

Just when it looked as though things could not get worse, Steldor came back into my life. My father called me to his study to inform me that our family would be dining on the morrow with Cannan's family in honor of Steldor's twenty-first birthday. While I was thankful that I would not be spending the evening on my own with Cannan's despicable son, I dreaded the occasion nonetheless. I had not seen him since he had rudely interrupted my shopping trip prior to Christmas, for the siege by Cokyri had been keeping all military commanders extremely busy, and that encounter hardly constituted a warm memory.

"In honor of the occasion, a small gift would be appropriate," the King was saying.

"Yes, Father," I said reflexively.

"I intend to discuss betrothal arrangements with Cannan, as I know of no other suitable candidate to be your husband. This decision can no longer be delayed, for your birthday is but three months away."

My entire body tensed, causing my temples to pound. While it had become clear to me that joy lay with Narian and heartache with Steldor, I felt ill-equipped to persuade my father of this, for the simple fact remained that my feelings would have no influence on his judgment as to whom I should marry.

"Temerson will escort Miranna. And, of course, Galen will be in attendance."

"Yes, Father," I repeated, curtseying to leave, but the King was not through with me.

"I desire your happiness. So does your mother," he said unconvincingly. "But you must desire it as well, and within the strictures of your position. Our hearts are not always wise, Alera, and cannot be relied upon in making certain decisions."

I nodded, wondering if he had perhaps read my thoughts, and left his study without further response, afraid my voice would betray my real feelings.

I arose early the next morning to make a hasty trip into the Market District, glad that February's sunshine was at last chasing away January's chilling rain. I had already decided what "small" gift would be appropriate for Steldor. As he had bestowed the exquisite and expensive sapphire pendant on me, I felt the need to match the lavishness of his gesture. When I came to the shop I had in mind, I surprised Destari by soliciting his advice on the purchase. Although he was uneasy about the nature of the item I was set on procuring, he assisted me in my selection and we returned to the Palace within an hour.

That evening, Miranna entered my quarters, already dressed for dinner, to wait for me to finish my preparations. While Sahdienne brushed my hair, my sister flounced about my bedroom, more animated than usual, and I smiled broadly at her.

"Are you perhaps a little nervous about Temerson joining us for dinner?" I asked.

"Is it that obvious?" she replied, sounding vaguely mortified.

"I'm afraid so. But don't fret about it. I'm sure he will be equally flustered."

"It's just that we have never joined Mother and Father on such an occasion before."

"I know. But he will pass the test."

"He will, won't he," she agreed, and the color high in her cheeks gave away her affection for the young man.

Miranna was radiant in a deep green velvet gown over a cream brocade dress. She had chosen not to put her hair up, and it fell loosely about her shoulders, adorned with a gold tiara set with emeralds. My gown was of white silk, with a bodice and tight-fitting sleeves of deep blue, and the skirt split to reveal a deep blue underskirt. Sahdienne had swept my hair back, then up off my shoulders, crowning it with the silver, double-banded sapphire and diamond tiara that I had worn for Semari's birthday celebration. The silver and sapphire pendant that I had received from Steldor encircled my neck.

Once I was dressed for the evening and had dismissed my

maid, Miranna and I chatted in my parlor until a Palace Guard arrived to inform us that our escorts had been shown to the small dining room on the first floor. Destari and Halias accompanied us down the stairs, then departed, off duty for the night since Cannan, Steldor, and Galen were more than capable of protecting the Royal Family.

Miranna touched my arm and we stopped in the corridor outside the dining room while she moistened her lips and pinched her cheeks. I smiled as she began to fuss with the placement of her tiara.

"Your beauty already exceeds mine, and there is no need to increase the disparity," I teased.

She giggled and stepped sprightly into the room, just a pace ahead of me.

Steldor stood to the right of the dining table, one hand resting negligently on a high-backed chair, the very portrait of elegance and charm as he casually swirled the wine in the glass he held in his other hand. Temerson, looking refined in a gold doublet, stood silently next to him, his brown eyes occasionally darting to Steldor, probably worried about being in his company.

The near end of the oblong table was covered in white linen and had been set for ten, with opulent golden plates and glass goblets. My father's place was at the head of the table, with my mother on his left and Cannan on his right. I would sit on my mother's left, with Steldor beside me, then would come Galen and whomever he had invited to accompany him. Faramay would sit next to her husband, with Miranna and Temerson likewise seated on the right side of the table.

Steldor, magnificent in a black silk doublet embroidered in gold, set his goblet of wine down on the table before he came to greet me. He inclined his head to kiss my hand, and I could tell that he was quite pleased to see the sapphire pendant resting just below the hollow of my throat.

I took his proffered arm and permitted him to lead me toward the refreshment table. Miranna hung back, looking expectantly at Temerson, who stumbled across the room to her side. They remained just inside the door, talking quietly, and I supposed that the young man needed to warm up to her before braving the rest of us.

As Steldor poured me a glass of wine, Cannan and Faramay arrived. Steldor's parents cordially greeted Miranna and Temerson, but then Faramay caught sight of her son and hastily crossed to us, Cannan a step behind. After giving me a curtsey, she adjusted the lacing on Steldor's shirt, her face radiant with joy, and I was again struck by the strong resemblance between mother and son —— her oval face, high cheekbones, straight and narrow nose, and perfect smile were mirrored in Steldor.

Steldor indicated his dislike for his mother's pandering with a roll of his eyes. I raised a hand to my mouth to hide my amusement, and chanced a glance at Cannan, who appeared disgruntled by his wife's overly solicitous behavior toward their son.

We continued making small talk, and it was but a short time later that Galen arrived with a young woman by the name of Tiersia. She was petite and feminine, but would have been rather plain were it not for her clear green eyes and long, bronze-brown hair. As she was two years my senior and rather reserved, I had never before spoken with her.

"Ah, Galen! Late as always I see," Steldor said, taking note of his friend's entry into the room.

"I'm never late," Galen returned good-naturedly. "You should know by now that the party doesn't begin until I'm here."

A mischievous glint flickered in Steldor's eyes as Galen guided Tiersia into our midst.

"And who is this lovely young lady who has somehow been

prevailed upon to accompany you?" he inquired.

"Take it easy. I'll get to the introductions in a moment." Like Steldor, Galen was in excellent spirits. Turning to me, he bowed and kissed my hand. "Princess Alera, may I present Lady Tiersia, the eldest daughter of Baron Rapheth and his wife, Baroness Kalena."

I nodded as she curtseyed, but my eyes were on Galen, for I couldn't help but notice that, other than Steldor, he was the only person who greeted me with a kiss on the hand.

Galen then addressed Cannan and Faramay.

"Lady Tiersia, I would like you to meet Baron Cannan, Captain of the Guard, and his wife, Baroness Faramay." Galen's manner remained formal, and he bowed his head in respect.

"It is a pleasure to meet you," Cannan responded cordially, but I saw Tiersia glance apprehensively at him, and I knew his mere presence was once again having an intimidating effect.

"And this, of course, is their son, Lord Steldor, whom I sometimes claim as my best friend," Galen finished with a flourish.

Steldor inclined his head to Tiersia and clapped an arm around Galen's shoulders.

"Let's get you some wine," he said, drawing Galen to the small table that held goblets and several different types of drink.

While the younger men served themselves, Cannan took the opportunity to lead Faramay across the room toward the well-stoked fire, and Tiersia moved to my side.

"How long have you known Galen?" I inquired, attempting to ease her nervousness.

"We met at a small holiday gathering, and he has called upon me twice since then."

She was soft-spoken and genteel, and I couldn't help but think that Galen was doing well for himself.

The two friends returned, extending to us glasses of wine. After taking a sip from his own goblet, which he had retrieved, Steldor addressed Tiersia, continuing in his earlier vein.

"So tell me, what type of bribe was used to entice such an enchanting woman into accompanying Galen tonight?"

Tiersia did not answer but cast her eyes toward her escort as her cheeks turned deep pink, uncertain how to react to Steldor. Lightly draping his left arm around her waist, Galen nobly intercepted his friend's remark.

"You may have had to resort to a bribe or two to persuade young women to accompany you, but I've never had to use such measures."

"No, no, your memory is flawed, Galen. It was *they* who bribed *me*."

"And how long was it before they demanded a return of their money?" Galen mocked, grinning widely, clearly enjoying the exchange of jibes.

Again addressing Tiersia, Steldor roguishly continued, "I should warn you about Galen. His charm wears thin about... well, about now, after which he becomes quite a bore." Motioning to the refreshment table, he added, a devilish glint in his eye, "So, feel free to partake of the wine throughout the evening, and when you are in need of... more stimulating companionship, come find me. I'm always willing to lend a hand to a desperate young lady."

Lifting his eyebrows, Galen gave Steldor a small shake of his head to let him know he was overstepping his bounds with Tiersia.

"I feel the need to remind you that Princess Alera is your companion this evening, while Tiersia is mine. Do try to remember that."

"I never forgot," Steldor smirked, then he slapped Galen on the back and pulled him a few feet away, saying, "Excuse us, ladies, as we have matters of the Kingdom to discuss."

Tiersia and I now stood together in confused silence. She did not know what to make of the best friends, and I was both annoyed and amused by Steldor's scandalously flirtatious style. Thankfully, the King and Queen were announced by Lanek right at that moment, thus saving Tiersia and me from awkward conversation about our escorts.

My parents greeted Cannan and Faramay, who were now standing by the fireplace on the near side of the room. Steldor and Galen came to reclaim Tiersia and me, and we approached our elders so that Galen could once again make introductions.

After a few minutes of polite conversation, the King and Queen moved to the table to seat themselves for dinner, and the rest of us followed.

The dinner would be served in several courses, although they would be less extravagant than usual, due to the rationing instituted throughout the city. Soup would come first, followed by bread and thick stew, then legs of beef and mutton. The final course would consist of pastries and fruits. The feast would last well over an hour, as formal dinners tended to proceed slowly and often seemed like a dance, with certain movements deemed appropriate and missteps duly noted by the older generation.

Despite the perceived pressure to display impeccable manners, the meal progressed pleasantly enough. Steldor was, naturally, on his best behavior in the presence of my parents and paid just the right amount of attention to me while simultaneously charming the rest of the room. I, on the other hand, was aloof and somewhat distant, knowing that my input was not needed in order to carry the conversation, and preferring to simply observe Steldor at his best.

The feast concluded, and my parents invited everyone to join them in the adjacent tearoom, where more intimate seating had been arranged. Steldor extended his hand to assist me to my feet as my father moved toward us, a broad smile upon his face.

"I would like to steal your young man for a few moments. I have some affairs to discuss with him. You can get along without him for a short time, can you not?"

I nodded, and my father put his arm around Steldor's shoulders and drew him companionably away from me and into the tearoom. I began to follow, walking with Galen and Tiersia, when I noticed Cannan standing by the doorway between the two rooms, his eyes upon me.

"Princess Alera, may I have a word?" he said as I approached.

Without waiting for an answer, he ushered me toward the dining room's bay window. I apprehensively complied, for it was clear he wanted no one to overhear us.

The candlelit chandeliers that had created a soft glow over the table where we had dined did not reach this part of the room. The moonlight filtering through the window kept the darkness somewhat at bay but created shifting shadows on the floor. Cannan gazed out the window into the West Courtyard as I waited for him to speak.

"I was once much like my son," he began, then turned to me, his face looking more lined than usual, deliberately choosing his words. "But war forged my temper into conviction, my ego into self-confidence, and my stubbornness into fortitude. Steldor has yet to face such trials, but when he does, he will change as well."

He paused, and his voice was heavy when next he spoke.

"I know that you are not in love with him, but I am convinced that he loves you, although I doubt his pride would let him admit it. This gives you some ability to influence him and to change him as well."

He turned his back to the window, his face now lost in darkness, but I knew not how to respond. I was unsettled by his frankness, and by his assessment of my feelings. As the silence between us lengthened, I searched for something to say, but then he continued, and his next statements were even more astounding.

"Although I believe in time that you would be able to open your heart to Steldor, I do not wish to force you into marriage. I will not give my permission for a betrothal until you indicate to me that such is your desire."

Gratitude broke over me in waves at the unexpected reprieve he was extending, immediately tempered by worry as to my father's reaction.

"But my father —— "

"Need not know my reasons. I can delay this decision without telling him that we have spoken." Anticipating my next concern, he continued. "I can also handle my son."

I nodded, almost inexpressibly grateful. "It may be Steldor's birthday," I finally managed, "but you have just given me a rare gift. I thank you for your kindness and will carefully weigh your advice."

"We had better rejoin the others," he replied, somewhat gruffly. His change in manner did not dampen my joy but merely confirmed he did not often reveal this sensitive side of his nature.

As soon as we walked into the tearoom, Steldor looked our way, a small furrow appearing in his brow as he contemplated his father, clearly curious about what subject the Captain and I had discussed. He was standing with Galen and Tiersia, his conference with the King having come to an end, and I knew from the blush in her cheeks that he and Galen must have again been tossing jibes at each other. As Cannan moved away from my side, Steldor took his place, but I was prepared for his arrival.

"I have something for you," I told him, tugging at his arm with a beguiling smile. "Come with me."

The tactic worked, for my rare show of affection drove all

thought of asking about my conversation with his father from his mind. I slipped my right hand into his left and led him into the corridor and down the hall to the King's Drawing Room, noticing as I did so that there was a slight ridge running across his palm.

We crossed the threshold, and I retrieved the package I had earlier set upon the massive oak sideboard that stood on the other side of the room, feeling a sudden chill, for no heat emanated from the barren stone fireplace. The room was appointed very similarly to the King's study, with brown leather sofas and chairs, and overflowing bookcases. Unlike the study, however, there were also gaming tables for cards, dice, and chess.

Steldor waited in the middle of the room until I returned to extend to him the narrow, tightly wrapped gift. When he reached for it, I impulsively took his left hand in mine, turning it over to examine it.

"I cut myself when I was a child," he explained.

"Badly, by the looks of it," I remarked, inspecting the pale skin of the scar that crossed from the base of his first finger to the heel of his palm. "It would appear that flipping daggers is a dangerous pastime."

I met his eyes as I relinquished my hold on him, expecting some reaction, but he merely smirked before turning his attention to the gift he held in his right hand. He studied the oddly shaped package, then quickly removed the wrapping. He glanced between the leather sheath lying in his hands and me, and slowly extracted a dagger with a black leather grip and a ruby set into the pommel.

"I didn't know you paid so much attention to my weaponry," he remarked with admiration and approval.

He drew his sword from its scabbard and compared the two blades, then flipped the dagger over in his hand as if checking its weight and balance.

"It is a magnificent gift, if a bit excessive," he said, his expression quizzical. "I can't help but wonder what led you to make such a purchase."

"I simply wanted to match the level of your gift to me," I explained with a satisfied smile. "I judge that we are now even."

"I see," he said with a hint of mirth that was mildly irritating. "And is there any other way in which you would like to even the score?" He shifted position so that he stood between me and the exit. "As you have managed to get me alone, I am quite at your mercy."

"We should return to the others," I stammered, flustered by his manner. "My father will be displeased to find we left without a chaperone."

"No one will begrudge us a little time alone —— especially not the King. He is quite interested in moving our relationship along."

He returned his sword to its scabbard and tucked the dagger into his belt, his eyes perusing my form, and the blush that burned in my cheeks seemed to spread throughout my entire body.

"As you are in a rather generous mood, and as it is my birthday, there is one other thing I would ask of you."

"And what might that be?" I queried, eyeing him with suspicion, certain he was goading me.

He smirked, then said, "Come closer and I'll show you what will please me."

I scrutinized him for a moment, trying to discern his intentions, then straightened my shoulders and stepped forward to stand directly in front of him. His eyes flicked across my face, and the back of my neck prickled, then he reached out with both hands and lightly ran his fingers over my cheekbones. My breath caught in my throat, but before I could react, he pulled the pins from my hair so that it tumbled loosely down upon my shoulders.

"I like it better this way," he said fondly, letting a few strands drape over the palm of his hand. Then he grinned and stepped back from me, motioning toward the door with his arm.

"I believe, dear Princess, that you expressed a desire to rejoin the others."

I nodded, too appalled to speak. I knew everyone would conclude from the change in my hairstyle that we had not just been conversing. Once more my cheeks flamed, this time from humiliation and anger, but as I could see no way out of my predicament, I moved to slip past him. Just when I was about to make my escape, he caught my arm.

"And exactly what was my father discussing with you?" His voice was a mixture of curiosity and suspicion.

"The weather," I sarcastically retorted. "He thinks we will have a good crop year."

To my relief, Steldor laughed, releasing my arm.

"Somehow I don't see my father discussing farming with the Crown Princess. But you can have your little secret, for now."

Wasting no time, I hurried back to the tearoom, Steldor's footfalls telling me that he was trailing. I waited just inside the room for him to join me and noted that our parents were comfortably seated on the chairs and sofa clustered near the bay window, sipping glasses of spicy mulled wine, with Galen and Tiersia standing nearby. Temerson and Miranna were seated at a small table away from the others, their foreheads almost touching as they conversed, his cinnamon brown hair a darker version of her strawberry blond tresses. I was glad to see that he had at least gotten over his shyness with her.

As Steldor stopped beside me, Faramay waved to him.

"Steldor, darling! Come to your mother! I didn't know where you were and was beginning to fret!"

I could feel Steldor stiffen. With a forced smile upon his face, he strode toward her. I followed a step behind, confused about his mother's odd exclamation. While Faramay was, at times, overly enamored with her son, I could scarcely imagine his absence would cause her distress.

"There's no need to be upset, Mother," Steldor placated as he went to her. "I only stepped into the corridor with Alera for a moment."

"You should have said something to me," Faramay pouted. "You know how I worry."

"Well, I'm fine. I went with Alera for she had a gift she wished to give me."

Having reassured his mother, Steldor glanced, frowning, at his father.

"She thought you had left without saying good night," Cannan explained bluntly. "As you obviously wouldn't do that, some horrible fate must have befallen you." I thought I detected a rare note of sarcasm in the Captain's words.

Moving away from Faramay, Steldor extended his new dagger to his father.

"I'm sure you will appreciate this," he stated with evident pride.

While Cannan examined the splendid blade, my father caught my eye, and I knew from his puzzled expression that he was trying to determine how the dagger qualified as a *small* gift. I smiled at him, knowing he would forgive my extravagance in light of how well the evening was proceeding, then blushed when he winked at me. I could only conclude from his manner that he was delighted that Steldor and I had stolen a few unaccompanied minutes, and that he viewed my disheveled hair as an encouraging sign.

After the dagger had been passed among our parents and appropriately praised, Steldor handed it to Galen, who immediately began to flip it in his hand, and the thought that the two friends were actually one and the same person flitted through my brain. With a slight motion of his head, Steldor indicated to Galen that he wished to move away from the older adults, but he turned dutifully to Faramay before we took our leave.

"We're going across the room to join Princess Miranna and Lord Temerson. You can keep an eye on us if you wish to do so."

Steldor's eyes darted toward me as the four of us joined my sister and her escort, and I could tell he was somewhat embarrassed by his mother's behavior. At my inquisitive glance, he gave a small shake of his head.

"Don't ask," he grumbled.

Galen handed the dagger to Temerson, and as he and Miranna admired it, Steldor spoke moodily to me.

"I'm going to get a glass of wine. Would you like one too?"

"No, thank you," I replied, for I still had not developed a taste for the liquid.

"I'll bring back two glasses anyway and be happy to drink them both," he quipped, with a touch of dark humor.

A short time later, my father rose to say good night, signaling that the evening had come to an end. We all left the tearoom together, but Galen and Tiersia bowed and parted from the group to walk toward the front entry of the Palace where Dameran, the older of Tiersia's two brothers, waited to escort her home. Before Faramay and Cannan departed, Steldor made a point of saying good night to his mother, resurrecting my curiosity about why she had become so upset when she had not known his whereabouts. Steldor then accompanied me to the spiral staircase, with Temerson escorting Miranna, the four of us following behind my parents. Miranna bid farewell to Temerson at the bottom of the stairs, but Steldor forestalled my attempt to do the same.

"I haven't properly expressed my gratitude for the birthday gift," he mused.

I looked pleadingly at Miranna, who grinned impishly before

she sashayed up the steps. Temerson adoringly watched her go and then exited as well.

Now that we were alone, Steldor reached out a hand to caress my cheek, and I watched him warily.

"It seems every kiss with you is a first kiss," he gently chided, "as too much time passes in between."

When I remained mute, he stepped closer to me, playing with a strand of my hair.

"Thank you for the generous gift, Princess."

Resting his hand on the back of my neck, he inclined his head and gave me a teasing and sensual kiss. As his intoxicating scent flooded my senses, my lips responded to his, and he placed his other hand on the small of my back, pressing his mouth more firmly against mine. Catching myself, I pulled back from him, and he released me.

"I am willing to take things slowly, Alera," he said, brown eyes smoldering. He gently ran a finger along my jawline. "I have a feeling you will be well worth the wait."

With a deep bow, he departed, and I traced my fingers over my unfaithful lips, unable to comprehend how I could enjoy a kiss from someone I so greatly disliked.

XXXII

ULTIMATUM

ver the next couple of days, I fretted over the conversation I planned to have with my father. I could no longer pretend that the King might be prevailed upon to embrace Narian as his successor to the Throne, when the primary objection to him was his trustworthiness. I also worried, given London's opinions, that my father would be unlikely to approve of him as a husband for me under any circumstances. I was well aware that the simple fact I was in love with Narian would not be enough to sway the King. But I had to try, for my happiness was now inextricably tied to the young man.

To add to my frustration, London and Destari had proved adept at keeping Narian away from me. I missed his company more than I would have thought possible and worried what London might have told him was the reason he could not see me. I tried to stay busy, but while I could keep my hands occupied with embroidery, gardening, and the harp, my mind and heart refused to be distracted. Then a simple solution came to me: I could have a servant deliver a note to Narian on my behalf. While I couldn't count on London or Destari to aid me, they could not prevent me from writing to him.

I was sitting in an armchair near the warm hearth, composing my note, when London exploded through my parlor door unannounced.

"Where is Narian?" he demanded.

"What?" I asked, completely baffled. "How would I know where Narian is?"

"If you know where he is, you must tell me."

"London, as you well know, I have not seen him in almost two weeks."

He spun on his heel, intending to depart.

"What is it you want of him?" I called, rising in pursuit. The insistent quality of my voice averted his exit, and he turned slowly back around, reluctant to explain his reasons to me.

"Cannan desires to speak with him." Seeing the question in my eyes, he added, "The Captain sent Elite Guards to retrieve him, but the boy could not be located within the Palace."

"He may just have gone into the city. He is not a prisoner, you know."

"I checked his room. He wouldn't take all his possessions simply to spend an afternoon in the city."

London's quiet words echoed like thunder. As I absorbed their meaning, I grew more and more alarmed.

"He wouldn't just leave!" I said, the color draining from my face.

London stepped toward me, and placing a hand on my arm, guided me back to my chair. As I sank into it, a harrowing thought hit me, and I glared accusingly at him.

"Did you tell Cannan about the Legend?"

"Yes, but that cannot be the cause of Narian's departure, as he could not have known of our meeting."

"But how did Cannan react?" I persisted.

"Not well. He is angry that Narian has not only failed to be forthcoming with him but has also failed to be honest. Cannan has little patience for those who deceive him."

"But why did Cannan send his guards? Why didn't he just go and talk to him?"

"I told you, Cannan is angry. He takes Narian's conduct personally and wanted to impress upon him the seriousness of the situation, as well as the seriousness with which Cannan will approach his transgressions."

I sat, still as death, trying to understand why Narian would suddenly leave.

"Alera, I must go. Cannan has sealed the city, and I may yet be able to find him."

"You won't hurt him, will you, London?" I whispered.

"Not unless I have to," he replied, but his words were contradicted by the steely edge in his voice. Then he left, and I shivered, for there had been no warmth or indecision in his eyes.

When Narian's bodyguard was discovered that evening bound and gagged in one of the other third-floor guest rooms, it was clear that Narian had indeed fled. After no trace of him was found in the city over the next few days, Cannan called off the search, certain he had gone over the wall within an hour of his departure from the Palace.

In the aftermath of his disappearance, I struggled to accept that I did not know him as well as I had believed. I began to reassess my own actions and feared that I had misinterpreted his feelings for me. The painful thought that London had been right about him kept recurring. I racked my brain for some other explanation, not wanting to believe that he had left because he did not think we could be together. I didn't want to consider that he had no love for Hytanica, no feelings for anyone other than me, and no desire for my friendship, even if it could not be something more.

The only other possibility of which I could conceive was that he had somehow learned of the discussion between London and Cannan, and had left because he judged himself to be in danger.

I knew, perhaps better than anyone, that Narian had an uncanny way of acquiring information, and that he would not stay and fight if retreat seemed the wiser course of action. I also knew that it would have occurred to him, just as it had to London, that much danger to Hytanica would be eliminated by his death.

Although Narian was gone, the Cokyrians had not abandoned the siege. I was baffled by this until London pointed out that it meant Narian had not returned to the land where he had been raised, for the enemy's purpose was to force us to relinquish him. While I prayed for the conflict to end, this gave me hope, for if Narian had not returned to the enemy, then he certainly felt some loyalty toward Hytanica. London, too, saw this as a good omen, believing that the young man was, in all likelihood, hiding in the mountains. It remained entirely possible that Narian would trust us enough to return, despite the horrible consequences he might face.

———

As we entered the month of March and the weather began to warm beneath the spring sun, there was a definite change in mood about the Palace. The tension brought on by the siege of the city was now tinged with excitement, and the gossip around the Palace was that we were preparing to attack the Cokyrians in an effort to push them back across the wide expanse of the Recorah River. The river now ran fast and wild, fed by rain and snowmelt in the mountains, and if we could force the enemy to the other side and then hold them at our boundary, we could reclaim our lands. The city's supplies were dwindling, and it would soon be imperative that we hunt and gather food, and that we be able to plant crops.

Despite this altered atmosphere, I could not seem to find any solace from my grief over Narian's departure. There was a sadness deep within my soul and an ache at the core of my being that could not be banished regardless of how I filled my day.

We launched our attack on a dark evening in early March, with London and two dozen scouts moving out first and on foot. As Destari was not one of the soldiers on the mission, I asked him what task this small group was to undertake and was shaken when he told me that our men carried bags of powdered poison. Their assignment was to add it to the food and drink of the Cokyrian soldiers at their various encampments. When I asked Destari why London was involved, he reminded me that London had begun his military career as a scout and told me that it was London and Cannan who had devised the scheme.

Several hours later, six torches flamed in the dark night, and numerous Hytanican troops, some on horseback, some on foot, moved out to try to rout the enemy. Destari was again my source of information about the course of the attack.

"The torches are a good sign. They are not only signals but mark the locations of the primary Cokyrian encampments, so we can target them in the dark." His black eyes were cold and unfeeling as he continued. "Those who survive the poisoning should be dealt with swiftly and ruthlessly by our soldiers. It is time we clear the enemy from our lands."

I could understand his feelings, in light of the losses we had suffered at the hands of the Cokyrians, but the level of hatred in his voice was disturbing.

"You may as well retire for the night," he advised, then added, his tone no longer laced with menace, "We aren't likely to hear anything until morning."

"I will, but you must wake me at once when you receive news."

"Agreed."

––––––

The sun was well overhead before our soldiers returned the next day. I was having a bite to eat in the tearoom, intent on avoiding any and all social encounters while I awaited news. Destari had accompanied me and stood just outside in the corridor.

Hearing loud and jubilant voices from the front of the Palace, I abandoned my meal, and Destari and I rushed toward the Grand Entry Hall to learn the news. Several Cokyrians, hands bound behind their backs, were kneeling on the mosaic stone floor, surrounded by Hytanican soldiers who were all speaking at the same time. Cannan emerged from his office through the guard room, and silence fell. Eyeing the captives, he gruffly ordered that they be taken to the dungeon.

"Kade will see to their interrogation. Unlike our other Cokyrian prisoners, perhaps one of them will value his or her skin enough to talk."

With a jolt, I grasped that our other enemy prisoners had probably died, no doubt unable to withstand our interrogation techniques. I glanced about at those being jerked to their feet, and I shuddered, realizing some of them were women. I could not imagine the agony about to be inflicted on all of the captives. I also knew I would not possess the strength or bravery required to face such an ordeal.

As Cannan's directive was carried out, London arrived, looking ragged, and I wondered what he and his men had suffered in the night.

"Report," Cannan ordered, eyes on his Deputy Captain.

"The poison worked most effectively, and one-third of the Cokyrian soldiers died or fell ill as a result. There was much confusion among the rest, as they tried to determine what had felled their comrades. Despite these disadvantages, they rallied to put up a ferocious fight, for they are exceptionally well trained. Eventually, we drove them toward the river, some managing to cross the bridge, but most plunging into the Recorah. It was impossible to tell in the dark how many drowned and how many made it across to the other bank." London sounded exhilarated that the mission had been successful. "Our wounded have been brought to the Infirmary, and I have stationed the rest of our troops along the river. They are tired, however, and reinforcements should be sent."

"I will see to it at once," Cannan answered matter-of-factly. When next he spoke, however, it was with an uncharacteristic touch of anxiety, and I realized that Steldor and Galen must have been leading some of the troops. "And how many died?"

"We did suffer casualties, but I cannot give a count at this time."

"I will send a detail to retrieve the bodies." His voice had hardened as he thought about the good men he had lost in battle. "Anything else?"

"There is also the issue of what to do with the Cokyrian dead."

"We should stack and burn the corpses," Cannan replied, without a trace of sympathy.

"I think we would be well served to bring the bodies to the bridge and let Cokyri retrieve its dead. Last night, we showed our strength; today, we can show our compassion." London spoke eloquently and persuasively.

Cannan considered his request for a moment. "Very well."

"I would like to see to the undertaking," London continued doggedly, and Cannan again agreed.

London turned to leave, then looked back at his Captain.

"I saw Steldor directing troops at the river's edge this morning. I did not see Galen, but I have heard that he is also well."

Gratitude flickered in Cannan's eyes, then he dismissed the rest of the soldiers who stood before him and retreated to his office. I knew he would soon inform my father of the details of our military maneuver.

————

Now that the Cokyrians had been driven across the river, the mood in the Palace and the city improved dramatically. The fighting was far from over, but our troops were managing to hold the enemy at the Recorah's far bank, assisted by the swollen river itself. As our supplies, even with rationing, were quickly being depleted, many of the men from the villages returned to the fields to plant crops, warily taking their weapons with them and working the soil closest to the city. Others hunted in the forest, replenishing meat stores with venison and wild boar. We needed to take advantage of the current favorable conditions, for the Cokyrians would pose a much greater threat once the Recorah began to ebb with the advent of summer.

Given our recent military assault, and the flurry of activity in the aftermath of our victory, my father had not yet revisited the pressing matter of my birthday. But when the middle of the month neared, the matter could no longer be ignored, and I was summoned rather abruptly late one afternoon to an audience with the King, a Palace Guard having been sent to escort me.

I self-consciously entered the Hall of Kings, aware of my father's eyes upon me while I walked across the wide expanse of floor to where he sat upon his throne. The Hall was quiet except for my footfalls, and it was strange to have no one else in attendance. My father had directed that Destari and all of the guards on duty in the Throne Room wait in the antechamber or the guard room, wanting his words to fall on no ears but my own.

I curtseyed and waited for him to speak.

"Alera, I am growing old and weary and, after almost thirty years, am ready to make way for a new King. I have also seen enough of war and have no heart to fight another."

His countenance was troubled as he scrutinized me, his left hand distractedly twisting the ring he wore on his right.

"I never should have ruled at all, but when my older brother died on the battlefield, I shouldered my responsibility as next in line to the Throne. There were many things I had thought to do with my life, but duty came first. Perhaps this is my failing, but I am not convinced that you understand the demands of duty, or the responsibility that comes with being my heir." He sighed, his heart obviously heavy. "It pains me to have to take this approach with you, but as you cannot seem to settle the question of a marriage partner, I will settle it for you."

There was disappointment in his usually kind eyes, and I could sense that some horrible fate was about to befall me.

"It is my decree that Lord Steldor be my successor to Hytanica's throne. A wedding will be held on the afternoon of your next birthday, and it is up to you whether you will be the bride or a lady-in-waiting."

I stared at him, unable to discern his meaning.

"You can choose to marry Steldor and be crowned alongside him as his Queen. But if you cannot see your way to being his wife, then you will forfeit your claim to the Throne in favor of your sister. Miranna *is* prepared to carry out her obligations as a Princess of Hytanica and has agreed to marry Steldor should that be your decision."

I felt as though he were speaking in a foreign tongue, and I stood frozen, unable to formulate a response to his ultimatum.

"May I talk to Miranna?" I pleaded, finally regaining my voice.

"No. She has made her decision. You do not need to talk to her to make yours." His voice was firm and devoid of compassion. "Your birthday is but seven weeks away, so you will give me your answer by this time tomorrow. You have already had abundant time to ruminate over this decision, and I no longer have the patience to wait for you to bring forward a young man of your own choosing."

"But Father, can't you give both Steldor and me more time?" I pleaded, hoping he would show the same compassion toward his daughter that I had often seen him extend to others. "He is young yet to be a king, and no law says I must marry on my birthday."

While it was traditional for a female heir to marry on her eighteenth birthday, my father was the King and as such was not bound by tradition. In fact, he would be breaking tradition by crowning Steldor at such a young age, for Hytanica's Kings were not usually crowned until their mid to late twenties. But putting the Kingdom in Steldor's young hands didn't seem a great risk due to the young man's background, his upbringing, and the fact that his father was the Captain of the Guard.

"I am your father and the King. You will not question my judgments," he said irritably, coming to his feet. "You have until this time tomorrow to make your decision."

Although I knew I was being dismissed, I could not force my body to move, my mind still struggling for the magic words that would persuade him without risk of offending or angering him.

"Alera, you may go now," he said more forcefully, breaking the spell that immobilized me.

I looked wretchedly at him, then turned and hastened from his presence, tears running down my cheeks. Destari watched me worriedly as I rushed through the antechamber, but he did not speak or try to stop me. Instead, he followed me as I turned down the corridor toward the spiral staircase. With the Palace walls seeming to close in on me, I wrenched open the doors into the garden to run down the pathway, seeking escape from my father, his decree, my thoughts, and my raging feelings. I was thankful Destari did not pursue me, and I collapsed upon a bench, burying my face in my hands.

In my misery, it took me considerable time to realize that someone had approached and was patiently standing several feet from where I sat. As I raised my head, my eyes fell upon London. I glanced gratefully down the path toward Destari, knowing he must have sent for him.

"London, help me," I sobbed, and he came to sit next to me, taking me into his arms.

I lay my head upon his shoulder, my tears soaking into the leather of his jerkin. After a long while, my crying subsided, and I rested wearily against him, gaining some measure of comfort from the presence of his strong arm around my waist.

"Do you want to tell me what this is about?" he asked at last, his tone so gentle my tears would have restarted had I any left.

"My father has decreed that I either marry Steldor on my birthday or forfeit the Throne in favor of Miranna, who *will* acquiesce to such a union. We are apparently interchangeable daughters."

London said nothing, choosing simply to listen to me.

"He demands my answer before sundown tomorrow, although in truth he could give me years for all the difference it would make. I know of no person but Steldor whom he would be willing to accept as King —— his list of criteria is designed so that only the Captain's son is a match."

My indignation flared, and I sat upright, brushing the tearstains off my cheeks with my hands.

"How can my father think so little of me? How can he ignore my feelings when it is I who will have to live with Steldor for the rest of my life? And what of Miranna? There is already a young man in whom she has an interest and with whom I believe she could find happiness."

With no answers to these questions, I sank into a stony silence. As my initial shock and hurt subsided, I began to shiver, for I had left the Palace with no shawl or cloak, and the temperature was falling with the setting of the sun.

"I had better return you to your quarters," London observed, "before you become chilled to the bone."

He assisted me to my feet and guided me back to the door, keeping me close to his side.

"Have some hot soup sent to her parlor," he muttered to Destari as we crossed the threshold. "She is quite cold."

A half hour later I was mechanically eating vegetable soup, staring vacantly at London, who had stoked the fire and was stirring the embers into a blaze. When he became aware of my eyes upon him, he stood and came to me where I sat upon the sofa.

"I'm going to leave you now, but Destari will remain outside your door for a few more hours, and your maid will be here soon to assist you in preparing for bed."

I nodded, not having the strength to form words.

"I will have Sahdienne bring something from the doctor to help you sleep," he continued, lightly brushing my cheek with his fingers. "I will see you in the morning. Maybe the world won't look so bleak in the light of a new day."

He turned from me, but I stammered, "Where are you going? Can't you stay a little while longer?"

"I have a pressing matter to address." He sighed, then confessed in response to my distraught expression, "I'm going to have a talk with your father."

Grateful tears pooled in my eyes, and he gave me a fleeting smile as he left the room.

London was wrong. The world did not look any brighter the next morning, despite the hope I now nursed that he had been able to affect my father's decree. But as the hours slipped by without my former bodyguard's return, my hope diminished, and the choice my father had put before me began to whirl dizzyingly through my mind. If only there were someone else I could marry, someone with whom I felt comfortable... but also someone to whom my father could not object. I reviewed every potential candidate but still could not find a suitable alternative to Steldor. I was sitting upon my sofa, bemoaning my circumstances, when London strode through the door, Destari having granted him entrance.

I eagerly met his eyes, but at the shake of his head, knew my father had been unyielding. He sat beside me and relayed the disappointing account of their conversation.

"The King is unwilling to give you additional time in which to make your decision, for he has a great desire to step down from the Throne, especially with the looming Cokyrian threat. He feels father and son would be best equipped to orchestrate our battle strategy, if it comes to that. He also feels, as do most men in Hytanica, that a father should not trust to a daughter's judgment a decision as important as the selection of a husband. As you well know, it is his right to arrange your marriage, and he regards your resistance to Steldor as unreasonable. From his point of view, Steldor has the makings of both a great King and a fine husband."

He paused, watching me closely as tears filled my eyes. "He thinks he is being generous, as he has enabled you to walk away from the match by forfeiting the Throne if you truly cannot give yourself to Steldor."

"Help me to see what I should do," I implored in a small voice, almost too miserable to make a sound.

"I'm afraid this is one decision you alone can make," he regretfully informed me.

I dropped my gaze, examining my hands as I wrestled with the choice that had been put before me, then raised my head with a jerk as a fresh idea surfaced.

"London!" I exclaimed, feeling a bit awkward, although I knew I had hit upon the ideal solution.

"What?" he said, perplexed by my change in attitude.

"Would you consider... I mean, what if we..." Words suddenly tumbled from my mouth, and my cheeks blazed. "My father would see you as having the experience and qualities necessary for a King. I'm sure he would give his permission for us to wed."

London looked shocked, then amused. "Are you proposing to me?"

"Yes, I suppose I am," I replied, almost delirious with relief. I could not believe it had taken this long for the idea to surface. "Don't you see, this is perfect! We care for each other, and you have a strong military background, and I know my father trusts your judgment, as he and Cannan already rely upon your advice. And you are a natural leader. The troops are willing to follow your orders the same as Cannan's."

He looked seriously into my eyes, then spoke, slowly but decisively.

"I am honored, Alera, but I cannot marry you. I do care deeply for you, and I would willingly give my life to protect you, but my feelings are not those of a husband toward a wife. And I cannot be King. I do not aspire to govern and am too independent to be comfortable in such a role. I am truly sorry."

I was not ready to give up, for I was certain that London would make a far better King and husband than would Steldor.

Giving him a furtive glance, I said, only half in jest, "As Crown Princess of Hytanica and future Queen, I could order you to marry me."

His posture stiffened as if he now expected the worst.

"If you order me to marry you, I will comply, but I ask you not to do so."

Despite how much I wanted to escape matrimony with Steldor, I could not force London into marriage against his will. I would be causing him the same pain my father was causing me.

"Very well," I said despondently.

London studied me for a long moment.

"While I want you to be happy, I am content with my life as it is," he said. "If you cannot see your way to marrying Steldor, then perhaps forfeiting the Throne would be the right thing to do."

I bit my lower lip as I tried to come to a decision, twisting my hands in agitation.

"I cannot let my sister marry Steldor, irrespective of my circumstances. That would be unfair to her, for Steldor is in love with me."

"But don't you think his feelings would subside over time?"

"I don't know. After all, we would both be living in the Palace and would continually come in contact with each other. I fear he would become bitter and resentful, and I don't have faith that he would treat Mira well. She has such a sensitive nature that she could never withstand his anger or indifference."

"But there's more to it than that, isn't there?" London astutely observed. "I suspect that you, who could never be discouraged from involvement in issues affecting the Kingdom, would have a difficult time walking away from the Throne."

I nodded a little sheepishly, for London understood me better than anyone else.

"Unlike me, Mira pays no attention to such matters. And even if she did, I doubt she would have the ability to influence Steldor's decision making. On the other hand, I can at least get him to listen to my opinions, although he may not act in accordance with them."

I rubbed my hands together, for like the rest of me, they had grown cold.

"Being the heir is my burden, and I cannot sacrifice Mira's happiness in an attempt to preserve my own. All of which means I am the one who must marry."

"It would appear that I previously misjudged you. You are quite grown-up after all." There was no hint of sarcasm in London's tone; rather, there was a touch of admiration.

I accepted his compliment with a nod, for it was too difficult to even force a smile. While the decision I had come to was the right one, that did not make it any less difficult or painful.

"Thank you for attempting to intervene on my behalf. But I would like to be alone now. I have only a few hours before I must meet with Father."

After London's departure, I nibbled at the lunch that had been brought to my parlor. As the hours continued to pass, and my despair deepened, I left my quarters to visit the garden, having always found its atmosphere soothing. I strolled among the wide variety of plants, noting the buds on the trees and the first tulips of the spring, until I recollected I had some other unfinished business. With a tiny surge of energy, I walked toward my bodyguard, who stood by the back entrance into the Palace.

"Destari, send someone to inform Cannan that I would like to see him."

My request surprised him, but he briefly stepped into the Palace to send a guard to find the Captain. I turned away and began to pace along the garden path, eventually sitting upon one of the stone benches to await Cannan's arrival. In no time at all, he entered the grounds, and I rose as he approached.

"Princess Alera, I have been told you asked to speak with me," he said, coming to a halt.

Forgoing the usual niceties, I came right to the point.

"Do you know of my father's ultimatum?"

"Yes, your father and I have discussed his decision. I am truly sorry it has come to this."

"You said you would withhold your permission for Steldor to marry me if I were not ready to wed. Would you likewise withhold permission with respect to Miranna?"

I held my breath while I awaited his answer, for my last hope rested on his response. If Cannan would refuse permission for my sister to marry Steldor, my father would have no choice but to give me additional time to find a husband.

The Captain examined me for a moment, and I could tell he understood where my thoughts had taken me. Despite the sympathy underlying his words, his response was not what I wanted to hear.

"No, as she is agreeable to the marriage. You must understand, both your father and I believe Steldor has the qualities necessary to be King. I made that offer to you so that you might find someone who not only would be a good King, but to whom you could give your love. I didn't make it because I wanted to prevent my son from taking the Throne."

I glanced away from Cannan toward the late-afternoon sun, knowing my time had run out. He stood patiently by my side while I came to the only decision my heart would permit.

"Then I am ready to wed," I reluctantly declared, my desire to protect Miranna's happiness far outweighing my desire to avoid marriage to Steldor. "Will you inform my father of my decision? I cannot bear the sight of him at the moment."

"As you wish," he said, not at all perturbed by the resentment I had expressed toward the King.

He bowed but spoke one last time before departing. "I can appreciate the complexity of this decision, but I believe you have made a wise choice. Your love for your sister and your devotion to duty are quite apparent. You have my utmost respect."

WITH THIS RING

he betrothal ceremony was held the following afternoon in the Palace Chapel. My father saw the necessity of moving with haste, due to the requirement that Banns be published on three consecutive Sundays preceding the wedding day. The Banns announced our betrothal and asked for anyone who knew of a reason we should not be wed to come forward and confess it.

Our parents were the only witnesses to the event. I wore the white gown that had been made for my seventeenth birthday, while Steldor wore his black leather military uniform. He and I had not talked beforehand, and I felt more awkward than ever before in my life as I stood beside him in front of the gray-haired Priest.

The ceremony itself was short, consisting of vows of intention and an exchange of rings. We joined our right hands, then the Priest, in an insufferably nasal tone, asked Steldor, "Do you promise that you will take this woman to wife if the Holy Church consents?"

"Yes, I will," Steldor answered.

The Priest then directed the same question to me. "Do you promise that you will take this man as your husband if the Holy Church consents?"

"Yes, I will," I woodenly stated, my heart hammering painfully against my rib cage.

439

"Let this be a symbol of your pledge," the clergyman intoned, pressing a ring into the palm of Steldor's left hand.

Steldor removed his hand from mine and slid the golden band onto the third finger of my right hand. The Priest repeated the ritual with me, and I rather clumsily slipped a golden band on the third finger of Steldor's right hand.

After blessing us, the Priest's final words were, "You may now seal your promises with a kiss."

Steldor stepped toward me and, placing a hand under my chin, pressed his lips briefly against mine.

Our parents stepped forward to congratulate us, then Cannan and my father proceeded in the direction of the Throne Room to discuss the marriage contract, and my mother and Faramay retreated to the Queen's Drawing Room to begin planning the wedding. As the Priest moved into the prayer room that contained religious tomes and artifacts, I was left alone with Steldor, who tossed me an impudent smile before sweeping me to him. He kissed me once more, only this time with greater insistence, and I found his passion almost frightening.

"A betrothal kiss should be a foretaste of things to come, don't you think?" he murmured when our lips parted, and there was hunger in his dark eyes.

I pushed against his chest, but his powerful arms held me firmly in place.

"Make no mistake, Alera. *You* are the daughter I have always favored to be my wife."

He released me, but before I could respond, he took my hand and led me down the corridor to the Grand Entry.

"I shall call on you tonight for dinner," he smirked. "A betrothed couple needs to spend time together, to get to know one another better before they are legally wed."

He turned and left the Palace, presumably headed for the Military Complex, and I wondered if he would be requiring me to dine with him from now on. Lamenting my loss of freedom, I climbed the Grand Staircase, fighting the impulse to disappear into the mountains as Narian had done.

———

I need not have worried about the amount of time I would be spending with Steldor during the six weeks that remained until our wedding. The Cokyrians had maintained their encampments on the other side of the Recorah River, watching and waiting, and Cannan countered with full troop deployments, which meant that Steldor and the other Field Commanders were deployed as well. On those few occasions when Steldor returned to the Military Base and seized the opportunity to dine with me, our meals were chaperoned by either his parents or mine, for the Church had strict rules governing the activities of betrothed couples.

My days also became exceptionally busy. Even in times of peril such as those in which we lived, a Royal wedding was an affair worthy of grand celebration, and our people needed a sign of hope. Invitations were inscribed and sent to all of the Hytanican nobility, the Banns were prepared and published, a menu was established for the wedding feast, a thorough cleaning of the entire Palace was underway, and the Ballroom and King's Dining Hall were being appropriately arranged and decorated. Unfortunately, given the Cokyrian threat, royalty from neighboring kingdoms would not be invited, as would normally have been protocol.

As my mother was in charge of the wedding preparations, the primary decision that fell to me was the design of my wedding gown. I called on my sister and mother for consultation, since they had more interest in fashion than did I. My sister and I had also not talked since before my father had presented his ultimatum, and I wanted to know how she had come to agree to marry Steldor if I refused the union.

We met the seamstresses in the Queen's Drawing Room, where bolts of fabric were displayed across the sofa and chairs. My head spun with the myriad possibilities, both in style and fabric, with which I was being presented. After a couple of hours, I looked pleadingly at my mother.

"Can't we just keep it simple?"

She smiled at me and held out a beautiful piece of cream silk against which she had laid a sheer fabric in deep gold.

"This would be lovely, and the colors are rich but simple."

I nodded in agreement, glad that at least one decision had been made.

By the time the sun was setting, I felt like a pincushion. Fabric had been draped yon and hither across my body, but we had at last agreed on the basic design of my gown. We had also made choices as to the fabric and style that would adorn Miranna.

It was getting late, at least by my mother's standards, so she dismissed the seamstresses and retired to her quarters. My sister and I were now alone for the first time all day, and a painful hush pervaded the room.

"I am not angry, Mira," I said softly, gesturing to the sofa. "Stay with me another minute."

Miranna looked at the door as if hoping to escape, then came to sit beside me, but she would not meet my eyes.

"Just tell me," I prompted, taking her hands in mine. "How did Father prevail upon you to be my second for marrying Steldor?"

Receiving no reply, I tried another approach.

"I was under the impression that you fancied a different young man, one by the name of Temerson."

I was gratified to see a small smile play at the corners of her mouth, only to disappear as regret crept onto her face.

"I'm not like you, Alera," she said, finally raising her head to meet my gaze. "I can't stand up to Father the way you can, and I have no strong opinions on most subjects. I also feel differently than you about Steldor. I know he is not always a gentleman, but that is part of his charm. And I agree with Father that he would be a good King." She again cast her eyes away from me. "As Father was insistent upon seeing Steldor take the Throne, I thought this might give you an alternative if you really could not conceive of being his wife. I'm sorry if I made your circumstances worse."

"You made the decision you thought was best, which is all any of us can do. I don't want this to come between us. Besides, you may recall that I offered him to you at my birthday celebration almost a year ago —— I can hardly blame you for taking me at my word."

"You did, didn't you?" she said, a genuine smile at last brightening her face.

"Now, tell me about Temerson. I believe he would have been sorely disappointed if you had been the one to marry Steldor."

"Yes, that was the one big drawback to Father's plan," my sister returned with a pretty blush, letting go of her nervousness and guilt.

We laughed together and continued talking comfortably for quite some time before retiring for the night.

After several more fittings, my wedding gown was finished, and the other preparations for the wedding were nearing completion as well. The final task that fell to me was the one I dreaded most. I was asked to choose a guest room on the third floor that would serve as my bridal chamber, although my mother would be the one to make it ready. After the wedding, as the coronation approached, my parents would vacate the King's and Queen's quarters so that Steldor and I could move into them, and rooms on the third floor would be renovated to suit their needs. My former quarters would remain vacant in anticipation of an heir. As I did not really care which room was prepared for our wedding night, the only criteria I used in making my choice was that it be as far away as possible from the room in which Narian had lived.

———

On the last day of April, but ten short days before my birthday and the day of my wedding, my mother hosted another afternoon tea party at the Palace for the young noblewomen in my age group. Unlike the other gatherings she hosted of this nature, my mother intended this one to be purely a social event rather than an opportunity to evaluate our manners, movement, and posture, which essentially meant there would be more than ample time for gossip.

Miranna, Mother, and I were met with a high level of chatter upon entering the first-floor dining room, the noise level reflecting the upbeat mood of the young women in attendance. As we began to greet our guests, the banter ceased and I felt as though all eyes were now riveted on me, confirming that I had moments before been the prime topic of discussion. Indeed, my nosiest friends soon clustered around me, irrepressibly curious about the plans for my wedding, for I would be the first among us to marry. After garnering as many details as I was willing to disclose, their conversation degenerated into a review of Steldor's charms, and I realized anew that I was the only girl in the group who did not aspire to be his wife. Deciding that my infatuated friends could explore this subject without me, I glanced around for my mother, intending to join her. I was about to move in her direction when Reveina's voice stopped me cold.

"If it were me, I would be most excited about the wedding night," she was dreamily saying, her brown eyes misty. "Lord Steldor once kissed me, and his very touch made me weak in the knees, and now Alera will have him all to herself."

Heads bobbed, the other girls enthusiastically agreeing.

"And he no doubt has experience with other women," Reveina continued, brushing back her dark hair. "I have been told that is desirable in a husband, as he will know how to make things comfortable for his bride."

Several of the girls giggled and blushed at her rather brazen remark, but I said nothing. It had not even crossed my mind prior to this moment that Steldor might have had intimate relations with other women, and this information substantially increased my anxiety.

"And what has become of Lord Narian?" Kalem, generally the romantic among us, abruptly asked. "He is also quite handsome, and after what happened at the Tournament last fall, I was hoping to meet him."

The other girls joined in assent.

"The skill he showed during the exhibition was quite astounding!" announced blond-haired Noralee, her blue eyes wide, reflecting her customary level of shock.

"Handsome, strong... and mysterious. Definitely a good second choice!" agreed Kalem. Then she looked sullenly at me, her light gray eyes shielded by her dark lashes. "Rumor has it that he showed quite an interest in *you* for a while. Really, Alera, you cannot have *both* of the most intriguing men in the Kingdom!"

"If he had not left, and you had been permitted to choose between them, whom would you have favored?" queried Reveina, always the bold one.

Everyone fell silent as they awaited my answer. I scrambled for a response, feeling self-conscious and ambushed. I was thankfully saved from further embarrassment by Miranna, who joined the circle and spoke up on my behalf.

"Narian is the brother of my best friend, so naturally Alera and I have become acquainted with him, but that's all there is to it."

Glancing appreciatively at my sister, I added, "And he departed because he missed the mountains and wanted to spend some time there."

Before the other girls could press the matter further, Miranna ended the conversation.

"Come, sister. Mother is preparing to take her seat and wishes us to join her." She took my hand and led me away, saying cheerily to our friends, "You should also find your places. This is probably your last chance to practice your manners before the wedding."

I walked by Miranna's side, my mood subdued. My friends' comments had brought all of my fears to the forefront. Where was Narian? Why had he left? And what would Steldor expect from his bride? I knew, even if Steldor did not, that I no longer had a heart to give, for Narian had taken it with him. I sat in silence through the serving of the tea, planning to depart at the earliest possible moment, for the agony of Narian's disappearance had resurfaced. The emptiness inside was like physical pain, and I wanted to run from it, but there was no escape other than in sleep. I felt as though I lived in a netherworld, where I could neither reclaim the past nor embrace the future, but was condemned to struggle through each day.

———

It rained the night before my wedding, which my mother told me was a good omen as it washed away past hurts and insults and permitted a fresh beginning. The morning of the wedding did indeed dawn fresh and clear, with the promise of a warm afternoon.

My mother sent a special wedding breakfast to my quarters, but I only picked at the food, too nauseated to eat. I next bathed in scented water and permitted Sahdienne to brush out my long hair.

Miranna, as my attendant, helped me into my wedding

attire in the early afternoon. My gown was made of the fabric my mother had selected, cream silk with a sheer overlay of gold falling from just below the bustline. The rounded neckline led to ruched sleeves, and the bodice was overstitched in gold thread. A sheer gold cape swept the floor and was attached at the shoulders so that it elegantly draped to reveal the gold lacing that ran all the way up the gown's back. Upon my head I wore a simple one-inch-wide gold band with three jewels set evenly across its front: sapphire for purity, emerald for hope, and red jasper for love. My hair was swept up and over the back of the band into a loose bun and tied with gold ribbon. A simple gold cross adorned my neck. I would carry in my left hand a small bouquet of flowers interspersed with herbs that were believed to bring good fortune.

The wedding was to take place in the Ballroom, followed by a feast in the King's Dining Hall, then a return to the Ballroom for dancing and socializing. My parents would escort me to the ceremony, and as the time for the service grew nigh, I waited for them in my quarters with ever-increasing dread.

The music of minstrels, along with the sounds of laughter and the clapping of hands, told me that Steldor was arriving. I could see the Central Courtyard through my open balcony doors and watched as he rode through the gates on his magnificent gray stallion, a footman treading off to one side. This was the only time I had ever seen a horse permitted within the Palace grounds, and my perception that nothing was the way it should be grew even stronger.

Steldor rode half the distance down the path that lay between the flowering lilac hedges, then dismounted, handing his reins to the footman and turning to wave at the crowd that had followed him through the city streets. The people would continue to gather in anticipation of the ceremony, and after our vows had been exchanged, the head of each family would be permitted to enter the courtyard to receive two gold coins symbolizing our union from a Palace Guard.

Glancing again toward the gates, I saw Cannan and Faramay step out of a carriage and begin to walk slowly up the white stone pathway. Other relatives and guests also arrived, parading in their wedding finery toward the open front doors of the Palace. Unlike me, who lacked uncles, aunts, and cousins, my father's only brother having died in the war and my mother's entire family likewise having perished, Steldor had a large extended family, with nine uncles and aunts, and seventeen cousins.

I stepped away from the balcony, so panicky I could scarcely breathe. Miranna crossed to me and held out a small glass of wine.

"Mother thought this might help calm you."

I took a sip and handed it back to her.

"Would you like to sit for a moment?" she worriedly asked. I shook my head and closed my eyes, consciously willing my breathing to slow.

"You look absolutely stunning," she continued, attempting to sound reassuring.

"You are breathtaking as well," I replied, opening my eyes to examine her.

Miranna's dress was of light blue silk with a fitted waist and full skirt. Its bodice was overlaid with sheer white lace, and its bell sleeves almost grazed the floor.

There was a knock on the door, and my mother glided into my bedroom, wearing a royal blue gown stitched with gold. Her beautiful blond hair was perfectly coiffed and topped with the official crown of the Queen, a circlet set with diamonds and adorned by a single cross in front that displayed five jewels, one each of sapphire, emerald, ruby, and amethyst, with a diamond in the center.

"I wanted to check on you, Alera, before your father joins

us." She gave me an airy embrace, then her serene blue eyes assessed me. "All brides are nervous on their wedding day, but you are marrying an exceptional young man, and everything will go smoothly."

"I'm fine, Mother," I assured her, although I did not feel fine at all. I felt like the condemned facing the gallows, rather than the excited bride my mother envisioned.

"The guests have arrived, as has the groom, and all is now ready. Is there anything you need before the ceremony begins?"

"No, I'm fine," I repeated, but the cracking of my voice argued otherwise.

"Then let us move into the parlor to await your father."

It wasn't long before a rap on the door told me the King had arrived, and he entered, attired in his royal blue robes, the crown of the sovereign with its four bejeweled crosses upon his gray-flecked hair. He beamed out of immense joy as he crossed to me and kissed my cheek.

"You are a vision, my dear. Are you ready to meet your groom?"

I nodded, cynically thinking it would be more apt to say I was going to meet my doom, and we left my parlor to walk down the corridor toward the Ballroom. When we arrived, we stopped just outside the wide doorway, and my mother stood to my left, my father to my right, their arms entwined in mine. A carpet of gold stretched before us, creating a path to the altar on the far side of the room. We would walk halfway into the Ballroom along the near wall, then turn left, Miranna following behind as my attendant.

"Shall we?" asked my father, and I took a deep breath before nodding.

We moved forward at a measured pace, then turned and stopped, and I wasn't certain I had the strength to make the long walk from where we now stood to the canopy and altar.

The festively attired wedding guests who filled to overflowing the benches to my left and right did nothing to calm me.

Steldor stood about halfway down the aisle, facing me, looking incredibly handsome in an embossed black leather jacket with extended shoulders, the sleeves and peplum of which were deep green velvet. He wore his tall black boots over black breeches, and his ruby-studded sword hung at his left hip, the dagger I had given him for his birthday at his right.

Faramay, stunning in a shimmering light green gown, stood to Steldor's left, while Cannan, clad in a dress coat of deep green velvet with gold embroidery, stood to his right. Despite my frame of mind, it came to me that this was the first time I had seen the Captain in anything other than military garb. Galen, his wavy ash-brown hair freshly trimmed, stood just behind the three of them, wearing a well-cut black dress coat.

As trumpets sounded, our wedding guests rose to their feet, and my parents and I walked forward until my father and Faramay stood side by side. The aged Priest slowly advanced from his position in front of the altar to meet us so he could ask the necessary questions to establish that Steldor and I could lawfully be joined in matrimony.

"Do you know of any impediment why you may not be lawfully joined?" the Priest intoned, the nasal quality of his voice somehow befitting my nausea.

"No," Steldor and I murmured.

"Are you of legal age to marry?"

"Yes," we both replied.

"Whose blessings accompany you?"

Our parents together answered, "The blessings of their entire families."

Faramay took a step back and moved to Cannan's right. My father removed my arm from his and rested my hand upon Steldor's, and then likewise withdrew to stand beside my mother.

"Have the Banns been published?" droned the Priest.

"Yes, on three consecutive Sundays," Steldor answered.

The Priest then asked the final, and perhaps most important, question. "Do you come of your own free will and accord to be joined in marriage?"

I glanced at Steldor, who had tensed almost imperceptibly.

"Yes, I come of my own free will," I stated. Steldor repeated the same, and I felt him relax, as though he had half expected a different answer from me.

The Priest then arduously approached the altar. Steldor and I came next, followed by our parents, with Miranna and Galen bringing up the rear. When we reached the front, my parents moved to the left to sit in the thrones provided for them, while Cannan and Faramay went right to sit in large padded armchairs. Miranna came to stand next to me, and I handed her my bouquet while Galen took his place beside Steldor.

The Priest joined my right hand with my betrothed's, and we turned to face each other as the exchange of vows began.

"Do you take this woman as your wife?" the Priest inquired.

"I receive you as mine, so that you become my wife and I your husband," Steldor said, gazing into my eyes. "And I commit to you the fidelity of my body; and I will keep you in health and sickness; nor for better or worse will I change toward you until the end." His voice was strong, for he suffered from no indecision.

The Priest then addressed me. "Do you take this man as your husband?"

I looked down and took a deep breath, my heart pounding so loudly in my ears that I wasn't certain I'd be able to hear my own voice. Then I forced myself to meet Steldor's eyes.

"I receive you as mine, so that you become my husband and I your wife," I said with a slight quaver. "And I commit to you the fidelity of my body; and I will keep you in health and sickness;

nor for better or worse will I change toward you until the end."

A smile flitted across Steldor's face as I finished, and we turned toward the Priest, who took the marriage ring from Galen. After blessing it, he handed it to Steldor.

Removing his right hand from mine, Steldor raised my left, palm downward, and partially slid the ring first on my thumb, then on my index finger, my middle finger, and my third finger, where it finally came to rest. With each placement of the ring, he made a pledge.

"With this ring I thee wed; this gold I thee give; with my body I thee worship; and with all my worldly goods I thee endow."

We turned to kneel on the padded step before the Priest and shared our first communion as husband and wife. After placing a veil over us to signify our union, the Priest blessed us, and we rose to our feet. Steldor removed the veil, then turned to me and untied the ribbon that held my hair in its bun, letting my dark tresses cascade loosely down my back to signify his dominion over me. His fingers lightly skimmed my shoulders, and he pulled me into his embrace, kissing me deeply.

A cheer went up from our guests, and Steldor and I walked briskly back down the aisle, into the corridor, and over to the King's Dining Hall, where we began to receive congratulations from our friends and family. I was glad to have the ceremony behind me, but fear clutched at my heart, for I had no idea what marriage to Steldor held in store.

WISHES

fter the King and Queen moved to the high table that was set for our newly united families, Steldor and I followed, and the rest of the assembled guests found seating as well. We waited for a blessing from the Priest, and then the meal began. The wedding feast was served in several courses, beginning with soup, bread flavored with ale, and an assortment of cheeses, to be followed by tortes filled with spicy veal and dates. Next came stuffed roast suckling pig, smoked fish, mutton, and all manner of roast birds, served with stewed cabbage. Fruit custard in a pie followed, along with spicy mulled wine. Rose-scented water was provided to the guests so that they could cleanse their hands between courses, and all was washed down with wine and ale. Throughout the meal, musicians performed, joined by acrobats, jugglers, and singers as the tables were cleared.

At the conclusion of the feast, Steldor stood and guided me to my feet. He took my hand and led me toward a round table that held a platter upon which our guests had been stacking the small cakes they had brought as gifts. With more than six hundred guests in attendance, the stack of cakes had grown several feet high. Tradition called for us to try to kiss over the top of the stack without toppling the cakes in order to be granted luck and prosperity.

Steldor removed my gown's cape from the clips at my shoulders and evaluated the task. He had an advantage as he stood four inches taller than me, but even he could not possibly lean over the cakes. We looked quizzically at each other, and then he called for benches. As Galen steadied Steldor's, and Miranna, assisted by Temerson, steadied mine, we stepped onto the seats and eyed each other over the tops of the cakes. Steldor rubbed his hands together, then held them out to me, and I reached out to join mine with his. Supporting each other, we leaned forward, trying to keep a bend in our waists so we would not nudge the stack of pastries. Our heads came together and our lips briefly touched as laughter and cheering erupted around us, but we recognized at about the same time that I was not strong enough to push myself away and back into a standing position. With a nod of his head to his right, Steldor indicated to me the direction in which he wanted us to fall. Pushing off each other's hands, we toppled to the right, Steldor agile and catlike. Somehow he managed to catch me before I hit the floor, and although the stack swayed precariously, it stayed upright. I laughed along with our jubilant guests, enjoying myself for the first time all day. Steldor set me back upon my feet, a grin brightening his features, and drew me into a firm embrace.

"Well done!" he exclaimed, his eyes alight, and I returned his smile.

Again taking me by the hand, Steldor led me through the crowd to return to the Ballroom for dancing and additional entertainment. By this time, the benches had been repositioned along the perimeter of the room, the altar and other items related to the wedding ceremony had been removed, and refreshment tables had been set against the near wall.

Steldor led me onto the dance floor, then flippantly reminded me of our last attempt at dancing.

"Remember, I'm the one who is supposed to lead."

I tried to relax in his arms, for I knew he was an excellent dancer, and as I did so, our movements became smooth and lithe. After a few turns around the floor, he gazed down at me, an amorous glow in the depths of his eyes.

"I trust this is a sign of submission in other ways as well," he murmured, and I was instantly wary of his meaning.

After a second dance, I felt the need for a break, and Steldor left my side to retrieve glasses of wine. London chose to confer with me in my husband's absence, approaching me with a melancholy smile.

"I hope you will find happiness," he wished me sincerely. "But I will also miss your company, for my duties will no longer place me within the Palace."

This had not occurred to me, and I found it quite upsetting.

"But we will remain friends, won't we?"

"Of course," he vowed, but his voice lacked conviction. "I thought you might be interested to know that I am leaving tomorrow to hunt for Narian in the mountains. If I find him, I will bring him back to Hytanica. Cannan believes he could be just as useful to us as to the enemy."

Steldor returned and handed me a glass of wine, looking askance at London, who bowed and departed. I had no time to reflect on London's words for guests continued to approach, wishing us health and happiness.

When the group of well-wishers finally began to dwindle, Lord Baelic, Steldor's uncle and Cannan's younger brother, approached. While I knew Lord Baelic's wife, Lady Lania, and his oldest daughter, Lady Dahnath, from my mother's tea parties, I had never before met him. I also knew little about him other than that he held the rank of Major and was the Cavalry Officer at the Military Complex.

Baelic was two inches shorter than his brother and an inch

shorter than his nephew, but otherwise bore a remarkable resemblance to Cannan, with hair so dark it was almost black, dark brown eyes, a chiseled jawline, and a muscular build. It did not take me long, however, to discover a glaring difference between the brothers, for Baelic was as smiley as Cannan was grave.

After Steldor had made the introductions, Baelic gallantly kissed my hand.

"Congratulations, Lord Steldor; Princess Alera, my sympathies."

Ignoring Steldor's groan of complaint, his uncle continued, looking playfully into my eyes.

"If you're ever in need of something you can hold over his head, come talk to me. I know everything about him that he would prefer to keep from his father." He glanced merrily at Steldor, then finished, "And that's my wedding gift to you."

"Is it impolite to refuse a gift?" Steldor retorted.

"It depends on the gift," Baelic countered with a slightly crooked smile. "Surely you wouldn't turn down one as high in quality as this."

Before Steldor could answer, I made my opinion known. "I have no intention of turning it down."

"I like her more every moment," Baelic said approvingly. "I still can't figure out what she's doing with you."

I almost laughed out loud at Baelic's willingness to needle his nephew and was irresistibly drawn to his light and engaging manner.

Steldor contemplated his uncle for a brief moment, the corners of his mouth pulling upward in amusement.

"She settled for a twenty-one-year-old charmer when she found that all the forty-three-year-old fools were taken," he parried.

"You cut me to the bone, dear nephew."

"Then I shall make up for it by hiring you as my court jester, dear uncle."

With a chuckle and another deep bow, Baelic said to me, "It was a pleasure meeting you. I shall leave my incorrigible nephew in your care, and I heartily wish you the best of luck."

He slapped Steldor good-naturedly on the shoulder and departed, leaving no doubt in my mind from whom my husband had inherited his innate charm.

As soon as Baelic left, my father drew Steldor away from me and began to speak with him. Feeling somewhat awkward, I cast about for my sister, but instead saw Galen walking in my direction. I presumed he was coming to talk to his best friend, so was at a loss when he strode over to me instead.

"May I have the pleasure of a dance?" he inquired, with a courteous bow.

I examined him skeptically for a moment before rebuffing him. "I would prefer to watch the other couples."

Although I did not know him well, I assumed from my brief encounters with him, along with his mannerisms, that he was much like Steldor and was therefore unlikely to win my favor.

He considered me carefully before responding. "'No,' you don't care to dance with anyone, or 'no,' you don't care to dance with me?" He sounded merely curious, no trace of offense in his tone.

Knowing that the truth would come across as rude, I started to tell a lie, but he put two fingers against my lips.

"Your hesitation speaks volumes, so I assume you would also be unwilling to keep company with me." He inclined his head, smiling ruefully. "I will leave you in peace, My Lady."

Stung by guilt for refusing his request, I reached out my hand and caught his arm before he could walk away.

"Please. A dance would be welcome after all."

"It will be my honor," he said graciously, and he escorted me onto the dance floor.

I quickly discovered that, like Steldor, Galen was an excellent dancer, and I moved elegantly in his arms as he guided me among the other couples.

"That wasn't so bad, was it?" he remarked when the song ended.

"Actually, it was quite pleasant."

I glanced toward Steldor, who was now bantering with Barid, Devant, and others of his military friends. I sighed, having no desire to mingle with that particular group, and not trusting that I would be welcome in any case.

"I would be happy to provide you companionship until someone more to your liking comes along," Galen declared, taking note of my dilemma as he led me from the dance floor.

I paused, unsure how to interpret his comment, but then smiled, for there was a twinkle in his soft brown eyes and a smirk playing at the corners of his mouth.

"Your company *is* to my liking, kind sir," I told him truthfully.

We did not, however, have further time to converse, for a group of young women was moving toward us, clearly of a mind to speak with me.

"As I am generally not *that* popular with the ladies," Galen teased, "and as my sisters are among the throng, I will leave you in their hands."

He bowed and departed, moving to join Steldor before my friends could trap him with me.

It wasn't long before I tired of the group's conversation, for my friends were obsessed with comparing the marriage potential of the remaining eligible men of noble birth. Seeing my mother, I excused myself and went to her, weariness seeping through me. She was standing with Faramay, Lady Hauna, who was Galen's mother, and Tiersia, who had once again come as Galen's date.

As I talked quietly with the women, I saw Steldor's eyes flit in my direction several times. The evening was growing late, as evidenced by the platters of food that servants were now bringing to the refreshment tables to provide our guests with the fortitude to celebrate until morning.

Breaking from his friends, Steldor advanced on me. He bowed to the Queen and kissed his mother dutifully on the cheek, then slid an arm around my waist.

"I think my wife is exhausted from the festivities, and that we should perhaps retire for the night."

A chill swept over me at the thought of what was to come, and the nausea that had dissipated in the aftermath of the ceremony returned.

With his arm encircling my waist, Steldor drew me with him to receive permission from the King for us to leave, then also bade good night to his father.

I climbed the front stairway to the third floor with Steldor, trailing the elderly Priest who had yet to bless the bridal chamber, feeling as though each slow and methodical step added a nail to my coffin. As we approached the room I had selected, Steldor guided me away from it, further down the hallway. We then approached the room that had most recently been Narian's. The Priest and Steldor entered, but I hovered in the doorway, confused and dismayed.

"This will serve us better," Steldor said, taking my hand, then he chastised in a low voice, "I will tolerate no ghosts in my home."

I entered the room, feeling nervous and humiliated, for Steldor had surmised that I did not want to intrude upon this space. I stopped a few feet over the threshold and surveyed my prison. The room had, of course, been refurbished by my mother in preparation for this night. Across from us was a large four-poster bed topped with a golden spread and

numerous pillows. Rose petals strewn across its surface added
a subtle fragrance. A small table adjacent to the bed held a lantern along with a jug of wine and two goblets. A large fireplace
took up most of the wall to our left, but no fire had been kindled
as the day had been quite warm, and a sofa and several chairs
were grouped about the hearth. The flower-filled urns from the
wedding had been brought up to the room and lined the wall
immediately to our right, adding a heady scent to the air.

The Priest had now moved to the side of the bed and was
beckoning for Steldor and me to join him. I stood in embarrassment at my husband's side as the clergyman blessed us and
our wedding bed in order to ensure good fortune and fertility.
The ceremony completed, I walked him to the door.

After the Priest's departure, I stood in the center of the
room, eyeing Steldor, painfully aware that I now belonged to
him, and that no one would interfere should he choose to assert
his husbandly rights. He perused me as he tossed his leather
jacket on one of the chairs and unlaced his white shirt, and I
could see his silver wolf's head talisman lying against his sturdy
chest. He came to me and unceremoniously kissed me, placing his hands on the sides of my face. As his now familiar scent
washed over me, he ran his hands down my body until they
rested upon my hips. I stiffened at his touch, and he stepped
back from me.

"Turn around, and I will help you out of your wedding dress."

I silently beseeched him, but, seeing no compassion in his
eyes, reluctantly presented my back to him. He began to loosen
the lacing of my gown, gently kissing my shoulders and neck as
he did so. I shuddered, and he immediately dropped his hands.
Fearful of his intentions, I pivoted and saw him standing with
his arms crossed over his chest, his handsome face clouded by
frustration.

"What am I to do with you? I would like nothing better

than to lie with you tonight, but it appears you would not come freely, but solely out of duty."

I cast my eyes to the floor, afraid to respond to his accusation. He stepped toward me once more, and with one hand against the small of my back, the other enmeshed in my hair, clasped my body against his, kissing me with greater passion. When I again involuntarily stiffened, he abruptly released me and retreated two steps. I waited in misery as he raked a hand through his dark hair, his eyes now flashing angrily.

"It is our wedding night, Alera. You are intelligent enough to know what is expected."

"I know what is expected but don't yet feel ready to submit, My Lord," I said faintly. I decided my best ploy would be to use his own words against him. "You told me not long ago that you were willing to take things slowly. I implore you now to be true to that promise and permit me time to become more comfortable with you... physically."

To my surprise, he laughed.

"You really are the devil, you know," he said drolly. "Fine, then, I will give you some time, but willing or not, you do have an obligation as a wife and a Queen to bear an heir."

He turned from me and moved toward the bed, pulling off his shirt, and in spite of myself, I couldn't help staring at his muscular form. Noticing my gaze, he raised a denigrating eyebrow.

"Just tell me how long you would like to look."

I averted my eyes, embarrassed yet again.

"As there is only one bed, it is your choice whether to join me or make use of the sofa," he callously added.

With one last disparaging glance my way, he snuffed out the lantern and crawled beneath the inviting covers, leaving me to stand in the dark in my wedding gown, with no creature comforts should I elect to sleep apart from him.

Disconcerted, I slowly moved toward the chair upon which he had tossed his jacket, gathering the garment into my arms and fumbling my way to the sofa. It was now too dark for me to find my nightdress, and with no maid to assist me in disrobing, it being expected that the groom would aid his wife on their wedding night, I was momentarily stumped. Then I tugged apart the lacing Steldor had loosened, letting the gown fall with a soft rustle to the floor. Using my husband's coat as a blanket, I lay down on my chosen bed in my chemise to stare sightlessly at the ceiling, knowing that I was in for a restless night.

Narian came to me in my dreams, enfolding me in his arms and whisking me away from all unhappiness. The dream was so sweet and real that I could feel his rough shirt brush across my cheek, breathe in his earthy scent, and see the love in his deep blue eyes as he bent to press his lips to mine. I abruptly awoke to lie motionless in the dark, tears trickling from the outside corners of my eyes, wondering where he was and if I would ever be with him again. I forced my mind to still, listening only to my heart and trusting in hope to be my guiding light. As I closed my eyes, I was filled with the certainty that he would find a way to come back to me, for his love was unwavering and as constant as the rhythm of my heart.

To Be Continued in *Allegiance*

ACKNOWLEDGMENTS

I want to take this opportunity to thank those people who helped *Legacy* come to life:

My mom, Kimberly, for her everlasting support and guidance. Without you, I would be nowhere.

My sisters, who define me in more ways than I can say.

My friends, whose critiques were invaluable in shaping the self-published edition of *Legacy*: Josie, Kriss, Laura, Susy, and my English teacher Ms. Kazeck (Mrs. White... never going to get used to that!).

My agent, Kevan Lyon, for her incredible work and dedication, and for always sticking up for me.

My foreign rights agent, Taryn Fagerness, for putting *Legacy* and its sequels, *Allegiance* and *Redemption*, out there for the world, and for being so enthusiastic.

The team at AmazonEncore for giving me this amazing new platform and being a pleasure to work with: Jeff Belle, Vicky Griffith, Daphne Durham, Terry Goodman, and everyone else who has contributed to the program.

At Melcher Media: Charlie Melcher and Duncan Bock, for their art direction and help with editing, and Shoshana Thaler, for her thoughtful support throughout. I also want to thank Paul Kepple for his design work; Rosemary Buczek, Kirk Caldwell, and Karen Gorst for their beautiful illustrations; and Amélie Cherlin for making copy edits a pleasure.

Thanks to Jim, Greg, Sue, and the rest of the gang who worked with us on the original paperback edition. I'll never forget the feeling of holding the first copy of the book in my hands.

Thanks to each and every person who reads this book —— you're holding my dream come true in your hands.

Until next time,

CAYLA KLUVER

ABOUT THE AUTHOR

Cayla Kluver lives with her family and her muse (Nina, her cat) in Wisconsin, where only the hardy survive. *Legacy* is her first novel and was published when Cayla was fifteen.

The first edition of *Legacy* won first place in the 2008 Reader Views Literary Awards, and a bronze medal in the 2008 Moonbeam Children's Book Awards for young adult fiction.